P9-CWE-725

Bodies, bodies, everywhere...

Carlotta Wren has always made a living on bodies–dressing them, that is. Over the years while working her retail job at Neiman Marcus, she's clothed some of the most successful, wealthy, famous and *hot* bodies in Atlanta. But her schedule and her personal problems (dumped by her blue-blood boyfriend, deserted by her fugitive parents and designated mom to her troubled younger brother) have left her lonely and longing for a warm body to cozy up to.

Then a meddling cop plows through her life....
And her prodigal boyfriend shows up....
And an intellectual body mover arrives on the scene....

Now that she has not one, but *three* hunky bodies vying for her time, what's a girl to do?

Eeenie, meenie, miney, mo...

TIPTON COUNTY
WITHDRAWN
PUBLIC LIBRARY

TIPTON CO. LIBRARY
TIPTON, INDIANA

Praise for the novels of

Stephanie Bond

"An engaging story and clever mystery
not to be missed."
–Romance Reviews Today on *In Deep Voodoo*

"A harmonious blend of humor, suspense,
friendship, and romance."
–A Romance Review on *Whole Lotta Trouble*

"Bond lays on the laughs with such enthusiasm
that 'comic suspense' might be a better
description [of the book]."
–Publishers Weekly on *Party Crashers*

A starred review! "DO read this novel."
–Publishers Weekly on *Kill the Competition*

"Plenty of suspense and sizzling romance."
–Romantic Times BOOKclub on *Kill the Competition*

"A sterling source of laughs and lighthearted fun."
–Publishers Weekly on *I Think I Love You*

"Bond's fun and frothy story keeps the
plot twists coming."
–Publishers Weekly on *Our Husband*

Stephanie Bond

BODY MOVER*s*

MIRA®

If you purchased this book without a cover you should be aware
that this book is stolen property. It was reported as "unsold and
destroyed" to the publisher, and neither the author nor the
publisher has received any payment for this "stripped book."

MIRA

ISBN-13: 978-0-7783-2333-4
ISBN-10:   0-7783-2333-1

BODY MOVERS

Copyright © 2006 by Stephanie Bond Inc.

All rights reserved. Except for use in any review, the reproduction or
utilization of this work in whole or in part in any form by any electronic,
mechanical or other means, now known or hereafter invented, including
xerography, photocopying and recording, or in any information storage or
retrieval system, is forbidden without the written permission of the publisher,
MIRA Books, 225 Duncan Mill Road, Don Mills, Ontario, Canada M3B 3K9.

All characters in this book have no existence outside the imagination of the
author and have no relation whatsoever to anyone bearing the same name
or names. They are not even distantly inspired by any individual known or
unknown to the author, and all incidents are pure invention.

MIRA and the Star Colophon are trademarks used under license and registered
in Australia, New Zealand, Philippines, United States Patent and Trademark
Office and in other countries.

www.MIRABooks.com

Printed in U.S.A.

First Printing: August 2006
10 9 8 7 6 5 4 3 2 1

Acknowledgments

The *Body Movers* story has been rattling around in my brain for several years, but it took the right characters to be able to pull it off, and the sister/brother team of Carlotta and Wesley didn't come to me until a couple of years ago in the midst of writing another book. When the story and characters finally came together, I had the feeling that I had an interesting premise for a series; next I had to find a publisher who shared my vision for bringing *Body Movers* to readers.

My thanks to Dianne Moggy, Margaret O'Neill Marbury and my editor Brenda Chin at MIRA Books for championing this project. Thanks, too, to my agent Kimberly Whalen of the Trident Media Group for handling the logistics. To my artist husband, Christopher Hauck, who assisted with the cover concept and who taught me how to smoke a cigar (for research). To William Waddell, high school friend and proprietor of the Globe Funeral Chapel in Olive Hill, Kentucky, who graciously provided information about the legal and proper handling of the deceased. (Some of the quirky things that happen in my story are from my imagination and do not reflect the reverence that William has for his job.) Thanks to Julie Giese for the forensics reference book and the (unused) body bag. My thanks to my critique partner, Rita Herron, for her ongoing support. And to my readers whose letters and e-mails keep me going. And finally, thanks to my wonderfully biased mom, Bonnie Bond, for the great cover quote.

1

"Does this make my ass look big?"

Carlotta Wren stood in the dressing room of Neiman Marcus in the Lenox Mall in Atlanta, Georgia, her arms full of designer bathing suits that Angela Ashford, one of her least favorite customers, wanted to try on. They weren't even halfway through the selections and already Carlotta wanted to murder the woman.

She dutifully glanced at Angela's surgically sculpted glutes falling out of a tiny patch of metallic-blue fabric. "No, your, um, ass looks...great."

Angela tossed her blond hair over her shoulder and pouted at her rear reflection in the three-way mirror. "You think?"

Carlotta's mouth watered to say, "Way better than it looked in high school," but bit her tongue. It was part of the game, after all—Angela played the role of poor little rich girl with a confidence problem, and Carlotta played the stroking, sympathetic friend. Both of them deserved an Oscar.

Angela turned around and carefully rearranged her newly

acquired breasts in the bikini top that barely covered her nipples. Then she slipped her narrow feet into the silver high-heeled sandals sitting nearby and performed a three-quarter turn to peruse her long, slender figure from all angles. Carlotta tried not to compare her own ample curves to the woman's lean lines. Or her own gap-toothed grin to Angela's perfect, Clorox smile.

She was *not* jealous of Angela Ashford.

"This suit is a definite maybe," Angela announced.

Carlotta managed not to roll her eyes—the sixth "definite maybe" so far. "I have to warn you that the trim on that suit won't hold up to chlorine."

Angela made a face. "Good grief, I don't actually swim in our new pool—I don't even know *how* to swim. I just want to look amazing."

Carlotta bit down on the inside of her cheek. "Do you want to choose from the ones you've set aside so far, or do you want to try on the rest of these?"

Angela looked irritated. "I'll try on the rest." Then she smiled meanly. "And I'll be needing several new spring outfits. With shoes, of course. Peter told me to treat myself to anything I wanted since he just got a *huge* bonus and our wedding anniversary is coming up. He's so generous."

Carlotta busied herself removing the next bathing suit from its hanger, trying not to react. Peter, as in Carlotta's former fiancé. Just like every time Angela came in for a shopping binge, Carlotta reminded herself that her relationship with Peter Ashford had ended over a decade ago. To be precise, one week after her father had skipped bail on his indictment for investment fraud and he and her mother had gone on the run. The local media had had a field day.

RANDOLPH WREN FLIES THE COOP
RANDOLPH WREN, FUGITIVE JAILBIRD
RANDOLPH WREN AND WIFE VALERIE ABANDON CHILDREN

Just a few weeks shy of eighteen, Carlotta hadn't been a child, but she'd led a rather charmed and sheltered life up to that point. Suddenly faced with raising her nine-year-old brother, Wesley, and with no extended family to rely upon, she had clung to her boyfriend, Peter. Too tightly, apparently, because after the headlines had exploded, he had explained over the telephone that their lives had grown too far apart—he was in college at Vanderbilt University in Tennessee, and she still had to finish her last semester of high school in Atlanta. Translation: *Your name is tainted and I don't want to be associated with your family scandal.*

With maturity and hindsight, she had come to understand why Peter had bowed out, but at the time, the rejection of the man she had loved for most of her teenage years, the man who had taken her virginity, had been akin to having her heart surgically removed.

"I hope it doesn't make you uncomfortable when I talk about Peter," Angela said as she yanked the tie to the bikini top, baring her rigid boobs. She kicked the two-hundred-dollar scrap of Lycra across the floor of the dressing room.

"N-no," Carlotta said, scrambling to rescue her merchandise. She straightened, then handed Angela a one-piece suit and gave a little laugh. "Why should it?"

Angela stepped out of the minuscule bikini bottoms and stood nude before Carlotta for a few seconds before stretching the next swimsuit over her tight bod.

"Because, well, you know, the whole pretend engagement you two had when we were in high school," Angela said, preening in the mirror.

The Cartier engagement ring was proof that it had been more than a "pretend" engagement, but Carlotta wet her lips and forced a casual note into her voice. "That was a lifetime ago. We were...kids."

"That's what he says," Angela offered cheerfully. "And that if the two of you had actually married—" she laughed at the improbability "—that it never would have lasted."

Carlotta's heart twisted, but she managed a smile. "Then everything worked out for the best, didn't it?"

In the mirror, Angela leveled her feline gaze on Carlotta. "I suppose so."

Carlotta steered the conversation back to clothes and, thankfully, Angela was distracted by the appearance of the "perfect" bikini (two of them) and the armfuls of designer dresses and pantsuits that Carlotta pulled from every couture department. A phone call to the shoe department on the lower floor brought Michael Lane to the women's clothing department. He headed toward Carlotta, pushing a hand truck laden with colorful boxes of Pucci and Gucci, Don Ciccillo and Donald J. Pliner. "Here's everything we have in size seven narrow."

"Thanks—you're a dear."

He gave Carlotta a wry smile. "How are you holding up?"

Carlotta scowled toward the closed door of the dressing room. "I'm ready to strangle her."

"Down, girl. Double-A is one of your best customers."

Carlotta smirked at Michael's use of her nickname for Angela. "I got an eyeful of her latest upgrade—let's just say she's no longer a double-A in the bra department."

He clucked. "Hey, what do you expect? The competition is tough in Angela Ashford's social stratum."

In Angela Ashford's social stratum. Michael didn't realize that he was talking about an arena that Carlotta herself had been destined for prior to having her life jerked out from under her. Michael wasn't a native of Atlanta, and she didn't go out of her way to tell friends and co-workers her entire sordid family history. In fact, she usually lied. She'd gotten quite good at lying and pretending.

"I suppose you're right," Carlotta conceded. "But, Christ, she always makes me feel like such a peon. And she's in rare form today."

He looked sympathetic. "Just remember that commission is the best revenge."

Carlotta laughed ruefully and waved goodbye as she wheeled the shoes toward the dressing room. Why did Angela insist on shopping with Carlotta at her beck and call? She could shop at any boutique in Atlanta or, as her own mother used to do, she could call the store and have a personal shopper select items and bring them to her home for her approval. Or she could simply seek the assistance of another clerk at Neiman's. But the woman seemed to take great pleasure in shopping under Carlotta's care, which, Carlotta realized, was a thinly veiled excuse for Angela to flaunt her successful life with Peter. It stung, but in truth, Carlotta needed the commission to pay the seemingly unlimited number of bills that she and Wesley, now nineteen years old, generated.

At the thought of her brother, a bittersweet pang struck her. Wesley had never fully recovered from their parents' abandonment and had suffered more than his share of emotional problems. When he was younger, those problems had manifested into behavioral issues in school, exacerbated by the fact that his IQ was higher than that of most of his instructors, especially in math. Despite his intellect, Wesley had barely graduated high school last year, and now as a directionless adult, his problems manifested into compulsive behavior—more specifically, gambling.

His affinity for poker had landed him in debt up to his neck— and hers. And he'd been foolish enough to borrow from some unsavory characters. A henchman for one of the loan sharks had come to see her at the department store a few months ago, threatening bodily harm to both of them if Wesley didn't make a payment. Inadvertently, her brother always seemed to drag her into his messes, but every time she'd considered telling him that he was of age and to hit the road, she couldn't. She couldn't abandon him as her parents had, yet the knot of worry in her chest never eased. She agonized over what trouble he might get into next, and how they might stay afloat.

Carlotta sighed. One of the worst things about living paycheck to paycheck was imagining Angela Ashford having a one-hundred-dollar lunch with her friends—many of them girls Carlotta had gone to school with and had once considered *her* friends—saying, "That poor Carlotta Wren, still single and working retail, can you imagine?" But if it was the price she had to pay for a hefty commission, so be it. If Angela spent true to form, the commission on this sale alone would be enough to pay this month's mortgage *and* electric bill.

Or at least last month's.

Carlotta opened the door to the dressing room to find Angela sitting on a bench, half-naked, drinking from a silver flask. She quickly swallowed and wiped her mouth. "Just getting a head start on my two-martini lunch."

Carlotta remained silent but knew that anyone who packed their own booze had a problem. Her mother had kept a similar flask in her purse for whenever the urge struck for a "drinkie-poo."

"I brought shoes," Carlotta said brightly, wheeling in the bounty.

Angela pushed to her feet shakily enough to tell Carlotta that she'd taken more than one "drinkie-poo" in Carlotta's absence, but apparently it had given the woman enough energy to embark upon another spending binge that included six outfits, eight pairs of shoes, including a pair of tall, exotic black boots that Carlotta coveted, plus a rather astonishing array of risqué underwear ("Peter likes me in black"). Angela even ventured into the men's department where she chose an exquisite cashmere jacket with a crest embroidered on the lapel—Peter's favorite brand, Carlotta recalled fondly. And the charcoal-gray would look great on Peter with his fair hair and dark skin. From the size, it appeared that he had filled out a little in the shoulders.

She hadn't seen him in ages, only once in the mall a couple of years ago. He hadn't known she was standing a mere ten feet from him while he ordered a double latte from a coffee shop. She had wanted to call out his name, to smile and say how nice it was to run into him, that she'd seen his and Angela's wedding announcement and photo in the *Atlanta Journal–Constitution* Sunday Living section and, hey, congratulations. But in the end she hadn't wanted to force an awkward exchange, to see the pity in his gorgeous cobalt-blue eyes for the way her family and lifestyle had imploded, so she'd simply watched him tip the clerk and walk away, her body straining after him.

Brushing her hand over the fine fabric of the jacket, Carlotta ignored the vibrating cell phone in her pocket and listened while Angela told her about the lavish parties that she and Peter threw at their palatial home located in a gated subdivision within the exclusive neighborhood of Buckhead. And how with the recent addition of a pool, spa and alfresco kitchen, they were the envy of their neighbors. And how well Peter was doing in his job at Mashburn and Tully Investments—which had once been Mashburn, Tully and Wren. The irony of Peter working for the same firm where her father had once been a partner seemed comically cruel.

"Did I mention that Peter was given a *huge* bonus this quarter?" Angela slurred as Carlotta rang up the enormous sale.

"Yes, I believe you did mention it," Carlotta said smoothly.

The encounter was nearly over—she could afford to be nice a little while longer, even if it killed her inside.

Angela smirked. "Of course, Peter makes all of *his* money legally."

Carlotta clenched her jaw but decided to allow the sly reference to her father's crime slide.

"Whatever happened to your parents?" Angela pressed, her eyes glinting with a gossipy light.

Carlotta wet her lips. "I really don't know."

"You mean you've never heard from them all this time?"

"That's right."

Angela made a pitying noise in her throat. "What kind of parents could just run off and leave their kids like that?"

Carlotta had her opinion but decided not to respond.

"I feel so sorry for you, Carlotta. I mean, it must have been hard for you to go from having everything you wanted to having nothing."

From the triumphant look in Angela's eyes, Carlotta could tell that by "everything," the woman meant Peter. Carlotta wanted to say that it hadn't been easy, especially since all of her so-called friends had seemingly vanished into thin air along with her parents. She and Angela hadn't been best buddies, but they had run in the same crowd—the crowd that had turned on her by high-school graduation. Angela had gone on to Vandy, which was where Carlotta assumed the woman had hooked up with Peter. Had "poor Carlotta" been a common topic of conversation?

"I managed just fine," she murmured.

Angela leaned in for a conspiratorial whisper. "That's why I always buy things from you, Carlotta, because I figure that you need the commission. It's my little good deed."

The scent of gin burned Carlotta's nose like the fiery mortification that bled through her chest. Years' worth of pent-up frustration suddenly flared to life. Her hands halted in the middle of ringing up the sale. "I don't need your pity, Angela," she said, her voice shaking, "or your effing money." She gave herself ten points for the verbal filter.

Angela's expression grew haughty. "You don't have to be nasty—I'm only trying to help."

"You're *trying* to make me feel like a charity case." And dammit, she was succeeding.

Angela swept her hand over the pile of merchandise that cost as much as Carlotta's car. "So you'd be willing to turn your back on this sale because of your stupid pride?"

Carlotta hesitated—she desperately needed the commission—and in her hesitation, knew Angela had won. As she looked into the woman's slightly unfocused but gloating eyes, comebacks whirled through Carlotta's mind, ranging from "Screw you" to "You're right" to "You got Peter—what else do you want from me?"

She wanted to throw something, to hit something, to push the Rewind button and be seventeen again, before her life had taken such a detour. To her horror, moisture gathered in her eyes. She blinked furiously and opened her mouth. "I—"

Her phone vibrated against her side and she pounced on the diversion. "I'm sorry, Angela, I have to take this call." But when she withdrew the phone and glanced at the caller ID, fear bolted through her chest. *Atlanta Police Department.*

Her heart lodged in her throat as images of Wesley's mangled body ran through her mind. He'd finally gotten himself killed on that damn motorcycle of his. She stabbed the Incoming Call button, missed, and tried again. "Hello?"

"Hi, sis," Wesley said, his voice tentative—like at age ten when he had put sugar in their neighbor's gas tank "just to see if it really would freeze up the engine."

It had.

Her initial flood of relief that he was alive was immediately overridden with a different kind of anxiety. "What's wrong?"

"Why do you assume something's wrong?"

She glanced up to find Angela listening intently. Carlotta turned her back and walked a few steps to be—she hoped—out of earshot. "Because, Wesley, the police department came up on the caller ID."

"Oh."

"So…what happened?"

"Okay, don't freak out, but I kind of got arrested."

Carlotta felt faint. "What? You *kind of* got arrested, or you *did* get arrested?"

She could picture him on the other end of the line, stabbing at his glasses and weighing his answer. "I *did* get arrested."

She closed her eyes and mouthed a curse.

"I heard that."

Okay, minus ten points for swearing at her kid brother. She counted to three, then exhaled. "What were you arrested for?"

"Well, it's kind of complicated. Maybe you'd better come down here."

"Where is 'here'?"

"The jail at City Hall East."

Christ, what did it say for her that she knew exactly where the jail was? She pinched the bridge of her nose, feeling a migraine coming on. "What am I supposed to do once I get there?"

"Uh...ask for inmate Wren?"

She clenched her jaw and disconnected the call, then gave Angela a flat smile. "I have to go. Someone else will be happy to ring up your purchases."

Angela's face reddened. "But I don't want someone else—I want *you*."

"Don't worry, Angela. I'm sure you'll still get a gold star for your little good deed." She swept by the woman, and when she passed Michael on the escalator, told him that she had an emergency and would return later if she could and would he take care of you-know-who?

Breaking into a jog, Carlotta retrieved her purse from her locker in the employee break room, fighting tears of frustration. What had Wesley gotten himself into now? Her feet moved automatically, carrying her to her car, which was a good thing because she couldn't consciously remember where she'd parked.

As she careened out of the mall parking lot, she imagined Wesley's mangled body again—only this time it was by her own hands.

2

Carlotta took a deep breath and made herself say the words. "I'm here to see i-inmate Wren."

The uniformed woman behind the Plexiglas rolled her eyes upward to glance over her bifocals. "Spell the name, please."

Carlotta did, glancing around the crowded waiting room nervously, hoping she didn't run into anyone she knew—or anyone who knew her. The place held bad memories; she'd been arrested once a couple of years ago for taking a tire iron to one of Wesley's bookies, but the charges had been dropped. And just before Christmas last year she'd been hauled in for questioning in a murder case. It turned out to be a big fat misunderstanding, but the experience had scared her straight. No more lying...no more pretending.

She frowned down at her outfit. One thing was certain— even in her last-season Diane von Furstenberg sundress and midi-jacket, she was a tad overdressed for the occasion.

The woman wrote down Wesley's name. "And you are?"

Carlotta lowered her mouth to the little hole in the Plexiglas and whispered, "I'm his sister, Carlotta Wren. And there must be some mistake. My brother would never break the law. At least not a big law."

The woman appeared to be unmoved. "Yeah. Have a seat and someone will be with you."

Carlotta cut a glance to the waiting room and noted the sagging bodies, the yawns, the general restlessness of people who had been waiting for hours. She looked back and flashed an ingratiating smile at the woman. "Look——" She peeked at the woman's name tag, then frowned. "Your parents named you Brooklyn?"

The woman smirked. "Everyone calls me Brook."

"Okay...Brook, I don't mean to be pushy, but I had to take a break from my job at Neiman Marcus to come down here, and I really need to get back ASAP."

The woman blinked slowly. "I need a million dollars and a good man. Have a *seat,* Ms. Wren."

Carlotta sighed——there went her overtime pay this week. As she turned toward the teeming waiting room, she made eye contact with a tall, striking man wearing a badge around his neck, pouring coffee from a corroded glass pot. A frown furrowed his brow.

"Did you say your name was Wren?" he drawled, hinting at his roots. South Georgia, she guessed, or maybe an Alabama boy. He was block-shouldered with black hair, a strong nose, fortyish, with bloodshot eyes, bad taste in ties and an apparent aversion to ironing. His haircut was rather good, she conceded, in her split-second scrutiny, reminiscent of George Clooney in his *E.R.* days. But this guy didn't seem to have much of a bedside manner.

"Yes," she said warily. "I'm Carlotta Wren."

He drank from the cup, then winced. "I'm Detective Jack Terry. I brought your brother in," he said and blew on the top of his coffee.

His nonchalance was beyond irritating. "May I ask why?"

He was still blowing. "I'll let him tell you. Hey, are you two any relation to Randolph Wren?"

She clenched her jaw. "He's our father. What does that have to do with this?"

"Nothing that I know of," he admitted, then took a slurpy drink. "I just wondered."

"When can I talk to my brother?"

"How about now?" He nodded at the woman behind the Plexiglas. "Brook, I'll take care of Ms. Wren."

Brook shook her finger. "Behave, Jack."

He grinned and Carlotta frowned. Judging from the woman's comment, some women apparently found his good-old-boy charm appealing. There was just no accounting for taste.

He waved his badge in front of a card reader, then opened a door that led to a noisy bullpen of cubicles. As he held the door for her, she stepped inside and was immediately engulfed by the clatter of conversation, the whir of machines and the drone of announcements over a public-address system.

Carlotta followed the detective through the obstacle course of overflowing desks, jutting legs and fast-moving bodies to an eight-foot-by-eight-foot cubicle marked with a nameplate that read, Det. J. Terry, Major Crimes.

Major crimes? Dread mushroomed in her stomach. This sounded serious.

Stacks of files and papers occupied every square inch of surface in the man's cubicle. His trash can was spilling over. A bag from the Varsity, Atlanta's famous fast-food joint on North Avenue, sat in a dusty corner on the floor, emitting iffy odors. The detective rummaged next to his computer, mumbling under his breath, until he found the phone, then yanked up the receiver, punched a button and said, "Janower, it's Terry. Bring the skinny computer jock to interview room two, will you?" He hung up the phone and gave Carlotta a flat smile. "It'll be a few minutes, if you want to have a seat. Here, let me clear a spot."

He leaned over and dumped the stack of files sitting in his visitor's chair on the floor, but at the sight of the dark stain on the dingy yellow upholstery, Carlotta swallowed. "Thanks, I'll stand."

He shrugged. "Suit yourself." Then he dropped into his own stained chair and took another drink from his coffee cup.

"So does my brother's arrest have something to do with computers?" Wesley had been tinkering with them since he was ten. He'd begged for his own PC, and later, when Carlotta couldn't afford to upgrade the machine, he'd rebuilt the old one himself. Over the years, he'd made spending money by upgrading computers for his friends and their parents, and had even helped some small companies with their software security. He had no less than six computers in his room at any given time, and sat rooted in front of them for the better part of every day, wearing headphones and generally oblivious to the outside world.

Possible scenarios whirled through her mind. Had he stolen

computer components? Or could this have something to do with his gambling problem? He was supposed to be on the wagon, but maybe he was running a bookie service or an illegal poker site. She held her breath and steeled herself for the bad news.

The detective worked his mouth from side to side. "Guess it won't hurt to tell you—it'll be a matter of public record soon. Your brother was arrested for hacking into the database of the Atlanta city government, specifically, the courthouse."

Panic blipped in her chest. "How much trouble is he in?"

"A lot," he said, his voice sober. "We're talking a felony here. And records tampering and identity theft is high on the department's priority list. Hackers are vigorously pursued and prosecuted. Accessing the records is bad enough, but we think he might have changed some things while he was in there."

Carlotta frowned. "Like what?"

"We're still trying to determine the extent of the tampering."

She stifled the spike of pride that Wesley was so damn smart—this wasn't the time to gloat.

"We're guessing that he might have been planning to sell the information."

Carlotta's jaw hardened. If money was involved, that damn Chance Hollander probably had something to do with it. That overgrown brat had been a friend of Wesley's since they were boys and he'd made a lifestyle out of talking Wesley into doing things that always seemed to result in Wesley getting into trouble and Chance getting a good laugh.

"This isn't like Wesley," she murmured, swallowing her rising panic. "He's mischievous, but he wouldn't break the law."

Detective Terry cleared his throat. "Wesley must have been a little fellow when your father, er—"

"Yes, he was."

"That has to be rough on a kid."

She nodded and averted her gaze. He had no right prying into their personal lives.

"Who raised your brother?"

"I did."

He seemed surprised. "What do you do for a living, Ms. Wren?"

"I work for Neiman Marcus."

He gave her a thorough once-over, his gaze lingering on her legs. The cad. "I hear that's a nice place."

She crossed her arms. "When and where was Wesley arrested?"

"This morning, at his residence. I assume it's your home, actually, since your name is on the mortgage?"

Her heart accelerated. "You were in our home?"

He nodded. "We traced his online activity to the house. I arrested him there and confiscated his equipment."

She covered her mouth. This couldn't be happening.

He gave her a little smile. "Don't worry—we didn't trash your place. That only happens on TV."

Carlotta narrowed her eyes. "You think this is funny?"

His smile vanished. "No. Sorry. Does your brother live with you full-time?"

She tingled under his scrutiny and felt her defenses rise. "Yes, it's his home, too. And for all that Wesley's been through, I think he's turned into a pretty decent kid."

He pursed his mouth. "He might still seem like a kid to you,

Ms. Wren, but your brother is an adult in the eyes of the law. And no offense, but he's making bad choices that are going to mess up his life, just like your father did."

His words cut her to the quick. For the past ten years, her consuming goal had been to do what was best for Wesley, to teach him right from wrong, especially considering the criminal legacy their father had left behind. It seemed she had failed... miserably.

She blinked back sudden tears. "What do *you* know about my father?"

The detective's face went stony. "I know that he made a living bilking people out of their hard-earned money while he lived like a king. And when he got caught, instead of facing his punishment like a man, he skipped bail and abandoned his children, one of whom seems on the verge of following in his footsteps."

Carlotta's defenses surged against his attack on her family. "What are you, a one-man judge and jury? You don't know everything, Mr. Terry."

"Detective Terry," he corrected amiably.

"*Detective* Terry, why aren't you out arresting real criminals instead of picking on my brother?"

His geniality fled. "Ms. Wren, your brother *is* a real criminal."

She wanted to scream a denial, to flail and blame everything on her parents, to rail against the unfairness of it all. She had given up her twenties because her parents had bailed on their responsibility, but had always told herself it was worth it to be the best possible replacement for their parents to her little brother. Had it all been for nothing?

Suddenly she felt so powerless. She sank into the yellow chair, stain and all, and summoned strength. She didn't have to like Detective Jack Terry, but right now he had the information she needed. "What will happen next?"

"He'll need an attorney."

"An attorney," she repeated in a weak voice. Where would she get the money for an attorney?

He checked his watch. "If his attorney can get here this afternoon, he'll probably have a bail hearing today."

"Bail hearing," she murmured.

"And since this is his first offense, he'll probably be released on bail."

Feeling like the most stupid person alive, she said, "How does that work exactly—bail? I...I don't remember from...I don't remember." From when her father had been arrested.

His expression softened, as if he realized that she wasn't nearly as street-smart as she tried to appear. "For a felony with no endangerment, the standard bail is five thousand. If you pay cash, you'll get it back after the case is settled."

She choked back a laugh. Where would she get five thousand dollars? If only their parents had left them a stash of ill-gotten gains to make up for the fact that they had abandoned their own children.

He coughed lightly. "If you don't have cash, you'll want to call a bail bondsman. That will cost you ten percent of the bail, which you won't get back."

Five hundred—she could probably scrape together that much, but it would be another expense that she didn't need right now.

He opened a desk drawer, revealing more clutter, and rooted

around, coming up with a curled business card. "If you need to, call this guy."

She took the card of Brumbee's Bail Bonds ("Call us anytime!"), a flush warming her cheeks. Had the detective guessed how deeply in debt they were, or had he already performed a credit check and confirmed it? At least her parents had left the house in her name. Although she suspected it was to shelter the property in case her parents' assets were seized during the criminal case, it was the one thing that had given her a financial toehold after they had disappeared, and the means to secure custody of Wesley. "I've heard of people putting up the deed to their house for bail."

"A property bond?" He splayed his big hands. "Yeah, people do that all the time. And then they get a lien placed on their home if the person doesn't show up in court." His lips flattened. "I wouldn't advise it."

She frowned. "Wesley would never skip bail."

The detective didn't say anything, but in the air hung the question *Like your father wouldn't skip bail?*

Carlotta lowered her gaze, burning with shame. She refused to cry. When Detective Terry's hand touched her arm, she could only stare at the blunt-tipped fingers, wishing it was the hand of someone she could rely on for the long haul rather than fleeting sympathy. They were, after all, on opposite sides of this issue. She inhaled to compose herself, then pulled her arm away and lifted her gaze to his. "After posting bail, then what?"

The detective looked contrite, then picked up his coffee cup with his errant hand. "Within a couple of days he'll have to appear in court to be arraigned."

"Arraigned," she said, nodding stupidly.

"That's where the charges against him will be read, and he'll enter a plea. If his attorney and the district attorney reach an agreement on the charges and the sentence, he can plead out." He hesitated, then added, "If not, his case will go to trial."

"Trial," she said like a sick parrot. She closed her eyes, thinking how sordid it all sounded—and how disturbingly familiar. It was all coming back to her, hearing the same terminology peppering her parents' conversations after the grand jury had indicted her father, her mother weeping drunkenly, her father professing his innocence—unconvincingly. And now it was starting all over again.

When she opened her eyes, Detective Terry was studying her intently. Upon closer inspection, his bloodshot eyes were hazel, almost golden, unusually pale with his dark coloring. And...dangerous. Unbidden, the thought darted through her mind that any woman foolish enough to hook up with this man was destined for disappointment.

Suddenly he leaned toward her. "Look, I didn't know about the connection between your brother and your father when I made the arrest this morning. Your brother will have to pay for his crime, but...well, off the record, I should warn you—the D.A., Kelvin Lucas, is the same man who had your father indicted."

A slow drip of panic entered her bloodstream, as cool as menthol. "Are you saying that the D.A. might be harder on my brother because he didn't get to prosecute my father?"

The detective's gaze was unflinching. "Ms. Wren, in this city, and especially in the D.A.'s office, your father's name is like a bad smell. All I'm saying is that you and your brother should prepare yourselves for the worst."

3

Wesley Wren whistled under his breath, a nameless tune that his father had always whistled when Wesley was a boy. He didn't remember too many moments with his workaholic father, whose angular face was hazy in his mind, but he remembered that when Dad was in a good mood, he whistled. And, despite sitting in the corner of a musty jail cell and the fact that Hubert, one of the dozen other guys in holding, had forced him to trade his new brown suede Puma tennis shoes for Hubert's worn-out no-name sneakers, Wesley was in a pretty good mood. It had taken him only a few weeks to find a way into the Atlanta courthouse records, and that wasn't bad for a hobby hacker.

His buddy Chance had given him the idea by asking if Wesley could expunge a couple of DUI arrests from Chance's record. He was willing to pay Wesley five hundred bucks per delete stroke.

Oh, sure, the extra cash had come in handy, but cleaning up Chance's traffic violations hadn't been the primary incentive.

For months now he'd been covertly accumulating details about his father's indictment and subsequent disappearance—covertly because Carlotta would murder him if she ever caught wind of it. He'd made copies of every public document he could find online and in crammed file cabinets around Atlanta, but the information was incomplete and dated. When he'd tapped into the courthouse records two days ago, he'd found a wealth of information on his father's last court appearance, and on sightings of his parents over the past ten years—Michigan, Kentucky, California, Texas. The thought of his polished, executive father wearing a ten-gallon hat made him smile, but he was sure that Randolph Wren could carry it off. His father was smart, savvy, and knew how to blend in to his environment—how else had he been able to elude the authorities for over a decade?

His chest swelled with pride when he thought of his father donning a disguise and slipping out of town under the nose of some cop out to make a career for himself by capturing Randolph Wren, The Bird. When Wesley was in grade school, he'd entertained his friends with daring stories that he'd imagined to be true. Having a notorious father had given him status in school. He was no longer the bespectacled runt who blew the curve in math class. He was the son of *The Bird*. He had told his classmates how he'd helped his father escape the feds by coming up with a fantastic math equation regarding engine speed and the timing of traffic lights, and how he continued to help his father from afar via secret code. As soon as his father had gathered enough evidence to prove that he had been set up, he would return to Atlanta and clear his name. They would be a family again, vindicated, and stronger for their trials.

It was true...sort of. He hadn't helped his father escape, of course, but he would have if his father had only asked. And there was no secret code within the abbreviated messages on the postcards they had received sporadically over the years—at least not one that he'd been able to crack. He'd spent hours poring over those postcards, eight of them in all, studying them under a magnifying glass, infrared light, black light, and had even managed to have a couple of them X-rayed on an eighth-grade field trip to a vet clinic. In hindsight, he realized there were no secret messages between the lines of "We're fine and we love you" or "You're always in our hearts," yet he remained hopeful that his father would someday contact him and ask for his help now that Wesley was an adult.

Unless his parents had forgotten how old he was.

He banished the thought as soon as it entered his mind. Of course his parents knew he was an adult now. Just because they'd never called or sent a special message on his birthday didn't mean that they'd forgotten that he was no longer a kid. Ditto for Christmas. They had sacrificed too much to risk being caught over something stupid and sentimental.

Yet every Christmas, in the back of his mind, he dared to hope that they might simply show up at his bedroom window, or maybe ring the doorbell. "We couldn't stay away any longer," they would say, then gather him and his sister in their arms.

But it never happened. Last Christmas he'd spent the day being a jerk to Carlotta when she'd only tried to make him happy by attempting to bake a chocolate cake with peanut-butter chips in the middle. It had been his favorite since he was a kid, a special cake that his mother had always made during the holidays. But Carlotta was hopeless in the kitchen. In fact, self-preservation had forced him to take over the cooking duties when he'd turned twelve. Carlotta's cake had been undercooked in the middle and burnt around the edges. He had snapped at her and at the time, had been unfazed by her wounded expression, just happy to lash out at someone.

But now he felt the sting of remorse over the mean things he'd said—that she'd never find a husband if she didn't learn to cook and that he hated the clothes she'd bought and wrapped up for him and that he didn't want to watch the dumb Christmas movie that she'd rented. The movie, he knew, had been her attempt to tether him, to keep him off the streets and away from the card tables. She meant well, but she smothered him.

Then he sighed. Damn, no matter what he did, he seemed to disappoint Carlotta. She'd be furious with him when she found out about the hacking. Although, if he was careful, he could at least keep her from finding out why he'd done it.

A buzzing noise sounded and the door to the holding cell slid open, revealing a uniformed officer. All the inmates who weren't sleeping or passed out perked up.

"On your feet, Wren. You have a visitor."

Wesley winced. Time to face the executioner. He pushed to his feet and waded through the jumble of funky-smelling bodies, enduring wolf whistles from his bigger, brawnier cellmates while the officer handcuffed him. Then he followed the officer to a room where his sister waited. Her anxious gaze darted from his face to his handcuffs, and she looked as if she was going to cry. God, he hoped not. Seeing her in tears tore him up, always had. When the officer left and closed the door, she gripped his shoulders hard, but instead of hugging him, she shook him with more strength than he'd known she had. "What the *hell* did you do, Wesley?"

When his eyes stopped spinning in his head, he said, "Relax, sis, no one was murdered."

She narrowed her eyes at him. "Yet. That Chance Hollander has something to do with this, doesn't he?"

"No," Wesley said because Carlotta already didn't like his best friend. And even though Chance had given him the idea to break into the courthouse records, *he* was the one who had actually done it.

"Tell me what you did. *Now*, Wesley."

He swallowed. He hadn't seen her this worked up since he'd broken the news that he wasn't going to apply for college. "I, um, sort of stumbled into a computer database that I wasn't supposed to."

One dark eyebrow arched. "Stumbled into, or hacked into?"

"Uh, hacked."

She crossed her arms. "Detective Terry told me that you broke into the courthouse computer and changed some records?"

He frowned. "That guy's a jerk."

His sister looked alarmed. "Did he hurt you?"

"Nah, but he gets off on that bad-cop routine."

She frowned. "I noticed. Now, why were you messing around in the courthouse records?"

He tried to look sheepish. "Just trying to get rid of all those traffic tickets I accumulated so I could get my driver's license reinstated and I wouldn't be such a pain to you." He could lie with assurance because when he suspected his access was being tracked, he'd unleashed a virus in the database that would be undetectable to the hillbilly programmers in the police department. No way they'd be able to tell what had been changed.

"Is that all?" she asked, her brown eyes hopeful.

Guilt stabbed at him, but he told himself that she wanted to believe him, and he'd only hurt her more with the truth. "Yeah, that's all."

She sighed in relief, then ran her hand over his cheek as she used to when he was little. "What am I going to do with you?"

His heart swelled with affection, but he tamped down his sissy emotions. "You have to keep me around, or you'd starve to death."

She smiled briefly, then sobered. "We need to get you a lawyer."

He shifted his feet. "I already called Liz Fischer."

Carlotta looked horrified. "Dad's attorney? Why?"

"Why not?"

"Well, for one reason, she'll probably charge an arm and a leg to represent you."

He shrugged. "Maybe not. She always told us to call her if we needed anything, and she sounded nice on the phone."

"I don't like the fact that everyone will connect her to Dad, and then him to you."

"Since we have the same last name, I think that's unavoidable, don't you?"

Carlotta frowned, her expression suspicious. "What did Liz say?"

"She'll be here. My bail hearing is at four this afternoon." He shuffled his feet again. "Can we make bail? I have six hundred dollars in a tennis-ball can in the garage."

Her eyebrows shot up. "You have six hundred dollars?"

More disapproval. He owed a lot of money to a lot of people, but he kept a secret stash in case a big card game materialized—something tempting enough to go back on his word to Carlotta that he wouldn't gamble. "My emergency fund," he mumbled. And now he'd have to find a new hiding place.

Her gapped front teeth worried her lower lip, then she sighed. "If the bail is set too high for us to pay cash, then I'll call a bail bondsman, assuming we can cough up ten percent."

"And if we can't come up with ten percent?"

"I'll have to put up the house."

Wesley's intestines cramped. For the first time, he doubted his plan. He hadn't counted on the trouble it would cause his sister.

Then she gave him a shaky smile. "Don't worry, we'll figure it out." She looked down and gasped. "Where did you get those revolting shoes?"

"Don't worry about it," he said, waving off her concern. "If I have to spend the night here, will you feed Einstein?"

She winced. "For that reason alone, I'll make sure you get out of here."

He grinned, glad to see she was back in good humor. His sister was a pretty woman, especially when she smiled. She was self-conscious about the gap between her two front teeth, but he thought it gave her character, made her look like a dark-haired Lauren Hutton…and his mother.

He worried about Carlotta. He'd seen men's eyes light up when she walked into a room, but she hadn't had a serious relationship since their parents had left, since that bastard Peter Ashford had dumped her. She'd never said so, but Wesley knew that he himself was much of the reason that his sister hadn't settled down. Not too many guys were keen on a kid brother as a package deal. Just one more thing for him to feel guilty over. "Thanks for coming, sis. I'll make it up to you, I promise."

Her expression was part dubious, part hopeful. "I'll hold you to that."

Wesley went back to the holding cell with mixed feelings pulling at him. For the next few hours he sat with his back in a corner trying not to attract attention from his cellmates, many of whom were finally rousing from hangovers and were spoiling for trouble…or romance. A muscle-bound guy wearing a headband and leg warmers kept looking his way and licking his lips. In desperation, Wesley pulled out a deck of cards he'd been allowed to keep and announced he was giving a clinic on how to play the ultimate game of skill and luck, Texas Hold 'Em Poker. His audience seemed suspicious at first, then crowded around. He sat cross-legged and dealt the four men closest to him two cards each facedown on the gritty concrete floor. Just the feel of the waxy cards in his hands sent a flutter of excitement to his chest.

"Those cards are your pocket cards," he explained. "I'm going to deal five community cards faceup—three, then one, then one more—and the object is to create the best hand possible from your two cards and the five community cards. Bets are made between rounds of revealing the community cards."

"We need chips," one guy said, then started ripping the buttons off his shirt. Everyone followed suit and within five minutes, a pile of mismatched buttons lay in the middle. Impressed with their resourcefulness, Wesley divided the buttons among the four players and gave them tips on betting. "If you have strong pocket cards, you'll want to bet. If not, you'll want to fold." Then he grinned. "Unless you want to bluff, and then you'll want to bet."

"What's a strong card?" a man asked.

"Any face card, or an ace,"Wesley said. "Two of a kind is great, two cards of the same suit can put you on your way to a flush, and two neighboring cards, like a nine and a ten can put you on your way to a straight." He went around, taking button bets on the pocket cards. "Now I'll deal what's called the flop cards." He tossed a discard card to the side, then dealt three cards faceup— a three of spades, a five of hearts and a queen of hearts. "We got a possible straight going with the three and the five, and a possible heart flush with the five and the queen."

Excitement built among the players and spectators as they studied the cards, creating possible hands. Wesley smiled to himself. There was something so sweet about evangelizing the game of games…and training potential players that he might someday face across the table and rob of every penny they had.

He tossed the top card onto the discard pile, then dealt another card faceup. "This is called the 'turn' card."

An ace of hearts. A murmur went up among the men. Wesley studied the players' "tells," the body language and betting techniques that told a more experienced player what the person was holding as surely as if the cards were transparent. The big guy on the far left was holding crap—probably a ten and a deuce, but he wasn't going to fold and look bad to the other guys. The guy next to him was grinning like a fool after the turn card, so he probably had a pocket ace to make it two of a kind. Beginners thought that aces beat everything else, no matter what.

The third guy also had nothing, else he wouldn't be gnawing on his nails and staring at the community cards as if he could will them to change. The fourth guy, though—he had something because he was holding his cards close to his chest as if they were winning lottery tickets. Wesley guessed he had pocket queens and was looking at three of a kind, which so far was "the nuts"—the best hand in the game.

"Here comes the river card," he said, and dealt a nine of clubs—not much good to anyone, he guessed, although the bidding was brisk. The aces guy was all in with his six wooden buttons and a jeans rivet. Pretty soon, everyone was all in, and Wesley asked, "Whad'ya have?"

The first guy turned over his ten of spades and four of clubs and took some ribbing from the other guys. The grinning aces guy turned over his ace of diamonds and seven of spades, giving him the expected pair of aces. The third guy cursed his mother and tossed in his jack of diamonds and six of spades, then stomped away as if they had been playing for real money instead of sewing notions. The last guy turned over his pocket queens to the cheers of the men behind him, and raked all the raggedy buttons toward him triumphantly.

While Wesley was shuffling for another hand, the cell door buzzed and slid open and he was being summoned again. "Your lawyer's here," the guard informed him.

Wesley handed off the deck of cards, stood and allowed himself to be handcuffed again, then followed the man to a room where Liz Fischer waited, tapping the toe of her pointy high-heeled shoe. She was a tall, athletic blonde in her mid-forties, a real looker who seemed to be in perpetual motion. Wesley recognized her from newspaper photos of his father's case, although her hair was shorter and she looked a little leaner.

"Hello, Wesley."

Her voice, for sure, was familiar—throaty and abrupt. He'd had more than one wet dream lately with that voice looping in his head. "Hello, Mrs. Fischer."

She smiled at his politeness. "I'm not married, so it's Ms.— in fact, call me Liz. How nice to finally put a face to the voice. I just wish it were under different circumstances."

When she sat down at the table, the scent of her cologne reached him—not a feminine, floral scent, but something earthy and strong that she might have gotten out of her lover's medicine cabinet this morning. Which could also explain the over-size white dress shirt she wore with her prim suit.

She clicked open her briefcase. "So, you got caught. I told you to be careful."

He splayed his hands. "I slipped up, but everything's fine."

She frowned. "The optimism of youth. Do you realize that you're facing jail time and a hefty fine?"

A vision of Leg Warmers licking his lips flashed through Wesley's mind. "How much jail time?"

"Probably less than six months, but it won't look good on your permanent record. Now, tell me what happened."

Wesley repeated the lie, that he had hacked into the courthouse records to clear his own traffic violations. "I'm really sorry," he added.

The woman's expression was bland. "You're going to have to do a better acting job than that for the district attorney. And you're telling me that this records break-in has nothing to do with your sudden interest in your father's cold case?"

"That's right."

She studied him suspiciously. Wesley imagined himself through her experienced eyes: a skinny, know-it-all kid who'd grown up without parents and likely wouldn't amount to much.

"You look like Randolph," she said, surprising him with intense eye contact.

His cock jumped—damn, he was going to embarrass himself. He shifted in his chair. "That's what my sister says when she talks about my father, which isn't often."

"Carlotta was bitter when your parents…left. Rightfully so. How is she?"

"Fine. A little upset with me at the moment."

"I called her occasionally after….afterward, and she always assured me everything was okay." The woman looked remorseful. "I should have looked in on both of you more often."

"We did okay," Wesley said, trying not to sound too reassuring in case she was inclined to reduce her fee out of some sense of obligation. "But Carlotta doesn't know that I've talked to you about my father's case. It would only upset her."

"She won't hear it from me, but you know that I agree with her, Wesley. You should let sleeping dogs lie, and get on with your life. Your parents seem to have gotten on with theirs."

Anger sparked in his stomach, but he didn't want to alienate this woman. She was too valuable in his search for the truth. Plus, she was wearing a pink satin bra beneath the white shirt, and that was really hot. "Do you know where my father is?"

Liz Fischer's expression hardened, giving the first hint of her age. "No, and if I did, I'd go straight to the police. Now, let's get back to the matter at hand and see if I can get you out of here."

After answering a few more questions and receiving a stern warning not to discuss his case with anyone, Wesley inhaled one last lungful of the woman's cologne, then went back to the cell with his cuffed hands in front of him to hide his hard-on. One of these days, he'd be a rich, accomplished man, and women like Liz Fischer would look at him with respect. When he won the World Series of Poker. When he cleared his father's name. He would be happy then, and everyone who meant something to him would be happy, too.

When he returned to the holding cell, a poker game was in full swing. He retreated to a corner to avoid Leg Warmers and to watch the interplay of the men and the game, nodding in satisfaction when he predicted hands correctly. He could do the odds in his head, but so could lots of cardplayers. He was good at poker because he was good at observing people, and he was willing to be patient for the payoff.

He would use the same skills to solve his father's case. He had time.

Less than an hour later, thank goodness, he was escorted to a small courtroom for his bail hearing. He spotted Carlotta's anxious face in the sparse gallery and gave her a thumbs-up that was somewhat hampered by his handcuffed wrists. Liz Fischer's presence next to him was assuring—and alluring—but his pulse ratcheted higher as he listened to the charges against him: federal charges of computer intrusion and unlawful use of passwords. Two counts each. *Federal.*

This might be more serious than he thought.

Addressing the judge, his attorney tried to pass off his hacking as a childish prank that he deeply regretted. "I request that my client be released on his own recognizance."

But the stern-faced judge seemed to be studying the papers in front of him rather than listening to counsel. When he finally lifted his head, he said, "It's been brought to my attention that your client is the son of a fugitive still wanted by the Atlanta Police Department."

Wesley shifted beneath the man's condemning gaze.

"Your Honor," Liz said, "with all due respect, I don't see what bearing my client's father's situation has on this case. My client hasn't seen his father since he was a little boy."

The judge frowned. "Still, I'd be remiss if I didn't take it into consideration. Bail is set at twenty thousand dollars. See the court cashier."

"Your *Honor,*" Liz said with alarm in her voice. "That will cause undue hardship on my client—"

"Then perhaps your client would be more comfortable in jail until his arraignment, Ms. Fischer." He banged his gavel. "Next case."

Wesley's mind churned at the unexpected turn of events. Twenty thousand dollars? They didn't even have the cash to pay ten percent to a bail bondsman. On the other hand, it was kind of cool that the judge thought he was worth that much.

"Wesley," Liz said slowly, "this is a little unorthodox, but if you need a loan—"

"We don't," Carlotta said, walking up to stand near him. She looked pale, and her hand shook as she held up a manila file. "I brought all the information to post a property bond."

"Hello, Carlotta," Liz said.

"Hello," Carlotta said.

His sister's voice was pleasant enough, but Wesley could feel the animosity rolling off his sister in waves toward the other woman. What was it with chicks?

"You certainly came prepared," Liz said lightly.

"I look out for my family. Wesley, let's go home." She turned and walked toward the exit.

He hesitated, then looked up at Liz Fischer. "Thank you for your help...Liz."

"No problem," she said smoothly. "Your arraignment is Monday morning. I'll be in touch." She picked up her briefcase and walked in the direction opposite from the one that Carlotta had taken. He noticed that the woman turned back and eyed his sister intently before continuing.

Escorted by a bailiff, Wesley caught up with Carlotta and watched with apprehension as she pledged the equity in their town home against the fact that he would appear in court when summoned. He had every intention of being there, but what if something happened? His sister's faith in him was a little unnerving. Even after his handcuffs were removed, his stomach was in knots, but he kept telling himself that the end justified the means.

As part of his sentence, he planned to offer his expertise to help the courthouse develop better safety firewalls, ones that only he could penetrate. If that failed, he had left himself a back door in the courthouse records database so when everything died down, he'd be able to go back in and explore. This arrest would be worth the inconvenience if it helped him gather information to help—and find—his father. He glanced at his sister's troubled profile and felt a twist in his gut. Someday, Carlotta would agree with him.

He hoped.

4

Carlotta's eyes popped open from a restless sleep, with elusive dreams of her parents sliding into the dark corners of her subconscious. Mercifully, the dreams had become less frequent over the years, and she hoped this recurrence was an isolated incident. A glutton for punishment, she allowed herself to wonder where her parents were waking up, and if she and Wesley ever crossed their minds. Then the events of yesterday—Wesley's arrest and bail hearing—came crashing back, and she squeezed her eyes shut.

Her family was going to be the death of her.

She turned her head on her pillow to look at the alarm clock and groaned. She'd meant to get up early to make up for the hours she'd missed yesterday, but now she'd be lucky to make it to the morning staff meeting on time. While she stood and yanked up the duvet cover to make her bed, she thought of Angela Ashford and the commission she'd walked away from yesterday. And she wondered how much of her phone conversation with Wesley the woman had overheard—enough to fuel another gossipy lunch with her girlfriends?

She tamped down her resentment toward Angela, recognizing that it was mostly rooted in the fact that the woman had married Peter, which, truthfully, only proved that Angela was... smart. Peter had graduated from Vanderbilt and returned to Atlanta to launch a successful career and join the ranks of his fabulously rich family. Angela enjoyed social status and all the perks that came with being a third-generation Buckhead wife.

Carlotta frowned. Although, considering the fact that the woman was sneaking booze in the department-store dressing room, her life might not be as rosy as the picture she'd painted for Carlotta.

After a quick shower, Carlotta opened the door to her closet, which always lifted her spirits. Working at Neiman Marcus for the better part of her adult life had afforded her a fabulous wardrobe on her employee discount. She had eased off her habit of "borrowing" clothes to wear for a special occasion and then returning them after nearly getting herself and her friends Jolie and Hannah in trouble last Christmas when they'd "borrowed" outfits to crash an upscale pajama party where a man had wound up dead. Since they'd been the only uninvited guests at the party and had drawn attention to themselves by accidentally falling into the pool fully clothed, they'd been fingered as the prime murder suspects. They'd managed to clear themselves, but had been stuck with paying for thousands of dollars' of ruined silk pj's and robes. She still hadn't paid off her Neiman Marcus credit card.

Thinking of Jolie made her smile. Her friend and co-worker

had moved to Costa Rica with the man of her dreams, and her parting gift to Carlotta had been a pink leather autograph book to replace the one full of celebrity autographs that had been ruined by the fall in the pool, and two thousand dollars in cash to satisfy the loan shark that had been hounding Carlotta for money that Wesley owed.

Jolie had saved their lives...or at least their kneecaps.

Carlotta flipped through her bulging wardrobe and decided to go all out today. Dressing to the nines always made her feel better.

She pulled out a black miniskirt, a teal-colored tunic, one of the vintage Judith Leiber huge "breastplate" necklaces from her mother's collection and tall Prada boots. She pulled her long black hair—her best feature, she thought—into a low ponytail, and added dangling glass earrings. She popped in her blue contact lenses, always amazed that they covered her dark brown irises so well. Blessed with good skin, she was able to skip foundation, but took time to stroke several coats of mascara onto her lashes to play up her eyes, add a touch of blush to the apple of her cheeks and smooth on red, red lipstick. When she made a final check in the mirror, though, she couldn't help but compare her dark coloring to Angela Ashford's golden good looks. Not only was Angela patently gorgeous and rail thin, she was well connected, with a long southern lineage. Yes, Angela was definitely the better match for Peter and the life he was destined for.

Carlotta sighed and turned to face the life *she* was destined for. She walked out of her bedroom and looked across the hall at Wesley's closed bedroom door and farther, at the end of the hall, to the closed door of her parents' room, left largely untouched except for the times she'd gone in to dust or to adjust the heating and air-conditioning vents. Daylight shining over the gray carpet in the hallway revealed large shoe prints, evidence of where the police had entered their home and confiscated Wesley's computer and phone equipment. A sense of violation permeated her skin—the cramped living space she'd tried to make a home for Wesley, compromised.

Using the toe of her shoe, she wiped out the footprints, wondering if they belonged to Detective Jack Terry. The mere thought of the man made a frown settle on her face and the knowledge that he'd been in her home made her feel naked, as if he knew intimate things about her. Had he peeked into her bedroom, sneered at the girlish white furniture, the pink Lilly Pulitzer linens and the fuzzy yellow chenille robe she always left draped across the foot of the bed? A flush climbed her neck when she remembered the way he'd looked at her when she'd told him that her father was Randolph Wren. He'd decided that she and Wesley were from bad stock. *Your father's name is like a bad smell.*

The friendly warning he'd given her about the D.A. notwithstanding, she had a feeling that Detective Terry was going to stir up more trouble before he exited their lives.

As she walked through the living room and into the kitchen, her thoughts turned to Liz Fischer. She didn't like the fact that Wesley had called the woman. She didn't trust Liz. After her parents had skipped town, Liz had tried to convince her that she was too young and ill equipped to raise Wesley, that his needs would be better served with a foster family until her parents returned.

This from the woman who'd had an affair with her father.

Carlotta had hated the woman for trying to fracture her family further, and it was Liz Fischer's insufferable words that had given her strength in the early years when she'd thought she would collapse under the stress of raising Wesley.

She knew what the woman was thinking now—that Carlotta had done a crummy job of parenting and that Wesley would have been better off with strangers.

And considering that he was head over heels in debt and now facing jail time, Carlotta couldn't exactly disagree. Maybe Wesley would have been better off with two authority figures who weren't bogged down with their own emotional baggage, who weren't struggling to make ends meet, who weren't, deep down, yearning for a life of their own.

Carlotta walked into the kitchen, massaging her temples and craving a Starbucks latte. But since they were facing unknown expenses, she poured water into the automatic coffeepot and waited for the homemade brew to trickle out. She walked around and straightened things that might have been moved by the police, or perhaps she was just being paranoid. What was it that Detective Terry had said?

Don't worry—we didn't trash your place. That only happens on TV.

Pushing the unpleasant thought—and the unpleasant man—from her mind, she glanced around the red-themed kitchen and contemplated repainting. All the rooms decorated under her mother's heavy hand were looking a little dated. In fact, she'd love to sell the town house outright and find another place for them to live, someplace with only two bedrooms and a larger living area, rather than having to walk by their parents' empty bedroom every day. But Wesley wouldn't hear of moving. He was afraid they would miss a postcard or a phone call...or the reappearance of their prodigal parents.

Heaving a sigh, Carlotta filled an insulated mug with coffee and cream to drink during the drive to work. Then she grabbed her purse and walked through the living room to the front door.

In the corner of the living room, the small aluminum fringe Christmas tree that had occupied the same spot for the ten years that her parents had been gone stirred anger in her stomach. Her mother had put up the tacky little tree the day after Thanksgiving and put a few presents under it, then had skipped town with their father two weeks later. Carlotta often wondered if her mother had felt guilty about abandoning her children just before Christmas, if Valerie had considered the tears that Wesley had shed Christmas morning when she and their father had failed to return, dashing his hopes for a Christmas surprise.

Carlotta loathed the raggedy little tree that had lost most of its luster, but Wesley had insisted that they leave the tree up and the presents underneath so they could celebrate when their parents came home. She had been eager to comfort her little brother in those first few weeks and months after her parents had left, but eventually she had begun to resent the tree's lopsided shape and the pathetic little pile of presents underneath. She'd long forgotten what she'd wrapped to give to her mother and father, and no longer cared what they had given to her. Several times over the years she had broached the subject of taking down the tree or, when money had been tight, of opening the gifts in the event that they contained cash, only to be met with

Wesley's curt refusal. He was obsessed with the tree, as if some-how by taking it down, they would be giving up on their par-ents ever coming home. That ship had sailed for her years ago, but she couldn't bring herself to hurt Wesley yet again by tak-ing it down. Turmoil rolled in her empty stomach. She was never sure how to handle her sensitive, quirky brother, so she usually erred on the soft side.

Too soft, apparently.

She opened the door, stepped out onto the stoop and bent to retrieve the newspaper. Around her, the neighborhood was peaceful, if a little shabby. Downsizing from their lavish home in a tony neighborhood to a town house in a "transitional" area had been a blow to her mother, who had chirped that it was only temporary and then taken another drinkie-poo.

"Carlotta!"

Carlotta winced, then turned to face her busybody neighbor. "Good morning, Mrs. Winningham. How are you today?"

The woman stood on the stoop next door with her head jut-ted forward, her eyes narrowed. "Why were the police at your place yesterday?"

Carlotta gave a hoarse little laugh. "Oh, that? It was a mis-take. They were at the wrong address."

Mrs. Winningham frowned. "I saw them carry a bunch of computers out of there."

"Everything is fine, Mrs. Winningham. I have to run—I'm late." Carlotta jogged down the steps and toward the garage while holding down the button on the remote control for the garage door. The noise of the door going up drowned out the woman's words, and Carlotta waved cheerfully as she swung into her dark blue Monte Carlo. She muttered a curse under her breath at the woman's snooping, then started her car.

The Monte Carlo was another sore spot—she loathed the car. Her beloved ten-year-old white Miata convertible sat like a sick and neglected pet next to her new car. Just before last Christmas, her Miata had died and she couldn't afford to have it fixed. So she'd taken advantage of a dealer's offer to test-drive a vehicle for twenty-four hours before buying it. Except the night she had taken the vehicle out for a test-drive was the night that she and her friends had crashed the party where a man had been murdered. She'd been taken to the police station for questioning and the car impounded. When she'd been released and had finally tracked down the car, the twenty-four-hour return period had expired and she owned the car by default.

The money that her friend Jolie had given her had kept Carlotta from having to sell her beloved, crippled Miata convertible to satisfy Wesley's debt. She still held out hope to have it back in working condition someday so she could get rid of the Monte Carlo—although what the Monte Carlo was worth amounted to less than what she owed on it.

Her life was a catastrophe.

Next to her Miata sat another thorn in her side: Wesley's newly acquired motorcycle, a fluorescent-green crotch rocket. He'd already received so many speeding tickets, his driver's license had been suspended, which only made him more prone to stay at home in his room and mess around with his computers.

Puffing out her cheeks in an exhale, she backed out of the

driveway, avoiding eye contact with Mrs. Winningham, and steered the car toward the Lenox Mall. She knew every curve of the road of her commute. The first traffic light would stay red long enough for her to take a long drink of coffee and scan the first three pages of the newspaper. The second light would stay red long enough to allow her to read any article that had caught her eye. The article that caught her eye this morning reported a rash of crimes in the area surrounding the mall where she worked—purse snatchings, muggings at gunpoint, even an attempted assault. There were also some disturbing reports of a ring of identity thieves operating in the Buckhead area. And then she saw it:

Man Arrested and Charged With Breaking Into Atlanta Courthouse Records—Wesley Wren, 19, of Atlanta was arrested yesterday and charged with hacking into the records of the Atlanta City Courthouse database, a federal offense. A police spokesperson wouldn't comment on how much data might have been compromised during the break-in, but maintained that records confidentiality and identity theft is a top priority for the department and that hackers will be prosecuted "vigorously."

Vigorously. Carlotta scowled. Since Detective Jack Terry had used that exact wording during their conversation, it wasn't a stretch to identify him as the officer who had leaked the story to the newspaper. And he had pretended to be sympathetic to her situation. The brute.

The sound of blaring car horns jarred her back to the traffic. The light was green and Atlanta drivers brooked no hesitation. She gunned forward, begrudgingly admitting that the Monte Carlo's engine *did* have some pickup, and fumed all the way to work. How many of her co-workers would see the article? And Angela Ashford would be able to tell her girlfriends that she was there when Carlotta had received the call from her jailbird brother—but then, like father, like son, of course.

With her exit looming, Carlotta wondered idly what would happen if she just kept driving up Interstate 75 and didn't stop until she was…somewhere else, far away from Atlanta. What would everyone think—that she'd been abducted, or perhaps had suffered some kind of mental breakdown? No, everyone would assume that she had run from her problems, as her parents had. Some might even think she'd gone to join them.

That thought, combined with the knowledge that she couldn't abandon Wesley, not when he was in so much trouble, made her put on her signal and take the exit, as she'd done thousands of times over the past ten years.

A few minutes later she slid into a parking place, jumped out and trotted toward the elevator. She was only a few minutes late, but the general manager, Lindy Russell, was still perturbed with Carlotta over the clothes-borrowing business and was keeping a close eye on her. When Carlotta opened the door to the meeting room, Lindy, who was standing, paused midsentence to frown. "Nice of you to join us, Carlotta."

Carlotta flushed and slipped into a seat in the back row, next to Michael Lane.

"You're late," he whispered.

"Did you take care of Double-A yesterday?" she whispered back.

"Yes. She was drunk on her pretty ass and not happy with you."

She winced. "Sorry."

"Don't worry—I rang up the sale under your employee ID."

She grinned. "You're a gem."

"I know."

She looked toward the front of the meeting room. "What did I miss?"

"Nothing. It's security update time."

Sure enough, the mall security director, a tall, wiry man with a crew cut, sat in a chair next to Lindy.

"With the upswing in crime in the area around the mall," Lindy was saying, "I asked our security director, Akin Frasier, to sit in on our meeting, and a representative from the Atlanta PD to join us and share some tips to help all of us be more safety conscious."

Since safety updates were fairly routine—and routinely bor- ing—Carlotta settled in to enjoy the rest of her coffee.

"Please welcome Detective Jack Terry."

Carlotta choked back her surprise, and then joined in the mild applause as the man rose from a seat near the front and nodded amiably to the crowd. He sent a special smile in her direction.

She frowned, sinking lower in her seat. Michael eyed her suspiciously.

"Good morning," the detective said. His voice was pleasant enough, but for some reason she suspected he hadn't volun- teered for this job. And she noticed his tie was as bad as yester- day's. Christ, the man must be color-blind.

"I want to tell you a few things you can do to minimize your chances of becoming a victim," he said, his voice almost too big for the room. "First, don't look like a victim. Always be aware of your surroundings. Try to buddy up when you walk to your cars, or ask for a security escort."

He continued with a litany of Safety 101 tips, but Carlotta found herself tuning out, distracted by the man himself, trying to ascertain something about him from his body language. He moved with athletic ease as he addressed the crowd, making eye contact and gesturing for emphasis. She wondered what would make someone choose law enforcement as a career. Maybe it was a family legacy. Or perhaps it was a career choice born of his size. A man with such a powerful build would naturally be drawn to a physical occupation. When he lifted his large hands in the air to make a point, she squirmed, remembering him touching her arm yesterday, as if to comfort her. She smirked, glad that she hadn't fallen for his act.

His left hand was bare of rings—no surprise there. Jack Terry seemed to fancy himself some kind of ladies' man, so a wife would probably cramp his style. No doubt he had a girlfriend or three, all of them working jobs that mandated a midriff-baring uniform. His nose and forehead were ruddy from a sunburn—he seemed like the kind of guy who played touch football with his back-slapping buddies on the weekends while consuming enormous amounts of beer.

"Any questions?" the detective asked, all smiles.

Carlotta raised her hand.

His mouth twitched. "Yes?"

"Detective Terry, doesn't the police department have better things to do than to go around scaring store clerks to death?"

Michael elbowed her. "That was rude," he hissed.

Everyone in the room shifted uncomfortably and Lindy rose to save the detective from answering, but he looked at Carlotta, smiled and said, "As a matter of fact, yes, we do have better things to do than to go around scaring store clerks to death. But we get a sick kind of pleasure out of it. Any other questions?"

Chuckles sounded around the room. She gave him ten points for being witty, then took them back because it was at her expense. Lindy glared at her, even more so when her cell phone's ringtone started its rendition of "Diamonds Are a Girl's Best Friend."

"Uh-oh," Michael muttered. "The boss lady is going to slay you."

But Carlotta didn't care at the moment because the caller ID said it was her home number. Wesley could be in trouble again. She scrambled out of the row and dashed out of the meeting room, pushing the Incoming Call button as soon as she cleared the door. "Hello?"

"Is this Carlotta?" a deep, sandpapery voice asked.

"Yes," she said, frowning. "Who is this?"

"I work for Father Thom, and he wanted me to tell you that your brother still owes him a shitload of money. He wants a payment, pronto."

Carlotta gripped the phone. "Wh-where's Wesley?"

"Right here," the man said pleasantly. "He didn't want me to call you, but I convinced him it was the right thing to do."

"Don't worry, sis," Wesley said in the background. "I got it covered."

The man guffawed into the phone. "Yeah, right. You have a week to come up with a grand. See ya soon, *sis.*"

The call was disconnected and Carlotta felt dizzy from the air being squeezed out of her lungs. Wesley must have squandered his "emergency fund" in the tennis-ball can in the garage. Otherwise he surely would have given it to the thug. Desperation clawed at her. How could she get a thousand dollars together in a week? A small cry escaped from her throat.

"Are you okay?"

She jumped, then turned to see Detective Jack Terry standing next to her, his gaze curious...and concerned.

She straightened her shoulders. "I'm fine."

"You don't look fine. You look like you just got an upsetting phone call."

She crossed her arms over her chest. "I said I'm fine." Then she narrowed her eyes. "You leaked Wesley's arrest to the newspaper."

He frowned. "No, I didn't."

"Liar."

His eyebrows went up, then he laughed. "Yeah, I've told a few whoppers in my time, but I'm not lying now. Besides, arrest reports are a matter of public record."

"This article quoted a spokesperson."

"Which is whoever answers the precinct phone. Look, Ms. Wren, I'm glad we caught your brother before he was able to do more harm, but I'm not out for his blood. The D.A.'s office, on the other hand, might be. They're probably the ones who called the newspaper, maybe thinking it would draw out your father."

She bit down on the inside of her cheek, irritated that he seemed to have a pat answer for everything.

He squinted. "Weren't your eyes brown yesterday?"

She frowned. "I should get back to the staff meeting."

"Okay." He nodded toward her cell phone. "But are you sure I can't help you with whatever is bothering you?"

He'd probably love to hear that on top of Wesley's legal trouble, he was in debt to two unsavory characters. That would seal his opinion that Wesley was no good, just like their father.

"I'm sure," she said evenly. "Goodbye, Detective Terry. Have a nice life."

He laughed. "Sorry to disappoint you, Ms. Wren, but I have a feeling that our paths will cross again."

Carlotta watched him stride away, ugly tie flapping, and muttered, "That's what I'm afraid of."

5

By Friday morning, Carlotta thought she might be having a nervous breakdown—four nights of stress-induced insomnia were taking their toll. "We have four days, Wesley. Where are we going to get the rest of the money to pay this Father Thom character?"

Wesley frowned and popped the top of a can of Red Bull, his standard breakfast drink. "Don't worry, sis. I'll think of something."

Her blood pressure ballooned. "Think of something? Wesley, your arraignment is Monday and you might be in *jail* Tuesday! How are you going to pay off these thugs if you're in jail?"

"Liz isn't going to let me go to jail."

She arched an eyebrow. *"Liz?"*

His cheeks colored. "She told me to call her Liz."

Weighing her words, she said, "I don't like the idea of you becoming chummy with that woman."

"We're not chummy," he said in a teenage-weary tone. "She's a good lawyer, and she's handling my case pro bono."

Carlotta's mouth puckered. "As if we're some charity case. And what makes you think she's a good lawyer?"

"Dad hired her, didn't he?"

She swallowed her words about what services her father actually had been paying for. "If he had so much faith in Liz Fischer, then why did he skip town?"

Wesley blanched, and immediately she was sorry. She had promised herself over the years that she would refrain from bad-mouthing her parents in front of her brother, thinking that when he became an adult, he would naturally reach the same conclusion that she had: that their mother was an unfeeling coward and their father an unfeeling, un*lawful* coward. But apparently he wasn't yet ready to let go of his childhood fantasies.

"Okay, time out," she said, sinking into a chair at the kitchen table and lowering her head into her hands. "I'm scared for you, Wesley. You're in big trouble here."

He downed the drink. "And Liz Fischer is the best chance I have to make things right and get back on track."

She sighed and looked up. "I still think I should go with you today to talk about your case. I don't trust Liz Fischer as much as you do."

He lifted his empty can high and aimed for the trash can across the room, let it fly, and grinned when it dropped in.

She glared until he sobered. Then he ambled over to the table, as if he didn't have a care in the world. "Sis, I know you want to help, but please let me handle this. I promise everything's going to work out."

Staring up at him, an overwhelming sense of déjà vu washed

over her. Ten years ago she had been sitting at this table, eaves-dropping on her parents' conversation in the next room.

"Let me handle this, Valerie. I promise everything's going to work out for us."

For us, her father had said, as in for him and her mother. Not for her and Wesley. They'd been left to fend for themselves.

She studied her brother's sharp, precise features, so like her father's, and the familiar sense of love tinged with helplessness crowded her chest. When had he grown up? It seemed like only yesterday she was putting Band-Aids on his knees and helping him with science experiments. And now suddenly he was an adult, with adult problems that she couldn't fix, and might even have contributed to...

"Sis?"

She blinked. "Yeah?"

"I said let me take care of this. Don't worry, okay?" He leaned down and dropped a fleeting kiss on her forehead on his way to-ward the door, but the rare display of affection was enough to distract her from her troublesome thoughts. She so wanted to believe him. "Do you want me to drop you at her office on my way to work?"

"Nope. I'll take the train."

"Call me and let me know what happened."

"Yup."

The front door banged closed, and she sighed, her shoulders drooping. A headache pressed behind eyes that were gritty and dry from lack of sleep. Despite Wesley's assurances, worry leaked back into her mind, and she suddenly longed for some-

thing to numb her senses for a while. Her gaze drifted to the li-
quor cabinet, which, out of deference to Wesley's age, held exactly two bottles of wine—a cheap chardonnay that she'd gotten
at a gift swap at the Christmas office party, and a decent pinot
noir that she had bought on impulse two years ago, thinking it
would be nice to have on hand in case someone special stopped
by unexpectedly for a romantic evening.

A dry laugh escaped her. What had she been smoking that
night? She'd had about a half-dozen dates since then, none of
them interesting enough to inspire an encore, much less the label
"special." Her friend Hannah claimed that she had been without
a man for so long, she was officially a re-virgin.

Thinking of her friend who was in Chicago on a field trip with
her culinary class, she sighed, missing Hannah, missing being
able to share her recent drama with the only person she knew
whose life was more tragic than her own. Carlotta glanced at
her watch. It was an hour earlier in Chicago. Hannah was a no-
toriously late sleeper, but if she called now, she could be sure to
catch Hannah before she was out and about for the day.

She dialed her friend's cell-phone number. On the sixth ring,
Hannah's sleep-muffled voice came on the line.

"Who the fuck is calling me at seven-thirty in the goddamn
morning?"

"Good morning, sunshine. And it's eight-thirty in Atlanta."

"Christ, Carlotta, this had better be important. Did you get laid?"

"No. I called because I miss you, you hag."

"Yeah, right. What's up?"

Carlotta sighed. "It's Wesley. He's in trouble…again."

"What's the little shit done this time?"

Hannah was the only person who could get away with calling Wesley names, because Carlotta knew that beneath her crusty veneer, Hannah was protective of him. "He got arrested for hacking into the courthouse database."

"I knew he was a smart little dude, but...*damn*. Why would he do something like that?"

"To delete his traffic violations."

"Wow, can he do that? I've got a couple of parking tickets I wouldn't mind having taken care of."

"*Hannah.*"

"Sorry. So how much trouble is he in?"

"I'm not sure yet, but he could go to jail."

"Yikes, Wesley's too pretty to survive in jail."

"I'm so regretting making this phone call."

"Sorry. Do you want my attorney's number? He did a great job of getting my assault charge against Russell dismissed."

Hannah had a thing for married guys—and for public breakups, which her last married guy had responded to by filing an assault charge. "Uh, thanks, but Wesley already has an attorney." Plus, she suspected that Hannah's ex dropping the charges had more to do with his reluctance to face the six-foot-tall, tongue-pierced, stripe-haired, goth-garbed Hannah in an open courtroom than with her attorney's expertise. "His arraignment is Monday."

"I won't be back until Tuesday or I'd go with you. Is there anything I can do from here to help?"

A rush of fondness swelled Carlotta's chest and she laughed. "Not unless you have a spare thousand you could wire me." Her friend would know she was kidding, of course. Hannah earned barely enough with her sporadic catering work to pay for her culinary classes.

"Uh-oh. Does this have to do with his case or something else?"

"Something else."

Hannah sighed. "His loan sharks again?"

"Yeah."

"Gee, Carlotta, you know I'd give it to you if I had it, but even if I did, that's only a temporary solution. How much does he owe now?"

She closed her eyes and swallowed bile. "Close to twenty thousand."

"Shit fuck fire."

"I know."

Hannah groaned. "Carlotta, I know you don't want to hear this, but don't you think it's time for little brother to grow up? I mean, Christ, when you were his age you were raising a *kid*."

Carlotta sank her teeth into her lower lip. She'd been the only eighteen-year-old at the middle-school PTA meetings, and she had sheltered Wesley so he could enjoy his childhood for as long as possible. But Hannah had a point. "You're right," she said with a sigh. "But I think he's trying to take responsibility for what he did. He wouldn't let me go to the attorney's office with him."

"Good, give him some rope, Carlotta."

"But what if he hangs himself with it?"

"Just make sure he doesn't have the other end tied around *your* neck. That boy needs some tough love, or you'll be bailing him out of jail and out of debt for the rest of your life."

"You're right. I'll try."

"Meanwhile, the little shit needs to get a job—how's that for a revolutionary idea? I might be able to get him some catering work, but he'd need a car."

"And a driver's license, so that's out. But thanks. And thanks for the pep talk. Sorry I woke you up."

"Ah, hell, we were awake…sort of."

"We?"

"My pastry instructor. I told you how cute he is."

Carlotta frowned. "And how married he is."

"That, too. Hang in there and good luck on Monday. I'll call you when I get back."

The call was disconnected, leaving Carlotta to shake her head. One of these days Hannah was going to meet up with a vindictive wife in a dark alley.

She drank from her coffee cup, but the liquid had gone cold. She winced, her mind still whirling with questions and what-ifs and worst-case scenarios. Then she pushed to her feet, thinking she might as well go to work. As much as the loan shark's voice haunted her, she could only deal with one crisis at a time.

First, they had to get through Wesley's arraignment on Monday. She didn't trust Liz Fischer, but she hoped that this time her father's former mistress had something helpful up her skirt.

6

Carlotta sat in the back row of the courthouse gallery, shooting anxious glances between the wall clock and the door. She and Wesley had arrived together, but he'd said he needed to visit the men's room and that was thirty minutes ago. Arraignments would begin in three minutes, and Wesley's case, Liz Fischer had warned, could fall anywhere in the lineup, so he had to be prompt if he wanted the deal that she'd managed to work out with the D.A.

The rows of chairs in the gallery were crowded with people of all shapes and sizes, some of them nervous and fidgety, others merely bored. Liz Fischer stood next to the front row and cast furtive glances at her watch. The district attorney, Kelvin Lucas, sat sprawled in a chair across the aisle wearing a smug smile as the seconds ticked away. Carlotta remembered the way the man had grilled her after her parents had disappeared.

"They must have said where they were going, or called to say they were okay. If you know something and you don't tell me, young lady, I'll have to charge you with accessory, and then who'll take care of your brother?"

But she'd stood her ground—she hadn't known where they were. If she had, she would've turned them in just to stop her brother's tears.

The man's hair was grayer, his neck thicker, but the arrogant set of his mouth was unmistakable. *"Tracking down Randolph Wren is my top priority,"* he'd said to a TV reporter ten years ago, a vein jumping in his forehead. *"Now it's personal."*

When his heavy-lidded gaze now landed on Carlotta, she swallowed and looked away. The man gave her the creeps, although she supposed that was part of his job description. She wondered if he had any idea who she was and how much he'd added to her nightmares at a time when she'd thought she might never sleep again.

"Did you lose your client?" Carlotta heard him ask Liz Fischer, his voice cutting through the noise.

"He'll be here," Liz responded, her tone cool.

Lucas gave a derisive laugh. "It's déjà vu, Counselor. Just like ten years ago."

Carlotta set her jaw. Ignoring the man, Liz strode toward her and leaned down. "Where the *hell* is Wesley?"

"He's in the restroom," Carlotta said hotly. "He'll be here in a minute."

"He'd better," the woman said. "I don't even want to think about what I had to do to get him this deal."

Carlotta gave her a pointed look. "I'm sure it's nothing you haven't done before."

"All rise," the bailiff announced as the judge walked in.

"Go find him," Liz said through clenched teeth.

Carlotta rose and exited the rear doors into the hallway, nodding at the guards stationed there. She scanned the area for Wesley, panic gathering in her chest. Had he fallen ill? Been detained in some way? Another thought slid into her mind and took her breath away. Had Wesley, who so adored their father, somehow gotten it into his head to imitate The Bird's behavior, to earn his own notorious reputation?

She asked one of the guards for directions to the men's room. She practically ran in the direction the man pointed and when she found it, hesitated only a second before barreling inside. There she found Wesley leaning over a sink, his mouth bloody and his clothes disheveled and a bulky man standing over him— Detective Jack Terry.

Her maternal hackles stood on end. "Get away from him!" She went in slapping at the bigger man like a windmill.

"Hey, hey, hey!" he said, arms raised to ward off her blows while he backed up. Then he grabbed her wrists and held her, his eyes blazing. "What the devil are you doing?"

"This is police brutality!" she cried. "Help, someone!"

He released her wrist to clamp a hand over her mouth. "Shut up before you get someone hurt, dammit. I walked in and found your brother like this. I was trying to help him get cleaned up before his court appearance."

She cut her gaze to Wesley for confirmation and her brother nodded. "He was trying to help," he mumbled through a fat lip.

She relaxed and the detective released her, her red lipstick bright against his fingers. "What happened?"

Wesley dabbed at the blood on his face. "Some guy jumped me, took my wallet."

She narrowed her eyes at him in the mirror but bit her tongue. She'd bet anything the "guy" had something to do with Father Thom, a detail that Detective Terry didn't need to know. "Liz Fischer sent me to find you. You need to get to the courtroom right away."

She moved next to him, her heart beating faster to see his puffy lip and bloody teeth. At least his glasses weren't broken. "Are you okay?" She reached for him, but he leaned away.

"I'm fine, sis," he said, then walked toward the exit, tossing the wet napkin in the trash. "Let's get this over with."

When the door closed, she turned to face the detective, who seemed bemused.

"Told you we'd be crossing paths again," he said. "I just didn't think it would be in the men's room."

She glanced around the slightly grubby tiled room lined with urinals. "Um, sorry for...attacking you."

"Don't mention it." Then he frowned. "Your brother seems to be having a string of bad luck."

"Yes. Thanks for helping him."

"Just doing my job," he said smoothly. "I hear that Liz Fischer made a deal with the D.A."

"Yes, thank goodness." Then she frowned. "Do you know Liz?"

"Sure," he said with a slow smile. "Liz and I are...friendly."

She pushed her cheek out with her tongue. "I so didn't need to know that."

He shrugged. "Just making conversation." Then he gestured

toward the urinals. "Now, if you don't mind, I actually came in here for a reason."

She lifted her eyebrows. "Hmm? Oh…" A blush climbed her neck as she turned on her heel and headed for the door.

"But I need to talk to you," he said behind her. "Save me a seat."

"Fat chance," she muttered.

When she entered the courtroom, she slid into a seat in the back row just as Wesley's case was being called. He and Liz Fischer stepped forward and took their place behind the defendant's table. Her brother looked so handsome in the brown suit that she'd pulled out of his closet, cut off the tags and forced him to wear. His normally shaggy hair was combed and his posture was arrow straight. But Carlotta's gaze was riveted on how Liz touched Wesley's chin and peered at his injury, then angled her head toward his ear as the judge situated his paperwork. Her body language seemed almost…intimate. Carlotta hardened her jaw. Had the woman transferred her affection to the son of her former lover?

"Don't look so grim," Detective Terry murmured in her ear as he took the seat next to her. "If the judge goes along with the plea bargain, your brother's getting off easy."

Carlotta frowned, and leaned away from the man who had somehow insinuated himself into their lives. Unbidden, thoughts of the detective and Liz Fischer together in bed popped into her head. She squeezed her eyes shut. Good grief, what was it about stick-thin women that drove men nuts?

"Can't bear to watch, huh?" the detective whispered, touching her arm.

She opened her eyes, exasperated. "Shut. Up." She looked down and pulled her arm away. "And I hope you washed your hands."

"I did—had to get the lipstick off." He pulled a handkerchief out of his pocket and handed it to her. "Speaking of which, you could use a touch-up."

She glared and snatched the hankie, then used a mirror to wipe her smeared lips and handed it back to him.

He looked at the now-pink hankie. "You can keep it."

She shoved it into her purse and looked to the front of the courtroom.

"And the state is satisfied with the plea agreement?" the judge was asking the D.A.

Kelvin Lucas dragged himself to his feet, then gave Wesley a long, slow look, before turning back to the judge. "The state is satisfied, Your Honor."

"Very well. The defendant is hereby sentenced to five thousand dollars in reparations, one hundred hours of community service, which will include collaboration with the city on computer security, and one year of probation." He banged a gavel. "Next case."

The sigh of relief she'd been saving remained pent-up in Carlotta's chest at the realization that yet more debt had just been heaped onto their already considerable pile. Add to that her credit card balances and the miscellaneous bills that were late, and the fact that tomorrow a big, hairy guy was coming by to collect a thousand dollars they didn't have, and she could barely push herself to her feet and toward the door. She just wanted things to be...good. She'd given up on easy years ago, but good would be nice.

To her chagrin, Detective Terry was on her heels. "Ms. Wren, I need to talk to you."

She turned and sighed. "What do you want, Detective—to tell me more about your manly conquests?"

A whisper of a smile crossed his mouth before his eyes turned serious. "Er, no. When was the last time you heard from your parents?"

She frowned. "I don't remember—oh, we received a postcard maybe two years ago."

"From where?"

"Texas, maybe. I don't recall."

"Where is the postcard?"

"I threw it away."

His eyebrows went up. "One of the few pieces of communication that you've had from your fugitive parents, and you threw it away? That's destroying evidence."

Anger surged in her blood. "So arrest me, Detective."

His mouth flattened into a thin line. "Ms. Wren, I think you and your brother both are keeping secrets. I think you might know where your parents are."

"Well, you're wrong."

"I can have your cell-phone records seized. And your mail."

For a second, she wondered if that might buy her time to pay her bills, but then she fisted her hands at her sides. "You'd be wasting your time. Besides, I figured you were too busy giving McGruff the Crime Dog speeches to salesclerks to be digging around in an old case that not even the D.A. cares about anymore."

"Wrong, Ms. Wren."

She turned to see Kelvin Lucas standing there, slump-shouldered, his hands in his pants pockets. "I do care. Funny thing, your brother's arrest got me all interested in your fugitive daddy all over again. I've reassigned the case to Detective Terry here because he always gets his man, don't you, Detective?"

A muscle worked in the detective's jaw. "Yes, sir."

Lucas smiled, but his eyes remained hard and cold. "So just in case this trouble that your delinquent brother's gotten himself into happens to smoke out your runaway parents, Detective Terry will be watching. And if I hear that your brother does anything to violate his probation, I'll nail his scrawny ass to the wall."

The D.A. walked away, his hard-sole shoes clicking against the floor. Carlotta scowled at the detective and he scowled back. "I know my rights," she said with more confidence than she felt, pulling herself up to her full height, which, even in heels, brought her only up to the man's chin. "Stay away from me and my brother or I'll...I'll..."

"You'll what?" he asked dryly.

"I'll sic your ex-lover Liz on you." She smirked—ten points for her.

But he barked out a laugh. "Lady, you're way more scary than Liz, and that's saying a lot."

She narrowed her eyes. "I don't like the idea of you watching me."

"You'll get used to it." He gave her a little salute and walked away.

7

Wesley swung his legs over the edge of his bed, put on his glasses and stared in the predawn light at the empty wall unit where a dozen monitors, hard drives, routers, keyboards, joysticks and printers had once sat, all interconnected. Damn, the police had cleaned him out. They'd even taken his software cabinet, games and landline phones.

He smiled to himself. It was a good thing that he kept all his good equipment at his buddy Chance's apartment.

He stood and stretched the kinks out of his neck, a bothersome side effect of spending so many hours bent over a keyboard.

Whew. Thank goodness the business with the police had been settled yesterday in court. Liz Fischer was a godsend…and a hottie. Too bad a woman like her would never take him seriously—movies like *The Graduate* and *PS* gave guys like him false hope.

Walking to the bathroom connected to his room, he rubbed his sore mouth, working his jaw. He wished he knew who had sent the guy who'd jumped him in the courthouse bathroom, but the thug seemed to prefer to talk with his hands. In truth, the guy could have been working for either one of the people that he owed—Father Thom being his biggest creditor. Then again, the guy robbing him could have been a coincidence.

But he doubted it.

The worst part was that he'd been carrying the fifteen hundred that Chance had paid him for deleting the speeding tickets—money he'd planned to take to Father Thom this morning. Instead, he'd have to scrounge together a few hundred from his various hiding places and beg for more time.

He thought about showering, but decided that fresh deodorant and mouthwash would suffice. If he got the ass-kicking he expected from Father Thom's thugs, a soak in a hot tub of water was probably in his near future anyway.

He rooted around the floor for a cleanish pair of jeans and pulled a T-shirt from the laundry basket of clothes he hadn't gotten around to folding. He dressed and shoved his feet into his old Merrell slip-ons, mourning his brown suede Pumas, and kicked Hubert's decaying shoes near his trash can.

In the fifty-gallon glass aquarium on the other side of the room, a mouse scurried around, terrified. A pang of remorse hit him and he walked over, unlocked the pin and slid the screen top aside. With a practiced hand, he captured the mouse and held it up by its tail.

"Relax, buddy, you got a reprieve. Einstein must be fasting again." He stared down at the black-and-gray spotted axanthic ball python, all six feet of his longtime pet coiled disinterestedly in a corner. "Finicky reptile, are you sure you aren't female? Or vegetarian?"

Einstein didn't move, and would likely stay in his stoic position for the next several hours. The police search, with all the activity and noise, must have traumatized him.

Wesley slid the cover closed, locked the pin, then returned the lucky mouse to a smaller container. Sometimes he thought that Einstein didn't eat out of sympathy for his prey. When he did feed, it was as if he would begrudgingly relent, then coil around and squeeze his prey to death before it had time to react, and swallow it promptly, as if to get it over with. Carlotta thought the snake was a man-eater, but Wesley could barely get him to eat enough to sustain his monstrous size.

Wesley sometimes wondered, though, what his pet could kill and consume if it were motivated.

Hearing a noise in the hallway, Wesley frowned. He'd hoped to be out of the house before Carlotta got up, partly because he didn't want to worry her, and partly because he didn't want to face her. The fact that she wasn't normally an early riser told him that she probably hadn't slept well, and no doubt he was the cause. Frustration tightened his chest. He just needed some time and space to get things worked out with his creditors and to investigate his father's case. Although he appreciated his sister's concern, her hovering was making things more complicated.

He made his way around the room and checked various hiding places—the hem of the curtain, the hollow leg of his metal bed, inside his worn copy of *The Catcher in the Rye*—and counted up three hundred sixty dollars.

He heard a muffled voice and realized that Carlotta was calling his name. God, he hoped she hadn't set the kitchen on fire again.

He grabbed his backpack and stuffed his iPod, cell phone and money inside. Then he stepped out into the hall and closed his bedroom door. It was a house rule that his bedroom door be closed at all times because Carlotta lived in fear that Einstein would somehow escape his enclosure.

"Wesley!"

"I'm coming," he yelled. But when he reached the living room, he stopped short. Sitting next to Carlotta on the couch was Tick, the tub of lard who had forced his way in the house last week and called Carlotta at work.

"Mornin', Wesley," the guy said, smiling and patting Carlotta's knee.

Carlotta, clutching the newspaper, looked terrified. Tick must have been waiting for her when she stepped outside to leave for work. Fury balled in Wesley's stomach—he wanted to kill the guy. He had always wished he was big and beefy like Chance, but never more so than at this moment.

"Leave her alone," was all he could say.

"Where's the money?" Tick asked.

Wesley pulled himself up to his full height. "Maybe you can tell me."

Tick laughed. "What are you talkin' about?"

"I was jumped yesterday. Guy took all that I was carrying. I figured it was for Father Thom."

Tick wagged his fat head. "Nope. Must have been someone else you owe."

Wesley couldn't tell if he was lying—but then, did it really matter?

Then the man's eyes grew mean. "So like I said, where's the money?"

Wesley reached into his backpack. "After yesterday, three-sixty was all I could get together."

Tick laughed. "You're shittin' me, right?"

Wesley extended the money and, as he hoped, Tick lurched to his feet to count it. "This ain't enough, Wesley. Father Thom gave me strict orders not to leave here with less than a grand. You don't want to get me in trouble with my boss, do you?"

Wesley swallowed. "No. But you can't squeeze blood out of a turnip."

Tick grinned. "Sure I can."

"Wait a minute," Carlotta said, her voice trembling. "Nobody's going to squeeze blood out of anybody. I have the money."

Wesley and Tick both looked at her. "You do?" they asked in unison.

Wesley frowned. "How?"

"Get it," Tick said. "I'm beginning to lose patience with you two."

Carlotta pushed to her feet and dropped the newspaper into a chair, then marched out of the room toward her bedroom.

Tick watched her leave and sucked his teeth. "Your sister's got a smokin' bod."

"Watch your mouth," Wesley said, clenching his fists.

The big man looked at him and laughed. "I guess if my sister looked like that, I'd be stupid about it, too." Then the man sobered. "But you *are* stupid if you think that Father Thom won't go after her if you're late again. Remember that real hard, little man."

Wesley opened his mouth to say something foul but stopped

himself when he heard Carlotta's footsteps. "Here's the other six hundred forty," she said, extending a stack of cash to Tick, her expression tight. "Now, please leave."

The big man took his time counting the money, then shoved it into his pocket and smiled. "See how easy that was? Do this every week and pretty soon, you'll be debt free, just like all those commercials on TV promise."

"Get out," Carlotta said through clenched teeth. "Or I'll call the police."

Tick laughed. "Yeah…right." Then he looked at Wesley. "Remember what I said, little man."

Wesley's throat burned with bile as he watched the man walk heavily toward the door. At the last second, Tick turned his head and glanced at the aluminum Christmas tree in the corner of the room.

"Merry fucking Christmas," he said sarcastically before banging the door shut behind him.

They were both quiet for a few seconds. He almost couldn't bear to look at his sister. When he did, her eyes were stormy, her arms crossed, her back rigid.

He gave her his best little-brother smile. "Where did you get the money?"

"A cash advance on my credit card," she said quietly. "My *last* credit card."

"Well…thanks," he said. "I'm sorry that had to happen here. I was going to take care of it—"

"Shut up, Wesley!"

He blinked.

"You. Have. To. Get. A. Job."

"I'm supposed to upgrade two of the Sheltons' computers this week."

"I mean a *real* job," she said, walking toward him slowly, stabbing her finger in the air, "with a paycheck and maybe even something as radical as health benefits. And you're not *allowed* to work on computers, remember? You're on probation for computer tampering! And that toad Lucas told me that if you violate your probation, he'd nail your ass to the wall. Is that what you want, Wesley? To go to jail?"

"Relax, sis," he said, raising his hands and backing toward the door.

"Relax?" Her dark eyebrows drew together and her finger started to shake. "Listen to me, Wesley, and listen good. The free ride is *over*. Get a job and start taking responsibility for your debt, or—" Her throat constricted. "Or get out."

Wesley reeled as if she'd slapped him. He blinked rapidly as she picked up her purse and walked past him and out the front door. He heard the dull hum of the garage door going up, and the growl of her car starting. When the garage door came back down, he exhaled.

Maybe it would be better if he slept on Chance's couch for a while. Maybe Carlotta would be better off without him. And maybe it would give him the space he needed to look into his dad's case.

He returned to his room and tossed a few things into a duffel bag. Chance wouldn't mind him crashing there for a while— his friend was stoned most of the time anyway. Einstein would be fine for a few days. Outside on the stoop, he locked the door and was heading down the sidewalk toward the Marta train station when a black Cadillac pulled up to the curb and the passenger-side window zoomed down. A man's face came into view, and Wesley's knees weakened.

"Hey, Wesley, where you going?"

Wesley shouldered his duffel bag higher. "Nowhere, Mouse."

"Really? Looks to me like you're trying to skip town."

"Nah, Mouse, I was just going to visit a friend."

"You missed your last payment," the man said pleasantly.

"I know. I ran into some trouble with the police."

"I read the papers," Mouse said. "Thought I'd give you a chance to get square with The Carver before you go to jail."

It occurred to Wesley that it was probably The Carver's guy who'd jumped him in the courthouse john. "I got probation," he said, trying to sound upbeat.

"Good for you," Mouse said. "So you're going to make your next payment on time?"

"Sure thing."

"Terrific," Mouse said, nodding amiably. "Because I wouldn't want to report back that you got the money to pay that crook Father Thom and not us."

Wesley considered lying but decided to remain silent.

"Don't be a stranger." Mouse nodded toward the town house. "We know where you live."

The car window buzzed up and the car pulled away from the curb. Panic curdled in Wesley's stomach as he stood watching the taillights, weighing his options. Stay and continue to expose Carlotta to the dangerous men he'd gotten himself involved with...or go and leave her at home alone where she might be even more vulnerable.

8

"Thanks for shopping with us," Carlotta said, forcing a smile for the guy who had made countless innuendos while selecting a skimpy red teddy.

He took the shopping bag and grinned, still leaning on the checkout counter. "I'd like to call you sometime."

She swallowed her distaste and nodded toward the bag. "I assumed this was a gift for your girlfriend."

"No, my mother."

"You bought your *mother* a red teddy?"

He laughed but didn't have the decency to look sheepish. "You got me there. Okay, it's for my girlfriend...but it's a breakup gift."

"Ah. Well, thanks anyway, but I'm not available."

He stared at her chest and made a rueful noise. "Too bad."

"Yes, well, have a nice day."

He took his time peeling away from the counter, looking back as if he just knew she was going to change her mind. Carlotta averted her gaze and busied herself straightening the counter. What an oaf. Were there any good men left in the world? She smirked, thinking of her friends' comments about her aversion to men. Would she recognize a good man if he crossed her path?

Then she sighed. Even if a great guy dropped into her life, who would want to sign up to share her problems? Fugitive parents, a delinquent brother, a mountain of debt—it didn't exactly make her the most eligible woman in Atlanta, not unless the guy had a laundry list of his own problems.

Take Detective Jack Terry, for instance. The man wasn't bad-looking if one could look past his ghastly taste in clothes. But even dressed in a Paul Smith suit, Jack Terry would still be a swaggering, arrogant, annoying pain in the ass. Oh, sure, he'd tried to help Wesley yesterday in the men's room, but now she knew it was only because her father's case had been reopened and he was trying to cozy up to them for information.

In her pocket, her cell phone vibrated. Since there weren't any unattended customers in sight, she pulled out the phone, hoping it was Wesley. She felt horrible about yelling at him this morning. Resentment toward her parents had never been stronger. She waffled between hoping the detective found them so she could tell them all the hateful things she'd been saving up for ten years, and hoping he didn't find them because their return would wreak so much havoc on Wesley. Better that he romanticize their plight than to know with certainty what she knew: that their parents didn't give a fig what happened to them.

But the caller ID read Hannah Kizer. Carlotta smiled and punched the call button. "Hi, are you back?"

"Yeah, I'm back. How did things go yesterday in court?"

"He got a fine, community service and probation."

"Wow, no jail time? His attorney must have been good."

Carlotta thought of Liz Fischer, frowned and changed the subject. "You'll be proud of me—I told Wesley he had to get a job."

"About damn time. Maybe now he'll be too busy to get into trouble. Have any of his thugs been around?"

Carlotta glanced around to make sure no one could hear her. "A guy forced his way into the house this morning, demanding money."

"You're kidding. What did you do?"

"Wesley had a little cash, and I'd gotten an advance on my credit card, so we had enough to pacify him."

"You should have called the police."

"Considering my family's history with the police, I didn't think that was such a good idea. Besides, the police would only make things worse."

Hannah sighed. "You're probably right. But you need something to protect yourself."

Carlotta pursed her mouth. "You mean a gun or something?"

The sound of someone clearing their throat made Carlotta turn her head. Her general manager stood there, frowning.

Carlotta's pulse spiked. "Gotta go."

"No, wait—I called you about a cocktail party tonight at the Four Seasons. Want to crash?"

Lindy was walking away, so Carlotta relaxed a bit. "I told you—I've sworn off party-crashing."

"Oh, come on, I'll let you in through the kitchen, so you don't have to worry about a counterfeit ticket. You're ready to clock out, aren't you?"

Glancing at her watch, Carlotta said, "Yes, but I really don't feel like going home to change."

"It's one of those business mixers for the upper crust, so the dress is business casual. Come on, it'll take your mind off things."

Carlotta wavered. She'd worn a rather conservative black suit and striped button-up shirt, so she would probably blend.

"I'll meet you at the kitchen entrance in an hour," Hannah said.

"Okay," Carlotta relented. "Just this once."

She disconnected the call and hurried to wait on a customer, who took up the time remaining on her shift. Afterward, she freshened her makeup in the employee break room. Michael Lane came in and removed a brown paper bag from his locker.

"Hot date?" he asked, cracking open a can of diet soda.

She smiled. "No."

"Hmm, I was hoping the reason you've been avoiding me is because you had a secret man in your life."

A pang of remorse struck her. She'd been avoiding Michael because he'd no doubt read about Wesley's arrest and she didn't want to discuss it. She and the gay man were friends, but she wasn't sure how much she could trust him where the gossip mill was concerned.

"I've just been busy, that's all."

"I understand," he said, his expression gentle. "Is everything okay at home?"

"It's getting better," she said evasively, hoping it was true.

"Let me know if I can help."

Gratitude swelled in her chest. "I will. And thanks again for the Angela Ashford commission last week."

He shrugged. "Everyone who works here knows she's your customer. You deserved it." Then he frowned. "So what's the connection between the two of you anyway?"

She married the only man I've ever loved. "Uh...we went to high school together."

"Oh. Was she a bitch then, too?"

Carlotta laughed. "In training."

"So what are you up to tonight?"

"I'm meeting Hannah at a party."

He frowned. "The vampire?"

"She's not a vampire. She just likes to dress...weirdly."

"Whatever," he said. "You'll never land a man if you keep hanging out with the likes of her."

She closed her locker door and swung her purse to her shoulder. "I'm not trying to land a man."

"Uh-oh," he said. "That's when it happens."

"When what happens?"

"Love. Just when you make up your mind that you have no intention of falling for someone—whammo!"

"I get hit by a truck?"

Michael stuck out his tongue. "Make fun, but mark my words—your Mr. Right is close at hand."

The door opened and the head of security walked in, looking all of a hundred pounds in his uniform, his pants gathered around his thin frame with a wide black belt, his nonexistent chest puffed up like Barney Fife.

"I came to do a routine check of your loading dock," Akin said, then looked at Carlotta and blushed furiously. "I want to make sure everyone here is safe on my watch." Then he saluted and strode out the double doors leading to the loading dock.

Michael looked at her and burst out laughing.

"On that note, I'm out of here," she said, waving goodbye.

She laughed at Michael's nonsense on the short drive to the Four Seasons Hotel. Despite her hesitation when she had been on the phone with Hannah, her chest clicked with anticipation as she parked her car—there was no money for valet service tonight—and walked toward the hotel entrance. There was nothing quite so exciting as fudging her way into a party where she wasn't supposed to be. The difference was tonight she wouldn't be incognito; if she ran into somebody she knew, it would be fun to see them stutter and fumble while trying to figure out how someone like her could afford the requisite two-hundred-fifty-dollar ticket that these events usually boasted.

She checked her watch as she walked into the hotel. Right on time. She rode up the elevator and when she alighted, turned away from the velvet-roped entrance where a hostess was taking tickets and headed down a narrow hall that led to the restrooms and to a set of stainless swinging doors marked Service Personnel Only. The door opened and Hannah, dressed in standard white culinary garb, her striped hair bound in a hairnet, thrust a folded garment into Carlotta's hands. "Put this apron on."

She did as she was told, crossing the long ties in front before securing them in back, then frowned. "You didn't tell me you were working the party. I thought we were going to hang out."

"I'm only standing in until someone else gets here, then I'll find you."

"Okay," Carlotta said sulkily.

"Cheer up," Hannah said, handing her a tray of mini quiches to carry through the kitchen. "I think I saw Gladys Knight. Didn't you say you wanted her autograph?"

Carlotta nodded, glad she'd put her new autograph book in her bag. "But why would she be here?"

"She's a businesswoman, has investments in town—including a tasty little restaurant in Midtown."

Considerably cheered, Carlotta followed Hannah through the kitchen maze, trying to look busy and intent as she balanced the tray on her hand. As soon as they cleared the doors into the hallway leading to the party room, she handed the tray to Hannah and removed the apron with lightning speed. "Thanks," she said, smoothing her hand over her hair.

"Have fun," Hannah said. "I'll see you as soon as I can get away."

Carlotta turned to the crowd, scanning for the singer of "Midnight Train to Georgia" among the preppily dressed, one-hand-in-their-pants-pocket crowd, and spotted her standing in a corner, sporting her signature dazzling smile and, fortuitously, signing an autograph. Carlotta made a beeline for the woman before she tired of autograph hounds. She stepped up and introduced herself, then explained that she'd once had the singer's autograph, but that her autograph book had recently been ruined and she was hoping to get a replacement. Ms. Knight was gracious and obliged, writing her name with a flourish in the new pink leather autograph book—the first among its blank pages.

Carlotta watched, starstruck, imagining all the glamorous, wonderful things the woman had done and seen in her lifetime and visualizing all of that luck and energy pouring into the bold signature that she would take home with her. "Thank you so much," she gushed when the singer handed the book back to her.

She turned, happy beyond words to begin filling another book with celebrity autographs. In the months since her last book had been destroyed, she hadn't realized how much she missed lying in bed and reading the names of famous people she'd met, if only for a few seconds.

"I'd know that smile anywhere," said a deep male voice.

Carlotta snapped the book shut, looked up, and froze. Peter Ashford, looking even more handsome than he had ten years ago, stood smiling at her.

9

Carlotta's heart stood still. "Peter. Hello."

His dark blue eyes turned wistful. "It's been a long time, Carlotta."

"Yes," she managed, wishing for something to lean against to keep from falling down.

"You look great," he said, sweeping his gaze over her. "The same...only better."

Obligatory chatter. She remembered his comment about recognizing her smile anywhere and was suddenly self-conscious of the gap between her front teeth that she'd never had corrected. She took him in—his dark, sun-kissed skin, his blond hair clipped in a trendy style that made the most of his cheekbones. He was still tall and lean but had filled out. What had once been boyish was all man, and she had to stop herself from reaching out to pull his body against hers, to breathe in the cologne on his neck, to knead the muscles in his back.

"How have you been?" he asked to fill the awkward silence.

"Oh, fine," she said quickly.

"And Wesley? He must be what—sixteen years old now?"

"Nineteen," she corrected, disappointed that he hadn't noted the passing of every year, of every day since their breakup. Immediately, she recognized she was being unfair. It hadn't been as traumatic an event to him as it had been to her.

"Wow, he's all grown up."

She nodded, wondering if he'd read of Wesley's arrest but was diplomatically avoiding the subject.

He pointed to the pink leather book in her hands. "And I see that you're still collecting autographs. I guess you filled up the black book you always carried around."

"That was a long time ago," she said, shoving the new book into her purse, not wanting to admit she'd replaced that black autograph book only recently—and not out of choice.

"Can I get you a glass of wine?"

Deciding there was nothing wrong with him using one of his drink tickets on her, she nodded.

"White zinfandel?" he asked.

"Pinot noir," she said, letting him know that her tastes had changed, matured. But while he ordered her drink, she devoured him with her eyes—tall, commanding, self-assured, polished. This was the man who would have been her husband. No…Angela had told her what Peter had said about marrying Carlotta. Even if they had married, it wouldn't have lasted.

But it was easy to put those troubling thoughts aside when he walked back toward her. Easy to pretend that Peter was her husband, returning with her drink. "Thank you," she said, taking the glass. His hand brushed hers, leaving her unreasonably flushed with pleasure.

"To the good times," he said lightly, lifting his glass.

She nodded and clinked her glass to his, then drank deeply of the rich red wine. The flavors burst onto her tongue, the alcohol pleasantly burning the back of her throat. Almost immediately she felt the effects of the wine and warned herself to take it slow on an empty stomach. Seeing Peter again had already knocked her senses off balance—she didn't need an accelerant.

He studied her as he drank from his glass and she wondered what was going through his mind. Regret? Relief?

Suddenly his nose wrinkled and he waved his hand in the air as the smell of cigarette smoke wafted their way from the bar. "Damn cigarettes. Let's get some fresh air," he said, nodding toward the patio doors.

She agreed, telling herself that it was perfectly normal that they should have a conversation after the way things had ended all those years ago. She fell into step next to him, careful to maintain a respectable distance in deference to the overwhelming urge to wrap her legs around him.

Dusk had settled on the patio where a handful of people stood talking quietly. Low light sparkled from luminaries hung all around that struck her as strangely romantic for what was supposed to be a business event. "What brings you here?" she asked.

He shrugged. "Thought it might be a good place to make some new contacts for potential clients. I'm an investment broker for Mashburn, Tully and—" He blanched. "Sorry, I still want to add your father's name to the partners list."

"It's okay," she murmured. "I knew you were working there. I saw your wedding announcement in the *AJC*."

"Ah."

"Is Angela with you?" she asked lightly, glancing around.

"No." Then he cleared his throat. "So what are you doing here?"

"I'm here with a friend."

One of his eyebrows arched. "Boyfriend?"

"No. My friend Hannah."

"Someone you went to school with? Would I know her?"

"No, I sort of...lost touch with the girls I went to school with. I hardly see them anymore." Then she decided to out the elephant in the room between them that he refused to acknowledge. "Except for Angela."

He took a quick drink from his glass. "Yes, she always tells me when she, um, runs into you."

Another stretch of awkward silence descended.

"I hear your home is very nice," she offered. "Angela told me about the new pool."

He gave a dry laugh. "Pool, outside kitchen, waterfall, hot tub and guesthouse."

"Oh. How...nice."

He looked up. "I wasn't bragging. It's all a little more grand than I had envisioned. I mean, it's just the two of us, and I'm not home—" He stopped. "I mean...I work long hours."

She thought about Angela's flask of gin. It didn't take a rocket scientist to figure out that Peter's "long hours" were taking a toll on their marriage.

And God help her, wasn't she just a little bit happy to know it?

The realization left her flustered and searching for safer ground. "How did you like the jacket that Angela bought for you last week? Gorgeous, isn't it?"

"I don't know what you're talking about."

She covered her mouth with her hand. "Oh, no, I've ruined a surprise. She said your anniversary was coming up and I completely forgot. Peter, I'm so sorry. Will you please act surprised?"

"Sure," he said quietly. "But our anniversary was three days ago."

Carlotta fumbled to cover her gaffe. "Well, perhaps she forgot about it, or is saving it for another special occasion...or she...changed her mind."

"Or perhaps she bought it for someone else."

Mortification bled through her chest at the implication.

"Such as her father," he added mildly, then smiled.

She laughed in relief at the obvious explanation. "Of course. I'm sorry I mentioned it. I was just..."

"Making conversation?" he supplied. "That's gracious of you, Carly, considering all the things you'd probably like to say to me after the way I behaved when...when your life fell apart."

Carly. His pet name for her. A name she'd used several times when crashing parties incognito, under the disguise of wigs and accents.

Her mouth opened and closed. Here stood the man who had ripped out her heart and abandoned her, and now when given the opportunity to ask him why, she didn't know what to say. She'd always known why, hadn't she? Would it really make a difference to hear him admit that he couldn't deal with the scandal of her parents' actions, and the responsibility of an instant family? Would it change anything other than to tear open wounds that had long since healed?

"We were young," she said, turning away from him, trying to keep her voice steady. "I understand why you did what you did."

He stepped beside her. "Then maybe you can explain it to me, because I don't understand why I did it—why I left you alone to deal with the fallout of your parents leaving, of raising a child."

"It wasn't your responsibility," she said, closing her eyes against his nearness. "It was mine. Your life was going down a different path." She looked up and smiled. "As it should have. Everything worked out for the best."

He looked as if he wanted to say something, but instead he drained his wineglass.

"Peter, hey!"

They both turned to see a middle-aged man walking toward them, all smiles. A memory chord vibrated in Carlotta's mind.

Peter straightened and even to her his body language seemed guilty as he extended his hand to the older man. "Hi, Walt."

"When did you get back from Boston?" the man asked.

"This afternoon. The meeting with Matthews went well."

"Glad to hear it," Walt said, then cut his gaze to Carlotta, his curiosity plain.

"Walt, this is Carly, an old friend. Carly, this is Walt... Tully."

Carlotta blinked—her father's former partner. No wonder he looked familiar. She'd been to countless company gatherings at his house, had gone to school with his daughter. And no wonder Peter was acting so strangely. But even though her father had stained the company's reputation, she had nothing to atone for.

She stuck out her hand and when the man took it, smiling, she said, "I'm Carlotta Wren, Mr. Tully. It's been a long time."

He seemed confused, then surprised, then uncomfortable. "Er, Carlotta, yes, of course. How are you, my dear?"

"Grand," she said with a big smile. "How's Tracey?"

"Hmm? Oh…she's fine. Married a doctor and lives in Buckhead."

One of Angela's lunch buddies, no doubt. "That's wonderful. Will you tell her I said hello?"

He frowned. "Of course." Then his gaze went back and forth between her and Peter.

"I was just leaving," she said cheerfully, setting her glass of wine on the nearest flat surface. "Peter, it was nice to run into you. Give Angela my best. Good evening, Mr. Tully."

She turned and fled, fighting tears as she wound her way through the crowd back into the kitchen. If she'd needed proof that being in Peter's life would have been a constant embarrassment for him, she had it. Walking blindly, she nudged a tray of fish-shaped pâté from a sideboard and sent it crashing to the floor.

"Who are you?" a man wearing a chef's hat bellowed. "Get out of here!"

She spied Hannah in the fray, who beckoned her toward the door where they'd met. "What's wrong?"

Carlotta bit her lip to keep her tears at bay, but failed.

Hannah grabbed her arm. "What happened?"

"It's nothing," Carlotta mumbled. "I don't feel well."

"Liar," Hannah said, herding her out into the hallway. "Did one of Wesley's thugs follow you here?"

"No," Carlotta said, then released a hysterical laugh at the absurdity of her life. "It was just a guy...I used to date."

Hannah frowned. "A guy? I've never seen you worked up over any guy you dated."

"This was a long time ago. I'm overreacting. It's nothing."

Hannah stared at her, more curious than concerned.

Carlotta wiped her eyes. "I shouldn't have come. I'm still worked up over Wesley's situation. I'll call you tomorrow."

Hannah squinted. "If you're sure."

"I'm sure." She turned and walked down the hallway to the elevator and stabbed the call button.

"Carlotta!"

She turned to see Peter leaving the main entrance of the party and making his way toward her. She turned back to the elevator and stabbed the button again. "Come on," she muttered.

"Carlotta, wait!"

When the door opened, she rushed aboard and pushed the button to close the doors, but Peter was too quick. The doors rebounded open and he walked on, his eyes dark and troubled. The doors slid closed, sealing her into an intimate space with the man she had loved for most of her adult life.

"What do you want, Peter?"

"I'm sorry about that," he said. "I was afraid if I introduced you, well...I was afraid that he would say something...inappropriate."

She watched the buttons light up as they descended slowly, then gave a little laugh. "It's okay, Peter. I'm used to being snubbed by people like Walt Tully. Do you want to hear something funny? That man is my *godfather*—that's how close our families used to be. But the last time I saw Tracey, she pretended she didn't even know who I was. It seems I'm invisible to most of the women I once thought were my friends." Her voice sounded surprisingly calm to her own ears. "Except for your wife, that is. Instead of ignoring me, she treats me like a servant when she comes in to shop. She flaunts her life with you and grinds me under her heel. She told me last week that giving me a commission is her little good deed, as if I'm some kind of pet project."

His mouth tightened and he shook his head. "I'm sorry."

She clenched her jaw, her chest aching. "Stop saying that." The elevator doors opened and she brushed past him. "Goodbye, Peter."

"Carlotta." He kept up with her until they reached the hotel entrance. "Give me your ticket, I'll have the valet send for your car."

She gave a little laugh. "I parked my own car, Peter, and *walked* one whole block to get here."

He looked ashamed. "Then at least let me walk you to your car so I won't worry about you."

It was something in his voice that weakened her resolve—the protective note that made her feel so cared for, so safe. Darkness had fallen and in truth, she wasn't looking forward to walking back to her car alone. And this might be her last chance to be with Peter, ever. "Okay," she said against her better judgment.

When they reached the sidewalk, away from the lights of the hotel, they slowed, as if by mutual consent. A spring chill had settled over Midtown, and Carlotta shivered slightly, although the goose bumps could just as easily have been caused by Peter's proximity. She glanced at him out of the corner of her eye, and more memories flooded back—the perfection of his profile, the way his brow furrowed when he was deep in thought.

The sidewalks in this area were nearly deserted, but cars zipped by on Fourteenth Street in a steady stream. Peter walked on the outside of the sidewalk, between her and the traffic, like a good southern gentleman. Carlotta desperately wanted to talk but didn't know what to say, afraid if she started talking, she might say too much. So she concentrated on putting one foot in front of the other, satisfied at the moment with breathing the same air as Peter.

"I can't believe it's been ten years," he said finally.

A response seemed unnecessary.

"Have you heard from your parents?" he asked gently.

"We received a few postcards over the years, but even those have stopped."

He looked pained. "I'm sorry."

"Don't apologize for something that isn't your fault."

"I'm sorry for leaving you stranded when you needed me the most."

Her heart thudded in her chest. She studied the toes of her shoes, afraid to look at him, afraid she would burst into tears over the admission that she'd longed to hear for over a decade.

"I was a coward," he said. "I let my family talk me into something I didn't want to do."

So, his family had pressured him to break off their relationship. She had suspected as much, but now that she knew, she wasn't sure what hurt the most—that they had considered her spoiled goods, or that Peter hadn't defended her.

He grimaced. "I'm not being fair to my folks, though. They were doing what they thought was right. I was the coward for not standing up to them."

She stopped next to her Monte Carlo Super Sport, which, she acknowledged, probably seemed garish to him. The damn car seemed to represent the sorry state of her life. She looked up and shielded her eyes against the lamplight. "What do you want me to say, Peter? Do you want me to agree with you?"

The pained look was back on his face. "I already know that you agree with me, Carly." He reached down and picked up her hand, sandwiching it between his. "I'm asking you to forgive me."

She felt the pulse in his thumb throbbing against hers, the warmth from his hands surrounding hers like when they had made love, with the kind of abandon that only two teenagers could possess. She had always teased that his body was like a furnace, and he had always said she put the fire in his belly. Her body tingled in response to his touch, as if answering some long-forgotten call.

"Is that what you need to be at peace, Peter? For me to forgive you?"

He looked into her eyes and squeezed her hand tighter. The tension between them crushed her ribs and constricted her airways. It was as if they were suspended, as if time stood still, poised to resume when one of them spoke or moved or breathed.

"No," he said in a raspy voice, releasing her hand. "Even if you forgive me, I can't say that I will ever be at peace."

She pushed her tingling hand inside her jacket pocket and tried to compose herself. "We can't turn back the clock, Peter. We're different people now. You have your life, and I have mine."

He smiled. "You're right. When did you become so pragmatic?"

"Ten years ago."

He sighed and nodded. "What choice did you have?"

She pulled out her car keys and hit the keyless entry button. "I should go." She opened the driver's-side door and dropped her purse inside.

"Carly."

She turned toward his voice—an old habit, easily resumed.

He stepped toward her and dropped a kiss on her cheek. The unexpected closeness of his body to hers sent a surge of desire rippling through her stomach. He groaned softly and suddenly the innocent kiss went from cheek to mouth, and his lips seared hers. She gave in to the overwhelming rush of longing and wrapped her arms around his neck, pulling him closer. His mouth devoured hers and instantly, she was home. She knew his mouth, knew how he tasted, how he liked to flick his tongue against hers, how he slanted his head just so for better leverage.

She moaned and kissed him with all the pent-up years of longing for him to come back to her, to climb into her bed and thrust his body into hers and whisper against her neck that he'd loved her all along. She kneaded the cords of his back and pressed her aching breasts against the wall of his chest. But when the hardness of his erection pressed into her stomach, warning bells sounded in her head. And when she heard footsteps approaching, reality came crashing back. She tore her mouth from his and stumbled back. She didn't know the couple walking by, but she was still awash with shame.

"Carly," Peter said on an exhale, then pulled his hand down his face. "You're killing me."

She covered her mouth with her hand, unable to believe what she'd just done—what she'd been about to do. "You're a married man, Peter."

"I know," he said, closing his eyes. "I'm sorry."

"Stop saying that," she said. "Stop *saying* that!" She brushed past him and swung into her car seat.

"Carlotta—"

She held up her hand to cut him off. "This was a big mistake. Go home, Peter. Go home to your wife."

She closed the door with a slam, separating herself from him. Somehow she managed to get the key in the ignition with a trembling hand, then cranked the engine. She pulled away, squealing tires and accelerating at a breathtaking speed. So the muscle car was good for something after all: rocketing her away from Peter Ashford.

She resisted the urge to glance in the rearview mirror, and broke every speed limit on the way home.

It wasn't until she pulled into her garage that her co-worker Michael's words came back to her. *Just when you make up your mind that you have no intention of falling for someone—whammo!*

She sighed and leaned her head on the steering wheel. "Whammo!" was right. She would have been better off getting hit by a truck.

Minus ten points.

10

When Carlotta's alarm went off the next morning, she slapped at it blindly, her eyes crusted shut from a river of salty tears. As she lay there rubbing her fists against her lids, last night came back to her in a horrible rush. She groaned. What had she been thinking? As soon as she saw Peter Ashford, she should've turned on her heel and run. Now she had fresh sensory details to torment herself with.

"Stupid, stupid, stupid," she lamented, hitting her forehead for emphasis. She wondered what Lindy would say if she called in to take a "mental health" day, meaning she was feeling more crazy than usual.

Knowing the answer, she pushed herself up on her elbows, hoping to motivate the rest of her body to get moving.

At the sound of muffled noise coming from the kitchen, she pursed her mouth. Wesley was never up this early. She raised her nose and sniffed the air. Hmm—bacon. She hoped he'd made enough for two. Throwing back the covers, she reached for her yellow chenille bathrobe and pulled it over her red Betty Boop pajamas, then padded barefoot toward the kitchen and the good smells.

Wesley, dressed in jeans and T-shirt, stood at the stove, stirring and flipping and...whistling?

"Good morning," she said warily.

He turned and grinned. "Mornin'. You look like hell."

She smirked. "Thanks."

"Are you sick? I got in kinda early last night and your door was closed—I thought that maybe you'd brought a guy home with you." He pointed an egg turner at her pajamas. "But I can see that isn't the case based on your god-awful sleepwear."

"Shut up," she said playfully, then went to the fridge for orange juice. "I'm not sick."

"What then?"

She sighed. "I ran into Peter Ashford last night."

"Peter Ashford? What's the asshole up to?"

She frowned. "Never mind."

"I thought he was married."

"He is. And it's not like I'm mooning for him. I guess seeing him just brought back bad memories. What are you making?" she asked to change the subject.

"Eggs Benedict with fresh sliced red and green tomatoes."

"Wow, what's the occasion?"

"I got a job." He took a bow, then waited for her reaction.

She squealed with joy, then jumped up and down, sloshing orange juice on her robe. "Oh, Wesley, that's wonderful. Doing what?"

He pressed his lips together and her joy dissipated.

"Wesley?"

"It's a great job," he said in a rush. "Flexible hours, good money, benefits, and I don't need a car."

"Good," she said, feeling somewhat cheered. "Doing what?"

"Uh...moving bodies."

She choked on her orange juice. "What?"

"Okay, don't freak out—it's a perfectly legitimate job. We pick up bodies and move them to the morgue."

"Pick up bodies from where?"

He shrugged. "Houses, hospitals...crime scenes."

"Crime scenes? And who is 'we'?"

The doorbell rang and Wesley smiled. "That would be my boss."

Her eyes widened as she looked down at her pj ensemble. "At this hour?"

"Coop is picking me up for a morning run to a nursing home," he said over his shoulder. "I told him to come early and have breakfast with us."

"Coop?" She only had time to tighten the belt on her robe and run her fingers through her tangled hair before Wesley reappeared with a tall man dressed in overlong jeans, black Converse Chuck Taylor tennis shoes and a black sport coat over a dress shirt and tie.

A *nice* tie.

He appeared to be about thirty-five, with light brown hair, long sideburns and funky dark-rimmed glasses. He looked more like a philosophy teacher who hung out in coffee shops than a...body mover.

"This is Cooper Craft, my boss," Wesley said. "And this is my sister, Carlotta. She usually looks better than this, but she's been crying all night over an old boyfriend."

She gasped, mortified. "Wesley!" She shot daggers at her brother while Cooper laughed, which only rankled her further. "I understand that my brother will be working for you, Mr. Craft," she said in her best never-cried-over-anyone voice.

"Call me Coop," he said, still smiling. "That's right."

"And what exactly is it that you do?"

"I work at a funeral home, but mostly I contract with the city morgue for body retrieval." Another smile. "That's where I need Wesley's help." He held up a newspaper. "I brought in your paper. Hope that's okay."

Carlotta nodded and took it, a little irritated that the man seemed to feel so at home in *their* home.

"Have a seat," Wesley said, gesturing to the table, where he had set three plates. "What do you want to drink, Coop?"

"You got coffee? I'll help myself," the man said, walking over to the table where he pulled out a chair for Carlotta. Feeling ridiculous, she tucked her bulky robe around her and slid into the seat. Coop poured himself a cup of coffee and took the seat opposite her. Wesley carried platters of food to the table and arranged them carefully, then took the seat between the two of them.

"This is incredible," Cooper said, unfolding the paper towel next to his plate and putting it in his lap as if it were linen. He looked at Carlotta. "Did you make all this?"

Wesley laughed. "Dude, Carlotta doesn't cook. I made it."

She bristled. "I cook…some things."

"Macaroni and cheese from a box doesn't count," Wesley said, filling his plate.

"Sure it does," Coop said, then winked at her.

Annoyed, Carlotta served herself then passed the tomatoes to Coop. "This body-moving business sounds very strange to me. Is it safe for Wesley to be around…dead bodies?"

Coop swallowed a mouthful of coffee. "We take precautions—gloves, masks, leak-proof body bags."

Carlotta looked down at the sauce on the eggs Benedict and her stomach roiled. "How long have you been doing this?"

"Working with stiffs?" he asked between bites. "Pretty much all of my life."

She picked at the food on her plate. "No offense, but it seems like an odd career choice."

"Really? What do you do?"

"I work at Neiman Marcus at the Lenox Mall."

He lifted his coffee cup. "Well, no offense, but to me *that* seems like an odd career choice."

Wesley laughed, then covered his mouth. "Sorry, sis, but he's got you there."

She frowned at her brother and concentrated on eating and not thinking about what Cooper Craft did for a living. Under her lashes, she stared at his hands—long, shapely fingers, with immaculate nails, clean from all the chemicals he used, no doubt. She wondered if he had been a weird kid, the kind that gave little funerals for roadkill. He seemed normal—mannerly, well-spoken, educated. But what normal person was attracted to his line of work?

Then she looked at Wesley and stopped midchew. Was there something wrong with *Wesley*? He did seem to have a fixation on feeding live rodents to that killer snake of his. Was he attracted to this kind of job? Good God, having her for a parent had affected him more than she'd ever dreamed. Not only was he a delinquent, but he was…morbid.

Coop wiped his mouth and groaned in satisfaction. "That was great."

"Thanks," Wesley said, then gave Carlotta's half-eaten breakfast a pointed look.

"Yes, it's great," she concurred weakly. "But I'm just not as hungry as I thought." The world was missing out on the eat-with-a-mortician diet.

"Ready to go?" Coop asked Wesley, then glanced at his watch. "All the folks at the nursing home will be lined up, expecting us. It's kind of a morning ritual. They have a send-off for their friends who have passed."

Carlotta winced.

"Yeah, let me grab my backpack."

"You got a shirt with a collar on it?" Coop asked.

Wesley frowned and looked at Carlotta, who smothered a smile behind her glass.

"Yeah," Wesley said, his spirits considerably dampened.

"How about a jacket?"

Wesley's face fell further. "Yeah."

"Good. The families expect us to look decent when we arrive to load up their loved ones."

Wesley nodded. "Give me a minute." He headed toward his bedroom, leaving her alone with creepy Coop.

"All these years I've been trying to get him to dress better," she said dryly, "and you accomplish it in five minutes."

"Seems like a nice kid," he said.

"He is…but he's been in a little trouble."

He nodded. "Wesley told me about the probation. I told him that everybody makes mistakes—it's how a person handles their mistakes that sets them apart."

Something in the tone of his voice made her wonder if he was talking about Wesley…or himself.

He stood and carried his empty plate to the sink.

"Leave it, I'll get it. That's our deal—Wesley cooks, and I clean up."

"It's okay," he said, rinsing the plate, along with his coffee cup. "I live alone. I'm used to cleaning up after myself."

Hmm—a bachelor. She wasn't completely surprised. An undertaker wasn't on the top of most girls' list of desirable dates. Unbidden, she wondered if the saying about undertakers having cold hands was true.

"Thanks for the hospitality," he said. "I hope you…feel better."

An embarrassed flush climbed her neck. The man must think she was a simpering fool for some loser guy. Not that she cared what he thought of her—he worked with dead people, for Christ's sake. "Thank you," she mumbled.

"I'm ready," Wesley said from the doorway.

Carlotta stared. "A tie, too?"

"Bye, sis. We're going in Coop's ride."

She frowned. "What kind of 'ride' would that be?"

"A hearse," Wesley said. "How cool is that?"

Her eyes went wide as she rushed to the window. Sure enough, a black hearse sat at the curb. "Mrs. Winningham will stroke out over this."

"I usually drive a van," Coop said, following her. "But the folks at the nursing home appreciate the classy extra touch."

Carlotta pushed her tongue into her cheek. "Classy—that's just what I was thinking."

Wesley pushed open the front door and galloped out to the curb to check out his "ride."

Coop laughed, then looked at her. "Nice meeting you." He stuck out his hand.

She swallowed before taking it, expecting his fingers to be frigid. Instead, they were warm and firm and...nice, actually. "Same here," she said, perplexed by the man's contradictions.

He nodded toward the dilapidated silver-colored tree in the corner. "I like your tree—very retro. You must really get into Christmas."

Carlotta gave him a flat smile. "Oh, yeah, it's Christmas every day of the year around here."

He grinned and walked to the door. "Guess I'll be seeing you."

She crossed her arms. "I have to be honest with you, Coop— I'm not sold on this idea of Wesley being a...a body mover."

Coop gave a little laugh. "Don't worry, you'll get used to it."

The door closed behind him and she frowned. Where had she heard *that* before?

She showered and dressed for work quickly, pushing away thoughts of Peter Ashford as soon as they entered her head. It was how she'd gotten over him before—by conditioning herself not to think about him and eventually the banished thoughts had diminished.

Although they had never quite disappeared.

When she walked out on the stoop, Mrs. Winningham was halfheartedly watering her yard, a ruse she promptly abandoned when she spotted Carlotta. "Why was there a *hearse* in front of your house this morning?"

Carlotta angled her head. "A hearse? I didn't see a hearse, Mrs. Winningham. Are you sure you didn't imagine it?"

The woman scowled. "If I did, I also imagined your brother getting in it."

Carlotta lifted her arms in a shrug. "Have a nice day, Mrs. Winningham."

She trotted to the garage, squeezing the remote control. The opener made a horrible grinding noise as it lifted the door—a sure sign it was ready to go out. She sighed, opened the car door and tossed her purse in the passenger seat. Just before she swung inside, she noticed a tennis-ball can on a shelf with old cans of spray paint and miscellaneous junk—Wesley's admitted hiding place for the cash he was hoarding. She frowned. If he was still holding out on her...

She walked over and stretched high to reach the tennis-ball canister. She assuaged her guilt for snooping with the knowledge that her credit card company had already hit her account with a twenty-two percent finance charge for the cash advance she'd gotten to pay off that odious Tick fellow.

She popped off the lid, peered inside and frowned. Empty. Then she squinted...no, there was something rolled up and nearly hidden because it was pressed against the lining of the canister. She wiggled her hand down inside, grabbed an edge with her fingernails and pulled it out slowly. Immediately, her stomach began to churn.

It was a postcard from her parents dated six weeks ago. The photo was an Ansel Adams landscape, a nondescript mountain scene mirrored by a lake. The note on the back was short and cryptic, as always. "Thinking of you both." It was her mother's handwriting. The postmark was Miami, Florida. She inhaled sharply. They had been only one state away when they'd mailed it?

She shook her head, wondering why Wesley would have kept the postcard from her and felt the need to hide it. Then she smirked. Hadn't she said the last time they'd gotten one—two years ago—that she hoped they didn't receive any more postcards, and that if they did, she would turn them over to the police? Wesley must have taken her at her word.

Detective Terry's question as to her parents' whereabouts echoed in her head. Should she call him now while the lead might still be warm? Or would that result in unnecessary surveillance of their home, their mail, their phones? She worked her mouth back and forth, debating. One thing was certain— she couldn't leave the postcard in case Wesley decided to hide it somewhere else. If he missed it and confronted her, she'd tell him the truth, which was more than she'd gotten from him. She returned the canister to the shelf, climbed inside her car, and, after studying the postcard again, stuck it inside her purse.

She'd hang on to the "evidence" until she decided what to do.

11

"This is too cool," Wesley said, nodding his head as he surveyed the inside of the moving hearse.

Coop looked amused. "Buckle up. It'd be embarrassing to die in a hearse."

Wesley clicked the seat belt home. "Where do you buy a hearse?"

"At a dealership, same as a regular car, or used from other funeral home operators. I only use it for funerals and pickups at the nursing home. Otherwise, I use the van."

Wesley studied the serious profile of the man next to him and had a feeling that there was more to him than met the eye. "How did you get into the business?"

Coop's mouth tightened and he looked away briefly. "The funeral home belongs to my uncle. I didn't grow up dreaming of working there, if that's what you're asking. It just worked out that way."

"And you like it?"

The man shrugged. "It's okay." He looked at Wesley. "It's better than jail." Coop's cell phone rang and he clicked on the hands-free button. "Coop here."

Wesley listened while the man talked to someone named Jim and arranged to pick up a body at the hospital, pondering Coop's comment about jail. He'd been referring to Wesley's predicament...hadn't he?

"I've got a trainee on board," Coop said into the mike and shot Wesley a smile. "This is his first call."

"Does he have a strong stomach?" asked the man on the phone.

Coop laughed. "Cut it out, man, you'll make him nervous, and you know how hard it is to find good help these days."

Wesley smiled, but his insides were churning—maybe eggs Benedict wasn't a good idea before his first-ever body run. He'd assumed the nursing-home call would be picking up some old geezer who'd died in his sleep with a smile on his face, but what if it were some kind of freak accident? Or what if they had died of some kind of flesh-eating disease? He wrinkled his nose. Or what if it were some old lady—naked? He wasn't sure if he was ready to see that.

Coop disconnected the call, and Wesley shifted in his seat, suddenly not feeling so well. "Is this going to be gross?"

"You ever seen a dead body before?"

"No."

"Lucky you." Coop made a rueful noise. "Death is never pretty, but some retrievals are more messy than others. Our job is to be calm and professional, no matter what. The relatives might be close by and it's not good if they see us react badly, no matter what the situation is."

Wesley swallowed hard. "What's the grossest case you ever had?"

"Garbage-truck compacter," Coop said without hesitation. Then he looked over. "That, my friend, is a bad way to go."

Wesley winced. "What happened to the guy who used to help you?"

"Couldn't hack it. I told you when you answered the ad, Wesley, this job isn't for everyone, but it's necessary and honorable work."

Wesley nodded solemnly, hoping he didn't let the man down.

"So," Coop said, turning the radio knobs, "your sister."

Wesley looked at him suspiciously. "Yeah, what about her?"

"She's cute."

"You like her or something?"

Coop shrugged. "Just making conversation."

"You should ask her out."

Coop was quiet for so long Wesley thought he might have misread him. "Think she'd go?" he finally asked.

Wesley laughed. "No. She doesn't date much and I don't think you're her type."

"Let me guess—she's into guys who wear moisturizer."

Wesley thought a minute. "I guess so. The guy she was crying over all night is some preppie dude she dated, like, ten years ago. He dumped her."

Coop frowned. "And she's still crying over him?"

"No—I mean, she hasn't seen him in years, but she ran into

him last night and I guess it upset her." He chewed on his lip, trying to decide how much of his life to divulge to his new boss. He didn't want to come across as some kind of drama case. "My sister's life hasn't been easy."

"How so?"

"She raised me since I was nine, and I've been kind of a shithead." Coop smiled. "What happened to your parents?"

Wesley looked out the window. "Long story, man."

"Some other time then," Coop said easily. "We're here."

Wesley's pulse kicked up as the nursing home came into view. It looked more like a shabby brick apartment building than a medical facility. Coop backed the hearse into a parking place near the door reserved for ambulances, climbed out and straightened his jacket as he walked toward the entrance. "Stay close and do what I tell you."

Wesley nodded. "Aren't we going to take in the gurney?"

"I like to go in first and assess the situation, greet the family if there's anyone around, maybe give them time to say goodbye while I make a trip back to get the gurney."

Wesley digested the info, nodding. His stomach was pitching now.

When they walked into the facility, the first thing that Wesley noticed was the smell—old building, old paint, old people. Mothballs, mold and Metamucil. They stopped at the front desk where a woman in a nurse's uniform stood at attention and smiled wide.

"Good mornin', Dr. Craft." She arched her back so that her boobs stuck out.

"Good morning, Sarah. Meet Wesley, my new sidekick."

Wesley exchanged greetings with the woman, but she quickly turned back to Coop, her eyes alight with interest that seemed to extend beyond gladness that they were there to take a body off her hands. "That jacket looks nice on you, Dr. Craft," she gushed.

Coop smiled. "Thanks, Sarah. I figured we'd have an audience."

"That you do." She handed him a folder. "Gentry Dunbar, third floor, room eighteen. The spectators are lined up in the hallway."

"Any family?"

"A sister, Ilse Dunbar—she has a room here, too."

"Thanks."

Wesley followed Coop down a long hall of gleaming green linoleum tile and white walls, past a dining room full of old people, some in their pajamas, some dressed up for breakfast as if they were going to church. The scent of scorched coffee and prunes nauseated him further. They passed a few residents in the hall, shuffling toward their destinations, bent from bone disease and sheer weariness, he assumed. God, he hoped he never grew old.

He frowned. Of course, that meant dying young...

Coop walked past the elevator, pushed open the door leading to the stairwell and began the climb to the third floor.

"That nurse digs you," Wesley said.

"You think?" Coop asked, looking amused.

"She called you doctor."

"Yeah," Coop said. "Sarah's a good girl. It takes special people to work with old folks and kids. But I don't mix business and pleasure, if you know what I mean."

All Wesley knew was that if he had a busty girl throwing herself at him, he'd go for it, screw business.

When they reached the third floor, Coop opened the door onto a hall where the green linoleum floor was dull and gray, the scarred walls a grubby off-white. Dozens of old people lined the hallway, some sitting in chairs that they had pulled out of their rooms, some leaning against the walls, some sitting in wheelchairs.

"Here's the body man," a woman announced loudly, probably in deference to those who were hard of hearing or had dozed off. Everyone perked up, calling greetings to Coop and making sorrowful noises about "poor Mr. Dunbar."

"He's in there," several people said, pointing to the only door on the floor that was closed.

"Thank you kindly," Coop said, stopping to pat arms and shake hands.

"Ilse is in there with him," a woman said sadly. "Poor thing has been sittin' by his bed, holding his cold, dead hand all mornin'."

Wesley suppressed a shudder as he waded through the spectators and followed Coop to the door. Coop knocked, then waited a few seconds before going in.

Wesley steeled himself for the sight of a cold corpse, then blinked at the empty bed. His gaze went to the man reclined in a ratty yellow La-Z-Boy chair, fully dressed in suit, tie and hat, as if he were going on a trip, his hands crossed over his lap, his eyes permanently closed. If the man in the recliner was ninety, the woman sitting next to him, her veined hand over his, had to be one hundred.

She looked up and smiled sadly at Coop. "How are you, Doc?"

"Fine, Miss Dunbar," Coop said, walking closer. "I see that Gentry here is in a better place."

She nodded, her eyes tearing up. "He told me he was going to die soon, but I didn't believe him. This is his burying suit, so he must have known before he went to sleep last night that he wouldn't make it 'til morning."

Wesley hung back, feeling weird and tingly. The dead guy didn't look real, more like a wax figure. Uneasily, Wesley looked to the ceiling and the corners of the room—he'd read something once about the spirit lingering for a while after leaving the body. Was the old man hanging around, watching them from the light fixture? He began to shake.

"You all right, Wesley?" Coop asked.

Wesley nodded curtly, put his hand over his mouth and inhaled deeply. He had to stop thinking about the dead guy. He was freaking himself out.

"God, how he loved that old chair," the old woman said, smiling, giving the ancient yellow tweed chair a thump that dislodged dust motes into the air. "I can't believe he's gone. I used to take care of him when he was a little tyke. Our parents died when he was young, so we've always been close. Neither of us married, and the rest of the family has died off." She gave them a watery smile. "We always looked out for each other. Now it's just me."

Coop touched her rounded shoulder. "You're in a nice place, Miss Dunbar. There are a lot of people here who care about you."

Wesley listened as Coop comforted the old woman, but he realized with the impact of hitting pavement that he could be looking at a future picture of himself and Carlotta—growing old alone, winding up in the same nursing home, for Christ's sake. Until this moment, he'd never considered the possibility that their parents wouldn't come back. The thought made him feel sick... and even more appreciative of Carlotta. Although, if he continued to get in trouble, how much longer would his sister stick by him? All the more reason to fix things, the sooner, the better.

"Has Mr. Gentry seen a physician recently?" Coop asked the woman.

"This morning, when Dr. Tessler came and pronounced him dead."

"Before that."

"About six weeks ago."

"If the person hasn't seen a physician within thirty days, an autopsy is automatic."

Her mouth twitched. "Can we still have an open-casket viewing?"

"Of course—the medical examiner will be respectful, I promise."

She nodded.

"Have you selected a funeral home, Miss Dunbar?"

The woman smiled. "Everyone here speaks highly of your family funeral home, Dr. Craft. I thought we'd have Gentry's service there."

Coop smiled. "Thank you. My uncle will take good care of him. We're going to give you time to say goodbye. We'll be back in a few minutes."

She nodded, smiling. "Okay."

They left the room and closed the door behind them. Wesley gulped non-dead air as their audience leaned in for details.

"Is he sure enough dead, Doc?" one of the old men asked.

"Sure enough," Coop said. "But it looks as if he was ready to go."

Agreement chorused through the hallway, and a few amens. They threaded back through the crowd to the stairs.

"This is going to be harder than I thought," Coop murmured.

Wesley frowned. "What do you mean? The guy even dressed up in the suit he wants to be laid out in. I wouldn't think it could get any easier than that."

"Ever tried to move a body in full rigor mortis?"

Wesley swallowed. "No."

"Let's just say that nothing bends."

"But the guy is sitting up."

"Exactly."

Wesley grimaced, feeling like he could lose his eggs on the spot.

They passed Sarah, who angled a sly smile at Coop, and then they walked outside to the hearse. The fresh air revived Wesley a bit as Coop unlocked the rear door and pulled out the gurney.

Staring at the flat surface, Wesley asked, "So how are we going to get a guy frozen in a seated position to lie flat on the gurney?"

Coop sighed. "Good question. It wouldn't be so bad if we didn't have an audience, but a sheet's not going to hide anything." He scratched his head, then worked his mouth from side to side. "In the back seat, there's a hand truck. Get it."

Wesley did as he was told, and soon they were back in Gentry Dunbar's room. His sister, sensing the end, was crying softly.

Wesley's heart went out to her and he wondered if the old man in the chair had put his older sister through as much hell as he had put Carlotta through.

Coop helped the woman to her feet and led her toward the door. "We need to move Gentry now, Miss Dunbar, but I was wondering—since he loved this chair so much, how about if we give him one last ride in it?"

Her eyes rounded. "You mean take him out in the recliner?"

"Yeah," Coop said, as if it were perfectly normal. "We'll make sure you get the chair back, of course."

The old woman smiled wide. "He'd like that. And just give the recliner to Goodwill."

"Fine," Coop said. "We'll be right out." When she left, Coop handed Wesley a pair of rubber gloves and donned a pair himself. Then he turned to assess Gentry.

"He's starting to smell," Wesley said, covering his nose with his sleeve.

"The cells begin to break down the second the heart stops beating," Coop offered calmly. He bent over and pried open the man's mouth with two gloved fingers.

Wesley winced but couldn't look away.

Coop made a noise in his throat. "Just as I suspected."

"What's wrong?" Wesley asked.

"The reason that Gentry here had prior knowledge of his death is because the old boy did himself in."

Wesley's eyes bugged. "Suicide?"

"Yeah."

"How do you know?"

"Look—his tongue is dry and flushed, probably an overdose of antidepressants." He closed the man's mouth, then walked over to a side table, opened a drawer and pulled out several prescription bottles. "Doxepin and trazodone—probably took a little of each, just enough to do the job."

Wesley bit his lip. "His sister will be crushed."

"She won't hear it from me," Coop said lightly.

"But won't it be on the death certificate?"

"Only if the medical examiner notices."

"You're saying he won't?"

"He, she, whoever is doing the autopsy. Gentry's an old man who died in a nursing home and probably was being medicated for a number of ailments. His autopsy isn't going to be a high priority in an office where hundreds of autopsies are performed every day."

"But you spotted it right away," Wesley said.

Coop was silent for a few seconds, then said, "I've been doing this for a while." He covered the man with the sheet, tucking it in around the sides of the chair. "Okay, when I tilt the chair, slide the hand truck underneath."

Wesley did and between the two of them, they managed to balance the chair on the hand truck. When they wheeled it out into the hall, there were guffaws of laughter, applause and an impromptu rendition of "I'll be Seeing You." Wesley couldn't help but smile as they wheeled the old man out to the hearse.

Getting the recliner into the back of the hearse was another matter, but they managed. In the process, Wesley's hand slid under the sheet and he accidentally touched the man's stiff fingers. He flinched, then realized the skin felt more like a cold bar of soap than anything sinister. A few minutes later when he swung into the front seat and banged the door closed, he was feeling pretty good about himself. "That wasn't so bad," he said to Coop.

Coop gave him a lopsided smile. "Don't get too cocky on me."

"Do you get a lot of funeral home business this way?"

"Yeah," Coop admitted. "There's decent money in contracting body retrieval with the morgue, but to be honest, it also helps my uncle's business. People get to know us. If they haven't already selected a funeral home, nine times out of ten, they'll go with us."

A shrewd businessman, Wesley decided, and wondered how much Coop was worth. Death was probably a pretty lucrative business, since it never let up.

"So when do I get paid?"

Coop's eyebrows rose and he laughed. "Jumping the gun a little, aren't you? We haven't even officially delivered the body to the morgue."

Wesley gave an embarrassed little laugh. "I have a fine to pay off, man." Not entirely the reason he needed the cash so soon, but it would do.

Coop nodded. "I hear you. I'll pay you every Friday, twenty-five bucks for every body you help me move."

Wesley nodded. "Sounds fair." His internal calculator kicked in. Even if they moved only four bodies a day, that was a hundred bucks, seven hundred per week, and with the crime rate and traffic fatalities in Atlanta, he was probably being conservative. Business would probably be even better on weekends and holidays.

Wesley's pulse began to drum with excitement. For the first time in his life, he was earning real money.

"You have to get that fine taken care of so you can clear your record and move on," Coop said.

"Right," Wesley said, half listening. With the kind of money Coop would pay him, he could eventually afford to buy into a high-stakes poker game. One big win would put him in the clear with everyone, and help him build a local reputation at the tables.

His promise to Carlotta that he would stop gambling rang in his head. Something akin to guilt stabbed him, but he shrugged it off as the familiar excitement of an impending card game began to build. He hated to go back on his word, but all he needed was one big win.

Just one.

12

"Well, at least Wesley's working," Hannah said.

Carlotta sighed into her cell phone. "But he's moving *dead* people."

"Somebody's gotta do it. I mean, when you think about it, it's really kind of cool."

"Christ, you sound like Wesley. All he talks about is how cool it is to ride around in the hearse, and how cool his undertaker boss is."

"Is his boss creepy?"

Carlotta thought of the long-legged, funky-looking man who had seemed so comfortable at their breakfast table. "He's not as creepy as you are."

"Funny."

"But how normal can the man be if he works around dead bodies all the time?"

"I don't know," Hannah said dryly, "some days it sounds preferable to working with live ones. Fridays suck, don't they?"

"Let me guess—trouble with your pastry-instructor lover?"

"Since we got back from Chicago, he's cooled way down."

"Do you think it might have something to do with the fact that he goes home to his wife every night?"

"Maybe."

Carlotta bit her tongue to keep from scolding Hannah for taking up with yet another married man—the memory of kissing Peter Ashford two nights ago was still too fresh for comfort. What a hypocrite she was.

She looked up and nearly dropped her cell phone to see Angela Ashford charging toward her counter. Had she somehow conjured up the woman with her illicit musings of Peter? "Oh, shit."

"What's wrong?" Hannah asked.

"Gotta go," Carlotta whispered, then disconnected the call.

Angela bore down on her, wearing the expensive black knee boots Carlotta had sold to her, black trench coat flapping. A paralyzing thought struck Carlotta: what if Peter had developed a guilty conscience and confessed the kiss to Angela? That vengeful-wife ass-kicking that she had been warning Hannah about for years might just be coming *her* way.

She swallowed and straightened her shoulders, and although her heart threatened to pound through her breastbone, she managed a shaky smile when Angela stopped in front of the counter. "Angela...hi."

"I'm glad you're here," the woman slurred, her expression dark.

Carlotta drew back slightly at the woman's flammable breath—another head start on her martini lunch, apparently. "What...what can I do for you?"

"Take it back," she said, leaning into the counter.

A sharp inhale tightened Carlotta's chest. "T-take what back?"

Angela swung a shopping bag onto the counter with a thud. "The man's jacket you talked me into buying. It was all wrong."

Carlotta was so giddy with relief that she decided to allow the gibe to slide. "It didn't fit?" she asked, reaching for the bag to hide her guilty flush.

"Hmm?" Angela asked, seeming preoccupied. "Oh...right."

Automatically, Carlotta's sales expertise kicked in. "Would you like to exchange the jacket for something else? Another size?"

"No—I need the cash."

Carlotta looked up, surprised. "Oh."

Angela recovered unconvincingly. "I mean, I'd rather have a refund."

Carlotta reached into the shopping bag and withdrew the charcoal-gray jacket that she had thought would look so handsome on Peter—the same jacket that she had inquired about at the cocktail party and that Peter seemed to have no knowledge of. Had Angela given it to him since? Had it spawned an argument? Had Peter admitted running into her and that she'd spilled the beans about the jacket just before allowing Peter to put his tongue in her mouth?

She glanced at Angela beneath her lashes and the fact that the woman was studying her with unveiled loathing did not put her at ease. She had the feeling that the woman knew something...or was it simply her own guilt getting the best of her?

Unnerved, Carlotta gave the jacket a shake. When the stench of cigarette—no, *cigar*—smoke reached her nose, she frowned. The jacket's tags had been removed, and it appeared a bit disheveled. She bit her lip. Exchanges and returns under her employee ID were being closely scrutinized since the trouble she'd gotten into over returning clothing that she'd bought and worn for a special occasion (or three). Since Peter had obviously worn the jacket, there was no way she could take it back without getting into trouble. "It, um, it looks like the jacket has been worn, Angela. I can't give you a refund, but I can give you a store credit."

Angela's head snapped up. "No way, I want cash."

"But—"

"Do you know how much money I spend in this store?"

"Yes, but—"

"And that I could buy and sell *you* if I wanted to?"

That stung. It was true, but the woman didn't have to remind her. People were beginning to stare. Moisture gathered on her neck and she cast about for something soothing to say. She put her hand out. "Angela, this isn't personal—"

"Personal?" Angela's eyes turned murderous. "Everything between us is *personal,* Carlotta, considering my husband is still in love with you."

Carlotta's throat convulsed. Did she know about the kiss? "Th-that's…not true, Angela."

"Yes, it is!" Angela shouted, her eyes watering.

She reached across the counter, grasped the gold-plated Judith Leiber fox pendant around Carlotta's neck and yanked her forward, until their faces were inches apart.

Carlotta's feet left the ground as she floundered forward onto the counter. Nose to nose with the wild-eyed Angela, she was too shocked and alarmed to speak.

Angela twisted the chain, tightening it against Carlotta's throat. "You're fooling around with him behind my back, aren't you?"

Carlotta flailed, gasping for air and kicking emptiness. She could hear commotion around them, but she couldn't process the noises because she was feeling light-headed. Even Angela's voice fused into one long droning sound. When the pressure on Carlotta's windpipe increased, self-preservation kicked in. She managed to get a handful of Angela's blond hair and yank with all her strength. She was rewarded with Angela's howl and her release. Carlotta fell back, sprawling on the floor, heaving and sputtering for air.

And suddenly Angela was on her again, this time crawling over her and straddling her, hair and eyes wild, hands circling Carlotta's throat. With what little air and energy she had left, Carlotta grunted and fought back, bucking and kicking, thinking that if she lived, she would probably be fired for creating a spectacle. Abruptly, Angela was dragged off her. Carlotta pushed to a sitting position, rubbing her throat, and saw a wide-eyed Michael Lane holding Angela, forcing her arms to her sides.

"Calm down," he ordered the woman who was struggling against him. "Security is on the way," he assured Carlotta.

"She's screwing my husband!" Angela screamed, then sagged against Michael, sobbing. He gaped at Carlotta and as soon as he loosened his grip, Angela sprang to life, jerking away, then running haphazardly toward the escalator. "Keep the damn jacket," she yelled over her shoulder. Michael looked back to Carlotta for guidance.

"Let her go," Carlotta said, sitting on the floor, dazed, trying to process what had just happened. A crowd had gathered, covertly looking over clothing racks and around shelving units. Her skin tingled, her face burning with shame as she pushed to her feet and righted her clothing. From the direction of the elevator Akin Frasier came jogging toward her, his head pivoting side to side, looking for potential perps. Her boss was right behind him.

"Are you all right, Carlotta?" Lindy asked.

"I got a report that you were being assaulted," Akin said.

"I'm fine," Carlotta said, growing more mortified by the moment. "It was...a misunderstanding with a customer."

"Was it someone you knew?" Lindy asked.

"Yes," Carlotta admitted slowly. "It was Angela Ashford, but I think that she'd been drinking. She wanted a refund on something and became a little...belligerent when I offered a store credit instead."

"What did she do?" Lindy demanded.

Carlotta swallowed. "She...uh..."

"She tried to choke Carlotta," Michael said dryly. "I was coming up the escalator and saw everything."

Akin's eyes narrowed as he reached for his phone. "I'm filing a police report."

"No," Carlotta said quickly, then gave a little laugh. "It was just a misunderstanding. I wouldn't want to blow it out of proportion." She gave her boss a reassuring smile, but Lindy Russell's gaze was wary. A flush burned its way up Carlotta's neck. The only thing that had kept Lindy from canning her over the clothes-returning business a few months ago was her exemplary sales record. An altercation with a customer was not helping her cause.

"I don't think a police report is necessary," Lindy said finally. "How much longer on your shift, Carlotta?"

Carlotta glanced at her watch. "Forty-five minutes."

"Why don't you straighten up here and then go home? If Ms. Ashford returns, someone else will deal with her."

Carlotta nodded, knowing she was getting off lightly. Akin and Lindy walked away and the knots of people dispersed, leaving only her and Michael.

"What was that all about?" he murmured.

"She was drunk," Carlotta said, picking up the jacket that Angela had left.

"She said you were sleeping with her husband."

"I'm not," Carlotta said, although she couldn't make eye contact with him. "Peter Ashford and I go way back, but he broke off our relationship years ago to date Angela, and then he married her. End of story."

"Wow, I knew there was tension between the two of you, but I had no idea a man was involved."

"It's all in her head."

"Are you sure?"

Carlotta looked up at her friend's concerned expression. "Yes. There's nothing between me and Peter Ashford." *Anymore.*

"Okay," Michael said, although his voice was still uncertain. "I have to get back to work. Are you sure you're okay?"

"Yes. Thanks for your help."

"No problem."

She watched her friend walk away and only then gave in to her frayed nerves. Her hands shook as she bagged and tagged the jacket with an ambiguous "hold" note. Then she made her way toward the employee break room, her legs still wobbly over the encounter.

She felt her neck where it would surely be bruised and wondered if Angela really meant to hurt her. The woman's accusation that she and Peter were having an affair reverberated in her head. What had Peter told his wife? Anger flared in her chest. He had no right to pull her into his marital difficulties.

Just as he'd had no right to kiss her the other night.

Her head was beginning to thump as she walked through the parking garage. She massaged the bridge of her nose and fought back sudden tears as the scene unfolded in her head. Good grief, hadn't she deserved the confrontation? Kissing another woman's husband—what had she been thinking? She couldn't blame Angela for being angry. Even if the woman didn't know the whole story, her intuition apparently told her that there were unresolved feelings between her husband and his former girlfriend. How maddening would that be?

Carlotta squeezed her eyes shut against the confusion assailing her, but the sound of an accelerating car jarred her out of her reverie. She jerked around to see a long, dark car with tinted windows speeding toward her. She stood frozen for a split second, then dived to the side and landed with a *whoomph* on the ground between her car and the vehicle next to it. She lay there, her heart beating wildly, expecting the driver to stop, apologize and ask if she was okay. Instead, the car sped down the ramp of the parking garage.

She pushed to her feet, cursing at the general craziness of Atlanta drivers who were too distracted by cell phones and road rage to be bothered with pedestrians. And she blamed herself for walking out in front of the car.

It was only after she was behind the wheel and backing out of her parking place that Angela Ashford popped back into her brain. Could the woman be angry enough to try to run her down? Then she almost laughed in relief. Angela drove a luscious red Jaguar. She'd seen the woman climb into it on more than one occasion at the valet stand.

The rash of crimes around the mall was another possibility— had someone targeted her for a mugging? That didn't seem likely since the driver hadn't even stopped to wrestle away her Coach bag. Then her blood went cold as the threat from her brother's creditor ran through her head. A henchman had come to visit her at the store once before. Was it possible that they were following her, that they had tried to run her down as a warning?

She shuddered and kept one eye on the rearview mirror as she drove home, but didn't see anything out of the ordinary, no dark cars with tinted windows following her. Still, as she pulled her car into the garage, she was thinking about the fact that in a few days, that thug Tick would be back, demanding another payment that Wesley wouldn't have. Even with his new job, he'd be lucky to have half of what the fat man would want.

And then there was next week...

She sighed, swung out of her car and slammed the door in frustration. Rounding the Monte Carlo, she gave it a kick in the back tire, wishing she could sell the redneck car but knowing that was impossible considering how much she owed on it and

what it was worth. She eyed her beloved white Miata, and conceded that even crippled, it could bring a few thousand dollars.
But that would be a last resort. Surely there was something else
she could sell.

She walked into the house and smiled at the noise and good
smells coming from the kitchen. "I'm home," she shouted.

Wesley came to the doorway and waved. "How does lasa-
gna sound?"

"Fantastic."

He eyed her up and down. "What happened to your clothes?
You look like you've been in a brawl."

She glanced down at the black marks on her skirt and
blouse—between the Angela Ashford incident and skidding
across the parking garage, she was a mess. And she wasn't about
to tell Wesley about her "brawl." "I walked out in front of a car
when I was leaving work and decided to sacrifice my outfit."

"Good call."

"I thought so."

"Go get cleaned up. Soup's on in ten."

"Okay," she said, moving toward her bedroom. She rubbed
the shoulder that she'd landed on, her mind still clicking with
worry over the bad element that continued to haunt their lives.
If only she could get her hands on enough cash to get the loan
sharks off their backs.

She turned on the shower, then backtracked to her bedroom.
From beneath her bed she pulled a small trunk, and from the
trunk, a red House of Cartier ring box. Her pulse raced as she
raised the hinged lid and stared at the glittering one-carat dia-

mond solitaire engagement ring that Peter had given her ten years ago. When he'd broken their engagement, he'd told her to keep the ring, to sell it if she needed to. And how many times had she been tempted to do just that to pay for utilities or school clothes or insurance? And how many times had she refused to part with her only remaining link to Peter?

Carlotta fingered the sparkling stone and bit down on the inside of her cheek. Perhaps it was time.

13

"*That* was amazing," Carlotta said, pushing away her plate and smiling at her brother.

"I know," he said with a smirk, still mopping up red sauce with crusty Italian bread. He pushed up his glasses. "I could teach you how to make it sometime."

She batted her lashes. "And spoil your pleasure in cooking for me? Never."

He wiped his mouth, then wadded up the paper napkin and threw it at her. Frowning, he leaned forward. "Hey, what happened to your neck? It looks like someone tried to choke you or something."

Her hand flew to her throat and she could feel the angry welts left by the chain that Angela Ashford had twisted around her neck. "It's...an allergic reaction to a necklace I wore, that's all." Wesley looked unconvinced, so she changed the subject. "When does your community service begin?"

"I have an appointment with my probation officer Wednesday. He's supposed to arrange for me to work with the city geeks on their lousy security."

"Good—maybe that'll lead to a full-time job."

"I already have a full-time job."

"And it's fine for now," she said carefully. "But you can't move dead bodies for the rest of your life."

"Why not? Coop does okay."

She frowned. "But this body-moving thing is just a side job for him too, right?"

"A side job from the funeral home, yeah. He contracts with the morgue when the M.E.'s office is short of vehicles."

Carlotta looked at the clock—almost seven. "You're not working tonight?"

"I'm on call. Coop said most weekend calls are late at night. Shootings, drunk-driving accidents, that kind of thing."

She winced.

"I think he likes you."

"Who?"

"Coop."

Her eyes widened. "Your creepy boss likes me?"

"He's not creepy. He's kind of…nice. And, yeah, he asked about you."

She frowned, remembering that she'd looked a fright the morning she'd met him, the morning after her crying jag over Peter. "Asked what?"

He shrugged. "You know, if you were single and stuff. He said he thought you were cute."

She raised an eyebrow. "Cute? What is he, in grade school?"

"Don't worry, I told him that he wasn't your type."

"Oh." She studied her nails—she needed a manicure badly. Then she looked up. "What's my type?"

Another shrug. "You know—smooth, slick. Coop said you were probably into metrosexuals."

She frowned. "And how could he possibly know that? When he met me, if I remember correctly, I was in my pajamas, wearing no makeup, and my hair was a foot tall."

"Yeah, but still, he could tell you were classy."

She smiled. "You think I'm classy?"

"Don't let it go to your head."

She laughed and in the wake of the cozy moment, she considered asking Wesley about the postcard she'd found from their parents. It had been a long time since they'd really talked about their parents. Maybe it was time to reopen that can of worms.

"Wesley—"

The chirp of his cell phone cut her off. He lunged for the tiny device sitting on the counter. "Hello?" He smiled. "Yeah, man."

Carlotta wondered if it was that Chance Hollander, calling to lure Wesley into some kind of Friday-night trouble. Rich little bastard. He surrounded himself with people like Wesley who were impressed by the toys and good times his money could buy—people who would do his bidding.

Wesley grabbed a pen and scribbled something on a napkin. "Got it. I'll get there somehow." Then he disconnected the call.

Carlotta set her jaw, gathering verbal arguments for Wesley not to meet up with his troublemaker friend.

"That was Coop," Wesley said breathlessly, his eyes shining. "We have a job."

"Oh," she said, her arguments vanishing as her thoughts turned foolishly to how she would greet Cooper Craft now that she knew he thought she was cute.

"But there's one little problem."

At the catch in her brother's voice, she was instantly on alert. "Oh?"

Wesley chewed his lip, then sighed. "It's a residential pickup, and Coop was close to the address when he got the call. Would you mind driving me there?"

"You're not serious?"

"Well, I could drive—"

"You know you can't drive on a suspended license!"

"I can't get there on the train."

Carlotta acknowledged that her brother was right, and felt herself wearing down. She'd hounded him about a job, and now he finally had one. It wouldn't kill her to drive him; it wasn't as if she had something better to do. "Okay, just don't make a habit of this."

He whooped. "Thanks, sis. I'll grab my backpack while you put on a bra."

She glared and swatted at his arm as he walked by, then pushed away from the table. The things she did for love. She went to her room wondering what would be appropriate to wear. She surveyed her flare-leg Levi's, Juicy Couture T-shirt, Michael Kors high-heeled Mary Janes, and decided the outfit would have to do. She donned a bra and added a brown shrug sweater against the evening chill, then slid chocolate-pink lip balm onto her lips to keep them from getting chapped, *not* because Cooper Craft thought she was cute.

"Come on," Wesley said from the doorway of her bedroom. "You're dropping me off. You don't need lipstick."

"It's lip *balm*."

"Whatever, come on already."

She swung her purse to her shoulder. "You owe me for this."

"Yeah, well, add it to the list."

They blew by Mrs. Winningham who was weeding her flower bed. "Wait! I want to talk to you two!"

"Some other time, Mrs. Winningham!" Carlotta promised the woman as they ran for the garage.

"But someone has been parking on the street and watching our houses! Don't you care?"

"No!" they yelled in unison, ducking under the opening garage door and bolting for the Monte Carlo.

"Christ," Carlotta muttered under her breath. "It's probably that Detective Terry snooping around."

"Yeah, probably," Wesley said in a noncommittal voice.

Or any one of several other undesirables, she conceded miserably. "Do you have the address?" she asked as she backed out.

"Yeah, it's in Buckhead." He read off the street name and number and Carlotta frowned. "Hmm, that's a nice area. Did he mention the neighborhood?"

"Yeah, it's Martinique Estates. Know it?"

She frowned. "Maybe. It sounds familiar, but I can't place it." She'd probably crashed a party there sometime, but didn't want to say so in front of her brother. Besides, those days were be-

hind her—no more party-crashing. She'd made an exception the
other night and it had put her in the path of Peter Ashford, a
scene which may have caused the humiliating takedown today
at work. Her skin crawled at the memory and she touched the
tender place on her throat. Thank God Lindy hadn't called the
police or the situation could have spiraled into something much
more messy.

"Did someone have a heart attack in their home?" she asked.

"Coop didn't say, but that's a good guess."

Unbidden, her parents came to mind. They would be in their
mid-fifties now. If her mother was still drinking, she couldn't
be in good health. And her father had smoked like a chimney
and enjoyed his bourbon. Occasionally she wondered if she and
Wesley would even be notified if they were sick…or worse. But
according to the postcard that Wesley had kept hidden, they
were still kicking.

She glanced sideways at her brother in the dark cab of the car,
unspoken words simmering on her tongue. But his face was a
mask of concentration. It wasn't an appropriate time or place
to bring up their parents' latest communication.

Ten minutes later they were winding through the community
of Buckhead, Atlanta's premier address, featuring enormous
tree-laden lots and even more enormous amenity-laden houses.
Old money met new money behind the soaring gates of the private communities where residents lifted a collective nose at the
rest of Atlanta. Carlotta knew, because she'd grown up in just
such a neighborhood.

"You missed the turn," Wesley said, exasperated.

She frowned and looked in her rearview mirror. "I'm doing the best I can. It's so dark out here!"

"Turn around!"

"Shut up and put on your seat belt!"

They bickered until they pulled up to the wrought-iron gates of Martinique Estates. A squad car with a silent, flashing light sat next to the gatehouse.

"Lot of commotion for a heart attack victim," she said, impressed.

A security guard accompanied by a uniformed police office approached the car as she rolled down the window. Wesley leaned forward and flashed an official-looking badge with his photo and something about the medical examiner's office. The policeman looked at it, then handed it back and signaled for the gatekeeper to let them in.

Recalling all the tickets that Wesley had counterfeited for her, she frowned. "Is that a fake badge?"

"What? No. Coop gave me this. I'm official. Turn here."

She did and again had the feeling that the street name was familiar for some reason. She stared up at the monstrous brick houses that looked more like compounds than homes and, God help her, she felt a stab of envy. Money didn't buy happiness, but it made certain aspects of life a whole hell of a lot easier. She'd lived on both sides of that wrought-iron gate, so she knew.

Wesley was craning for house numbers, but that became a moot point when they both caught sight of a squad car and an ambulance, lights flashing, and various other official-looking vehicles parked at angles on the curb and in the downward-

sloping driveway. The megamansion sat below curb level, judging by the way the land fell away and by the downward gaze of
the onlookers. "I think we found the right house." She guided
the car closer, picking up an approaching cop in her headlights,
then stopped and zoomed down the window.

"You need to keep moving, ma'am."

"We're here to help transport the body," Wesley said, sounding amazingly mature. He handed the badge to the cop, who,
after scrutinizing it, handed it back. "Okay, but you'll have to
park here and walk onto the property. The pool is down there."

"Pool?" Wesley asked.

"The woman drowned," the cop said curtly.

Carlotta shuddered, then looked at Wesley. "Do you see your
boss's vehicle?"

"No, but he's probably parked near the house."

"I'll pull over and wait a few minutes. If you don't come back
or call my cell, I'll know you found him and I'll go."

He sighed. "You worry too much."

"I know. Go."

He scrambled out of the vehicle and disappeared down the
driveway. Carlotta pulled over to the curb and put the car into
Park, giving the cop a little wave. Headlights shone in her rearview mirror, and then a car parked behind her. A suited man
climbed out and walked by her car, his destination obviously the
house. With a shock she realized it was Detective Jack Terry, just
as he turned and recognized her. He stopped and tapped on her
window. Reluctantly, she zoomed it down.

"Ms. Wren, what are you doing here?"

"Just dropping off my brother, Detective. He got a job with a local funeral home operator who contracts with the morgue to…uh…move bodies."

He pursed his mouth. "Did he now? Well, that explains why a hearse was parked in front of your place a couple of days ago."

She glared. "Stop spying on us."

His gaze raked over the Monte Carlo and one side of his mouth lifted. "I like the car—not exactly what I thought you'd be driving, though."

She put her hand on the gearshift to keep from swinging at him. "*Good night,* Detective."

Suddenly another set of headlights shone in her rearview mirror, these from a smaller car approaching very fast. Detective Terry flattened himself against the Monte Carlo as the little car careened past and screeched to a halt at a haphazard angle, leaving the smell of burnt rubber in the air. It was a dark Porsche, but she couldn't discern the model.

"Looks like the husband is home," the detective said, his voice rueful. "This is always the hard part."

Carlotta felt an unexpected stab of compassion for the detective as he walked toward the man who flung himself out of the car. How horrible it must be to work with angry, distraught, and sometimes violent people, day in and day out.

And based on the body language of the man who was trying to push past the detective, those were just the survivors.

Riveted, she watched as Detective Terry visibly tried to calm the man. They were about the same height, but the detective's bulk gave him the advantage of leverage. He led the man to where they could look down upon the house. From the way the man bent over and gripped his knees, she presumed they could see the pool from where they stood—and the body. Then the husband turned, as though to gather himself, and lifted his head in Carlotta's direction.

The breath froze in her chest as recognition slammed into her.

Peter Ashford, looking disheveled and inebriated.

She glanced at the monstrous house, eerily illuminated by up-lights and headlights. This was Peter's house?

Which meant, she realized with dawning horror, that the woman who was dead was...Angela Ashford.

14

The lost look on Peter's face made Carlotta's heart swell in agony. Before she had time to think, she was out of the car and moving toward him in the semidarkness. "Peter?"

He turned at the sound of her voice and when he saw her, his face creased in confusion. "Carlotta? What are you doing here?"

"I dropped off Wesley. He's here...in an official capacity," she said vaguely. "We had no idea this was your house...that Angela—" She broke off, at a loss for words.

He embraced her and she could feel desperation palpating through his heated skin. She could also smell the gin on his breath and on his shirt. He was drunk, and she wondered how much his clinging to her was to keep himself upright. Then he buried his face in her hair and pulled her body against his. She ached to give him the comfort he sought, but when she realized that Detective Terry was gaping at them, she reluctantly pulled away and cleared her throat.

Detective Terry's eyebrows sat high on his forehead. "I take it you two know each other?"

"Old friends," Carlotta supplied quickly, then her gaze caught on the pool about twenty yards below them, shrouded in the mist that rose from the surface of the heated water. Angela's body, clad in black, lay on the pale background of the concrete pool surround, her limbs at awkward angles. Carlotta swallowed hard against the cold truth that Angela was dead.

Peter looked at the scene and dragged his hand down his face. "I have to go to her," he said, and the detective relented with a nod, falling into step behind him.

Carlotta didn't know whether to stay or to go, or to walk down with the men. She didn't relish seeing the body up close, but she also didn't want to just leave. She hugged herself, running her hands up and down her arms to ward off the damp chill that blanketed everything that didn't move—which would include Angela's body, she noted ruefully.

Peter turned back. "Carlotta…I could use a friend right now."

She hesitated, darting a glance at the detective, who looked extremely irritated at the idea of her going with them.

"Try to stay out of the way," Detective Terry said, then continued tromping down the incline.

She followed them, careful to stay behind while still in Peter's peripheral vision. She couldn't take her eyes off him. He seemed so…so…disconnected. She wondered if he was in shock. No tears, no prostrate hysterics. Maybe the alcohol had numbed his senses, but back when they had dated, alcohol had always made him more emotional.

He moved like an automaton, staring straight ahead, his hands hanging limply by his sides as he walked by the vehicles parked in the paved turnaround in front of the house, including a car with the medical examiner's shield on the side and a plain white van that Carlotta assumed belonged to Cooper Craft. As they approached the tall wrought-iron fence that enclosed the pool, Carlotta glanced around nervously.

She took in the palatial lines of the brick house, the sweeping steps that led from the turnaround, the huge fountain, the two-story entryway and the soaring Palladian windows, eerily dark. The house looked cold, empty...dead. By contrast, the gated pool area adjacent to the house was blazing with lights, the deep water an unnatural blue. With steam rising from the surface, the water resembled a witch's cauldron. Taking deep breaths against the turmoil in her stomach, she followed the men down a short lighted stone path to a gate that had been propped open. The scent of chlorine burned the air, which seemed swollen with humidity and sadness.

Wesley and Cooper stood off to the side of the pool next to a small waterfall, apparently waiting for the police to complete their investigation. A youngish man with Medical Examiner on his jacket stood over Angela's body, taking photos. Carlotta made eye contact with Wesley, who looked confused at her appearance. Then his gaze went to Peter and back to her, wide-eyed. She nodded, trying to answer the questions that must be whirling through his mind, and walked over to where they stood.

"Isn't that Peter Ashford?" Wesley whispered.

"Yes," she murmured.

"And that's his wife?"

"Yes."

"Jesus," Wesley said. "Nice place."

"Wesley!"

He looked contrite and pressed his lips together.

"Do you know the family?" Cooper asked them asked under his breath.

"That's sis's old boyfriend," Wesley offered. "The one she was crying—"

"Do you know what happened?" she cut in, shooting Wesley a lethal look.

"Accidental drowning is what I was told," Cooper offered quietly. "She must have fallen in."

Her gaze cut to Angela's still body and the gray wetness around her on the concrete from her saturated clothing. When she'd been shopping for swimsuits, Angela had mentioned that she didn't know how to swim. She was still wearing the chunky-heeled black knee boots that Carlotta had sold to her—they must have felt like lead when she'd gone under the surface of the water. The pool was about twenty-five feet wide—she would have been a mere body's length from safety. The vision sent a shudder through Carlotta. The entire scene was surreal, an unimaginable nightmare.

"The maid found her," Wesley added, nodding to an open sliding glass door leading into the house. A small, older woman stood in the doorway, her shoulders hunched, a handkerchief covering her face.

The uniformed officers apparently had been waiting for Detective Terry to arrive because when they saw him, they straightened from the body. Peter's knees buckled and Detective Terry steadied him, guiding him toward the open door into the expansive house. She heard the detective say something about coffee. The maid scurried aside and turned on a light. The wall facing the pool was made almost completely of glass. From where Carlotta stood, she saw Peter sink into a chair around a table in a room that appeared to be a sunroom or a casual dining room. He covered his face with his hands.

Carlotta's body strained toward him, but she forced her attention away from the man with whom she had been so recently and so bizarrely reunited and back to the scene unfolding around the pool.

The officers talking to Detective Terry gestured toward the water, perhaps indicating where they had found the body. At the end of the pool sat an outdoor kitchen with a stone fireplace, appliances and a bar. From her vantage point she could see at least two bottles of gin, along with a silver flask that looked like the one Angela had drunk from in the dressing room. Behind the bar area was a small cottage—the guesthouse, Carlotta presumed, recalling what Peter had said about the pool addition being more than he had envisioned.

But she silently applauded Angela's ambition. It was a garden paradise, with huge sago palms in clay pots, beds of lush flowers and a flagstone path to a hot tub lined with mosaic tiles. It was a picture out of *Better Home and Gardens*...except for the body lying poolside. Angela Ashford hadn't lived to enjoy the luxurious addition to her posh home.

Next to the pool, Detective Terry had been in discussion with the medical examiner, and now knelt over the body, pulling a set of plastic gloves from his jacket pocket. He snapped them on and lifted the mass of golden hair that had fallen across Angela's neck. Then he lifted her lifeless hands, one at a time. Carlotta tried to reconcile the still form lying on the concrete with the animated, angry woman who had been so alive just hours ago. Her stomach rolled, sending acid to the back of her throat; she thought she might be sick.

"Maybe you should go," Cooper suggested quietly, his mouth near her ear. "This isn't something that everyone should see, especially if you have a connection to the deceased."

She nodded, breathing deeply, and turned to leave. She walked to the open door where Peter sat, staring off into the distance, his jaw clenched. He looked up and a desperate look came into his eyes. He lifted his hand to her. With her heart clicking, she stepped into the house, immediately assailed by a sense of grandeur—the scale of the wood-lined ceilings alone was awe-inspiring.

"Will you close the door?" he asked, turning his head away.

She did, glad to shut out the sounds of hushed voices and staticky police radios. The vacuum of the door closing sealed her into a room where the air was surprisingly stale, as if the house was rarely used. Through the wide doorway in the back of the room Carlotta caught a glimpse of the maid bustling around in a large kitchen. Hallways and stairways that extended out of her line of vision spoke of the house's spaciousness. The scent of strong coffee wafted on the air.

The room she stood in was another designer feat, a den with a soaring brick fireplace, built-in cherry-wood cabinets jammed with expensive-looking bric-a-brac, overstuffed leather couches and chairs, plus a long carved mahogany table and twelve matching chairs. Peter sat in the chair near the end of the table, his back to the pool, fingering the tip of a flower in what had to be the most hideously huge silk flower arrangement that Carlotta had ever seen.

"We argued about this stupid flower arrangement," he said, still staring straight ahead.

She stood motionless, letting him talk.

"It didn't matter that it was ugly," he said with a laugh. "What mattered was that some upscale florist came to our house and designed it especially for Angela. He even gave it some ridiculous name, and I'd be ashamed to tell you how much it cost. Do you believe that we had a party so that people in the neighborhood could come and look at the damn flower arrangement?"

He looked up as he finished, the anger in his voice traveling to his startling blue eyes, hardening the drunken lines of his face until he looked almost…mean.

Carlotta was glad when the maid appeared with a coffee tray and set it on the table. The woman filled a cup and slid it in front of Peter, then offered Carlotta a watery smile. "Coffee, miss?"

Carlotta shook her head. "I don't think—"

"Please," Peter implored. "Sit with me, just for a little while."

She hesitated, then took the chair opposite him. Too late, she realized it gave her a direct view of Angela's body. The woman's pale face was turned toward Carlotta, her eyes slightly open. It was as if she were determined to watch Peter and Carlotta, even in death.

Just as the maid set a cup of steaming coffee in front of Carlotta, the glass door slid open, revealing Detective Terry. He stepped in without being asked, although he did make a perfunctory pass at wiping his feet on the doormat.

He scowled at her briefly before addressing the maid. "I understand, ma'am, that you found the body?"

The old woman's eyes teared and she nodded.

"What's your name, please?"

"Flaur Stanza."

He made a note on a palm-size notebook he carried. "Can you tell me what happened, Miss Stanza?"

"I...come home from store," she said in broken English. "I see Miss Angela's purse, so I know she is here. I call her name to see if she want tea, and she no answer. I come out here to sweep, and...and——" She began to sob, her shoulders shaking.

"Take your time, Miss Stanza," Peter said, his voice strangely calm.

"I see her...in deep end...floating facedown," the woman said. "She fell in, I think."

"Had she been drinking?" Peter bit out.

Detective Terry frowned. "Mr. Ashford, if you don't mind, I'll ask the questions. Miss Stanza, did you see anything else, any signs of where she might have fallen in?"

She nodded and pointed to the far end of the pool. "A broken glass on the edge. I show policeman when he get here."

Detective Terry made another note. "Anything else?"

"Black marks, I think from her boots."

The detective nodded. "And you called 911?"

"Yes, sir. And Mr. Peter." She shot a quick glance at Peter and her face crumpled again.

"It's okay," Peter soothed, patting her arm. "It's not your fault. I was afraid something like this was going to happen."

Detective Terry perked up. "Oh? Has something like this happened before?"

Peter pursed his mouth. "You mean Angela drunk? Only all the time. And she was a poor swimmer."

Detective Terry told the maid that she could go. The woman looked to Peter for confirmation, and he nodded. "Go home, Miss Stanza. I'll call you tomorrow." When the woman left the room, Peter gestured to the tray. "Would you like some coffee, Detective?"

"No, thank you." Then Detective Terry looked at Carlotta. "Ms. Wren, will you excuse us for a moment?"

Realizing that he was asking her to leave, she started to stand, but Peter's hand on her arm stopped her.

"Stay," he said, his voice beseeching, then he turned to the detective. "I have no secrets. Ask me anything."

The detective looked back and forth between them until Carlotta averted her gaze. This was really beginning to feel... wrong.

"Okay," Detective Terry said with a sigh. "Mr. Ashford, was your marriage in trouble?"

Next to her, she felt Peter stiffen. "No more so than any other marriage, I would suspect."

Outside, the medical examiner and the police had stepped away from the body. Cooper unfolded a white sheet, whipped it open and allowed it to float down over Angela's body. Carlotta stared until the woman's face was completely obscured by the sheet. Wesley lowered what resembled a long plastic tray with scooped sides and black handles. With care that impressed her, Coop rolled the covered body toward him until Wesley had slid the tray underneath. Then he gently lowered the body and situated it onto the carrier. Both men tucked the sheet around the body with respectful concentration. She felt a swell of pride for Wesley, that he was handling such a terrible job with professionalism and obvious detail.

"Were the two of you discussing a divorce?"

The question yanked her attention back to the conversation.

"No," Peter said defiantly.

Carlotta shifted in the uncomfortable chair, the memory of their kiss now even more sordid. She closed her eyes briefly and when she opened them, found Detective Terry studying her before he turned his attention back to Peter.

"Has your wife ever threatened to hurt herself?"

"No, of course not." Peter's expression darkened. "You're not thinking that she did this on purpose."

"Just covering all the bases, Mr. Ashford. Was she taking any medication?"

Peter rubbed his eyes and sighed. "Sure, it was always something with Angela. She had insomnia and back trouble, and she took a ton of vitamins. You can check the medicine cabinet in her bathroom if you want the specifics."

Detective Terry cleared his throat. "Perhaps we should both go check, to see if Mrs. Ashford left a note."

Peter's jaw clenched. "There's *no* note."

"How can you be sure?"

Peter pulled his hand down over his faced and sighed. "Because...I asked Miss Stanza to look for a note when she called me. She didn't find one."

"So you suspected suicide?"

Peter lifted his hands in a helpless gesture. "I didn't know what to think, but it crossed my mind. You didn't find one on...on her?"

"No. The guesthouse was also checked, plus the sedan in the garage—I assume that's Mrs. Ashford's car?"

"No, actually. Her Jag is at the dealership for regular maintenance. The sedan is a loaner."

"Mr. Ashford, where were you when Miss Stanza called to give you the bad news?"

Peter's mouth tightened. "If you must know, I was at a bar, Geary's, not far from my office."

"Where do you work?"

"Mashburn and Tully Investments. I'm a broker."

Recognition flashed in the detective's eyes and his gaze flicked to her, then back. He'd made the connection that her father had once been a partner there. A harmless yet suspicious coincidence.

"Were you alone at the bar, Mr. Ashford?"

"Yes. What's that got to do with anything?"

Detective Terry shrugged his big shoulders. "I just wondered why I got here before you, that's all."

"There was construction on the connector," Peter said hotly.

Warning bells sounded in Carlotta's brain. Surely Detective Terry didn't suspect that Peter had something to do with Angela's death? She bit her lip, wondering whether to say that she'd seen Angela earlier that day and what her state of mind had been. But if she did, she'd have to admit that Angela thought that she and Peter were having an affair, and wouldn't that only throw more suspicion on Peter?

She clamped her mouth shut, telling herself that she was doing the right thing. Angela's death was just a tragic accident, a result of a bad vice and bad balance. She felt the detective's gaze on her and decided that her presence might be doing more harm than good. She pushed to her feet. "Peter...it's time for me to leave." Her throat convulsed. "I'm...so sorry for your loss."

"Before you go, Ms. Wren," the detective said, holding up his hand, "I'd like to ask one more question." Then he gave Peter a pointed look. "Were you, sir, having an affair?"

Carlotta's pulse skipped and she forgot to breathe. Peter put his hands on the table, then slowly pushed to his feet. "No, Detective, I wasn't having an affair. My wife's death was an accident, pure and simple. I'd think that the police have enough on their plate without trying to turn this tragedy into a crime."

Detective Terry closed his notebook, then looked contrite. "How right you are, Mr. Ashford. My sincere condolences." Then he swung his gaze to her. "Ms. Wren, since I'm leaving, too, I'll walk you out."

She couldn't think of anything less appealing, but since she couldn't think of a way to refuse, she simply nodded. "Peter, call me if...I can help."

He looked at her for a long while, then nodded. "Okay."

Aware that the detective was hanging on their every word, she quickly walked to the door, slid it open and stepped outside. Detective Terry was on her heels. She retraced her steps down the stone path back to the front of the house where Wesley and Coop were closing the door on the back of the van.

"You okay, sis?" Wesley asked, his face contracted in concern.

"I'm fine," she said, slowing her pace. "Wesley, you remember Detective Terry."

"Hard to forget," Wesley said wryly, then nodded. "How's it going, man?"

"Glad to see you got a job," Detective Terry said.

"This is my boss, Cooper Craft."

The detective nodded. "The doctor and I know each other."

Coop nodded, but his eyes were...wary? Carlotta wondered about the men's history. And had the detective called him *doctor?*

Detective Terry looked around. "I see the M.E. already left. Do you have the report?"

Coop nodded and handed it to him.

Detective Terry looked over the form, then glanced up. "Do you agree, Coop?"

Coop hesitated. "It's not my place to agree or disagree."

The detective's mouth tightened. "I'm asking."

"Since you're asking...no, I don't agree with the report."

Carlotta pressed her lips together. This couldn't be good.

The detective grimaced in thought then said, "I want an autopsy. Take her to the morgue."

"But—" Coop began.

"I'll handle the paperwork," the detective cut in.

Coop gave a curt nod, then said, "Let's go," to Wesley.

"We have another call after this one," Wesley said to Carlotta. "Coop said he'd give me a ride home."

"Okay." She turned to walk up the steep driveway, eager to be away from death and all this talk about the morgue.

"Ms. Wren," the detective said, catching up to her easily, "how exactly are you acquainted with Peter Ashford?"

Her skin tingled as she pumped her arms to manage the climb in her high-heeled Mary Janes. "Peter and I used to date, ages ago, when we were kids. He's older and when he went to college, we broke up, just like a million other teenagers." She was proud of herself for how nonchalant her voice sounded.

"He seemed pretty eager to rekindle your friendship. When was the last time you saw him?"

In another few steps they were at the top of the incline in front of their vehicles. She stopped and turned to face him, breathing hard and blinking into the glare of a streetlight. "I've seen him twice in the past ten years, Detective, once at the mall when he wasn't aware of it, and once at a cocktail party."

"When?"

"Three nights ago."

His eyebrows climbed. "Is that so?"

"There's nothing going on between me and Peter Ashford, Detective."

He studied her as if trying to determine whether she was telling the truth. Then suddenly he leaned forward and she had the insane notion that he was going to kiss her. She jerked back. "*What* are you doing?"

"What happened to your neck?" he asked, squinting.

She raised her hand to the welts on her skin that still felt raw and tender. Panic bolted through her chest that she bore marks left upon her by a woman who was now dead. "Nothing happened. I'm fine." She turned and walked to her car, fumbling in her pockets for her keys before remembering she'd left them in the ignition.

He followed her, wearing a dubious expression. She fisted her hand that hid the marks from his prying eyes. "Detective, would you please stop staring at my chest?"

He lifted his gaze, but took his time. "Yes, ma'am. Good night, Ms. Wren. I'll be seeing you."

"*Stop* spying on us. You're making my neighbor paranoid."

"Wouldn't have to if you'd cooperate."

She glanced at the purse that she'd left on the car seat and thought of the postcard from her parents tucked inside. "I don't know what you're talking about."

"Right," he said, then turned and walked toward his own car.

Carlotta stuck her tongue out at his back, then glanced down at the house just as Coop turned the white van around. When he pulled away, the open garage was fully lit, revealing a dark sedan sitting inside. Carlotta recalled the morbid conversation about checking Angela's car for a suicide note, and grimaced.

But as she stared at the loaner car, a memory chord strummed in the back of her mind. She couldn't be sure, but the car looked like the one that had nearly run her down in the parking garage today.

She jerked her attention away and hurriedly swung into her car, frantic to be gone. In her haste she nearly flooded the engine, but finally the ignition caught and she pulled away from the house, her hands clammy, her mind ringing with one truth: It was a good decision to have kept her mouth shut about her run-in with Angela, or that pesky Detective Terry might try to implicate *her* in the woman's death by pointing out that she had plenty of motivation for wanting Angela dead.

Carlotta rubbed at her temple where a headache had settled. As if she didn't already have enough problems to deal with.

15

From his seat in the van, Wesley watched his sister career out of the neighborhood and shook his head.

"She's in a hurry," Coop observed wryly.

"I guess this scene shook her up. She was engaged to that Ashford guy."

"Hmm."

"Kind of weird that she ran into him just a couple of days ago, then again tonight, huh?"

"Hmm."

"And now his wife is dead."

"Hmm."

Wesley looked at his boss. "Are the husbands usually that calm in a situation like this?"

Coop took his time answering. "Not usually, but sometimes. Ashford looked drunk to me."

Wesley stabbed at his glasses. "Well, I didn't like the way he cozied up to Carlotta, seeing as how his wife isn't even in the ground."

"It's good that you watch out for your sister," Coop said with a little smile, "but I have the feeling that she can take care of herself."

His mind flew to the disheveled state of Carlotta's clothing when she'd arrived home. What had she said? That she'd walked out in front of a car when she'd left work and had decided to sacrifice her outfit.

No way would Carlotta sacrifice her outfit unless she truly thought she was going to bite a car grill.

And even though it was probably some soccer mom from Alpharetta trying to beat rush-hour traffic, there was the possibility that it had been someone who'd targeted her, someone who wanted to scare her, to send a message…to him. A sour taste backed up in his mouth. He'd heard rumors about The Carver running people down, and the bumper on his black Caddy did look as if a few objects had bounced off it.

"Say, Coop, do you know where I could get a gun?"

Coop's head pivoted. "Why on earth do you need a gun?"

Wesley shrugged. "You know—for protection."

"You're on probation, chief, or have you forgotten? Besides, I think you're overreacting on the protective-brother thing."

He chewed on his response for a while, then decided to talk to Coop man-to-man. "Look, I owe money to some bad dudes. One of them keeps showing up at the house and hassling my sister. I just want to be able to protect her, if necessary."

Coop scowled. "Maybe you should call the police."

"Yeah, right. And the next body-moving call you get will be me."

Coop didn't respond and Wesley wished he hadn't brought

up the subject. His buddy Chance would probably know where he could get a gun with no questions asked. "That detective back there, he's the guy who arrested me. Jerk."

"Jack Terry? We don't always see eye to eye, but he's usually just doing his job."

"He called you doctor, just like that lady at the nursing home."

"Uh-huh."

"And he asked your opinion on the M.E.'s report."

"Uh-huh."

"So what's up with that?"

Coop stretched in his seat and Wesley thought it was another one of those questions his boss would avoid.

"I used to be a doctor," Coop said finally.

"Used to be?"

Coop shot him an impatient look. "Yeah, as in I'm not anymore."

"What happened?"

The man's profile hardened and he seemed to turn inside himself. "Long story," he said, mimicking Wesley's response of a couple of days ago when Cooper had probed about his family.

"Some other time, then," Wesley said.

"Yeah. We're here," Coop said, pulling the van into the parking lot of the city morgue.

Wesley looked at the nondescript building, the third time he'd accompanied Coop to the place. They pulled around to the back where two guys in scrubs were just finishing a smoke break and going back into the building.

"Working in a morgue, you'd think they'd know better than to smoke," Wesley said.

"Yeah," Coop replied, "but sometimes the people who know better have the worst vices of all."

Something in his voice made Wesley think once again that Cooper Craft had secrets and maybe a shady past. And the set of the man's mouth told him that something about this body pickup had bothered him more than usual.

When Coop parked, Wesley jumped out to help him unload the body from the van and place it on a gurney. They rolled it up a ramp where Coop pressed a button on a call box and identified himself and their "delivery." A few seconds later a buzz sounded, unlocking the door.

A slender, suited man, maybe in his fifties, met them just inside the door, a thundercloud on his bushy brow.

"Hello, Dr. Abrams," Coop said pleasantly.

The man didn't acknowledge the greeting. "Is this the Ashford body?"

"Yes."

"My medical examiner just phoned in. He said he ruled the death an accidental drowning."

"He did," Coop said.

"So why is she here?"

"Detective Jack Terry told me to bring her here after he interviewed the husband," Coop said, his voice even. "The M.E. had already left, Bruce."

The chief medical examiner's expression changed to one of suspicion. "And I suppose *you* had nothing to do with the detective overriding the M.E.'s report."

Coop lifted his hands. "Just following orders."

The man expelled a long sigh and jammed his hands on his hips. "You're putting me in a hell of a spot. I extended the transport contract for your family's funeral home because we go way back, and in spite of everything, I respect you, Coop. But I can't have you on the scene second-guessing my people."

Coop frowned. "Well, maybe I wouldn't have to if your people would do their job. The guy barely looked at the body before writing the report and taking off. He didn't even talk to the next of kin, only the maid."

Dr. Abrams made an exasperated noise. "Coop, you of all people know how it is—everyone here is overworked and underpaid. We're lucky to fill the entry-level jobs, and we got bodies stacked up in here."

"Then one more won't matter," Coop said, his voice challenging.

The older man's expression hardened and his chin went up in the air. "No, Coop. That's not the way things are run around here anymore. We follow the rules to the letter."

Coop's mouth tightened, and then he shook his head, his eyes full of disdain. "That's why you'll never be a great M.E., Bruce."

The man's eyes narrowed. "You arrogant son of a bitch. You have the nerve to criticize me after the disgraceful way you behaved?"

Wesley took a step back. The men obviously had history.

Coop set his jaw and looked away. When he turned back, his expression was contrite. "I'm sorry, Bruce. You're right—I was out of line. You don't have to do an autopsy, but I'll have to leave the body here while I make another run. I'll pick it up when I make the next dropoff in about—" he looked at his watch "—two hours. Okay?"

Dr. Abrams drew back, his eyes still wary despite Coop's apology, his chin stubbornly set. "Take her to the crypt for now."

Coop nodded in acquiescence and told Wesley where to turn once they reached the end of the hall. He seemed to know his way around the place.

The morgue was a cold, sterile building with industrial surfaces and a hushed, echoey atmosphere. At this time of day, the corners were dark, the glaring overhead lights ruthless. They passed workers wearing scrubs, their eyes and shoulders sagging in fatigue. A few of them recognized Coop and murmured hello, although their body language seemed awkward and their eye contact furtive.

Wesley slid his gaze sideways to his boss. The man was indeed a mystery, but he had a feeling now wasn't the best time to ask questions.

As they rounded a corner, the body shifted in the gray body bag they had transferred her to. Wesley jumped back and Coop smiled as they repositioned her.

"Relax, man, she's not going to hurt anyone."

Even in the voluminous body bag, her breast implants were obvious, jutting up, pushing the plastic taut.

"It freaks me out a little because she was so young," Wesley said.

"Unfortunately, you'd better get used to that."

"But she's, like, my sister's age."

"Uh-huh."

"So you don't think her drowning was an accident?"

Coop pursed his mouth and resumed pushing the gurney. "As a matter of fact, it probably *was* an accident. I have a tendency to look for a devious angle even where there is none." He smiled. "I can be rather morose, if you hadn't noticed."

"I guess this job will do it to you."

"Yep."

They reached the stainless-steel doors marked Crypt. Coop knocked and handed some paperwork to the young orderly who came to the door and said, "We'll take it from here."

Wesley handed off the gurney and turned to go. Coop took a little longer and cast a lingering glance over Angela Ashford's body as it disappeared through the doors. Then he turned to Wesley and clapped him on the back. "Louis Strong at the Sonic Car Wash on Monroe Avenue."

Wesley frowned. "Who's that?"

"The man who can get you a decent handgun without a lot of questions. He's not cheap, but he has a good reputation. Tell him I sent you, and don't shoot your damn foot off, okay?"

Wesley grinned. "Okay."

"Wipe that grin off your face. I'm doing this because I don't want to see anything happen to your sister, capisce?"

Wesley's grin widened. "Capisce."

16

By the time Carlotta parked the Monte Carlo in her garage, she was shaking uncontrollably. A hot shower did little to dispel the chill that had seeped into her skin, a reminder that Angela Ashford would never again be warm. Sleep was out of the question. Instead, she huddled against her headboard wrapped in the fuzzy chenille robe, watching the Style Network through a haze of tears that wouldn't fall and aching all over from a misery that she couldn't define. Hovering along the edges of guilt over how many times she'd wished terrible things upon Angela was a profound fear that she'd never felt before——her own mortality.

She and Angela were the same age, and Angela had been surrounded by everything that Carlotta had once thought would be hers someday, including Peter. In Carlotta's eyes, Angela had been the luckiest woman in Atlanta, yet it all had been snatched from her in the time it took to fall into a quarter-of-a-million-dollar swimming-pool addition and drown.

How long did it take for a person to drown? Carlotta wondered. One minute? Three? Five?

All that time, Angela would have been thrashing in the water in those boots that Carlotta had coveted, trying to hold her breath until at last giving in and drawing chlorinated water into her burning lungs.

Had Angela's last thoughts been of Peter, of the man she'd married? Had she died thinking that her husband was having an affair with his former fiancée? Had she mourned that her life hadn't turned out the way she'd hoped?

If so, Carlotta thought sadly, then she and Angela actually had a lot in common.

With her bedroom lights blazing, Carlotta listened to the comforting hum of voices from the television as the pretty people on the entertainment news show floated through their glamorous lives, smiling wide and lifting one-hundred-dollar glasses of Clarendon Hills syrah, climbing in and out of their European sports cars, wearing couture clothing from Milan. Their lives seemed so perfect…the life she'd always aspired to have.

She picked up the Cartier ring box from her nightstand and fingered the marquis-cut engagement ring that Peter had given her when she was seventeen. She'd been much too young to be thinking about marriage, she knew that now, but her love for Peter had obliterated any other goal she might have had for herself. The fact that the ring he'd given her surpassed what most adult women received spoke of the incredible wealth that Peter had at his disposal. Too young, too clueless and too wealthy… completely unprepared to deal with reality.

She sighed. After ten years of hard knocks, sometimes she still felt unprepared to deal with reality. Her mind churned, consumed with the quandary she'd put herself in by kissing Peter Ashford the night of the cocktail party. After ten years, she had run into him and fallen into his arms, and only a couple of days later, his wife was dead.

Life was nothing if not uncanny.

But as she dwelled on the horrific coincidence, the terrible thought that she had managed to keep at bay stubbornly worked its way through the nooks and crannies of her brain and presented itself: What if Peter had killed Angela?

As soon as the notion materialized, she dismissed it as absurd. Why would Peter kill Angela?

Because of you.

Angela's accusations rang in her head like a gong. *My husband is still in love with you. You're fooling around with him behind my back, aren't you?*

Carlotta shook her head, refusing to believe any of her own foolish conjectures. How conceited would she be if she thought that Peter would murder his wife just so he could be free? The idea was positively ludicrous.

The blaring ring of the phone on her nightstand startled her so badly, she cried out. The clock radio displayed the time as just after midnight. She set down the ring box and answered, thinking it was Wesley because she hadn't heard him return yet. "Hello?"

"Carly, hi. It's me…Peter. Did I wake you?"

Her chest constricted painfully at the rasp of his voice. He sounded as if he'd been drinking again. "No, I was awake. How…how are you?"

"Not good," he admitted. "I just finished calling everyone in the family. Angela's parents are on a cruise, so it took me a while to track them down."

"I'm so sorry, Peter."

"I know," he said. "I just called to thank you for…staying this evening. You didn't have to."

"It's okay," she murmured, struck by an overwhelming sense of déjà vu. How many times had she lain curled up in bed talking to Peter on the phone? Hundreds? Thousands? "I only wish that I could help you."

"You did, simply by being there. I'm just sorry that you had to hear all the hateful things that Neanderthal detective said."

She twisted a hank of hair that had fallen next to her ear, a nervous habit she'd given up years ago after her hairdresser had chastised her. "I'm sure he was only doing his job."

"Still, he tried to make it sound as if…as if I had something to do with her death."

Carlotta's heart pounded and moisture gathered around her hairline, but she remained silent.

Peter gave a little laugh. "I almost got the feeling that he thought you and I were having an affair or something."

She tried to mimic his laugh, but the noise that emerged sounded high-pitched and strangled, a noise similar to what she imagined Angela had made in the throes of death. "Well… we're not."

"I know," he said, "but I don't have to tell you that if the police knew that we ran into each other earlier this week and that we...kissed...they might be suspicious. I'd hate to see you dragged into this mess over a misunderstanding."

"Right," she said, her mind spinning over his words and the memory of his searing kiss.

"Did the detective question you?"

"Yes. I told him that we dated when we were kids, but...I didn't mention the kiss." *Or the fact that I'm still crazy in love with you.*

His sigh of relief whistled over the line. "Good. Of course, the M.E. ruled the death accidental, so I guess there's no reason to worry—about the police somehow involving you, I mean."

His reaction raised warning flags in the back of her mind. On the heels of such a tragedy, was it normal for Peter to be concerned about such trivial things? Unless...unless he had a *reason* to be concerned. And hadn't she heard with her own ears Detective Terry tell Coop to take the body to the morgue to be autopsied? Should she mention it to Peter?

"Peter, Angela came into the store today."

"And?"

"And she wanted to return the man's jacket that I told you she'd purchased."

"She did?"

"Yes. But it looked, um...worn. And when I told her that I couldn't give her a refund, she went berserk."

"What do you mean?"

"She...attacked me."

"*What?* Did she hurt you?"

"I'm fine," she said. "She'd been drinking, and she accused me of fooling around with you behind her back. Why would she think that?"

He made distressed noises. "I don't know. And I'm so sorry that Angela made a scene. I hope it didn't get you in trouble at work."

"Don't worry about it. I'm only sorry that the jacket must have been a sore spot between the two of you."

"When a marriage is going south, petty things tend to get blown out of proportion."

"I thought you'd love the color," she said, fishing. "Brown always looked good on you."

"Thanks," he said. "It was thoughtful of Angela."

Her hand tightened on the phone. The jacket was gray. Maybe Angela *had* bought it for someone else. But if so, why would Peter pretend otherwise? Or maybe he was just too overwhelmed with everything else to remember details like the color.

"Peter," she said carefully, "I'm not sure it's a good idea for you to call me, considering everything that's happened."

"Oh," he said, his voice colored with disappointment. "I thought you were my friend, but you're right—it was wrong of me to call."

She closed her eyes, frustrated with her warring emotions. She was suddenly afraid—afraid he would ask her to come over, to comfort him in his grief, and that in a moment of weakness, she would. "I am your friend, Peter. I'm trying to advise you as to what's best, that's all."

"I know, Carly. You're the only person in my life who ever truly cared about me, and I ruined everything."

She bit down on her tongue. The pain helped to clear her head. "Peter, I don't think now is the time to discuss the past. You have other things to worry about. You're not going to be alone tonight, are you?"

"Sort of. I couldn't stay at the house, so I checked into the Ritz-Carlton for a while. Room 539."

"That's good," she murmured, shifting on the bed but unable to find a comfortable position. Did he think she'd offer to come to the hotel and keep him company? She couldn't do that, but somehow she wound up writing the room number on a notepad next to the phone.

Peter heaved a sigh. "Angela and I were having problems, but I never thought it would end like this."

A chill went through her at the despair in his voice. Was he on the verge of making a confession? "Peter, I really don't think I'm the person you should be sharing this with."

"You're right, of course. I won't bother you anymore, Carly."

"You're not bothering me," she said quickly, her mind racing. "But you need to take care of yourself. Try to sleep, okay?"

"Okay," he said, sounding disoriented and childlike.

She gripped the phone, not wanting to let him go. "Good night, Peter."

"Good night, Carly."

She put down the receiver, her heart squeezing painfully, her head spinning. Why did life have to be so hard? Useless tears pressed on her eyelids as she fought the push-pull emotions she felt for Peter. She wanted to believe him, but could she? He had betrayed her trust once, and now he seemed remorseful, but the timing couldn't be worse. Shouldn't he be too consumed with grief to be worried about anything else?

She huddled down in the covers, turned up the volume on the television and immersed herself in the figures moving across the screen. As always, watching the exotic lives of the rich and the beautiful helped to remove her from the turmoil raging in her life and in her heart.

Even after paid programming came on at 3:00 a.m., she fought sleep. She didn't want to go where she couldn't control her thoughts and fears. There were too many faces to haunt her, too many questions pulling at her—her parents' disappearance, the loan sharks' lurking presence, Peter's betrayal and their illicit reunion, and now, Angela's death.

And the chief tormentor in her fitful dreams was Jack Terry, who prodded and poked at her, demanding to know the truth about her parents, about their lives, about her feelings for Peter, about her suspicions regarding Angela's drowning. He pursued her, crowded her, menacing and relentless, his eyes all-seeing, his big hands reaching for her, as if he were going to wring the truth out of her—

"*Carlotta.*"

Her eyes popped open and she shrieked, scrambling away from the voice.

"Sis, hey, it's just me."

She blinked through the morning light and Wesley's concerned face came into view. "Oh." Her muscles relaxed in abject relief.

"Hard night, huh?"

She nodded against her pillow, then alarm seized her anew and her gaze flew to the clock. "What time is it? Oh my God, I overslept. Lindy's going to fire me for sure!" She flung back the covers and swung her legs over the edge of the bed.

"I left you some breakfast on the table," Wesley said. "I have to take off—I'm working with Coop today."

"Okay, thanks," she said, her head heavy as she stood. "What time did you get in last night?"

"Late." He was headed toward the door, talking over his shoulder. "We ran into some trouble at the morgue with the Ashford woman's body, and then—"

"Trouble?" she cut in, pushing her hair out of her face. "What kind of trouble?"

"The chief M.E. almost refused the body, said his examiner determined the death accidental and he wasn't going to do an autopsy. There's some history between the guy and Coop— they argued. I think they used to work together, but Coop didn't want to talk about it."

Carlotta waved her hands to dismiss the details about Coop— who cared? "Is there going to be an autopsy or not?"

"Not, from what I could tell. We had to leave the body there because we had another run, but we picked it back up a couple of hours later."

No autopsy. She went limp with relief.

"I'll be late again tonight," he said. "Weekends seem to be a popular time to die. Don't wait on me for dinner."

"Okay," she said, but he was already gone. Another glance at the clock had her jogging into the bathroom for a quick dip in and out of the shower before the water even had time to warm up. As she toweled off, her mind raced ahead to the things she had to do today and suddenly, the events of last night came rushing back full force. Angela Ashford was dead. And Peter Ashford was behaving suspiciously.

Before her thoughts became paralyzing, she pushed them away and forced herself through her morning routine at lightning speed, pulling a red jersey DKNY "emergency" dress from her closet. A gray cashmere shrug would pass for a jacket and trusty black Miu Miu slingbacks would get her through the day sans Band-Aids. She turned on the local-news radio station, and just as she was flossing her teeth, there was mention of Angela's death.

"A Buckhead woman, Angela Ashford, was found drowned in her home pool yesterday. Alcohol is believed to have been involved. In other news…"

Carlotta paused in her flossing. Two sentences? Angela's life and death had been acknowledged in two lousy sentences. She was here, now she's gone, with the implication that her death had been her own darned fault. The woman was no saint, but still, it hardly seemed fair.

But life wasn't fair. Hadn't that lesson been her own constant companion over the past ten years?

Traffic was surprisingly light, so she wasn't as late as she might have been when she crashed through the door and tossed her belongings into a locker in the break room. Still, Lindy Russell glared at her as she slid into place behind an available counter and offered to assist a customer. Carlotta moved like a zombie through the morning hours. Her department was busy, even for a Saturday, but everywhere she turned, she pictured Angela Ashford's body lying next to the pool, with water streaming from clothes that she had bought here. She felt detached from what she was doing, as if she were floating above her own body. She kept telling herself that Angela's death being ruled an accident was a good thing, but her conscience nagged at her.

Michael appeared midday, his eyes glittering and wide. "Did you hear about Angela Ashford?"

"I heard," she offered noncommittally.

"She *drowned*," he barreled ahead, "in her own pool. Can you believe it?"

"No," she replied honestly.

"After that drunken scene that she caused yesterday, I'm not surprised that she fell in. Sad, though."

"Yes, it is."

He leaned in close. "I have a friend who works in a Botox clinic on Piedmont. She said that Angela was a patient there and always showed up drunk on her ass. Guess it was only a matter of time before she hurt herself or someone else."

Carlotta chewed on her lip. Everyone seemed eager to believe that Angela had brought her untimely death upon herself. It did seem like the simplest, neatest explanation...but was it true? She hadn't particularly liked the woman, but it was starting to dawn on her that she was in a peculiar position to ensure that Angela's death received more than a passing glance.

Michael frowned. "Are you okay?"

Carlotta managed a nod. "It's just such a shame, to die that way. She was so young and so beautiful."

"That's pretty big of you considering that yesterday the woman tried to kill you."

"You're exaggerating, don't you think?"

"No," he said flatly. "I still think you should have filed an assault charge. Your neck is bruised where she tried to choke you."

She covered her neck with her hand. "It doesn't really matter now, does it?"

"No," he agreed, then sighed dramatically. "She's gone, along with her big fat commissions. Poor you."

"Yeah," she said, trying to mimic his light tone.

"Of course, there's always her husband," he said, wagging his eyebrows. "Not to be tacky, but any chance that you'll hook up with the grieving widower, or are you two really just friends?"

I thought you were my friend, Peter had said. But what if he was playing her so that she would protect him instead of revealing that he might have had a motive for killing his wife?

But how could she report the facts without implicating herself?

"Hey, I was only joking," Michael said.

She exhaled and gave him a reassuring smile. "It's not you. I didn't get much sleep last night."

"Hmm. Guilty pleasure or guilty conscience?"

She flushed under his gaze and murmured, "I need to find an aspirin."

"Don't dawdle," Michael said softly. "Lindy is watching your every move."

With his threat ringing in her aching head, Carlotta moved

through the rest of her shift fighting bouts of paralyzing para-
noia. If she went to Detective Terry with details about Angela
and Peter's relationship, things were bound to get a lot worse
for her, and she couldn't afford to draw more negative attention to herself at work.

No, she decided as she clocked out and made her way toward the mall, she would leave Angela Ashford's death to the
professionals.

And for now, she'd try not to think about the fact that Peter,
the love of her life, was now a single man, and what that might
mean to her life.

She wove her way through the Saturday crowds, dodging
packs of suburban kids and in-town kids making their rounds,
young marrieds on their way to the cinema, and pathetic people like her who had convinced themselves that an evening of
window-shopping was better than a date.

With her new autograph book in mind, she decided to cruise
by the Sunglass Hut to see if anyone famous was trying on the
new Maui Jim sunglasses. Next to Blue Pointe restaurant in
Buckhead and the Fulton County Courthouse, it was the best
place in Atlanta for celebrity sightings.

She had just sidestepped a teenage couple who only had eyes
for each other when the back of her neck prickled and she was
overcome with the feeling that someone was watching her. She
swallowed hard and tried to shake the eerie feeling, chalking it
up to the events of the previous day and her frayed nerves. But
as she continued walking, the feeling grew stronger. Fighting
panic, she turned into the sunglass shop. From the display case,

she picked up a pair of retro Ray Ban aviators and jammed them on her face, then adjusted the mirror to see behind her.

There…a few feet back in the mall stood a man, his torso and face obscured by a newspaper—a cartoonish ruse. She could tell little from the jeans-clad legs other than that he was a big man. Her pulse spiked. One of Wesley's thugs, following her? Maybe planning to jump her on her way to her car and take her cash?

Fear coalesced into anger. She punched 911 into her cell phone, then whipped off the sunglasses and charged out into the mall and up to the man, wielding the phone like a weapon, her thumb over the Send button. "I'm onto you, mister, and I'm going to call the police."

The corner of the newspaper came down, revealing Detective Jack Terry wearing a dry smile. "I don't think that will be necessary, Ms. Wren."

17

At Detective Terry's nonchalant declaration, Carlotta's anger detonated. "How dare you follow me like I'm some kind of criminal!"

He folded the newspaper carefully and tossed it into a nearby trash bin. "I wasn't following you. I just happened to be out shopping." He lifted a ratty Dick's Sporting Goods bag as proof.

"Really? That's funny, because there's no Dick's in this mall." Then she angled her head. "Of course, if you're talking about just plain old dicks, I could probably point one out for you."

"A muscle car *and* a sense of humor—wow, you're just full of surprises."

"And you're full of crap. What the hell do you want?"

"Like I said, I'm off duty, just doing a little shopping. But since I ran into you, I'd like to talk to you for a few minutes. How about we grab a cup of coffee?"

Instantly wary, she asked, "What do you want to talk about?"

He smiled again. "The weather, the Braves, your parents—there are so many things."

Through clenched teeth, she said, "I told you, I don't know where my parents are."

He held up both hands, Dick's bag swinging. "I've been reading the files, and I just want to clarify a few details, that's all." A cajoling smile transformed his big features into almost handsome, dammit. "Come on, let me buy you a cup of coffee for all the trouble I've caused you."

She hesitated.

"Ms. Wren, you're going to have to talk to me sooner or later. Let's try to keep this as informal as possible."

She narrowed her eyes. "This doesn't have anything to do with Peter Ashford?"

"Should it?"

"No," she said quickly. "I just thought…after last night…"

"No, I got final word from the coroner's office this morning. They stand by their accidental-death ruling. Case closed."

"Oh." So even the police had put the matter to rest.

"How about that coffee?"

She frowned. "Don't you have something better to do on a Saturday night?"

"Apparently not. Did I interrupt some kind of sunglass-shopping emergency?"

A flush warmed her cheeks. "I wasn't looking for sunglasses. I was looking for celebrities."

"Excuse me?"

She tapped her purse, not caring whether he thought she was silly. "I collect autographs, and this is a great place to spot famous people."

He pursed his mouth. "Good to know." Then he gestured toward the food court. "Shall we?"

She nodded curtly, then fell into step with him. He had traded his suit and shoddy tie for Levi's, a black T-shirt and a pair of black western boots. Ten points for the boots since western wear was back in style, although she suspected that Jack Terry didn't know or care that he was accidentally in vogue. She became hyperaware of his size as they walked. The man was a mountain, with a thick torso and long legs. More than one woman turned to look at him as they made their way toward a coffee shop. The two of them must look like quite the odd couple, she realized.

Not that they were a couple…or that anyone watching them could mistake them for a couple.

"Is this table okay?" he asked, gesturing to a tiny café table with two chairs.

She nodded and awkwardly lowered herself into the chair he held out for her. With a shove, he scooted her so close to the table she felt as if she were in a high chair.

"I'll get us some coffee. How do you like yours?"

"I'll have a double latte with fat-free soy milk and a bottle of Pellegrino."

He gave her a small smile that told her he had no idea what she'd said. "I'll be right back."

She watched him walk up to the counter, obviously out of place at the yuppie establishment. Dread ballooned in her stomach as she pondered the questions he had for her. Just the thought of him reading the files on her father's case made her tingle in embarrassment—he knew all the family secrets and scandals, and seemed intent on making her relive the part of her life that she most wanted to forget.

Her fingers itched. Christ, why had she stopped smoking?

"Here we go," the detective said, setting a tray on the table. "Two coffees with cream, a bottle of springwater and two chocolate éclairs."

She frowned. "Thanks."

"You're welcome." He sat down on the diminutive chair and slurped his coffee, then bit into the éclair and chewed heartily. "How's your brother?"

"Fine. Better, I think. Although I can't say that I'm crazy about his job choice."

"There are worse jobs. It might scare him straight, confronting death like that."

"I noticed last night that you seemed acquainted with his boss."

"Cooper Craft? Yeah. When I first joined the force, he was the coroner."

She frowned. "The coroner? As in, a doctor?"

"Yeah, Dr. Cooper was the chief medical examiner."

"But I thought he worked for his family's funeral home."

"He does now. He had some problems with alcohol and there was some kind of blunder with a high-profile case. There was an inquest and he lost his license—and his job. I think he might even have served some jail time."

Carlotta was astonished. The tall man with the long sideburns who thought she was cute had quite a colorful past. "So now he works for a funeral home and moves bodies for the morgue."

"Yep. And he seems to have put the booze behind him. He'll be a good influence on your brother."

"Good. Wesley worships the man."

"He's probably just starved for a father figure." He cleared his throat, reached into the Dick's Sporting Goods bag and pulled out a folder. "Speaking of which, I was hoping you could help me fill in a few gaps regarding your father's disappearance."

Her spine stiffened as she sipped from the cup of surprisingly good coffee. "I doubt it, but I'll try."

He opened the folder that contained a half-inch sheath of papers, most of them printouts and official-looking reports. "Do you remember the day your father was indicted?"

She nodded and looked into her coffee, recalling the tension that had blanketed the town house, overrun with a constant stream of lawyers and the addition of a bay of file cabinets to keep up with the paperwork. "Everything seemed to be leading up to that day. Wesley and I stayed home, but we heard the news on the radio before my parents returned home."

"So they did return home?"

She nodded. "My mother was crying and my dad was angry, saying that he'd been framed and that he'd get even with everybody."

"Did they mention that they were thinking of leaving town?"

"No."

"You had no idea?"

"No," she said evenly. "My parents said they wanted to go to dinner alone, to talk about some financial issues. They left about seven o'clock and...they simply never came home."

His expression darkened. "That was the last time you and your brother saw them?"

She nodded. "When we got up the next morning, their bedroom door was closed. I assumed they'd gotten in late and were sleeping in. I got Wesley ready for school and we left. When we came home from school, Liz Fischer was waiting for us. She'd been looking for my father all day."

His eyebrows went up. "Liz?"

She squirmed, remembering that he and Liz had history. "You were aware that she was my father's attorney?"

"Yeah, it's in the files, but I thought she was simply on the defense team. I assumed she was handling things behind the scenes."

Her smile flattened. "She was. Liz and my father were—how did you put it? Oh, yes. *Friendly*."

He scratched his temple. "Are you saying that something was going on between them?"

"Why don't you ask her the next time you...see her?"

"I will," he said smoothly. "So you were saying that Liz was waiting for you?"

"Right. She said she'd been trying to reach my father all day. From the look of my parents' bedroom, it appeared as if they hadn't been there since they'd left the previous evening."

"Did they leave a note?"

She swallowed more coffee. "No."

"Did they call?"

"No."

His mouth twitched downward. "Do you remember the date?"

"December second, three weeks before Christmas." She heard the bitterness in her own voice.

He sipped from his coffee. "Does that have something to do with the little Christmas tree in your living room?"

She looked up sharply.

"I noticed it when I went there to take your brother in. It's hard to miss."

She picked at the éclair in front of her. "Yes. Wesley wouldn't let me take it down."

"Even after all this time?"

"Even after."

He made a rueful noise in his throat. "When did you first hear from your parents?"

She looked off into the distance, and tried to make her voice sound detached from the information she conveyed, as if it had happened to someone else. "It was about six months later, in June. We received a postcard from Michigan, I think."

"Do you have family in Michigan?"

"None that I know of. My mother's parents were deceased before I was born, and she was an only child. My father's parents died when I was in grade school. He has a half brother in New Zealand, and a couple of extended cousins somewhere in Utah, but he wasn't close to them. I believe the police followed up with them, though."

He scribbled on a piece of notepaper. "Where did your family go on vacations?"

She shrugged. "Where didn't we go? All along the eastern

coastline, north and south, France, Germany, England and Ireland, cruises to the Caribbean. My father liked to live large."

The only vacation she and Wesley had taken since then were the three days they'd spent at Walt Disney World when he was eleven. It had taken months of saving every dime and had been marred by Wesley's conviction that Carlotta was holding out on him—that their parents were going to join them in Orlando as a big surprise. Of course that hadn't happened, and Wesley had cried the entire eight-hour drive back to Atlanta. She straightened. "How much longer, Detective? I'm rather tired, and I haven't eaten yet."

"Jack."

"Hmm?"

"Why don't you drop the detective stuff? My friends call me Jack."

She glanced at the notes in front of him and reminded herself that the man was manipulating her to get the information he needed to bring her father home, which would only plow another furrow through her and Wesley's lives. She stood and smiled down at him. "Goodbye, Detective."

He nodded. "Ms. Wren, before you go…was there something you wanted to tell me about the Angela Ashford case?"

Her hand moved automatically to cover her neck as she tried to look innocent. "Uh…no."

His gaze went to her neck. "Really? Because if you know something…"

She knew she had reached the point of now or never. "W-well, it probably doesn't mean anything."

He slurped his coffee. "Why don't you let me decide?"

"Angela was a customer of mine," she blurted before she lost her nerve. "She purchased a man's jacket last week. A couple days later I ran into Peter at a party and asked him about the jacket, but he didn't know anything about it." She decided to leave out the fact that she'd asked Peter about the jacket again last night and he hadn't corrected her when she'd said it was brown.

The detective frowned. "I don't get it."

"Well, I started thinking that...perhaps she had bought the jacket for...someone else."

"You mean a lover?"

"I have no idea. I'm just telling you what I know."

"You mean what you think."

Carlotta gritted her teeth. "Anyway, she returned the jacket yesterday."

"When yesterday?"

"In the afternoon."

"Was she acting strangely?"

"She'd been drinking," Carlotta admitted. "The man's jacket had been worn and when I told her I couldn't give her a refund, she became...verbally abusive."

"What did she say?"

"She had the idea that...Peter and I were having an affair."

He lifted his cup to his mouth. "Why would she think that?"

Carlotta fidgeted. "Perhaps because he and I were engaged before they were."

"But you said that happened years ago."

"Yes. Peter ended our relationship about the same time my parents left."

He frowned. "He dumped you when the going got tough, huh?"

"He was just a kid," she said defensively. "I was hurt, but I eventually understood why he did what he did."

"So maybe Mr. Ashford has been pining for you all these years?"

She shook her head. "I don't think so."

"But Mrs. Ashford seemed to."

She pinched the bridge of her nose. "Look, what I'm trying to tell you is that Angela might have been the one having the affair. I don't know if it means anything, but I felt obligated to tell you, so there." At this point, mentioning that the woman had also tried to strangle her seemed like overkill.

He leaned back in his chair and shook his head slowly. "You want to know what I think? I think that you imagined this thin story of Angela Ashford having a lover to make yourself feel better over the fact that whatever was going on between you and her husband might have made her take a flying leap into that pool all on her own."

Carlotta's mouth opened, then closed as denial washed over her.

He lifted his cup to her. "This theory that you have—where I come from, we call that borrowing trouble. The truth is, Ms. Wren, you and Peter Ashford both should be thankful that the M.E. ruled the death an accident." He smiled. "Now you can carry on with a clear conscience."

White-hot anger whipped through her. "You don't know what you're talking about."

He looked her up and down over the top of his cup, then he gave a little laugh. "Maybe not, but I know guilt when I see it, lady."

Carlotta glared at him, then wheeled and stalked away as fast as her high heels would allow. The man was insufferable!

And dead on.

18

Carlotta pulled up in front of Hannah's apartment building just as Hannah bounded outside, long black leather skirt flowing, thick buckles and silver chains clanging. She opened the passenger-side door of Carlotta's car and slid inside. "Hiya."

Carlotta stared at the goth garb. "Hannah, for Christ's sake, this is a funeral not a Halloween party!"

"I'm wearing black," Hannah said, unfazed as she buckled her seat belt.

"*When* are you going to let me give you a makeover?"

"Let me see...uh, never. Besides, what does it matter what a person wears to a funeral?" She snorted. "I can promise you the person in the casket doesn't give a crispy crap."

Carlotta frowned. "Funerals are for the living, and I can promise *you,* everyone at *this* funeral will be dressed as if they were going to the Oscars."

"Do you think they'll have food? I'm starving."

"No, they won't have food, you idiot. It's a *funeral*. Haven't you ever been to a funeral?"

"No," Hannah said. "Have you?"

"No," Carlotta admitted. "But I've seen them on television, and there's no buffet."

"I don't know why you want to go to your ex-boyfriend's wife's funeral anyway. It's like you're rubbing it in that you're still alive and she's...not."

"That's a terrible thing to say. I knew Angela—we went to school together, and I told you, she was a customer of mine."

Hannah gave her a sideways glance. "But what aren't you telling me?"

"Nothing."

"Huh?"

"Nothing."

"Huh?"

Carlotta sighed. "Okay...the other night when I ran into Peter at the party..."

"Yeah?"

"When I left, he followed me."

"And?"

"And...we kissed."

Hannah whooped. "You kissed a married man? After all the shit you've given me over the years?"

"It's not something I'm proud of."

Hannah hooted. "This is great." Then she stopped. "Oh, wait. You kissed the man and a couple of days later, his wife drowns in a pool. That's not great, that's...weirdly coincidental."

Carlotta wet her lips. "I know."

"Oh my God, do you think he killed her?"

Her hands tightened on the steering wheel. "Of course not."

Hannah jumped up and down in her seat. "Maybe he killed her because he's still in love with you! Oh my God, that's so romantic!"

Carlotta was starting to regret her decision to ask Hannah to attend the funeral with her, but she'd thought she'd stick out more if she went alone. Now with Hannah's getup—and her oozing mouth—the only thing she needed to draw more attention to them was a flare.

"Peter didn't kill Angela," Carlotta said carefully. "She was drunk and fell into the pool. The coroner's office ruled her death an accidental drowning."

"Mighty convenient for you," Hannah said slyly.

"That's not remotely funny."

"But it's true. You must still have feelings for this guy, Carlotta. I saw how shaken up you were the night you ran into him. I've never seen you have anything more than disdain for men. In fact, I was beginning to think that you might prefer women."

"Also not funny. And my reaction to Peter, well, I was just so shocked seeing him after all these years, I was disoriented."

"So...you don't have feelings for him."

Carlotta rolled her shoulders. "I didn't say that. I'm confused. Besides, I don't think it's appropriate to lust after a man who's grieving for his wife."

"Are you kidding? If he's as rich as you say, there'll be single women stacked up at this shindig to wipe his tears. If you want him, you'd better be prepared to claw your way to the top of the pussy pile."

Carlotta frowned. "I have no intention to claw my way anywhere. Here's the place," she said, slowing and signaling to turn into the Motherwell Funeral Home, a stately white plantation-style home in front with some less attractive additions jutting off the back.

"Damn, look at the cars," Hannah said.

Indeed, Carlotta felt self-conscious parking her muscle car next to the Beemers and Mercedes and Bentleys, but it couldn't be helped. She climbed out, aware that their arrival had garnered a few stares from other attendees who glanced at her car—and Hannah—with faint distaste as they strolled by. Seriously suited men and severely coiffed women made their way toward the entrance of the funeral home.

Carlotta's pulse pounded harder as they fell in with the crowd, still questioning her decision to attend but unable to deny the compulsion that had grown since her encounter with Jack Terry. Damn him, he was right about her guilt. Her conscience wouldn't let her rest and no matter what she'd told the detective, or Hannah, for that matter, she wasn't at peace with the M.E.'s ruling of the cause of death. She had convinced herself that attending the funeral might settle her mind, give her a sense of closure.

She dearly hoped so.

They were almost to the entrance when a man's voice sounded. "Carlotta, hello."

She turned her head to see Walt Tully and next to him, his

daughter Tracey. Recalling that her last encounter with her estranged godfather had been during her accidental reunion with Peter, Carlotta almost panicked, but pulled a smile out of thin air. "Hello, Walt, Tracey."

"Carlotta, it's been just ages," Tracey said, raising her left hand to her cheek in a way that sent the sun beaming off the knuckle-spanning cluster of diamonds. "Daddy said he ran into you the other night…with Peter, of all people."

"That's right."

"I can't believe Angela drowned in her own pool," the woman said, her voice melodramatic. "And I can't imagine a more horrific way to die."

"Actually," Hannah interjected, "I read on the Internet that the most painful way to die is in a garbage-truck compacter, but drowning ranks near the top."

Tracey glowered at her, then turned her attention back to Carlotta. "Didn't Peter used to date you?"

"We used to date each other," Carlotta clarified quietly. "A long time ago."

"Oh…right," Tracey said, then looked puzzled. "So…are you here for Peter?"

To support him, or to nab him? The innocent question was loaded with catty suspicion. Carlotta pushed her tongue into her cheek. "Actually, I'm here because I know—*knew* Angela."

"Really? That's strange because Angela was a very good friend of mine and never mentioned you…in that way."

Carlotta wondered in just what "way" Angela had mentioned her name—in tandem with the *C* word, no doubt.

While Carlotta cast about for an ambiguous response, Tracey changed tack. "What is it that you do again, Carlotta? Seems like I remember that you worked for Neiman's years ago."

"Still do," Carlotta said cheerfully.

"Oh."

Only her mother had been able to inject more disapproval into one word.

Hannah dug her elbow into Carlotta's side. "Aren't you going to introduce me to your friends?"

"Uh, Hannah Kizer...Walt and Tracey Tully."

"Lowenstein now," Tracey gushed, flashing her ring again. "Mrs. Dr. Lowenstein."

"Mrs. Dr.?" Hannah asked, feigning awe. "I'll bet that looks great on your vanity license plate."

Tracey's eyes narrowed, then she huffed and tugged on her father's arm. Walt gave Carlotta a suspicious, lingering look that unnerved her before he hurried away.

"Behave," Carlotta hissed. "That's my godfather."

"Damn, I'd hate to see how they treat complete strangers."

"Shh," Carlotta said as they stepped into the crowded wood-paneled foyer of the funeral home. The sickeningly sweet smell of live flowers rode the air as they shuffled forward on industrial-grade beige carpet toward what appeared to be the main parlor. At the far end of the entryway, a tall man in a striking brown suit nodded to her over the heads of the crowd. Surprised, she smiled and nodded back.

"Who's the deep dish?" Hannah said into her ear.

"It's Wesley's boss, Cooper Craft. I guess this is his family's funeral home. I had no idea."

"Yowza, he's hot."

"He's a funeral director," Carlotta reminded her friend, but she had to admit, the man knew how to wear a suit.

"So? What's the saying—cold hands, big schlong?"

Carlotta shook her head in exasperation as they were swept up in the crowd and herded into the burgundy-and-hunter-green parlor where low organ music played. They seized two of the few remaining empty seats, and the walls were quickly lined with overflow guests.

Standing room only, Carlotta thought morosely. Angela would be thrilled, if only she weren't dead.

But she *was* dead, lying, presumably, inside the gold-and-white casket on display at the top of three steps at the front of the long room, flanked on either side by countless baskets and wreaths of flowers, crammed into every square inch of space, each seemingly more huge than the next.

"Christ," Hannah groused, "how many acres of hothouse flowers were depleted for this send-off?"

Carlotta ignored her and as discreetly as possible looked for Peter. She spotted him in the front row, head bent as he spoke to the tanned, older couple next to him—Angela's parents, no doubt. On the other side of him sat his own parents, spines ramrod straight, the picture of propriety. The same propriety that had driven Peter to end their engagement ten years ago. How different things might have been if only...

A few rows in front of them, Tracey Tully bent her head to

whisper into the ear of the woman sitting next to her, and the woman turned around to send a laser stare Carlotta's way. She watched as Tracey's companion then whispered to the next woman, who turned to gawk. One by one, the entire row of women turned to look, all of their noses identically chiseled, their mouths tattooed with permanent lip liner.

"Are the clones friends of yours?" Hannah asked dryly.

"Hardly," Carlotta murmured, "although I'm sure I went to school with some of them."

The rise of organ music signaled that the service was about to begin. A minister strode down the aisle and stopped to shake hands with Peter and with Angela's parents before ascending to the podium. He read a short, dry eulogy in a detached monotone and as he droned on, Carlotta realized that the man had probably never met Angela Ashford or, if he had, that he didn't *know* her. He divulged no personal details, nothing to conjure up images of Angela as a living, breathing human being.

The same was true for the three women (all of them with names ending in "i"), who had apparently requested or had been asked by the family to talk about Angela.

"She loved Peter more than anything," Staci gushed into the microphone. "The day they were married was the happiest day of her life."

"She worked out and took care of herself," Lori said. "Everyone on the tennis team is really going to miss her."

"Her house was her pride and joy," Tami said, "down to the last flower arrangement."

"Egad," Hannah whispered behind her hand. "If that was her life, she's probably glad she's dead."

Helplessness tightened Carlotta's chest as she remembered the two sentences the radio announcer had used to sum up Angela's life and death. The indifference was heartbreaking, but Carlotta had expected more out of the woman's friends.

"Would anyone else like to share their memories of Angela?" the minister asked, giving the audience a cursory glance.

Stand up, Carlotta willed Peter. *If you had any feelings for this woman, don't let people leave here thinking that the sum of her existence was being your wife, going to the gym and living in a big house.*

"Very well," the minister said.

"Wait," Carlotta said, lurching to her feet. She felt everyone's heads turn toward her and the weight of their attention fall on her.

"Yes?" the minister said. "You'd like to say something?"

Now what? her racing mind screamed. Her gaze flitted over the expectant crowd and to the bewildered expression on Peter's face.

"Go ahead," the minister urged.

Carlotta wet her lips and clamped her hands on the back of the seat in front of her. "Angela and I were friends a long time ago," she said, her voice high and shaking. She took a deep breath, then exhaled. "A lifetime ago really—we were just kids, trying to make sense of things." She gave a little laugh. "Angela had a talent for drawing cartoons. She would make up characters and stories about them and put together her own little comic books. She was really good at it, and said that she'd like to draw comics for a living someday."

The room was deadly quiet now, and Carlotta's throat tightened. Fervently wishing she'd never stood up, she pressed on. "Angela bit her fingernails to the quick, she always dreamed of owning a pinto-colored horse and she could hit the high note in 'The Star-Spangled Banner.' I remember her saying that one of her favorite movies was *Awakenings*—she was captivated by the fact that people could be frozen inside themselves, and how agonizing it must be to want to get out and not be able."

People were gaping at her now, and she realized that this crowd didn't really want to hear anything deep or meaningful about the woman in the casket. They simply wanted to do their duty as neighbors and club members and put in ass-time at the funeral. Some of them were already glancing at their watches. Angela's parents seemed confused and although Peter was smiling, based on the way people were looking back and forth between them, she wasn't so sure that was a good thing.

"She'll be missed," Carlotta finished abruptly, then sat down.

"That was memorable," Hannah muttered.

As the minister brooked the awkward pause with a thank-you and some throat-clearing, she could feel people's sideways glances land on her and whisperings ensue.

"Who is that?"

"Is she drunk?"

"What was she talking about?"

In front of her, the Clone Club was practically buzzing. Her face flamed as she shifted in her seat. In trying to reveal a side of Angela that no one else seemed privy to (or would own up to), she'd simply made a spectacle of herself. And the kicker was, she couldn't explain what had made her do what she'd done.

At the side of the room, she caught the eye of Cooper Craft, who was staring at her with a little smile. He inclined his head as if to say "well done," but she couldn't be sure that he wasn't making fun of her.

She stared at her hands for the rest of the service, standing at the end to join in the processional past the casket and to shake hands with the family. Her feet felt like lead as she made her way up the aisle, but she shuffled along until she stood before Angela's parents and Peter. Even as she shook hands with the stoic couple, she felt Peter's gaze on her. When she finally looked at him, his blue, blue eyes bored into her, and she could sense that he was holding himself back from embracing her. He clasped her hand and squeezed her fingers, sending wholly inappropriate sensations tumbling through her body. Her heart expanded painfully.

"Thank you for coming," he said, just as if she were anybody…or nobody.

"You're welcome," she said, then pulled her hand away and followed the crowd out into the parlor where people were pouring out the front door, moving toward their cars, already discussing where they might have lunch. On the other side of the foyer, Cooper Craft stood erect with his hands folded in front of him, a serene expression on his face, the picture of poise and comfort.

"There won't be a graveside service?" an older woman was demanding to know.

"Um, no, ma'am."

"Why not?" the woman pressed, clearly affronted.

"Mrs. Ashford requested that her body be cremated, ma'am, rather than be buried."

"Cremated? Burned alive?"

He wiped his hand across his mouth, but to his credit, kept a straight face. "It's a very respectful procedure, ma'am, and good for the environment."

The woman hmphed and walked away, shaking her head. Coop smiled in Carlotta's direction, and Hannah nudged her from behind. "Introduce us."

Carlotta threw Hannah a withering look, then stepped toward him. "Hello," she said as they walked up.

"Hi," Coop said, his light brown eyes crinkling in a smile. The man had nice eyes, she conceded, and wondered what he looked like without his glasses.

Hannah bumped her from behind. "Oh, um, Cooper Craft, this is my friend Hannah Kizer."

Coop stuck out his hand. "How do you do?"

"Thoroughly," Hannah cooed, practically licking her lips as she clung to his hand.

Carlotta laughed nervously. "I didn't realize that Motherwell's was your family's funeral home."

"My uncle's," he clarified. "I just help out. By the way, that was nice, what you said in there."

She smiled weakly, then looked behind her to see that the main parlor had almost emptied. The family would be coming out soon. "Hannah," she said, pressing her keys into her friend's wayward hand, "would you mind waiting for me in the car?"

Hannah scowled. "Yes, I would."

"Hannah."

"Okay," Hannah said, then turned a wry smile to Coop. "Guess she wants to keep you to herself."

"Hannah, *go.*"

Carlotta watched her friend stomp away in her black combat boots, then looked back to Coop. "Sorry about that. Can I...talk to you?"

He lifted his eyebrows. "Isn't that what we're doing?"

"I mean about Angela Ashford."

He frowned. "What about?"

She leaned forward. "I overheard what you said the night that...it happened. You told Detective Terry that you thought the body should be autopsied. Why?"

He shrugged slowly. "Because it would be easy to tell if she drowned accidentally...or not." Then he angled his head. "Why are you asking?"

Carlotta squirmed and told him what she'd told the detective, about the men's jacket that Angela had bought and returned, and that Peter had denied knowing anything about it.

"You think that Angela had a man on the side?"

She lifted her chin, prepared to be laughed at again. "I have no idea, but I had to tell someone."

"You should be talking to the police."

"I did. Detective Terry blew me off."

"Why?"

She sighed. "Because I have history with Peter Ashford."

"Yeah, Wesley told me."

Carlotta frowned. "My brother talks too much." She glanced

over her shoulder, then back to Coop. "Look…I guess I'm asking if you saw anything peculiar about the, um, body when you…did whatever you do to bodies to get them ready for viewing."

He pursed his mouth and appeared to be chewing on her words. "Maybe."

Her pulse ratcheted higher. "You did?"

"That doesn't mean I can do anything about it."

"Jack Terry said you used to be a medical examiner."

Coop frowned. "Jack Terry talks too much, too."

"Is it too late to check?" she asked, her heart thudding against her breastbone.

"No," he murmured. "Not until the body is cremated." Then he folded his arms. "Carlotta, you must have been close to Angela Ashford."

"Not really," Carlotta admitted. "Like I said in there—friends, a lifetime ago. But no matter what's happened since, I can't just let her be overlooked."

Coop glanced in the direction of the parlor, then back. "Not even if it means your former boyfriend might somehow be involved?"

Carlotta swallowed hard, battling a bout of vertigo, as if she were balanced on a precipice, rocking back and forth between the past and the future. "N-not even."

She said goodbye and walked out the front door, staring straight ahead and ignoring the people and things in her peripheral vision. Hannah stood leaning against the car, smoking a cigarette.

"Got another one of those?" Carlotta asked, opening the driver's-side door.

"You betcha."

Carlotta swung into the driver's seat and accepted a cigarette that Hannah offered but her hand was shaking so badly, Hannah had to light it for her.

"Jeez, what did you and the delectable undertaker have to talk about that's got you so hot and bothered?"

"Nothing important," Carlotta said, then took a deep drag on the cigarette and exhaled in blessed release. She looked at the cigarette. "God, this is good. Why did I stop smoking?"

"Because it'll kill you?"

"Oh, yeah," Carlotta said, then thought of Angela and the fact that there were lots of things that would kill a person faster than smoking. "If I start up again, I can't let Wesley know—he'll start up, too." Thoughts of her brother sent pangs of anxiety to her stomach. Tomorrow, and every Tuesday into the foreseeable future, was pay-up day. There was no way her brother would have a grand pulled together to pay that brute, Tick. Her gaze went to her Coach bag with the Cartier ring box stowed inside.

"Hannah, do you know a reputable pawnshop?"

"Sure. What do you want to sell?"

Carlotta took another drag on the cigarette and exhaled slowly. "My soul."

19

The woman behind the counter sucked her teeth. "Name?"

"Wesley Wren. I'm here to see—" He checked the slip of paper he held. "E. Jones."

The woman tapped on a computer keyboard. "Spell the name."

"J-O-N-E-S."

Eye roll. "I meant *your* name, hotshot."

"Oh. W-R-E-N."

"Date of birth?"

He told her. More tapping ensued, then the woman jerked her thumb to the left. "Down the hall, second door on the right. Knock before you go in."

He did as he was told, but dread cramped his intestines. With his luck, his probation officer would be one of those hard-ass military types with a crew cut and ripped arms, bent on scaring his charges straight. Wesley stopped at the door and knocked.

"Come in," a muffled voice sounded.

He opened the door and stared at the back of his probation officer—all five foot and ten willowy inches of her.

"Park it," she said over her shoulder as she walked her fingers through hanging files in a cabinet drawer.

Wesley settled into a chair facing the desk and busied himself studying the shapely E. Jones's rear end, encased in snug khaki-colored pants. No crew cut here—instead, glossy auburn hair was twisted in a knot on the back of her head and secured with a pencil stuck down through it. But her arms were ripped—lean and tanned beneath the short-sleeve yellow shirt she wore. He could only hope that her front was as hot as her back.

She whirled around and pinned him to the chair with blazing green eyes. Damn, she was...*gorgeous.*

"What's your name?" she barked, dropping into the chair behind her desk.

Name? "Uh, Wesley," he stammered. "Wesley Wren." He leaned forward and handed her the slip of paper that he'd received in the mail.

She glanced at the paper, then sifted through a stack of folders on her desk and pulled one from the pile. She didn't look up, but Wesley didn't mind because it allowed him to study her unobserved. She looked to be in her mid-twenties, and she moved like a cat, with no wasted motion. Her lashes were dark and incredibly long, her nose petite, her mouth full and pink, although it was at the moment tightened in a disapproving little bow.

"So, Mr. Wren," she said without looking up, "you're a bad computer hacker."

He bristled. "I got in, didn't I?"

"Yes, and you got caught." She sat back in her chair and assessed him with narrowed eyes. "You're what, eighteen?"

"Nineteen," he said, sitting straighter.

She seemed unimpressed. "Okay, I'm supposed to help you get a job."

"I already got a job," he was glad to report.

"Where?"

"It's not in a location. I'm a body mover."

"Excuse me?"

"I work with a guy who contracts with the morgue for body retrieval."

She pursed her pink mouth and nodded. "It's a niche. But I'll need a note from your employer, or a paycheck stub."

"Okay."

"And you need to set up a payment schedule with the court to pay your five-thousand-dollar fine."

He winced. "How will that work?"

"Make regular payments to the court cashier, with a check or money order, preferably every week."

Another weekly payment. He was still feeling queasy over the fact that Carlotta had met Tick at the door yesterday morning and handed over a grand before fatso had a chance to ring the doorbell. His sister didn't want to say where she'd gotten the money, but when he'd insisted on knowing, she'd admitted that she'd pawned the engagement ring that Peter Ashford had given her. She'd mooned over the guy for ten years, and now that he was available, she'd pawned the ring.

If he lived to be five hundred years old, he'd never understand women.

Of course, between Father Thom and The Carver, his chances of living to be a hundred didn't look too good.

The rapid snapping of fingers caught his attention. "Are you with me?"

He flushed, embarrassed to be caught daydreaming. "Sorry."

She frowned. "Are you high?"

"No."

She pulled open a drawer and produced a cup. "Then you won't mind giving a urine sample before you leave."

His neck and ears warmed. "No."

"Drug use, possession of a firearm and any other legal violation will land your ass in jail, do you understand?"

"Yes, ma'am."

"Your probation also stipulates that you aren't to access a computer, except when you begin your community-service work with the city to improve their computer security."

"Right."

"And I see from your file that your driver's license has been suspended for multiple speeding violations."

"Right again."

"How do you get around?"

"I ride the train or walk."

She frowned and reached inside yet another drawer and pulled out a Marta train pass. "Here."

"Thank you."

"Now…back to paying off your fine. Can you swing fifty dollars a week?"

"Probably."

"Can you or can't you?"

"Yes, ma'am."

She made a note in his file. "How soon can you begin your community-service work?"

He perked up. "The sooner, the better."

"What about your work schedule?"

"My boss knows my situation. He'll work around it."

"Okay, I'll make a couple of phone calls and get back to you." She asked for and wrote down his cell-phone number. "Regardless, you'll need to meet with me once a week. Are Wednesdays okay?"

He nodded.

"Any questions?"

"Yeah. What does the 'E' stand for?"

"I beg your pardon?"

He stabbed at his glasses, then pointed to the nameplate on her desk. "Your first name—what does the 'E' stand for?"

Her pink mouth twitched downward. "You don't need to know." She handed him the cup for his urine sample. "Down the hall, to the right. Leave the sample with the officer there. I'll see you next week. Don't forget to bring your paperwork."

Feeling thoroughly dismissed, Wesley stood and walked to the door.

"Mr. Wren?"

He turned back, eager to have more contact with the intriguing E. Jones. "Yeah?"

She tapped his file with an ink pen. "For some reason, your probation has been flagged by the D.A.'s office for close scrutiny. Why is that?"

Deciding he could be mysterious, too, Wesley shrugged. "You'll have to ask the D.A."

For the first time, he detected a light of curiosity in her green eyes. "I will."

He left her office with a bit of a spring in his step and, after depositing a sample of his whizz with the dour-faced guard in the john, walked out of the building, whistling under his breath. Suddenly, probation was looking like a more pleasant prospect. He certainly could get used to looking at E. Jones every week.

With his probation officer's warning about possessing a firearm ringing in his head, he used the pass she'd given him to take a Marta train to the Midtown station, then made the several-block walk to the Sonic Car Wash, a huge enterprise that was always jammed with business. He asked a fellow in the exit lot who was hand-drying the windshield of an SUV to point out Louis Strong. The man pointed across the lot to a short, raw-boned guy supervising the tire-cleaning of several vehicles, shouting orders and waving cars forward.

Wesley walked over to the man who sported tattoos across his knuckles. "Louis Strong?"

The man turned and eyed Wesley up and down. "Who wants to know?"

Wesley leaned in. "Cooper Craft gave me your name. I need a gun."

Panic flared in the man's eyes as he grabbed Wesley by the

shoulder and looked around. "Keep your voice down, man. Are you trying to get me arrested?"

"No." Wesley pushed his glasses up. "Sorry."

"Where's your car?"

"I don't have one."

"Well, come back when you get one," he said, disgust in his voice. "If people just walk up and start talking to me, my boss is going to get suspicious, got it?" He walked away, shaking his head, leaving Wesley feeling like a fool.

Cursing under his breath, Wesley walked off the lot, dialing his buddy Chance Hollander's number.

"Yeah?" Chance answered.

"Dude, it's Wes."

"I thought you'd died or something, man. Where you been since you got out of jail?"

"Working."

Chance laughed. "Working? You flipping burgers?"

"No, man, I'm moving stiffs to the morgue."

"You're fucking with me, man."

Wes's chest expanded. Chance wasn't easily impressed. "No, I'm serious."

Chance guffawed. "That's righteous."

"Listen, dude, I need a gun."

"What kind?" Chance said, instantly all business.

"Handgun."

"You in trouble?"

"A little."

"You can borrow one of mine."

Wesley's shoulders dropped in relief. "You sure, man?"

"Absolutely. Come on over."

"I'm on foot. I'll be there when I can."

"Oh, right, you don't have a license." Chance's hearty laughter sounded over the line. "Man, you should've taken care of your own speeding tickets, too."

"I know," Wesley said, hating to pretend that he was dumb.

"Where are you? I'll come and get you. I'm bored as shit anyway."

Wesley told him where he could pick him up, then walked to the corner and waited. A few minutes later, Chance's black BMW coupe came into view. He stopped in traffic and gestured for Wesley to get in. When a car horn sounded behind him, Chance gave the guy the finger and swore out the window.

"Fuckers need to chill," Chance said. His chunky body was dressed in Tommy Hilfiger and sprawled in the driver's seat. He smiled behind his Oakley sunglasses, but even without seeing Chance's eyes, Wesley knew he was stoned.

"Did you bring the gun?" Wesley asked as they pulled away from the curb.

"Glove compartment," Chance said happily. "In the black case. It's a .38 special, easiest gun in the world to fire. There's a half box of shells in there, too."

Wesley opened the case and removed the small revolver to heft its weight in his hand. His heart beat faster as he stroked the cold metal. "Thanks, man."

"Don't worry about it," Chance said. He was always generous when he was high. "Just find a good hiding place."

"Is it registered to you?"

Chance snorted. "No way. It's practically untraceable."

Wesley nodded, thinking that his friend was pretty street-smart for a frat boy. He put the revolver and the shells in his backpack, then asked, "So how's school?"

"Sucks a big, hairy one. You're lucky that you don't have to go."

"Yeah," Wesley said, thinking that Chance didn't realize how lucky he was that his parents provided the means for him to go to school, have a great apartment and car, and all the spending money he wanted. They would've paid for an Ivy League school if Chance could've gotten accepted, but as it was, he'd barely scored high enough on the SAT to get into a state college.

"So tell me about this body-moving gig," Chance said.

"Oh, it's cool. We go to hospitals, people's houses, any-where there's a stiff, and transport them to the morgue or to a funeral home."

"Worked any traffic accidents yet?"

"A couple."

"How bad was it?"

"Not pretty," Wesley said, bracing himself against the car's dash as Chance zigzagged through traffic and wondering if some day he and Coop would be peeling his buddy off a guardrail.

"So you got probation in your case, huh? You must've had a kick-ass attorney."

"Yeah, she was great, not bad to look at either."

"Did you fuck her?"

"What? No. She's a *woman*—she's not interested in me."

"Don't be so sure," Chance said. "And trust me, older women are *great* in bed."

Wesley smirked. Chance had more women than he could count. The guy was legendary in his conquests, and bragged that he'd once bedded four women at once. Wesley didn't doubt it. Girls loved Chance's money and his parties and to hear Chance tell it, his dick.

The guy had it made, Wesley thought, shaking his head. As his friend guided the little sports car down the street toward the town house, he said, "Thanks for the ride home, man. And the piece."

"Call it a bonus for taking care of the speeding tickets." Chance laughed. "I pretended to be an employer doing a background check and called to see if the tickets were gone. My record is clean as Clorox."

"Great." Wesley jerked his thumb toward the town house. "Want to come in?"

"Nah, I'll pass," Chance said. "All that talk about women got me horny. I think I'll go get a massage, if you know what I mean."

He did. Chance liked paying for sex, even though he didn't have to. But his trust fund had to be spent somehow.

"Catch you later," Wesley said.

"I keep hearing rumors of a high-stakes poker game being put together. When it happens, I'll give you a call."

"Okay," Wesley said, and stepped away from the car. He approached the house with trepidation, looking up and down the street for suspicious cars. Seeing none, he breathed a little easier and went inside.

After he reached his room, he closed the door and inspected

the gun again, taking a couple of test aims in his mirror. Then he glanced around for a hiding place, trying to think of somewhere that Carlotta—and the police—would never look. He considered and discarded the top of his closet, the clothes hamper and a boot. Then he glanced at Einstein's enclosure and smiled. No one would look there.

He unlocked the pin, slid the screen top aside and reached in to place the small revolver and box of shells in the base of a driftwood decoration that he seemed to like more than Einstein did. As he expected, Einstein barely moved.

"Hungry yet?" He retrieved the squeaking mouse from its temporary home and dangled it in front of the python, without consequence. "A few more days and I'll have to force-feed you," Wesley warned, returning the mouse to its container. "Just don't swallow my gun. I'd have a hell of a time explaining that one to the veterinarian."

And to Carlotta. She'd never understand that having the gun within reach made him feel better able to protect her. He smirked, thinking of his green-eyed, flame-haired probation officer. If she knew he had a gun, she, too, would have his hide.

He lay down on his bed and crossed his hands behind his head. Of course, *that* might be fun.

Yes, things were definitely looking up.

20

"Is everything okay, Carlotta?"

Carlotta started from her reverie as she nodded to her boss. "Fine, thanks."

"Glad to hear it," Lindy said. "You've seemed preoccupied of late. Last week's sales reports just crossed my desk and for the first time that I can remember, your name wasn't at the top."

A flush burned its way up Carlotta's face. "Um, I guess I'm going through a little slump."

"It happens," Lindy said. "I just hope it doesn't last too long. There are lots of sales associates who'd love to have a crack at your department."

Carlotta's stomach did a little flip and she dipped her chin. The fact that Neiman's prided itself on having the best, sharpest employees was what had attracted her to the company in the first place—next to the employee discount, of course. "I understand, Lindy. Don't worry, things are...back to normal."

"Good," Lindy said. "Carry on."

Watching her boss stride away, Carlotta gave herself a mental shake. She had to get her mind back on her job and off the preoccupations that threatened to drive her insane, namely, Angela's death, and Peter's possible involvement.

Oh, and then there was everything else that was wrong in her life.

It had been three days since Angela's funeral, three days since she'd spoken with Coop about the men's jacket and her suspicions concerning Angela's death, and the more time that passed, the more she wished she'd kept her big mouth shut.

Detective Terry was right—her deep-seated guilt over her feelings for Peter were driving her to make preposterous assumptions about the jacket issue, which could've been innocent and completely unrelated to Angela's marriage and drowning.

Scowling at her own stupidity and determined to be rid of the jacket, she went to the dressing-room area and searched through a long rack of items tagged to be returned to the floor or to the manufacturer. She located the jacket and decided the best place for it was the trash—it was paid for, and no one was going to claim it. And with the heavy scent of smoke clinging to it, clearly it couldn't be returned to the floor.

She took the jacket from the hanger and wadded it up, cursing herself for even getting involved, and felt something unyielding in the inside breast pocket. Curious, she reached inside and pulled out a cigar encased in a small plastic bag with a zip top. Peter had an aversion to smoke—surely the cigar wasn't his. She held up the jacket and checked the size. When Angela had purchased the jacket, Carlotta had assumed that Peter had filled out in the past ten years, but now that she'd seen him, this jacket was way too big for Peter. She squinted, recalling the thin frame of Angela's father. This jacket was way too big for him as well.

The hair on the back of her neck tingled as she considered the jacket and the cigar. She carefully rehung the jacket and covered it with a garment bag. There was no way she could smuggle it out and take it home—employees' bags were checked when they left the store.

But the cigar...

She studied the eight-inch brown cylinder, wondering if it could help her locate the person who had purchased it. On the back of the plastic zip bag was a gold seal. She squinted to make out the letters: Moody's Cigar Bar, Atlanta, Georgia.

She considered calling Detective Terry and telling him about this new development, but the thought of his sarcastic reaction stopped her short. She had enough trouble with the man as it was. Besides, the cigar might lead to nothing at all, and it would be easy enough for her to locate Moody's and ask a few discreet questions herself. A quick check of the phone book at the checkout counter gave her a street address—on the fringes of downtown Atlanta in an unpredictable part of town.

Despite her promise to Lindy and to herself to get her mind back on her job, she was distracted and jumpy until her shift ended, then blew off Michael in the employee locker room in her rush to get to her car. Traffic was horrible, as usual, the roads choked with commuters vying to get home and tourists flocking to the aquarium. She craved a cigarette in the worst way—God, it didn't take long to fall back into a bad habit.

Like Peter, for instance.

Toying with the radio buttons and tapping on the steering wheel helped to keep her hands busy, but her mind continued to rehash the events of the past couple of weeks. She had hoped that selling his engagement ring would help her to sever the bond she had foolishly maintained with Peter's life. Yet with this little field trip, would she open yet another can of worms? Insinuate herself further into his affairs? She kept telling herself that she should just let it go, but something compelled her to keep moving.

She got lost twice trying to find the address, but finally spotted the small neon sign—Moody's—in a dark window, and darted in front of another car to nab a lone parking space. The area was on the verge of gentrification, but Moody's, sandwiched between a new trendy-looking coffee shop and an adult video store, appeared to be part of the old neighborhood.

She climbed out, dropped a few coins in the parking meter and made her way inside. A brass bell tinkled when she opened the big, solid door with a leaded glass insert. The shop was what the name implied—a dark, atmospheric space housed in a deep, narrow storefront with tall ceilings, art deco light fixtures and original black-and-red checkerboard linoleum tile floors. The lazy swirl of low-hanging ceiling fans did little to dispel the acrid odor of tobacco that permeated the air, tickling her nose and throat, making her want a cigarette even more.

A horseshoe-shaped black lacquered counter dominated the center of the store. The walls were lined with glass cabinets housing boxes of cigars and clear canisters filled with fragrant blends of loose tobacco. A scratchy recording of big band music sounded from an unseen source. The crammed, quaint space gave her the feeling that she'd stepped back in time, back to when pompadours and polka-dot dresses were in style, when men wore sock suspenders and hats with their suits.

She liked it instantly.

The sound of footsteps drew her attention to a stairway near the back of the room that she hadn't noticed. A pair of shapely legs preceded a gray pencil skirt hugging slim hips, a prim white blouse straining over generous breasts and a nice double strand of pearls. The woman's face appeared, and the words *steel magnolia* sprang to Carlotta's mind. The pink-lipstick smile was welcoming, but beneath the teased pouf of bleach-blond hair, the kohl-lined eyes were piercing.

"Hello," the woman said as she made her way down the stairs, her drawl low and smooth. She was well into her fifties, and looked as if she'd kicked some ass in her day—and could still cause some serious harm if the situation called for it. In her elegantly manicured hand she held a half-smoked cigar, its smoke plume wafting behind her. At the bottom of the stairs a sign with an arrow pointed to a martini and wine bar on the upper level and Carlotta realized suddenly why the parking places were full and the store empty.

"Hello."

"Can I help you, darlin'?"

"Maybe," Carlotta said, suddenly nervous as she reached into her purse and withdrew the cigar. She walked deeper into the store and could hear the buzz of a crowd overhead. "I'm looking for the person who purchased this cigar from your store."

The woman stepped forward with a little frown between her eyebrows. She set her cigar in one of the dozen colored glass ashtrays lining the massive black bar, then reached for the plastic bag. A young man wearing a waiter's waist apron came clopping down the stairs and, referring to a notepad, moved from case to case, selecting cigars, obviously filling orders.

A knot of customers came down, businessmen all of them, ties loosened and voices raised. "See you next time, June," they said to the woman, and she called them each by name when she said goodbye.

When the door closed behind them, the woman handed the plastic bag back to Carlotta, then picked up the cigar she'd been smoking and took a hearty puff. "That is a very expensive cigar, Miss——?"

"Um, Carlotta. Carlotta Wren."

"I'm June Moody," the woman said with a slow nod. "May I ask how it came into your possession?"

"I...found it," Carlotta said, hedging.

The woman's mouth twitched. "Do you smoke, Carlotta?"

"Not cigars."

June Moody smiled. "You ever tried?"

"No."

"Would you like to?"

Carlotta hesitated. "Well...sure."

The woman's smile lit her eyes and Carlotta had the feeling that she'd just passed some sort of test. "Why don't you join me upstairs, and we can talk about how you happened to *find* such a fine cigar."

Intrigued and edgy, Carlotta followed the woman upstairs.

"Carlos," June said as they ascended, "would you please bring me an Amelia when you come up?"

"Sure thing, Miss Moody."

They walked upstairs, where the furnishings were plush and the air was rich with smoke. The martini and wine bar resembled an old-fashioned parlor, with deep velvet chairs and thick rugs. The bar lined one side of the landing, surrounded by groupings of chairs and couches around low tables. Most of the seats were occupied by businessmen, with a stray woman here and there.

Behind the bar was an older gentleman with a ponytail. He nodded to the women, his gaze raking Carlotta with appreciation.

"May I offer you a drink, Carlotta?" June asked. "On the house."

"A martini, thank you," Carlotta said to the man, taking in the art deco barware, decanters and glasses. "Nice place."

"I'm glad you like it," June said, nodding her approval when the man dropped two olives in each crystal-clear martini. "Thank you, Nathan. Will you ask Tonia to keep an eye on the shop? Carlotta, let's take our drinks in here."

Carlotta picked up her martini and followed the woman into a room where more tables and chairs were situated around a fireplace that, even unlit, was a welcoming feature. It was easy to see why Moody's was a busy little place and Carlotta wondered with consternation why she hadn't heard of it before now.

"How long have you been in business?" she asked June as they sat in sumptuous gold-colored club chairs.

"It was my father's business," the woman said, taking a sip of her drink. "He passed away four years ago. It's been my place since then."

Carlotta surveyed all the men sitting back, cradling drinks and puffing on cigars. "I wondered where all the straight men in Atlanta were hiding."

June laughed. "They're right here, darlin'. Bring in your girl-friends sometime."

Carlotta smiled at the thought of bringing Hannah and Michael to this place. They wouldn't exactly "blend."

Carlos appeared and handed June a small, slender cigar about five inches long. June thanked him, then handed the cigar to Carlotta. "I hope you don't mind. I took the liberty of choosing a cigar I thought you'd like."

"Not at all," Carlotta said. "But I don't know what to do first."

"Some people take off the band, but I like to leave it on so that the tobacco doesn't stain my fingers, at least until it burns down."

She read the colorful band: Key West Havana Cigar Company. "Okay."

"Here's a cutter," June said, handing her one of the small guillotine-looking devices that littered the tables next to enormous art-glass ashtrays. "The tapered end is the cap end. That's the end that you cut and light. See the cut line?"

Carlotta scrutinized the cigar, and saw the faint impression. "Yes."

"Don't cut beyond the line or you'll risk cutting the wrapper leaf."

Carlotta situated the cutter and severed the cap with surprising little effort.

"Good. Do you have a lighter?"

She withdrew from her purse the trusty mother-of-pearl lighter that she'd unearthed from a bureau drawer yesterday—just in case a cigarette fell into her lap.

"Hold the cigar in your hand and rotate the cigar tip near the flame. It's best if you don't actually touch the tip to the flame. Just let it char from the fumes."

Carlotta did as she was told, fascinated. When embers began to appear, June said, "Okay, now put the cigar to your mouth and draw by pulling in your cheeks, like this."

She imitated the woman, noting the unfamiliar, but not unpleasant, taste of the leaf upon her lips. She was gratified when the tip of the cigar began to glow.

"Good." June sat back in her chair and raised her martini to her mouth. "It's like giving a blow job, only more enjoyable."

Carlotta inhaled sharply at the unexpected comment and her lungs rebelled, sending her into a coughing spasm.

"Don't inhale," June said, laughing. "Take it slow, puffing occasionally to keep it lit." She smiled. "Also like a blow job."

Carlotta recovered, thinking it was a good thing that her memory was long, or the comparison would be lost on her. But she acknowledged that she liked the feel of the cigar in her hand, and that she was very tempted to like the woman across from her, although admittedly, June Moody was difficult to read.

"So," June said, turning her head to exhale, "tell me about the Dominican Cohiba."

Carlotta recognized the name as the brand of the cigar she'd brought in. Her mind whirled for an explanation more reasonable than the real one. "I work in a department store, and someone left it. I'm just trying to find the owner."

"I see," June said mildly. "That's mighty generous of you."

Carlotta smiled guiltily.

"Did you actually see the person who left it?"

"N-no."

"You just found it?"

"In the pocket of a men's jacket that had been returned."

"Ah. So why couldn't you just check the sales receipt?" June puffed on her cigar casually, but her eyes were wary.

Carlotta averted her gaze and pretended to concentrate on her cigar.

"If you expect me to give you the name of my best customers," June said, "you're going to have to come up with a better story than that."

With a sigh, Carlotta decided to come clean with the woman. What choice did she have? "The jacket that I found the cigar in was purchased by a woman named Angela Ashford, who's… dead."

She had June's full attention now. "Go on."

"Angela drowned, but the circumstances around her death are suspicious and I thought…that is, I wondered…if she could have been involved with a man who had…hurt her."

June exhaled, then gave Carlotta a pointed look. "You mean, killed her?"

"I don't know."

"If her death is suspicious, then why aren't the police involved?"

"Let's just say they're not interested."

"So you thought you'd do a little investigative work on your own?"

Carlotta nodded.

"Were you friends with this Ashford woman?"

"Sort of," Carlotta hedged.

"Was she married?"

"Yes."

"So this jacket, the cigar——they don't belong to her husband?"

"No."

June's eyebrows shot up. "I see. So the person who bought the cigar could have been a lover?"

"Maybe. Again, I don't know."

June sat forward and tapped ash into the beautiful ashtray. "So you're asking me to divulge the names of the customers who bought this particular kind of Cohiba, knowing that it could lead to an investigation?"

Carlotta nodded again. "If it's an expensive cigar, it couldn't be that many customers."

"Only a handful," June confirmed.

Carlotta's heart began to beat faster, partly due to the nicotine infusion, partly due to the feeling that she was onto something. She puffed on the cigar, then exhaled in a frustrated sigh. "Are you going to help me?"

June studied her for a few seconds, then leaned forward and used her cigar to gesture to the people around them. "Carlotta, most of the guys in here are decent fellas who come to hang out because their wives don't want cigar smoke stinkin' up the living-room curtains. But some of my customers——well, they aren't the nicest people. Are you sure you know what you're getting yourself into?"

Carlotta swallowed a mouthful of the martini, then shook her head against the sting of alcohol. "No. But this feels...necessary." Besides, she was starting to get used to having "not nice" people in her life: a fugitive father, lurking loan sharks, a detestable detective.

June lifted her glass. "Fair enough, darlin'. I'll give you what you want. But you'd better watch your step. If your suspicions are correct, one dead girl is plenty enough."

21

"Mrs. Susan Harroway," Carlotta read from the napkin on which she'd written the names that June Moody had given to her the night before, after the cigars had been smoked and another round of martinis exhausted.

"Harroway is an old Atlanta name," Hannah said, reclining on Carlotta's bed in full goth getup and fingering the silver barbell piercing her tongue. "I don't know a Susan in particular, but I've catered parties for various Harroways."

"I'll ask Michael at the store. Maybe he'll know something about her." Carlotta worked her mouth from side to side. "But June told me the woman said the cigar was a gift, so that could mean her husband, her father, a brother."

"Or a boyfriend," Hannah added.

Carlotta frowned. "Not everyone cheats on their spouse."

"Sure they do, if they live long enough. Who else is on the list?"

"Dr. Joseph Suarez. I looked him up in the phone book and he's a plastic surgeon. His office is in Buckhead."

"A plastic surgeon in Buckhead? Ooh, big surprise."

"Michael mentioned that he had a friend who worked in a clinic where Angela got Botox injections. Maybe Dr. Suarez works there."

"Hmm. Next name?"

"Bryan D'Angelo. June says he's an attorney and I got the feeling that he's a little shady." She bit the end of her fingernail. "Maybe Liz Fischer knows him."

"Who's that?"

"Wes's attorney," she said dryly. She hated the thought of calling the woman. Liz's history with Detective Terry made her even less palatable in Carlotta's eyes.

"Do you have a beef with Liz?"

"She was my dad's attorney, too."

"Oh?" Hannah's voice rose in curiosity, probably, Carlotta presumed, because she rarely mentioned her father.

"What about Dennis Lagerfeld?" Carlotta asked to redirect Hannah's attention.

Her friend squinted, as if the name was familiar.

"His is the last name on the list. June said he used to be a professional athlete."

"Oh, right," Hannah said, nodding. "Receiver for the Falcons, maybe ten years ago. Man, he was fucking gorgeous. I wonder if all that muscle has gone to fat."

"There's no obvious connection to Angela."

"They could have met anywhere—at a party, at the club, at a day spa."

"Or he could be a client of Peter's," Carlotta murmured.

Mashburn and Tully prided themselves on representing the investments of athletes and celebrities. Part of the reason she had first begun collecting autographs when she was a teenager was due to the access her father had once had to famous people.

"So what if you find out that one of these people does have a connection to Angela Ashford? Are you going to confront them, Nancy Drew?"

"I don't know." Carlotta sighed. "I'll cross that bridge if I get there."

"Any news on whether there's going to be an autopsy?"

"No. I haven't talked to Coop since the funeral."

"What, you need an excuse to talk to the hunky undertaker? Step aside and let me at him."

Carlotta smirked. "You just want to have sex in a coffin, don't you?"

"Doesn't everyone?"

"You need help, you know that?"

Hannah smirked. "So have you heard from the grieving husband?"

Carlotta laid the napkin on her nightstand. "He's called a few times." Six, to be exact. "But I haven't answered."

"Did he leave messages?"

"Just that he called and would like to talk to me." In the last couple of messages, though, she'd detected a bit of desperation in Peter's voice.

"Are you going to call him?"

"Probably," she admitted. "Eventually."

Hannah held up a pack of menthol cigarettes. "Want a smoke?"

"Yes," Carlotta said, then moaned. "No. I have such a head-ache after smoking that cigar last night…of course, the martinis probably didn't help."

"I can't believe you didn't take me with you."

"You were working."

"Still."

Carlotta smirked as she reached for a cigarette. "I'll take you back sometime—you'd love it. Everyone there looked married."

Hannah clapped her hands. "This is great. I thought when you gave up the party-crashing, you were going mainstream on me. But then you kissed a married man, and now you're smoking again!"

"I can't *afford* to start smoking again. I'm already broke, and do you know how much cigarettes cost these days?"

"Yeah," Hannah said holding up the box of cigarettes from which Carlotta had taken a smoke. "I kind of bought these. And for someone who's always broke, you always seem to always have money to spend on clothes."

Carlotta looked at her closet that was too full for the double doors to close. Designer bags and shoes, belts and coats, dresses and jeans bulged past the door frames. She thought of the money from her pawned engagement ring that was rapidly dwindling. "Too bad I can't sell some of *this* stuff."

"You can," Hannah sang. "eBay."

"Under the rules of Wesley's probation, we can't have a computer in the house."

"Oh. Bummer." Then Hannah brightened. "I know a place— Designer Consigner, in Little Five Points. They'll take all this name-brand crap off your hands."

Carlotta frowned. "For how much?"

"You set your price, and they add a percentage. You get paid when it sells, and you know this shit will sell, like, instantly."

Carlotta picked up the purse she'd carried last night—last season's Coach, but still in prime condition. And she had at least two dozen more like it, all different brands. Even if she could sell them for a third of what she'd paid for them, she could pay down her credit cards and maybe have her Miata fixed. The thought of being able to get rid of the dreadful Monte Carlo made her giddy.

"Why don't you load up a few things and we'll take them in," Hannah suggested.

Carlotta narrowed her eyes. "You despise designer clothes. How do you know about this place?"

"It's next door to a place I shop, and the same people own it. Stop stalling." She grimaced at the overflowing closet. "Good grief, Amelia Earhart could be in there."

Carlotta emptied the contents of the Coach bag on her bed, then went through her closet, choosing purses that she'd grown tired of but that were still in great shape, many of them protected by dust bags. Hannah began pulling out clothes in clumps. "How long has it been since you wore this?"

Carlotta studied the fitted orange tweed jacket. "I can't remember."

Hannah tossed it on the bed. "It goes."

"Wait a minute!"

"Jesus, Carlotta, the closet rods are bowed. You couldn't wear all this stuff in ten years!"

With a sigh, Carlotta relented and thirty minutes later, they were piling clothes and shopping bags of accessories into Hannah's retro refrigerated catering van that was covered in graffiti.

"When are you going to get this thing painted?" Carlotta asked.

"It *is* painted," Hannah said, clearly annoyed. "Some of the best graffiti artists in Atlanta live in my neighborhood and have left their mark on my ride." She stepped back and gestured to the words *Do yourself* written in stylized white lettering, highlighted to look three-dimensional. "See the signature—Zemo. He's huge. This van is going to be in the Smithsonian one day."

"Right," Carlotta said as she rearranged the bags stuffed full of clothes. She sniffed and wrinkled her nose. "It smells like garlic in here."

"Last night's gig," Hannah said, closing the rear half-doors. "I made so many garlic rolls I swear this morning I crapped a clove."

"You really should write poetry."

"I just might someday."

Carlotta climbed up and swung into the cracked blue vinyl bench seat and slammed the door hard to get it to stick. When Hannah pulled away from the curb, Carlotta waved at a frowning Mrs. Winningham, then rolled down the window and lit the cigarette she'd been playing with for an hour.

It was a breezy, cloudless spring day and she couldn't stave off the pang of sadness that Angela had been dead for mere days and the world had marched on, with hardly a pause. She wondered what Peter was doing—if he'd returned to work yet, sold Angela's car, spread her ashes, ordered her grave marker. Would he order a double headstone, with thoughts of someday being buried next to his young wife, or was he already thinking ahead to inviting another woman into his life?

Like *her*.

"Why can't you let it go?" Hannah asked, wrestling with the huge steering wheel with one hand, holding her cigarette in the other.

"What?"

"You know what—Angela Ashford's death. Everyone but you thinks it was an accident. And if it was an accident," she said lightly, "doesn't that sort of clear the way for you to get back with the love of your life?"

Carlotta flicked ash out of the window. "I suppose so."

"Well, I'm no shrink, but either you think Peter killed her or you're conflicted about your feelings for him and are going to some pretty extreme lengths to avoid the situation altogether."

Carlotta studied the cigarette she held, asking herself why people did things that they knew would hurt them eventually, and if she had a particular propensity for self-destruction. She took a long draw, then exhaled. "Well, like you said, you're no shrink."

Hannah frowned and replied by leaning forward and turning up the volume on the radio, blasting Marilyn Manson into the cab for the short ride south into Little Five Points.

Carlotta felt torn over shutting out her friend, but she was already so confused about Peter, she was afraid that talking about him, that putting words to half-baked feelings, might send her into an emotional abyss. What if she did give in to years of pent-up longing and allow Peter into her life...and into her heart? Would he tire of her after he felt he'd paid penance for abandoning her? After all, how much did they really have in common now?

She slid her gaze sideways at Hannah, the tongue-pierced, stripe-haired, smoking and cursing bondage queen...with a heart of gold. Her best friend, but would Peter accept her and her eccentricities? And how would he feel when he discovered that she herself had had a couple of, er, *misunderstandings* with the law? And she doubted that Peter's boss, Walt Tully, would look kindly upon him taking up with the daughter of the man who had stolen hundreds of thousands of dollars from their clients, the man responsible for an embarrassing asterisk on the company records.

So what could she really ever be to Peter—a pastime... closeted?

"This is it," Hannah said, throwing the van into park.

Carlotta looked up and took in their eclectic surroundings. The people and shop owners in Little Five Points prided themselves on their individuality. Antique bookshops, organic restaurants, futon stores, bike shops, alternative-music stores, hip T-shirt shops. The theaters and playhouses and trendy eateries had caught on with the younger Buckhead crowd determined to prove that they were get-real cool despite their black American Express cards, so the clientele was slowly changing from students with pocket change to young professionals with loads of disposable income. Ergo, next door to a retro used-clothing store called Rebound Rags sat Designer Consigner.

They loaded up armfuls of bags and clothing and headed for the door. Carlotta felt a little sheepish to be taking her personal items in to hock—it smacked of desperation. Her mother, she thought, would be appalled at the notion of Carlotta selling her clothes——consignment stores and yard sales were too pedestrian for the Wrens.

Embezzlement, bail skipping and child abandonment, on the other hand, were acceptable.

She followed Hannah into the store that was remarkably well merchandised for a consignment shop. A petite Asian woman with a sleek bob and wearing a Chanel suit as well as anyone Carlotta had ever seen looked up from a table where she sorted items that, presumably, the two women standing in front of her had just brought in.

"I'll be right with you," the Asian woman said in a clear, cultured voice.

The two customers turned and Carlotta blinked in surprise—one was Tracey Tully...er, Lowenstein. Mrs. Dr.

"Carlotta," Tracey said, her voice chilly. "How utterly bizarre to see you again so soon."

"Hello, Tracey." A flush blazed its way up Carlotta's neck as she saw Tracey take in the bulging shopping bags she and Hannah held. Humiliation washed over her.

Tracey gestured to the dry-cleaner bags of clothing stacked on the table. "My friend Courtney and I were just dropping off some items for the Women Helping Women clothing drive."

The other woman smiled tightly without making eye contact, as if Carlotta and Hannah might qualify as some of the women who needed help.

"Well...what a coincidence," Carlotta said, lifting her chin. "So are we."

She ignored Hannah's strangled noise as she lifted the shopping bags to the table. After she jerked her head meaningfully, Hannah did the same with the bounty she'd carried in.

From the top of one of Carlotta's bags, Tracey plucked a nearly mint Kate Spade leather hobo bag from two seasons ago. "Yes, underprivileged women will appreciate these items, even if they are hopelessly dated." Then Tracey made a face. "This stuff smells like garlic."

Carlotta smiled through clenched teeth as the woman carelessly tossed the expensive purse back into the bag.

"You're very generous, ma'am," the salesclerk murmured to Carlotta.

Carlotta tried to keep smiling as the woman gathered up the bags and disappeared with them in a back room. There went the extra cash she'd hoped to have.

When the salesclerk returned, Tracey snapped her fingers, as if she were talking to a servant. "I'll be needing a receipt so I can deduct this from my income taxes. I'm a doctor's wife and in our tax bracket we need all the deductions we can get."

Hannah coughed, disguised her muttered "bitch" as a wheeze.

"Yes, ma'am," the salesclerk said, then she smiled at Carlotta. "If you'll write down your name and phone number, I'll give you one as well."

Not that it mattered in *her* tax bracket, Carlotta thought miserably.

Tracey snatched the receipt from the woman's hand, then turned to Carlotta. "Now that Angela is gone, I guess I'll be seeing you at the club."

Carlotta frowned. "What's that supposed to mean?"

Tracey tossed her hair. "I mean, it's pretty clear that you and Peter Ashford are going to pick up where you left off...if you ever stopped." She gestured toward the back room where the salesclerk had taken the shopping bags. "You're probably giving away all your old things because you think that Peter is going to buy you whatever you want now. Poor Angela, not even cold in her grave."

Anger flared in Carlotta's chest and she struggled to keep her voice steady. "You don't know what you're talking about."

"Oh, it's not just me talking,"Tracey assured her with a cocked hip. "After you made a spectacle of yourself at the funeral and the way that Peter fawned over you afterward in front of everyone, trust me, *everyone* is talking." Then Tracey smiled meanly. "But considering the way you were raised, no one is surprised."

Carlotta flinched as if she'd been slapped, but Hannah apparently wasn't nearly so traumatized. "Mrs. Dr., how'd you like my pointy-toed boot up your charitable ass?"

"We're leaving,"Tracey said, looking them up and down with contempt as she and her friend made their way toward the entrance—but not without a parting shot. "Really, Carlotta, you've gone to the dogs."

Hannah lunged toward them, but Carlotta grabbed her arm. Still, it was enough to send Tracey and her sidekick scrambling out the door.

When Carlotta turned back to the salesclerk, the woman had a faint smile on her face. "Sorry about that," Carlotta murmured, then bent to write her name and number on the receipt book.

"They have history," Hannah added unnecessarily.

"So I gathered," the woman said, her dark eyes shining. She

extended the receipt she'd written to Carlotta. "Thank you very much for the donation."

"You're welcome," Carlotta said, feeling guilty as hell as she took the slip of paper.

When their hands brushed, a strange look crossed the woman's face. She clasped Carlotta's hand. "Wait."

From the sharp tone in the woman's voice, alarm blipped through Carlotta's chest. "What is it?"

The woman had turned Carlotta's hand palm up and was studying it, a crease between her perfectly arched brows. Carlotta glanced at Hannah, who only shrugged. After a few awkward seconds had passed, the woman looked up.

"I don't mean to worry you," she said quietly, "but you are facing danger."

Carlotta squirmed. "Why would you say that?"

The woman's cheeks turned pink. "I'm sorry. Sometimes I have a gift…for seeing things. When I touched your hand, I felt danger. Do you have a big, strong man in your life to protect you?"

Hannah snorted. "No."

Carlotta nervously withdrew her hand. "We'd better be going, Hannah."

The woman smiled. "My name is Amy, Amy Lin. I didn't mean to scare you, but please be careful."

Carlotta studied the woman's body language for some sign of a con or impending sales pitch. Instead, Amy Lin's eyes burned with sincerity and…concern.

Without responding, Carlotta backed away and left the store, with Hannah at her heels like an excited puppy. "Oh my God, that was a psychic moment!"

"I don't believe in psychics," Carlotta said as she climbed into the van.

Hannah catapulted herself into the seat and slammed her door. "Well, I do, and I've always wanted something like that to happen to me."

"If it makes you feel better, I wish it had happened to you, too. That kind of stuff is wasted on me."

"I wonder what she meant by you facing danger?" Hannah bounced in the vinyl bench seat. "Ooh, ooh—maybe Peter Ashford is the danger, and you need someone to protect you from him."

Carlotta sighed, exasperated. "It doesn't mean anything, Hannah. It's one of those blanket statements that could apply to anyone, anytime." She gestured to the cars around them as Hannah wedged the van between two moving cars. "I'm in danger just sitting in traffic in this city."

"Still," Hannah said solemnly, "you shouldn't dismiss something like that."

Carlotta laid her head back. "Just take me home. This is turning out to be a lousy day."

"Hey, what's up with you giving all your loot to charity back there? That was probably hundreds of dollars' worth of stuff."

"Thousands," Carlotta corrected, closing her eyes.

"Jesus God, even worse."

"I just couldn't stand the thought of that woman spreading stories to her friends about me selling my clothes. Everyone will think I'm broke."

"You *are* broke."

She expelled a long sigh. "I know." Her chest and head ached when she thought about the things that Tracey Tully had said. Did everyone assume that she and Peter were having an affair, or perhaps had been all along? If Angela had thought so, it made sense that the woman had confided in her friends. And *she* hadn't helped matters by making a spectacle of herself at the funeral.

Good grief, when had life gotten so complicated?

Hannah rattled on about a psychic moment she'd had with a dog, until they arrived at the town house. Cooper's white van sat in the driveway.

"Wesley must be going on another body run," Carlotta said as they parked.

"Let's go with them!"

"Are you nuts? I'm not getting involved this body-moving business."

"Why not? It's fascinating."

Cooper Craft came out of the house dressed in jeans and a dark sport coat, and strode toward his van.

"And so is he," Hannah murmured.

"Down, girl," Carlotta said before opening the door and dropping to the ground.

Coop glanced up and smiled as they approached. "Hi. I didn't expect to see you."

"Are you and Wesley going out on a...job?"

"Yeah, he's changing."

Carlotta swallowed at the force of his eye contact behind his glasses. When had the man gotten so…appealing? His hair was nicely rumpled, his shirt had French cuffs and his jeans were snug against long, muscular legs.

"Remember me?" Hannah said, stepping up and practically bursting out of her tattooed skin.

"Sure I do, Hannah," Coop said cheerfully, but his gaze snapped back to Carlotta.

"Right," Hannah said dryly. "Okay, I'm taking off. Call me later, Nancy Drew."

Carlotta glared at her friend as she climbed into her graffiti-van.

"What was that all about?" Coop asked with a laugh.

"Nothing," Carlotta said. "Except I think that Hannah is crushing on you."

He smiled and his eyes crinkled at the edges. "It must be the spring weather. I'm feeling a pretty intense crush coming on myself."

The way he looked at her made it obvious that Hannah wasn't the object of his affection. Carlotta's chest tingled with pleasure, but she didn't believe in starting something that she couldn't finish. What the man did for a living just creeped her out too much. And since he was going to be around a lot, she thought she should be honest.

"Look," she said, breaking the pregnant pause, "you're really nice—"

"Oh, God," he cut in, lifting his hand. "Spare me the 'you're really nice' speech. If you're just not into me, I understand."

She wet her lips. "We're just so different, that's all."

He leaned toward her. "How so?"

"Well…" She gestured vaguely in the air, disconcerted by his nearness. "You're…an intellectual, and I'm…not."

A little frown crossed his face and he shook his head, his gaze boring into hers. "I think you're smarter than you want people to know. You hide behind that froufrou job of yours, pretending to be happy selling five-hundred-dollar blue jeans to Atlanta's finest, but I think there's more to you than meets the eye." Then he grinned. "Not that what meets the eye isn't pretty darn spectacular."

His little speech left her a little angry, a little frustrated, and…a little turned on. Her breasts perked up as if they had ears. Her thighs tingled like peppermint. Her overloaded senses effectively cut off the signals between her brain and her tongue.

The front door slammed and Wesley leaped down the steps in threes. "Hi, sis! I don't know when I'll be home. Don't wait up."

"Okay," she said when her voice decided to reappear. Then she looked at Coop. "So you think I'm smart?"

Coop flashed her another smile as he opened the driver's-side door to the van. "Yeah. Thanks to you, I was able to convince the M.E. to do an autopsy on Angela Ashford." He inclined his head to her, then swung inside the van and closed the door.

Carlotta swallowed hard as she stepped back to allow the van to leave. An autopsy…thanks to her.

Suddenly panic billowed in her lungs. What had she done? What if, as Hannah had pointed out, her neuroses over Peter had caused her to set a series of events into motion that could endanger more than just her heart?

She rubbed her thumb across the palm of the hand that Amy Lin had "read." Was she indeed facing danger?

Carlotta watched the van pull away, with Coop at the wheel.

And was Dr. Cooper Craft—a big, strong man—offering his protection...and more?

22

"Stop the van," Wesley said. "I'm going to be sick."

Coop veered to the shoulder of the road and brought the van to an abrupt halt. Wesley practically fell out the door and made it two steps before he grabbed his knees and projected his half-digested Homewrecker burrito from Moe's onto the weeds.

Damn, it had been so good going down.

"You okay?" Coop yelled.

Wesley nodded but maintained the position a few seconds longer to make sure the queasiness had passed. He gulped air and closed his eyes, but was immediately assailed by the visions of the teenage boy he'd just helped Coop to peel off Interstate 285 westbound. The teenager, at least, was in only three pieces. His motorcycle was in about a million, recognizable as a motorcycle only because one of the side mirrors had been lodged in the kid's unhelmeted head.

Another wave of nausea hit him and he hurled the chips and salsa he'd eaten as an appetizer. Man, that tomato sauce was like battery acid on the flipside. He felt like a moron, puking his guts out on the side of the road in broad daylight.

"Breathe through your mouth," Coop yelled.

He did and gradually the graphic images in his head began to diminish. Slowly he stood and waited for the horizon to right itself, then stepped back to the van.

"Sorry, man," he said as he pulled himself up into his seat.

"No problem," Coop said, then pointed to the glove compartment. "There's a package of wipes in there."

Wesley pulled out a couple and wiped his mouth, feeling like a kindergartner. "Am I fired?"

"What?" Coop laughed. "Of course not. That was a rough scene back there. I'd be worried if it didn't affect you a little." He clapped Wesley on the shoulder before pulling out into traffic. "At least you waited until we left the morgue. The CSI folks tend to frown upon upchucking at the scene."

Wesley eased into the seat, grateful to be let off the hook.

"That's it for the day," Coop said. "And you're not on call this weekend."

"Why not?"

"I have other commitments," Coop said, his closed expression indicating he didn't care to elaborate. "But don't worry, we'll make up for lost time next week."

Wesley nodded, looking forward to a free weekend. "Today's payday, right?"

Coop pulled an envelope out of his jacket pocket. "Here you go. Don't spend it all in one place."

Wesley pulled out the check and smiled in satisfaction. Thirty-two body retrievals in one week—eight hundred dollars. His fingers began to twitch. He could almost feel the ridged edges of the poker chips in his hand.

"Did you go see the guy at the car wash?" Coop asked.

Wesley didn't want to tell Coop that the guy had blown him off when he'd been stupid enough just to walk up to him. "I changed my mind." Which was sort of the truth—after Chance had given him his loaner piece, he *had* changed his mind about buying one.

"Good," Coop said. "Then you can put some of that money toward your debts."

"Right," Wesley said, still fingering the check. The urge to gamble was building inside him. He could feel it—the nervous energy, the anticipation. He tried to distract himself. "So, I saw you making moon eyes at my sister before we left. Did you ask her out?"

"No," Coop said, then grinned. "She needs time for me to grow on her."

Wesley laughed. "Dude, that could take a while."

"I got nothing but time," Coop said in a way that made Wesley think that the man spent a lot of hours alone.

"Carlotta said that Hannah digs you, though."

"The one-woman chain gang?"

"She's all right, a little kooky sometimes, but cool."

"How in this world did the two of them get to be friends?"

Wesley laughed. "My sister tried to crash a ritzy party for celebrities a few years ago and got busted with a counterfeit ticket. Hannah was working for the caterer and saw the whole thing. I guess she was impressed with sis's chutzpah because she let her in through the kitchen. They've been friends ever since."

"Your sister crashed a party?"

"Lots of them—I used to design and print the tickets for her. She had real fun with it sometimes—wore disguises, changed her name, spoke in accents."

"Your sister did all those things?"

"Yeah. Then last year she crashed a house party where some guy wound up murdered. Because she and her friends were the only people who weren't supposed to be there, they got in a shit-load of trouble with the police."

Coop was staring. "For real?"

"For real, man. They got off, of course, but I think it scared my sister straight. On the other hand, Satan couldn't scare Hannah straight."

"I *knew* your sister had a wild streak."

"Dude, it ain't gonna happen with Carlotta. Especially now that Peter Ashford is back on the scene."

"Back on the scene? You mean he's been in touch with Carlotta?"

"He's called, like, a dozen times. I've seen his number on the caller ID."

Coop shifted in his seat and covered his mouth with his hand.

"Sorry, dude. Maybe he'll drop out of sight."

"Maybe," Coop said as he pulled up to the town house. "I'll call you next week."

"Later," Wesley said, loosening his tie as he jumped out of the van. Whistling under his breath, he waved to Mrs. Winningham, who was peeking out the living-room curtains, and ran up the steps. He was hungry and rich—not a bad combination.

But when he put his key in the lock, the front door swung inside freely. A curse flew out of his mouth.

Someone had been there...or still was.

He stood motionless and listened for noises in the house but didn't hear anything. He glanced around the living room and noticed one of the desk drawers was slightly open. He shot his gaze to the tinsel Christmas tree, and was flooded with relief to see that the little pile of gifts with faded paper seemed untouched. A pang of embarrassment barbed through his chest. He shouldn't care so much about the stupid tree, but he couldn't help it.

He closed the door behind him and walked from room to room, noticing things that had been disturbed—a cabinet door here, a drawer there. When he opened the door to Carlotta's room, he inhaled sharply. Half of her clothes were gone from the closet—she'd freaking levitate when she found out. Strangely, though, her collection of big clunky necklaces seemed untouched, and they were supposed to be worth something. His room seemed undisturbed, although upon closer inspection, the lock on his door had been tampered with. He checked Einstein's enclosure, relieved to see that his pet seemed fine, if unresponsive. It looked as if nothing other than Carlotta's clothes was missing.

He dropped onto his bed and pulled out his paycheck, wondering who could have broken into the house.

Tick had collected Father Thom's payment on Tuesday, so he should've been satisfied, although the man certainly knew his way in and out of their house. The more likely scenario, though, was that The Carver knew that Wesley was paying Father Thom and had sent someone to ransack the town house. Or maybe Carlotta had simply left the door unlocked when she'd gone to work—she hadn't exactly been herself lately.

Staring at the check, he wished like hell it was for more money. He needed to make a big payment to The Carver, keep out fifty bucks to pay the court, and geez, a guy needed some pocket change.

His cell phone rang and Chance's name came up on the screen. Something told him not to answer it, but then he remembered how Chance had come through when he'd asked about a gun. Wesley pressed the call button. "Yeah, dude, what's up?"

"You know that big amateur-game rumor I've been hearing?" Chance asked, his voice more animated than usual. "It's happening tonight, man. An all-weekend tournament."

Wesley's pulse picked up. The promise he'd made to Carlotta not to gamble reverberated in his head even as he asked, "Where?"

"Basement of an office building in Brookwood on Peachtree. It'll be a bunch of lawyers and telecom execs—you'll clean up. Only twenty-five seats, and the top five players are in the money. The grand prize is twenty-five thousand, man."

Perspiration beaded on Wesley's lip. "What's the buy-in?"

"Twenty-five hundred. You got it?"

Wesley hesitated. He could probably scrape together another two hundred from his various hiding places. "I have a grand."

"I'll loan you the rest, man, for half of your take."

Wes swallowed. He'd vowed never to borrow money from Chance—somehow, it seemed even more dangerous than borrowing money from loan sharks. He'd have to make up something to tell Carlotta where he'd be, but he'd have his cell phone with him if anything came up.

"Wes, are you there?"

"Yeah."

"Are you in?"

Wesley's mind raced. He'd been studying cards like crazy since he'd last played, since he'd made that promise to Carlotta. He'd watched marathon poker tournaments on television and practiced at free online poker sites until his computer had been confiscated. He'd become adept at reading other players' tells and disguising his own. If the cards fell his way, he could probably double his money, or triple it. And if he won...he'd be debt free and would have earned enough of a reputation to get a backer for the World Series of Poker tournament on a regional level. An opportunity like this didn't come around very often.

"Come on, man—shit or get off the can. Are you in?"

Sending silent apologies to Carlotta, Wesley stood and grinned into the phone. "I'm in."

23

"You okay, Carlotta?"

She snapped out of her reverie and turned to see Michael retying his tie in a mirror in the employee break room. She nodded, realizing she was staring into her open locker. What had she been looking for? She was so worried about Wesley that she couldn't concentrate.

"Are you sure?" he asked more gently, coming over to stand next to her.

She closed the locker door and put a smile on her face. "I'm fine. Just being a big sister."

"Is Wesley giving you trouble again?"

"Actually, no. He has a job, he's looking forward to doing his community service, and he even *asked* if he could stay with a friend this weekend."

"So he's behaving himself and you have the place to yourself. Did I miss something?"

She smiled. "Mothers know that when kids are on their best behavior, that's the time to worry."

"Except you're not his mother," Michael chided. "He's an adult, sweetie."

"I know," she said, realizing that Michael wouldn't understand the sixth sense she'd developed where her brother was concerned. He was up to something, she just knew it. And the fact that he was staying at Chance Hollander's apartment did little to soothe her anxiety. She hoped that he simply wanted a little privacy—that he was meeting up with some girl that he didn't want to bring around. Thinking about Wesley's sex life made her a little queasy, probably because it made her think about her own sex life, which was fictional. But still, thinking about Wesley hooking up with a girl was preferable to all the other trouble he and Chance could get into.

But Michael was right—there was no sense in borrowing trouble, especially since she already had plenty. Peter had called again last night, and it had taken all the willpower in her body (and a cigarette) not to pick up the receiver. She wanted to keep her distance to give Peter a chance to grieve, and to give the police a chance to sort things out where Angela's death was concerned.

"Michael," she asked casually, "do you know a Susan Harroway?"

He squinted. "I can't keep the Harroway women straight—they're all perky blond paper dolls. Why?"

She shrugged. "No reason. I heard her name mentioned the other day and wondered who she is, that's all."

"I *think* Susan is married to Davidson Harroway. He's a bigwig at the CIN cable news network. If she's the one I'm thinking of, she's some kind of local tennis phenom who was chosen to play a round with Chris Evert when she came to town to raise money for charity."

Carlotta's pulse picked up. Angela played tennis—at the funeral hadn't one of her teammates mentioned how much they would miss her?

They walked out to the sales floor and she followed Michael to the shoe department. "You mentioned the other day that you had a friend who worked at a Botox clinic."

"Uh-huh," he murmured, readying his cash register.

"What was the name of the clinic?"

He glanced up. "Why?"

She didn't have to fake the blush. "I'm considering a little work."

He snorted. "Your skin is flawless and Cindy Crawford would kill for your bone structure. What gives?"

"I'm just thinking about a consultation."

"I hope this doesn't have something to do with that Ashford guy."

Carlotta swallowed hard. "Of course not."

"Good, because I'd hate to see you start changing yourself for a man."

"Are you going to give me the name of the clinic or not?"

He tore off a piece of sales receipt and wrote on it. "Here's the name of the clinic. A consultation will set you back three hundred dollars."

She raised her eyebrows at her friend.

"So I've been told."

Smothering a laugh, she said, "Thanks."

Michael leaned in conspiratorially. "Don't look now, but there's an action-hero type headed your way."

Carlotta turned and broke into an instant sweat to see Detective Terry, dark suit and hideous tie, heading her way. "Gotta go," she murmured and pushed away from the counter.

Her first thought was that Wesley was in trouble again, but then she realized the detective could be here about a number of things—her parents...Angela. Christ, her life was way too intertwined with the Atlanta PD.

"Good morning, Detective," she said as he strode up to her.

"A private word with you, Ms. Wren?" He didn't wait for a response, simply grabbed her by the elbow and steered her toward a dressing room in the adjacent men's department.

She trotted to keep up, trying to shake off his grasp. "I'm coming, you don't have to manhandle me."

"I have a feeling," he muttered, "that you couldn't be handled even if a man wanted to."

She was still mulling over the meaning of his remark when he propelled her into a changing room, followed her in and closed the door behind them.

Carlotta crossed her arms, more to protect herself from his towering nearness than anything else. "Really, Detective, must you be so dramatic?"

He narrowed his eyes. "You've got some explaining to do."

She tried to remain aloof but failed miserably. "What are you talking about?"

"You were questioned in a murder case last year?"

She hugged herself tighter. "So?"

"So, you didn't think it was worth mentioning to me at some point?"

"I fail to see what business it is of yours. Besides, I wasn't arrested. And they caught the murderer."

"I know." He frowned harder. "And you also were arrested for assault?"

"Those charges were dropped! Besides, the big galoot deserved to have a tire iron wrapped around his head, trying to entice my brother into gambling so he could get him deeper into debt."

The detective jammed his hands on his hips and shook his head. "Cooper Craft asked the M.E. to autopsy Angela Ashford based on questions you raised about that men's jacket she bought."

"And?"

"And after the fact, he and I both find out that your credibility is...tainted."

She glared. "Tainted how? I didn't kill anyone!"

"You tried to—a tire iron isn't a toy, Carlotta! The bottom line is that you don't look so good on paper."

She was thrown off guard by the fact that he'd used her first name...and by the strange feeling that despite his condemnation, he seemed slightly impressed with her outlaw status. She swallowed the retort on her tongue because there was something bigger at stake. "So there's not going to be an autopsy?"

He pursed his mouth and took his time answering. "Actually, the autopsy took place this morning."

She inhaled. "And?"

"And...the M.E. found signs of a struggle. Angela Ashford was probably held underwater by her neck. Her death has been reclassified as a homicide."

Mixed feelings stabbed at her—relief that her hunch had been right, but horror that the woman had died at the hands of...someone.

Then she frowned. "So what was all that crap about me not being credible?"

He frowned harder. "If you ask someone to pull in a professional favor, it's only fair that you put everything on the table so there aren't any surprises. Coop really went out on a limb for you on this one."

Coop, the man who thought she was smart. She angled her chin at the detective. "Then I guess it's a good thing I was right."

"Guess so...except now you realize, don't you, that your boyfriend is our prime suspect?"

"Peter Ashford is not my boyfriend."

"Really? I found a valet driver at the Four Seasons hotel who saw Peter Ashford kissing a dark-haired woman standing next to a Monte Carlo the night you said you ran into him at a party there."

Wow, the man had eyes and ears everywhere. Did he also know that she'd crashed the party? "That kiss was...spontaneous. It didn't mean anything."

Detective Terry leaned in and pressed one hand on the wall behind her, effectively pinning her in, his body mere inches from hers. His dark gaze lowered to her mouth. "I could see how that could happen," he murmured, his voice throaty.

She moved her head back and held her breath, taking in his cleanly shaven jaw that hinted of the beard that would reappear in a few hours. She wondered how often the man shaved, and if his propensity for hair extended to his broad chest. She'd never been much for hairy chests, although suddenly the idea wasn't repulsive.

"But you have to admit," he said, his breath close to her cheek, "the fact that someone saw you kissing in public a couple of days before the man's wife was murdered is...coincidental."

Her breathing became shallow. Carlotta lifted her hand and pressed against his chest until he stepped back, giving her room to breathe, although her lungs still didn't work as well as she would've liked. Her hand tingled with awareness of the wall of muscle beneath his shirt and tie. "Peter and I weren't and aren't having an affair," she said as steadily as she could manage. "I told you that our relationship ended years ago."

"Really? Then why does Peter Ashford carry a photo of you in his wallet?"

She blinked. *"What?"*

His eyebrows went up. "You didn't know?"

"Of course I didn't know."

"But his wife probably did. Which might explain why she attacked you here the day she was murdered."

Her throat convulsed. "I...I...you know about that?"

He gave her a tight smile. "Your security department has been helpful. The question is, why didn't *you* tell me that she became violent?"

"I didn't think it was...relevant."

"Oh, well, that makes everything okay," the detective said sarcastically. Then his jaw hardened. "It's starting to look as if Peter Ashford killed his wife over you."

"He didn't," she said with conviction. "I know Peter and he could never do anything like that."

One eyebrow quirked. "I thought you said the other night was the first time you'd talked to him in years."

"That's right. In over ten years, in fact."

One side of the detective's mouth slid back. "People can change a lot in ten years."

"I know," she conceded. Look at her, for instance. "But Peter simply isn't capable of murder."

He gave her a flat smile. "Everyone is capable of murder, Ms. Wren. And some people just might think that you were in on it with him."

"Th-that's ridiculous."

"Is it? I spoke to your associate, Michael Lane. He said that you'd threatened to strangle Angela."

She gasped. "That was a joke. I didn't mean it!"

"You and Peter became reacquainted and the spark was still there, wasn't it?"

She locked gazes with him, then looked away, wondering if men could ever understand the power of young love, a woman's emotional connection to the person with whom she had lost her virginity. It was a memory that bonded her to Peter.

The detective gave a little laugh that said her body language told him everything he needed to know about how she felt about Peter. "Angela was in the way, and angry about the two of you."

"She was angry," Carlotta said, "but she was wrong." A hysterical little laugh escaped from her. "Besides, if I were in on this, why would I push so hard to make sure the body was autopsied?"

"Maybe you got scared," the detective said. "Maybe you didn't think he'd go that far, and now you're having second thoughts."

She gritted her teeth. "Peter's not a murderer. If his marriage had deteriorated so badly, he would've divorced Angela."

"Really? He's not one of those guys caught up in family image?"

She turned her head to prevent him from seeing the sudden moisture in her eyes. Wasn't family image the reason that Peter had abandoned her, leaving her alone and bewildered? "Not if it meant murder," she said finally.

"For your sake," he said quietly, "I hope that's true."

His unexpected compassion caught her off guard. "Have you questioned Peter?"

"Yes, and he denies killing his wife."

Carlotta exhaled, then caught herself—if she truly believed that Peter was innocent, why was she so relieved? She straightened, aware that Detective Terry was studying her every move.

"Did you ask him if Angela was having an affair?"

"Yes. He said if she was, he didn't know about it."

She bit her lip. Or perhaps he didn't want to know?

"But Mr. Ashford is behaving suspiciously," the detective added. "He already had his wife's things removed and destroyed, and hired a cleaning service to clean the house and the guesthouse top to bottom."

The information startled her, but she tried to hide her reaction by lifting her shoulders in a slow shrug. "That sounds to me like a man who's trying to get on with his life."

"Exactly," the detective said, eyeing her. "One more thing—

Mr. Ashford knows that you were the one who raised questions about Mrs. Ashford's death because of the men's jacket his wife purchased and returned."

She closed her eyes briefly and in her mind's eye saw any second chance that she'd had for happiness with Peter go up in flames. "I suppose you told him?"

"I had to. Sorry if it makes things tense between the two of you," he said, not sounding sorry at all. Then he stepped back and pulled out a notebook. "What time did you leave work last Friday?"

"About five-thirty—you can check my time card."

"Where did you go?"

She pressed her lips together and decided not to mention the incident in the parking lot—it would only make her (and Peter) look more guilty if they discovered it was Angela who had tried to run her down. "I went straight home. It's about a fifteen-minute drive. Wesley was there, he'd made dinner."

The tiniest smile came over his mouth, easing the tension. "Your brother cooks?"

"What's wrong with that? Men cook."

"Not this man," he said with a laugh.

"Then together we'd starve," she said cheerfully, "because I don't cook either. I guess it's a good thing we don't like each other."

"Right," he said, nodding. He cleared his throat and looked back to his pad. "You ate dinner, then what?"

"We were still eating when Coop called Wesley for a body-moving job."

His mouth twitched. "I think the official term is 'body retrieval.'"

"Whatever. I drove him because his license is suspended and Coop was already on the scene."

"And you had no idea it was the Ashfords' house?"

"None. You were there when Peter pulled up. I was shocked."

"Both of you seemed surprised to see the other," he conceded mildly. "Hell of a coincidence, though."

The entire conversation was wearing on her, and so was his proximity. "Are we finished? I'm on the clock. You're going to get me fired, Detective."

He frowned. "I'll need the jacket that Angela Ashford returned, if you still have it."

"Lucky for you, I do," she said, happy to escape the intimate confines of the dressing room. When they walked out, more than one salesclerk cut her a sly look.

"You could wipe that smirk off your face," she hissed at him. "People think we were in there messing around."

"That's impossible," he said. "If we'd been in there messing around, we would've been in there *much* longer."

She raised an eyebrow and gestured to his NASCAR tie. "Are you sure you don't want to replace your cartoon tie while we're in the men's department?"

He looked outraged and flipped the tie over. "Mark Martin signed this tie."

"Who?"

He frowned. "I thought you were into celebrities. This tie is probably worth a hundred dollars."

"Then you should definitely sell it."

A scowl settled on his brow. "The jacket?"

"Right this way." She headed toward the escalator and as they rode up, she watched him looking around, taking in the expensive displays and the pretty people. He tugged at his tie and she felt a little pang at having made fun of it—the big man obviously thought he had scored a winner.

His body language left her unsettled. He hovered close like her personal mountain, crowding her space. Inching away was useless—the man seemed to expand like foam insulation to fill the space around him. He was a head taller than she, and his head was in constant motion—scanning, registering. It was, she presumed, his training, so ingrained that he probably wasn't even aware of his actions. His hands on the rubberized rail were huge, like the rest of him, and surprisingly well manicured, although she'd bet he cleaned his nails with a pocketknife. A large crested ring on his right hand had something to do with law enforcement. The man obviously had to shop in the big and tall section, but his suit was well cut. His rumpled blue shirt, however, was tight since he had the top button undone, and his belt was a bit too...gadgety. His shoes were black and plain with a high polish. His western boots suited him better, she decided.

Her foot caught abruptly. Too late, she realized that while she was daydreaming, they'd reached the top of the escalator. She flailed and suddenly those large well-manicured hands closed around her waist and lifted her off her feet, moving her forward as he walked off the escalator. He set her down and smiled. "Are you okay?"

"I...yes, I was just...distracted."

He grinned. "I have that effect on women sometimes."

Flustered, she could only glare and slap his hands away. Burning with humiliation, she led the way to her department, trying to regain her composure. "This is where I spend most of my day."

He looked around at the sparse racks of the couture department and gave that universal man-nod that meant he just didn't get it. "No offense, but I'd rather dodge bullets."

She managed a wry smile and walked to the storage area outside the dressing rooms where she had put away the jacket. When she found it, she unzipped the bag and handed it to him. "The bag was brand new, so there's no chance that trace evidence from a used one could have been transferred to the jacket."

He frowned. "Somebody who looks like you shouldn't be home at night watching *CSI* on television."

She frowned back and vowed not to make any more slips about just how pathetic her social life really was.

He carefully removed the jacket from the bag and held it up. "This is too big for Ashford."

"That's what I tried to tell you," she said dryly. "It's too big for Angela's father, too."

"Did she have brothers?"

"No."

"Brothers-in-law?"

"No sisters."

He brought the jacket to his nose and sniffed. "Cigar smoke."

"Right. And Peter is allergic to cigarette and cigar smoke." She flushed, thinking that her own smoking would be one more thing that Peter would disapprove of. "There was a cigar in the breast pocket."

He patted the pockets. "Was?"

"I...took it out."

He looked up. "What happened to it?"

She suddenly remembered what she'd been looking for in her locker that morning—the cigar. "I don't know. I put it in my purse and now...it's gone."

"You lost it?"

She winced and nodded. "But I can describe it. It was a Dominican Cohiba, very pricy. Purchased from Moody's Cigar Bar downtown, and only four people have bought them in the past six months."

He pinched the bridge of his nose. "Don't tell me you've been playing detective."

She bristled. "Someone had to. If you'd believed me, I wouldn't have had to take matters into my own hands."

"You compromised evidence. There were probably fingerprints on the cigar."

She swallowed. "I didn't open the bag it was in."

"No, instead you lost it."

"Well, I didn't mean to!"

He glared at her like a disapproving teacher, then shook his finger. "*Find* that cigar. And when you do, call me."

Carlotta frowned. "Do you want the names of the people who bought the cigar or don't you?"

From the confounded look on his face she couldn't tell if he wanted to strangle her or shake her hand. His mouth tightened and she thought she heard a muttered curse as he reached for his notebook. "Okay, but this is where your pretend investigation ends, got it?"

24

As her shift wore on, Carlotta stewed over the crack that Jack Terry had made about her "pretend investigation" in tracking down the origin of the cigar—jerk. She'd saved him hours of legwork. June Moody might not have been so willing to share the names of her customers with a behemoth detective. Carlotta nibbled on her thumbnail, feeling miffed.

It was *her* persistence that had led to Angela's case being re-opened. Now she was supposed to just step back and put Peter's fate into the hands of the police? Detective Terry was already convinced that Peter had done it. How diligent would he be at following every little lead?

Besides, she might be in a better position to get *some* answers.

Pulling out the piece of paper on which Michael had written the name of the plastic surgery clinic, she picked up the phone at the register and dialed information, then the clinic.

"Buckhead Expressions," a honey-voiced woman answered.

The name made the place sound more like an art gallery than

a cosmetic surgery center. "Hello. Does Dr. Joseph Suarez work for your clinic?"

"Yes, would you like to make an appointment for a consultation?"

Her pulse ratcheted higher that the man was connected to Angela, if only indirectly. Since her next day off was Tuesday, she asked about availability that day.

"There's an opening at ten o'clock Tuesday morning."

"I'll take it," she said, then listened as the woman explained that they didn't accept insurance cards unless a procedure was deemed a medical necessity, so Carlotta should come prepared to pay the three-hundred-dollar consultation fee.

She could think of a thousand other things to spend three hundred dollars on, but at least she didn't have to worry about having money next week for that gangster, Tick. Wesley had gotten his first paycheck from Coop and promised her he'd be able to cover his payment to that Father Thom creep.

Thank God Wesley was finally starting to behave responsibly.

On her lunch break, she stopped by the administrative office and looked around for a deserted cubicle where she could snitch a few minutes on the Internet. M. Smith's cubicle in a nice secluded corner looked adequately abandoned and M. had even left a cryptic note on the monitor that read: "Be back at 1:30." Nice of him. Or her.

She had twenty minutes.

Hoping the machine was minus a keyboard password, she rolled the mouse and was rewarded with the monitor coming to life, the desktop studded with little icons, most of which were alien to her. But Wesley had insisted that she learn some basics about browsers, so she was able to locate one fairly quickly. From there she moved to a search engine and typed in "Dennis Lagerfeld Atlanta." Big mistake, she realized as over a half million hits were returned. She narrowed her search by using tricks Wesley had taught her, but was at a loss as to how she could connect the man to Angela. Then on a hunch, she entered "Dennis Lagerfeld" and "Martinique Estates" and got a hit on a lifestyle article in the *Atlanta Journal–Constitution:*

"...Martinique Estates, tucked away in a lush Buckhead basin, has become home to many local celebrities, including supermodel Danielle Finnie, former Falcon Dennis Lagerfeld..."

Her heart sped up. Dennis Lagerfeld, one of the people who happened to buy the same type of expensive cigar she'd found in the jacket that Angela had returned, lived in the same neighborhood as Peter and Angela. And if the man was a former professional football player, he was probably a big man—big enough to fit the jacket. She clicked on the images filter and looked for photos of Dennis Lagerfeld. There were many of him in the black-and-red uniform, but she finally found one publicity shot.

He was handsome, with dark hair and caramel-colored skin, large, exotic features and piercing pale-colored eyes. But there was a slight curl to his mouth that made her think that Lagerfeld was a jock who wasn't above exploiting his celebrity status.

She glanced at her watch and rushed to do a local search on Susan Harroway. Lots of hits were returned, but most of them were mentions of her husband, Davidson, with Susan at his side. She scanned images of the couple, then clicked to enlarge a photo of them walking into a benefit. Davidson Harroway was puffing on a long cigar, with Susan's hand tucked under his arm.

So, chances were, the Cohiba that Susan had purchased was for hubby. Carlotta moved the mouse to close the browser just as a man's face appeared over the top of the cubicle.

She started, then manufactured a smile for Akin Frasier, security officer extraordinaire. "Hello, Mr. Frasier." She was never sure how to take the intense little man with the big attitude. He was either a little off in the head, or the most dedicated security officer she'd ever encountered in retail.

"Hi, Ms. Wren. Just making my rounds. I was told that no one is supposed to be in here except the people whose names are on the cubes."

She hurriedly closed the browser window and stood, replacing the owner's sticky note and scooting the chair in close. She gave a dismissive wave. "Smithy told me I could check my e-mail, but I'm all finished."

She sashayed by.

"Ms. Wren?"

She winced and turned back. "Yes, Mr. Frasier?"

"I ran into that Detective Terry this morning and told him all about that awful Ashford woman attacking you last Friday. I thought he should know, even if the woman is dead. He seemed appreciative—even asked for the surveillance film."

She managed to maintain a watery smile. "Thank you."

He tipped an imaginary hat. "You're welcome, ma'am. We had

a report of a purse snatcher in the area. If you need an escort when you walk to your car, just let me know."

"I will, Mr. Frasier."

She returned to her department, her nerves frayed. Because of her, Peter was being investigated for the murder of his wife, and even though she believed he was innocent, somehow she managed to keep giving the police more and more motive for him to have done it. Now they had footage of his wife attacking his presumed girlfriend the day she was murdered.

She felt numb the rest of the afternoon as she waited on customers, worried sick over Peter's fate and mulling over the information she'd learned. She was going to be fired if she continued to obssess over the case.

She clocked out a few minutes early, then found a quiet corner in the employee break room and made a call on her cell phone that she didn't want to make. After the third ring, she was hoping to be able to leave a message, but after a click a voice came on the line. "Liz Fischer speaking."

Carlotta's throat tightened. "Um, hi…Liz. This is Carlotta Wren."

"Hello, Carlotta," Liz said, although her voice was laced with concern. "Is everything all right? Is Wesley okay?"

"Everything's fine. In fact, Wesley's little run-in with the police has helped him to grow up. Probation seems to agree with him." She wet her lips. "I didn't thank you, Liz, for helping him. I know I didn't act like it at the time, but I do appreciate it."

"It was no problem," Liz said, her voice now suspicious. "But surely you didn't call me on a Friday evening just to thank me for helping your brother out of a jam."

"No," Carlotta admitted. "Actually, I know I don't have the right to ask, but I need another favor."

"Okay," Liz said warily.

"Do you know an attorney named Bryan D'Angelo?"

"Sure. But he's not an attorney now. He was just appointed to fill a vacant bench on the circuit court."

"He's a judge?"

"Yes. Why are you asking questions about D'Angelo?"

"A friend of mine died," Carlotta said slowly. "Actually, she was killed. And I found a cigar in her possession that I'm trying to trace back to an owner. Bryan D'Angelo's name came up as a possibility and I thought you might be able to tell me what kind of person he is."

Liz made a thoughtful noise. "I've only worked with him a couple of times on cases, but my experience with him wasn't pleasant. He's a big, arrogant son of a bitch. On the other hand, I can't see him killing someone."

"But he's a big man?" Carlotta asked, thinking of the jacket size.

"Not fat, but tall and kind of bulky. Listen, Carlotta, I'm sorry about your friend, but this sounds serious. You should turn over whatever information you have to the police and let them handle it."

"I have, but I'm afraid the investigating officer has already set his sights on another suspect, who is also a friend of mine." She thought it best not to mention that she herself had given them plenty of reason to scrutinize her "friend."

"Who was the woman who was killed?"

"Angela Ashford."

"Yeah...she belonged to my club. I thought it was an accidental drowning."

"Her death has been reclassified," Carlotta murmured, wondering if she was giving away too much. On the other hand, it
would be public knowledge all too soon.

"Who is your friend that the police have fingered?"

"Um, her husband, Peter Ashford."

"Oh," Liz said mildly. "You're friends with the vic's husband?"

"Just friends," Carlotta said, closing her eyes. *Liar, liar, Prada
pants on fire.*

"Who's the investigating officer?" Liz asked. "I can call and
have a word with him, if you like. Tell him to keep an open mind."

Carlotta pursed her mouth, annoyed at the idea of having Liz
call up her old boyfriend on Carlotta's behalf.

"Carlotta?"

"Uh, actually, it's Detective Jack Terry."

"Oh. I know Jack," Liz said, her voice turning wistful. "I
wouldn't mind giving him a call."

Carlotta had a vision of the woman on the other end licking
her pencil. "No, I don't want you to go to any trouble—"

"Oh, it's no trouble at all," Liz said, practically purring. "I've
been meaning to give Jack a call and see what he's up to. Don't
worry, your name won't even come up."

"Thanks," Carlotta said with a sour frown. "But back to D'Angelo—can you tell me anything else about him? Is he married?
Does he have a reputation as a womanizer?"

"I don't know, but I can put out some feelers and get back to you."

"I'd appreciate it. Goodbye." Carlotta disconnected the call and sighed. She'd just guaranteed that Jack Terry was going to get laid soon—probably tonight. But hey, as long as it meant he'd be more cooperative and *she* didn't have to sleep with him.

Not that she'd sleep with him under *any* circumstances.

Unbidden, an image of the two of them together entered her head, of his powerful body covering hers. She frowned and pushed herself to her feet. The lack of food was making her hallucinate.

As she walked out to her car, dread accumulated in her stomach. She wasn't looking forward to going home to an empty house. Maybe she should've taken Hannah up on her offer to sneak her into a party at the High Museum tonight. At the time the prospect had seemed dull, but now she knew she would only go home and spend the night thinking about Peter and sifting through mementos. How pathetic was that?

"Carlotta."

At the sound of her name, she looked up to see Peter standing next to her parked car in the dim lighting of the parking garage. For a split second, she thought she had conjured him up from a memory. His tousled blond hair, long-sleeve polo jersey and loose jeans sent her back in time, to when the two of them were all that mattered and every minute of her day hinged on his touches and phone calls. It was easy to imagine that he had just stopped by to pick her up for the movies.

She inhaled to clear her head and bring herself back to the

present as she walked closer. She stopped about five feet away, her breathing compromised. "Peter…what are you doing here?"

"I had to talk to you," he said, his voice hoarse. "You wouldn't answer my calls."

"I…I didn't think it was a good idea. And I wanted to give you space to grieve for Angela."

"I am grieving," he said, his eyes clouding. "The police came back this morning, to question me. Now they're saying that Angela was murdered, and they think I did it."

"If that were true," she said carefully, "and they had evidence, they would have arrested you."

"The detective said that it was you who told them that Angela had been murdered." His eyes were heavy with hurt and he shook his head. "How could you think that?"

Her heart cracked a little to see him in pain and to know that she had caused it. At the same time, a chill inched up her back as she realized they were alone. Was Peter angry? Had he been drinking? "I—I don't think you killed Angela, Peter. I was suspicious of how she might have died, but I never said you did it. In fact, I told the detective just the opposite." She lifted her hands. "Don't you see? The police are trying to pit us against each other. Detective Terry even insinuated that we were in on it together."

He frowned. "That's ridiculous."

"That's what I said, but that's why I haven't returned your calls. I didn't want to give them more ammunition."

He exhaled and dropped his head. When he looked up, she was relieved to see a small smile and a glimmer of the old Peter. "I knew it couldn't be true. I knew you of all people couldn't think that I was a murderer. You still know me better than anyone, Carly, even after all these years."

Her chest warmed and she walked forward, extending her hand. He clasped it between his two hands, his eyes shining with—hope? His touch still made her tingle, she realized, still made her feel as if they shared something special, a bond that neither time nor tragedy could break.

"Can we go somewhere and talk?" he asked.

She bit her lip, so tempted to leave with him. But they were both so vulnerable right now, it would only lead to more complications. "We can sit in my car," she suggested.

"I'll take what I can get."

With her heart tripping faster, she unlocked the doors with her keyless remote and slid into the driver's seat. Peter lowered himself into the passenger side, then adjusted the seat to accommodate his long legs. They closed their doors and Carlotta was immediately assailed with the intimacy of the small space. The late hour had cast the parking garage in shadows; it was darker still in the car, but she welcomed the obscurity. Having Peter so near was unsettling enough, inhaling his earthy cologne and feeling the warm energy of his body across the short distance. If she had to look at him she was afraid she wouldn't be able to form words for a coherent conversation.

For a few seconds, only their breathing sounded in the car, and she suspected he, too, was struggling for words.

"Peter—"

"Carlotta—"

They both stopped and laughed, easing the tension a bit.

"Me first," he said softly. "I'm so sorry that you've been pulled into this mess, but I'm so glad to have you on my side."

Guilt stabbed at her. Was she on his side?

"I feel so guilty," he said, and suddenly picked up her hand.

Alarm bells sounded in her head. "Why?"

"Because I can't help but think if I had been more of a man, that I would have married you instead of Angela. She was a great girl. Deserved someone who loved her more than I did."

Something inside her softened to hear the sincerity in his voice—he had cared for Angela. She weighed her words. "Do you think she...found someone?"

"You mean, was she having an affair? No. Besides, I suggested divorce several times, but she wouldn't hear of it. If she'd wanted out of the marriage to be with someone else, she knew I would've given her her freedom."

Carlotta recalled Angela's shopping sprees, her drinking. How awful to want to cling to a loveless marriage.

"I don't know why she wanted to stay married to me," Peter said. "I was never mean to her, but she knew that she'd never have my heart, not entirely." His voice grew strained and he slid his palm over hers, sending little shivers over her arms. "I left a piece of it with you."

Her own heart expanded in response. "You took a piece of me, too," she murmured, entwining her fingers with his. "At the time I thought I was going to die."

"Me, too," he said, his voice thick. "I was so worried about you, but too ashamed to call and check on you. I kept telling myself that your parents would return soon, that you would be okay." He made a choking noise. "Oh, God, Carly, I'm so sorry. I screwed up everything, including Angela's life. And now, this."

Tears gathered behind her eyes for the random events in life that threw people together and pulled them apart. Angela had been caught in the middle. The woman must have hated her, Carlotta realized sadly.

"What do you think happened to her, Peter? Who would have wanted to kill her?"

"I can't think of anyone," he said solemnly, his voice tinged with anger. "A stranger? I don't know. It's just such a waste." He squeezed her fingers. "The only good thing to come from all this horror is that it's brought you back into my life."

"Peter," she said, swallowing her tears, "the detective said you had a picture of me in your wallet."

He sighed. "That's right."

"Did Angela know?"

"She found it…the morning she died."

Carlotta closed her eyes. "That's why she came to the store and accused me of having an affair with you." And a few hours later, she was dead…murdered. The timing was suspicious at best.

"I'm so sorry. I never meant for her to see the picture."

"That wasn't fair to her. Or to me."

"No, it wasn't," he agreed. "I was an idiot, withholding a piece of myself from my wife, and pining for a woman that I lost because of my own stupidity."

"We've discussed this, and I told you that I understand why you did what you did. We have to put it behind us."

He stared at their fingers twined together and gave a little laugh. "This brings back memories, huh? Being in a car together."

She smiled. "The Crown Vic."

"My dad's hand-me-down. He couldn't understand why I didn't want a new sports car. He didn't know that the back seat of the Vic was like a full-size bed."

"Our Holiday Inn," Carlotta said, her body warming at the memory of their progression from sweet kisses to heavy petting to the night he had taken her virginity with Rod Stewart's "Have I Told You Lately That I Love You" playing on the stereo. Peter had been such a gentle, thorough lover. She'd never felt so completely connected to a person before...or since. Her eyes burned furiously as emotion overwhelmed her.

Peter shifted in his seat to face her in the semidarkness. "I love you, Carly. I never stopped loving you."

His admission caused her breath to catch in her lungs. The times she had lain in bed and cried in her pillow, had he been equally miserable, but strapped with guilt and shame on top of having lost the woman he loved?

He reached for her and despite a tiny part of her conscience telling her to resist, she went to him. He slanted his mouth over hers and kissed her hungrily. She responded in kind, swept up in the sweet familiarity of Peter, of picking up where he had left her hanging emotionally over a decade ago. Peter moaned into her mouth, then wrapped his arms around her and pulled her over the console to straddle him. With her skirt pulled up, she settled onto his lap and lost herself in his arms. Nothing had changed. He still had the ability to make the rest of the world fall away. All that mattered was that they had found each other again.

A sharp rap on the window next to her brought her head up and around. Oh geez, it was probably Akin Frasier doing his rounds. While Carlotta scrambled to straighten her clothes, Peter wiped the steam they'd generated from the inside of the window. To her abject horror, Detective Jack Terry frowned in at them.

Peter uttered a curse, and Carlotta wondered hysterically if it were possible to actually die of humiliation. After Peter opened the door, he helped her out first, then climbed out after her, unaware that his hair stood on end from where she had run her fingers through it. Detective Terry stood there with his hands on his hips, wearing a bemused expression. "Sorry to interrupt you two lovebirds."

"So why did you?" Peter asked hotly.

The detective frowned. "There've been reports of trouble in the parking garage. I was in the area and thought I'd cruise through. I recognized Ms. Wren's car and saw the commotion inside and thought she was being assaulted." He looked at her, his expression dark—and disgusted. "The car was bouncing, for heaven's sake." He nodded to her blouse, then averted his gaze.

She glanced down and gasped to see her button-up shirt gaping open, revealing her white lacy bra. She turned her back and fastened her shirt, feeling like a fool...and a slut.

"Do I have to tell you," the detective practically bellowed, "how bad it looks for you two to be caught together right now?"

"No, you don't," Peter said, lifting his chin. "But I don't care how it looks. I didn't kill my wife."

Detective Terry took a menacing step toward Peter. "If you don't care how it looks on you, Ashford, think of how it looks on Carlotta." He made a derisive noise. "For God's sake, next time at least get a damn room." Then he stalked away stiffly, opened the door to a dark, unmarked sedan. He hesitated, looking back at Carlotta with disapproval and—anger?—before swinging into his car, gunning the engine and driving away.

"I have to go," she said to Peter absently, walking around to get back into her car.

"Carlotta—"

"*Don't,* Peter," she said, holding up her hand, her voice shaking. "Don't." She ignored the helpless look on Peter's face, got into her car and, after grinding a few gears, pulled away. The entire way home, Carlotta's skin stung with shame. What must Jack Terry think of her?

Whatever it was, it couldn't be as bad as what she thought of herself.

Minus ten points, Carlotta.

25

Wesley blinked at the pile of chips in front of him, so tired after thirty-six hours of cardplaying and so wired from all the caffeine he'd consumed, he was practically seeing double. The faint tolling of church bells was the only indication that Sunday morning had dawned. The basement of the Peachtree office building had no windows, one mark of a good card house. Casinos employed the same tactic to prevent gamblers from realizing just how much time had passed since they had entered the establishment.

Casinos also pumped uber-oxygenated air into their facilities to help keep gamblers awake and feeling fresh. The converted basement card room was not quite that advanced—the air was pungent from the industrial trash cans overflowing with discarded beer cans and take-out bags, from the smoke of about a thousand spent cigarettes (which probably violated numerous no-smoking ordinances), and from the unwashed bodies of the twenty-five players who had entered the tournament on Friday and who had, even after they'd been eliminated, stuck around to see who would make it to the final table.

The last five players standing would all be in the money, ranging from the top prize of twenty-five thousand down to three thousand. Four names had been written on a dry-erase board that had likely been filched from an accounting department. The fifth name would be either Wesley's or the man sitting across from him—"Quinn," a CFO of some tight-ass company who had so many facial tics, it was difficult to know what was a "tell" twitch and what was just the guy's natural neuroses.

They shared their table's $12,500 of chips, with Quinn having the slight advantage. But Wesley could sense that the guy was wearing down, taking longer and longer to make bets, his eyes and mouth drooping.

Time for the kill.

As the dealer shuffled, Wesley downed the rest of his third Red Bull in an hour and scanned the room.

A few feet away, his buddy Chance gave him a thumbs-up, his energy level suspiciously high—Wesley wouldn't put it past him to have done a couple of lines of coke in the john. Besides making up the difference for Wesley's buy-in, Chance had forked over the dough for his own spot in the tournament, too. But as much as Chance liked the action and the atmosphere of a card game, he was lousy at poker. Guys with big egos usually were. They sulked when they got bad cards and slapped backs when they got good ones. They also thought that drinking alcohol improved their judgment. That's what Wesley liked most about the game of Texas Hold 'Em— it was the game of the underdog, the thinker, the mathematician.

His game.

"Post your blinds," the dealer said, to call for the mandatory bet to initiate a hand. Dealers only had to "announce" in amateur gatherings like this one—at casino tables, the dealer rarely spoke.

It was his turn to post the "big" blind, set at two hundred dollars in this game. He pushed two hundred dollars' worth of chips forward. Moving in slow motion, Quinn posted the "small" blind, set at one hundred. The advantage of Wesley having the big blind was that Quinn would have to place the first bet after the cards were dealt.

The dealer dealt them each two cards facedown, then tossed one into a discard pile.

Wesley lifted the corner of his two cards, but instead of glancing down, he watched Quinn look at his cards, irritated when the man's mouth twitched violently. Good? Bad? The beginning of an epileptic seizure?

Looking at his own cards, he willed himself not to react. Pocket kings, spades and clubs. ThankyouJesus.

"Your bet, sir," the dealer said, nodding to Quinn.

Quinn hesitated, then glanced at his cards again. "I'll raise four hundred," he said, then stacked the chips and pushed them forward.

Good. The man's cards were strong enough to keep him in the game. For now, he'd slow-play Quinn to draw up the pot. Wesley fidgeted on purpose, then called the man's bet and pushed forward three hundred in chips to make them even at five hundred all.

"Here comes the flop," the dealer announced, then dealt three cards faceup on the table—the five of spades, seven of spades and king of hearts.

Three. Of. A. Kind.

He studied Quinn's reaction to the flop, but the man was smothering a yawn and his eyes were watering. The best pocket cards Quinn could have were aces, which didn't stand a chance against his own three kings. Or Quinn could be holding the other king and either a five or a seven, giving him two pairs, which still wouldn't beat the three kings. With the five and seven community cards, he could be working a straight, or less likely, a straight flush *if* he held the eight and nine of spades.

Across the table, his opponent's eyes were bleary and blood-shot. He looked like he wanted to quit and go home to his Sleep Number Bed. Quinn frowned, then put his hands on his chips. "I'll bet a thousand."

Wesley nodded thoughtfully. With that kind of a bet, the man must have the two pair, or, like him, three of a kind. But if so, the best three of a kind the man could have was sevens, and that wouldn't beat his three kings.

He could practically smell the frankincense and myrrh.

The urge to raise was strong, but he resisted. "I'll call," he said, and added a thousand dollars' worth of chips to the center.

"Here's the turn card," the dealer said, then flipped over the king of diamonds.

FOUR. OF. A. KIND.

Wesley tamped down his excitement, schooling his expression into a practiced mask, with a hint of a frown for good measure.

Across the table, Quinn rubbed his eyes with his palms, then said, "Oh, hell, I'm all in," and pushed his chips toward the center. A murmur moved across the room, and a few people crowded closer.

Wesley waited for the hubbub to subside before he smiled. "Call." Then he pushed the rest of his chips toward the center. With nothing left to bet and no card in the deck that could improve his hand, he turned over his pocket cards with a flourish, gratified at the crowd's rousing reaction.

"Four kings!" Chance bellowed. "My buddy has four kings!"

Wesley almost felt sorry for Quinn...until the man turned over his cards: an eight and a nine of spades. With the five and the seven of spades from the community cards, that put him one card short of not just a straight, but a straight flush, one of only two hands that could beat four of a kind.

The crowd went crazy and Wesley swallowed hard. He was still in good shape—the man had only one "out" card to beat him, the six of spades. Including the discards between rounds, eleven cards had been dealt, leaving forty-one undealt. The chances of the next card being a six of spades was about two percent. On the other hand, the chances of the next card *not* being a six of spades was about ninety-eight percent.

If the next card was anything other than a six of spades, he'd won a seat at the final table, was guaranteed to go home with more money than he'd come with and had a good shot at the twenty-five grand. That kind of cash could make all his problems disappear, and put him back in Carlotta's good graces.

If the card was a six of spades, he was out the one grand he needed to pay Tick on Tuesday, owed Chance fifteen hundred bucks, and Carlotta would flay the skin off his body with a stiletto heel.

"Here comes the river card," the dealer said, then paused before turning the final card faceup on the table. Half the room erupted in cheers, half the room cried out in dismay.

Wesley stared down at the six of spades.

He was so fucked.

26

Carlotta looked over the dinner table at Wesley, who was moving the salmon with dill sauce around on his plate more than he was eating it.

She paused in her chewing—something was definitely wrong. When he'd come home yesterday, he'd gone straight to his room and spent the evening there, and since she'd arrived home from work today, he'd barely spoken more than a dozen words. She hadn't pressed him because she'd been preoccupied with her own problems, but she was truly becoming concerned. Had he intercepted another postcard from their parents?

"The salmon is terrific," she ventured.

"Thanks."

"You're not eating."

He set down his fork and picked up his glass of iced tea. "Not hungry, I guess."

She took another bite, chewed slowly, and swallowed. "How was your weekend?"

His hand tightened on the glass. "Fine. Yours?"

"Fine."

They ate in silence for another minute or so, then Carlotta tried again. "How's your job?"

"Good. Four pickups this morning, and I'm on call this evening." His voice was low and indifferent.

She took another bite. "Thanks for doing the laundry."

"No problem. I, um, noticed that there were some things missing from your closet when I set the basket on your bed."

"Oh, I gave away a bunch of stuff Friday."

He gaped. "You did?"

"Hey, I'm a charitable person." Accidentally, but still.

Wesley resumed eating. "By the way, I found a man's handkerchief in your laundry."

She frowned, then her memory kicked in. "Oh, it's Detective Terry's."

"Huh?"

"Don't get any weird ideas. He loaned it to me the day of your arraignment." But the thought of the man put her in an instant funk, and she wasn't sure why. He already thought she was from bad stock, so why should she care what he thought of her lapse with Peter?

In her car.

In the parking lot where she worked.

With a man suspected of murdering his wife.

She pressed her fork on her mound of garlic mashed potatoes, flattening it. Christ, what had she been thinking? The detective was probably convinced that she and Peter had conspired to kill Angela.

"Are you okay?" Wesley asked.

Carlotta frowned. "I was getting ready to ask you the same thing."

The chirping of his cell phone broke into the silence. He seemed relieved at the distraction and answered quickly. After a few cryptic "uh-huhs" and "okays" he disconnected the call and looked up, chewing his lip. "Got any plans tonight?"

"Why?" she asked warily.

"That was Coop. He's at the scene of a murder, and wants me to meet him there if I can. Can you give me a lift?"

She set down her fork. "Not again. Good grief, Wesley—another murder scene?"

"A woman was strangled at Martinique Estates," he said solemnly. "I thought you might be...interested."

Her hand flew to her mouth. Peter's neighborhood! She could only nod.

"Give me a few minutes to change." Wesley's chair scraped the floor, and he disappeared.

Carlotta sat frozen in her chair, considering the implications. Was a killer targeting women in the upscale subdivision? As awful as that would be, it would exonerate Peter in Angela's death. Peter had mentioned that perhaps a stranger had murdered Angela. Maybe she'd simply been in the wrong place at the wrong time.

Pushing to her feet, Carlotta cleared their plates, her heart thumping and nerves tingling.

"Ready?" Wesley asked from the doorway.

She was still dressed in her work clothes, so all she had to do was grab her bag on the way out. As they drove toward the neighborhood in the falling darkness, Wesley turned to her and grinned. "This is kind of cool, us working together."

She gave him a chastising look. "We're *not* working together. I'm simply dropping you off." And getting the scoop on what had happened.

"We could probably work independently for Coop, you know, as a brother-sister duo. All we need is a van. Hey, what about Hannah's van? It's even refrigerated!"

"Are you crazy? Her van is for storing food not cadavers."

"Still, Coop is always looking for extra help."

"Well, don't give Hannah any ideas. She's already fascinated by this stuff, and she doesn't need any more creepy hobbies."

"It's really not too bad most of the time," he said, cajoling. "Being around dead bodies kind of demystifies death."

"I don't mind being mystified. In fact, I prefer it. I've been to the morgue."

He frowned. "When?"

"Last year when my friend Jolie dragged me there to identify her boyfriend's body. They had him in a drawer, like some kind of human file cabinet." She shuddered at the memory. "Besides, I have a job, remember?" Unless she got fired due to her plummeting sales. "By the way, how much was your check last week?"

"Uh...I've been wanting to talk to you about that."

Dread filled her chest. "What is it?"

"Okay, don't be mad."

"What?"

He sighed. "I messed up."

She gripped the steering wheel tighter. "Wesley, I swear I'm going to drive us straight into traffic if you don't tell me what you don't want to tell me."

"The money's gone."

She tapped the brake, as if she could stop the words that had already come out of his mouth. "What happened to it?"

"I...lost it."

"Lost it, as in dropped it down a manhole, or lost it, as in gambled it away?"

The look on his face told it all. "I'm sorry, sis."

She closed her eyes for as long as she dared while driving, then counted to five to keep her fury at bay. "You *promised* me you would stay away from the card tables."

"I know, I'm sorry, but I was *so* close to winning big."

"That's what all gamblers say, Wesley, just before they file bankruptcy. Except you don't owe a bank, you owe two big, beefy loan sharks!" She inadvertently stepped on the brake again, causing the car behind her to blast the horn. "Oh my God, tell me you didn't borrow any more money from those horrible people."

"I didn't."

"Are you just saying that because you're afraid I'm going to kill us in this car?"

"No," he said, bracing his arm against the dashboard, "but maybe we should talk about this later."

"Later? Wesley, tomorrow morning that hoodlum, Tick, is going to show up at our door and demand a thousand dollars. You told me you had it covered. There's no way I can get that kind of money together between now and then."

"Don't worry, I'll take care of it."

"How?"

"I'll think of something," he said. "Turn here."

She bit her tongue and made the turn, her thoughts chaotic. Wesley was playing with fire. This entire situation was going to explode in his face...and maybe hers.

She stopped at the gated entrance for Wesley to show the identification badge that Coop had given him. The security guard radioed ahead to someone, then opened the gate to let them drive through.

It was about the same time of day, she noticed, as when she'd last driven into the neighborhood, unaware that she would know the victim. She slowed to make out the street signs in the waning light, then made two more turns, the last one away from the Ashford house.

"There it is," Wesley said, pointing up ahead to the left where the lights of two police cruisers flickered. She pulled in behind a familiar dark sedan and frowned. Not again.

"Come on," Wesley said.

"They won't let me in," she protested.

"You're with me. Besides, you've talked your way into places more sensitive than crime scenes."

So true—although she hated having her little brother remind her of it. Burning with curiosity, she followed him and nodded curtly at the officers who studied Wesley's identification.

"We're here to remove the body," Wesley said, his voice deep and formal.

The officer glanced at Carlotta, then waved them both through.

"If you start working with me and Coop," Wesley said as they walked toward the huge stucco mansion blazing with lights, "you could have your own badge."

"Tempting, but no."

Coop's white van sat in the driveway, next to a car with the medical examiner's insignia on the side. The door to the house stood open, with light streaming out. Wesley led the way inside and Carlotta followed. The palatial foyer, painted in whites and yellows, featured a sweeping staircase to the right. To the left, the house opened into cavernous rooms, the decor pale and exquisite, with nothing out of place.

"Wesley, up here. Don't touch anything."

They looked up to see Coop gesturing from the catwalk. Carlotta followed, hanging back, her heart tripping faster as she climbed the steps. At the top, the six-foot-wide catwalk gave way to luxurious rooms on either side—a sitting room, a music room, most with French doors, all of them standing open. A couple of gloved CSI guys, carrying a camera and several brown bags, came out of a room at the end of the hall and walked by them. Coop disappeared into the room and Wesley followed. When Carlotta caught sight of a woman's scantily clad body lying on a bed inside the room, she shrank back against the wall. A split-second glance was enough, though, to brand the horrific scene on her mind—the blonde's limbs lying at awkward angles, her pale skin glowing through the transparency of the black lingerie she was wearing, one high-heeled shoe on her foot, one lying on its side on the floor.

Manolo Blahniks—she'd know them anywhere.

The woman's face was beautifully sculpted, her blond hair in loose, crimped waves. A chord of recognition vibrated in the back of Carlotta's head but refused to surface—maybe the woman was a model. She squinted, recalling more detail. The lingerie...black, maybe French, definitely upmarket.

Wanting a better look, she stepped to the bedroom door, only to have her view blocked by a set of panoramic shoulders.

"Ms. Wren," Detective Terry said, his expression wry. "I almost didn't recognize you without your skirt hitched up to your waist."

Carlotta flushed. "Well, if it isn't Detective Peeping Tom."

"You shouldn't be up here," he said, looking supremely annoyed. "You need to leave."

She crossed her arms. "Are you the only detective in the police department? You seem to be everywhere."

He glared at her. "Buckhead happens to be my jurisdiction. What's your excuse?"

She bristled. "I brought Wesley to help Coop. When I heard it was in the same neighborhood as...before, I thought it might have some bearing on Angela Ashford's case."

A thundercloud descended on his brow as he grabbed her elbow and steered her back down the hall. "All the more reason you shouldn't be here."

"Wait." Carlotta shook off his hand and turned to face him. "What's the woman's name?"

"I can't tell you."

She sighed, exasperated. "I'm going to find out in tomorrow's paper, or when Wesley comes home, for that matter."

His mouth tightened. "Lisa Bolton. Mean anything to you?"

She repeated the woman's name under her breath. "It sounds familiar. Can I see the body?"

"*No.* I can't believe this conversation has lasted this long. Scram."

"Is she married?" Carlotta pressed.

He pulled his hand down his face, then sighed. "Widowed, about a year ago."

"Who found her?"

"A neighbor walking her dog noticed the front door was open, knocked to see if anyone was home and then called the police when no one came to the door."

"Do you have any suspects?"

He leaned in, looking as if his head might explode. "Am I going to have to forcibly remove you from the scene?"

She picked up the end of his orange-and-blue-paisley tie and made a face before dropping it. "I was just leaving," she said, then turned to make her way back downstairs.

"I got a call from Liz Fischer."

She turned back and gave him a bland smile. "Was it good for you?"

A muscle worked in his jaw. "Let me do my job, Carlotta. The last thing I need is to have to worry about what trouble you're getting into."

"Worry about me?" She angled her head up at him. "Watch out, Detective, I might start to think that you care."

He shifted his big body and looked as if he had developed a bad taste in his mouth.

"By the way," she said casually, "Dennis Lagerfeld, one of the persons who bought the cigar that I found in the jacket that Angela returned, lives in this neighborhood."

She made her way to the bottom of the stairs, then glanced up to find the detective leaning on the handrail of the catwalk, studying her, his mouth pursed. She locked gazes with him, wondering if they were destined to butt heads on every front. Given their differences and all the unresolved issues in her life, it seemed likely. She dragged her gaze away from his and walked out the door.

She couldn't get home fast enough. It was one thing to hear about a murder on the eleven o'clock news or to read about it in the Metro section of the *AJC,* but to actually see the room where a woman had had the life squeezed out of her and to see how her body had been abandoned for a passerby to find... It took a gruesome person to treat a life so carelessly.

Visions of the woman's body twisted in the sheets plagued her. Had the killer been on top of her when he'd strangled her? She touched the skin on her throat, remembering when Angela had attacked her and what it had felt like to have her airway cut off. The woman would have been flailing, fighting for her life.

And judging by the way she was dressed, Lisa Bolton had known the person who had killed her...unless the woman lounged around the house in black French lingerie and Manolos.

Which, she conceded, she had done herself once...okay, twice, while Wesley was at band camp.

Then she recalled other details that hadn't registered at the time—a bottle of champagne next to the bed, a tray of some kind of food—chocolates, maybe? Lisa Bolton had been expecting company, but not expecting a violent end.

Her cell phone rang and she glanced at the screen——L. Fischer. Great.

But she'd asked for the woman's help, hadn't she? She sighed and pressed the call button. "Hello?"

"Carlotta. Hi, it's Liz."

"Hi...Liz."

"Just wanted to let you know that I made a few inquiries about Judge D'Angelo. I don't know if he knew your friend, but he didn't kill her. He's been in San Francisco for three weeks at a technology-law conference."

At least that was one name to cross off the list. "Thanks for checking, Liz."

"Oh, no problem. Actually, it gave me a good reason to reconnect with an old friend."

She smirked into the phone. "Detective Terry said that you'd called."

Liz's lubricated laugh slid over the line. "I hope that's all he told you, that devil."

Carlotta rolled her eyes, then held the phone away from her mouth. "I'm losing you, Liz...ack...ola...meng." Then she disconnected the call.

She sighed. Two murders in ten days, both beautiful young women in their prime. Such a waste...and terrifyingly casual. The arrogance of someone just to snuff out someone's life. The person had to be a sociopath.

And still out there somewhere.

By the time Carlotta arrived at the town house, her nerves were unraveling. When she stepped out of her car, the air was cold and the wind brisk, bending branches and sending fingers of black shadows over the ground between the garage and the front door. She ignored the prickle on her neck, telling herself that she was still spooked from the crime scene. She'd made the quick dash countless times in the dark, and not once had a serial killer jumped out of the bushes to grab her.

She hugged herself and put her head down, leaning into the wind as she ran across the front yard and up the sidewalk. Just before her foot hit the bottom step, a large body stopped hers and a sweaty hand covered her mouth.

There was, Carlotta realized with dismay, a first time for everything.

27

Carlotta's mind whirled with panic to feel the bulky body behind her. Why hadn't she listened when Detective Terry had given that little talk at the mall on safety and self-defense?

Reacting out of instinct, she bit down on the meaty fingers covering her mouth and was rewarded with a howl and the relaxing of his grip on her. Then she brought her heel down hard on the man's instep. Another howl sounded, this one twice as loud. Carlotta lunged forward to get away, but the man grabbed her from behind, spun her around and held her jaw in the vise of his big hand. His face was fleshy and pockmarked, his eyes small and mean. "Stop fighting me, bitch. Where's your deadbeat brother?"

She gasped for air. "Who...are...you?"

"I work for The Carver. Wesley owes him a bunch of green, and he's way late on his payments. My boss is pissed because he knows Wesley's been paying Father Thom and not him, so he sent me to collect an installment, if you know what I mean."

"W-Wesley's not here."

The man gave her a rough shake, gouging his big fingers into her face. "Money will do."

"I don't have any money," she said as well as she could with her jaw being held shut.

The man licked his lips. "Then maybe we can work out a little trade, sis. Just how much do you care about your little brother?" He squeezed harder and she cried out, terrified. She was no match for his strength. The man could do anything he wanted to her and she would be powerless to stop him.

He started walking her toward the house when suddenly a heavy *thunk* sounded and the man grunted, staggering back and releasing her.

She spun around, surprised and weak with relief to see Peter standing there, holding a hefty tree branch like a baseball bat. Before the man stopped reeling from the first whack, Peter lifted the branch and swung again, this time landing a blow on the side of the man's head, drawing blood. The thug went down on his knees, wincing and holding his head. He wore a long, dark coat and nice clothes that betrayed him as more than a run of the mill criminal.

"Reach for a gun," Peter said, standing over the man with the club in swing position, "and I'll *end* you."

The fury in his voice left no doubt that he meant what he said. Carlotta blinked at a side of Peter that she'd never seen before. Physical, yes, but violent?

The man shook his head and lifted his hands to indicate he had no intention of fighting back.

"Why are you bothering Carlotta?" Peter demanded.

"Her kid brother...owes money...to my boss...The Carver."

Peter looked at Carlotta, and after a humiliating hesitation, she nodded. Peter's mouth tightened, then he looked back to the man. "How much?"

"Ten grand," the guy panted, touching the gash on his head. "But a payment...will do."

To Carlotta's mortification, Peter reached into his back pocket and withdrew his wallet.

"Peter, don't," she implored.

Peter handed her the makeshift club, then opened his wallet and withdrew all the cash inside. "Here's a little over a grand. Now get the hell out of here."

The man pushed to his feet, took the money and lumbered off.

The light on the stoop next door came on and Mrs. Winningham emerged, wearing a nightcap and wielding a broom. "What's going on out here?"

"Nothing, Mrs. Winningham," Carlotta called. "Sorry we woke you."

"I heard a big commotion," the woman insisted.

"Good *night,* Mrs. Winningham," she said as Peter touched her arm.

"Let's get you inside," he said, staring in the direction the man had gone.

Scrambling toward the front door, she half expected a gunshot to ring out from the shadows, but apparently the man was satisfied with the money.

She fumbled to unlock the door, her hands trembling. Finally,

Peter took the key from her and within a couple of seconds, the door opened. Carlotta practically fell inside.

Peter dead-bolted the door behind them, then walked to the window. "Don't turn on any lights yet." She watched him part the curtain, then peer out, scanning the yard. "He drove off," Peter said. "All clear."

She sighed in relief and turned on a corner lamp, bathing the small living room in warm light. Realizing how the incident might have ended if Peter hadn't shown up when he did, she started to shiver uncontrollably.

"Are you okay?" He came up behind her, then rubbed her arms up and down. "Did he hurt you?"

"No." She turned around and, at the sight of his handsome face drawn in concern, her heart expanded with love and gratitude. "Thanks to you."

He put his finger under her chin. "Has this kind of thing happened before?"

"Nothing this...serious."

His eyebrows converged into a frown. "What kind of trouble is Wesley in? Drugs?"

"No, thank God. He gambles—which is bad enough."

"And he borrowed money off some thug named The Carver?"

She nodded. "The name alone should've been a tip-off, huh? And he's in debt to another guy named Father Thom—he's the one who usually sends a...collections agent."

"Usually?" His face darkened. "You mean these thugs have been harassing you on a regular basis?"

The angry concern in his voice made her feel warm and...

protected. And it made her mourn even more all the years they'd been apart. How many times had she yearned for him for this very reason, because he had always looked out for her?

"Have you ever called the police?" he asked.

"It would only make things worse, and Wesley is already in enough trouble with the law."

Peter looked sympathetic. "I read about the computer-hacking charges in the paper."

Her cheeks burned with humiliation to have all the sordid details of their lives revealed to Peter. "He received probation and has been doing...better." If she didn't count his gambling lapse over the weekend. "He has a job, contracting with the morgue for...well, you know," she said, her voice trailing off.

He nodded. "I saw him the other night. He's all grown up."

"Yeah, with grown-up problems." She swallowed. "I'm sorry about the money, Peter. You didn't have to do that. I'll pay you back."

He gave a dismissive wave, as if a thousand dollars was pocket change—and for Peter, she realized, it was. "I don't want you to pay me back, Carly. And I can send you more if it will help. It's the least I can do."

After abandoning you. The unsaid words plucked at her. Was Peter trying to buy his way back into her good graces?

"No," she said hurriedly, "that won't be necessary. I appreciate your offer, but Wesley and I will work it out." Then she clasped her hands together. "But thank you for taking care of that guy. I didn't realize...you had such a temper."

"Threaten someone I care about," he said, his nostrils flaring, "and I turn into a dangerous man."

She swallowed hard as a rogue thought slid into her head: Had Angela told Peter that she'd confronted Carlotta at the store? He'd acted as if he'd known nothing about it, but what if he had and the incident had triggered his anger?

"I'm just glad I was there," he said fiercely, running his finger along her tender jaw.

"Peter," she said, then wet her dry lips, "why *were* you here?"

He hesitated, his expression contrite. "I've been sitting out there in my car for over an hour, waiting for the chance to see you. I just wanted to say that I'm sorry for what happened in the parking garage the other night."

She managed a little smile, despite the sensations buzzing through her body at his touch. "It was both of us."

"When I look at you," he said earnestly, "I can't help myself. I just want to touch you, to feel your skin against mine. I've fantasized about you so much over the years, when I see you and you're so real and beautiful—more beautiful even than I remember—I just…lose my mind."

She knew the feeling. When she looked at Peter, her brain emptied of common sense in order to process the torrent of sensations pummeling her body.

"Like right now," he said, sounding desperate. He dipped his head slowly to her mouth, giving her plenty of time to retreat.

But she didn't. After years of hoping that he would magically appear and save her, he had. She lifted her mouth to meet his and melted into his arms for the most intense, powerful kiss of her life. He tasted sweet, yet his lips were firm and demanding. Their young kisses had been born of first love, lust and discovery, but this kiss was born of adult hunger, denial and deprivation.

He slanted his mouth over hers and speared his tongue inside, flicking the tip against her teeth, bringing back in a flood of sensory signals the memory of other delights they had shared. Her body had a long memory, coming alive under the slide of his hands down her back and over her hips, pulling her against his hardness.

At the intimate contact, her breasts grew heavy and molten need swelled in her stomach. She moaned into his mouth, overcome with the desire to relive the earth-shattering lovemaking they had always shared. Peter broke their heated kiss long enough to pick her up and lay her on the couch. Then he covered her body with his, his eyes hooded with banked desire. He kissed her neck, blazing a trail to her collarbone, then slid his hands beneath her shirt to cup her breasts. Her nipples budded under the sensitive strokes of his fingers and she felt his erection surge against her thigh.

"I want to be inside you," he whispered, tonguing her ear.

She sighed, rocking her hips against his, gratified at his groaning response. She tugged his shirt from the waistband of his pants, massaging the warm, smooth skin of his back. "I want that, too."

Suddenly, he stiffened, and she realized the phone was ringing, pealing through the empty house.

"Leave it," she whispered, reveling in the indention of his spine. But a few seconds later, she realized that something had changed, that Peter was pulling away from her, his expression dark and unreadable.

"I can't do this."

"Yes, you can," she urged, pulling on his arm. "I want you to." The phone continued to ring.

"No," he said, standing and shaking his head. "It's not right. I'm only thinking of myself. That detective was right—I'm not considering how this affects you, and I should."

She sat up, feeling as if she'd been unplugged from an electrical socket.

He looked at her, his gaze deep and passionate. "I love you, Carly, and I want to be back in your life, but not until this mess is over. I have to make everything right."

His words reminded her of where she'd spent most of her evening. She stood and straightened her clothes, her body still humming from his touch. With the phone ringing in the background, she said, "Peter, I went with Wesley on a call earlier this evening...in your neighborhood."

He frowned. "*My* neighborhood?"

"A woman was strangled in her home. Lisa Bolton."

He froze, his expression anguished. "No...no. Oh, God, this changes everything," he said as if he were talking to himself.

She had expected a reaction, but his detached distress alarmed her. The clanging phone in the background strung her nerves tighter. "Did you know the Bolton woman?"

He blinked and stared at her. "I should go. The police are probably looking for me."

The back of her neck tingled. "Why would you say that, Peter?"

"They think I killed Angela. They're probably going to want to question me about this, too."

He seemed inordinately calm for someone who'd just learned

he might be a suspect in a second murder. Deadly calm. Still ignoring the phone, she followed him to the door, drawing hope from the fact that he'd seemed genuinely shocked when he'd heard of the Bolton woman's death. He couldn't be involved... could he?

"Lock this door behind me," he directed. "If that guy comes back, call the police, understand?"

She nodded, wishing things were simpler, but knowing that things were likely never to be simple again. Life had been lived...things were complicated, and seemed to grow more so every day. "Thank you again, Peter, for...being here."

He reached up and caressed her cheek. "You're welcome. Carly, if things go bad, just remember that I love you and that I tried to do the right thing. But I'm begging you, please stop asking questions."

Truly alarmed now, she asked, "Why? What do you mean?"

But he simply opened the door and walked out, disappearing into the night.

After she closed the door, she realized the phone had stopped ringing. No sooner had the thought left her mind than it began to ring again. With a sigh, Carlotta walked over and picked up the receiver, sure it was a bill collector because her and Wesley's personal calls always came through their cell phones. "Hello?"

"Ms. Wren, this is Detective Terry."

Just the man's voice triggered an instant headache. "What now, Detective?"

"I called to make sure you'd made it home safely, that's all."

She blinked. "Oh." The memory of being overpowered by The

Carver's thug rushed back to her, but there seemed to be no point in mentioning the encounter, not when she'd have to admit that Peter had emerged from the shadows to save her. "I'm fine, Detective. Thank you," she added as an afterthought.

"No need to thank me, just doing my job. If we have a killer on the loose, who knows who his next victim might be."

Something in his voice told her that he had a suspicion who the killer might be…and was warning her to be careful. The palm reader's cautionary remarks came back to her: *You are facing danger.* And then the woman's advice that she needed someone big and strong to protect her.

Yet Peter was the one who might have saved her life tonight, or at least her honor.

"Okay, then," he said in her silence. "Good night."

"Good night, Detective," she murmured, and slowly hung up the phone. She put both hands to her head and groaned, thinking of how her life had spun out of control since being reunited with Peter.

And then a fleeting memory snagged on something in her brain and held. Lisa Bolton's face had seemed vaguely familiar, and now Carlotta knew why.

She had seen the woman at the party she had crashed, the one where she had run into Peter.

28

After a restless night, Carlotta woke feeling groggy and miserable. Peter's touch haunted her, and his words tormented her. He was so close, yet at the same time, out of reach. The push and pull of emotions was wreaking havoc with her judgment. And in the back of her mind, she agonized over the possibility that he might have done something awful that would forever keep them apart. How could she both long for a man and fear that he was capable of murder?

She threw back the covers and swung her legs over the side of the bed.

And if she didn't have enough of her own problems, she expected that Tick character to ring the doorbell any minute, demanding cash. Wesley had promised he would "handle" it, but since he'd admitted to gambling away his check, she had no idea where he'd get the money.

Unless he had more hidden stashes.

She showered and dressed quickly, dreading the consultation

appointment at the clinic where Angela had been Botoxed, but looking forward to having lunch with Hannah afterward. When she emerged from her room, she found a note from Wesley on top of a covered plate of French toast.

Sorry about last night. Made my payment this morning. Lamb chops for dinner.

Carlotta shook her head. Wesley obviously thought he could soften her up with food.

She dragged her finger through the powdered sugar and syrup, then licked it off. He was right, the little turd.

As she left for the appointment, she scooped the newspaper from the stoop and dropped it into her bag. On the drive, she resisted the urge to smoke a cigarette, but stopped to get an expensive nonfat latte. American vices, she decided, were driving the economy.

Case in point: Buckhead Expressions was a five-story building with a luxurious lobby studded with gorgeous coeds dressed in pale blue lab coats sitting behind a black counter and wearing phone headsets. After she'd forked over the requisite three hundred bucks and was settled in the waiting room, she noticed the headline on the newspaper a person sitting across from her was reading.

BUCKHEAD SERIAL KILLER?

She nearly choked on her coffee, then yanked the paper from her bag and scanned the lead story.

The police were investigating two murders that had occurred in the same upscale neighborhood in the space of ten days. The first murder, previously thought an accidental drowning, had been reclassified after questions surrounding the victim's death had triggered an autopsy.

Carlotta bit down on the inside of her cheek—at least she hadn't been named.

The second murder was more brazen, with the woman being attacked inside her home, in her bedroom, in broad daylight.

The implication was clear—a killer was on the loose targeting beautiful, rich women, and his violence seemed to be escalating.

Her heart thumped wildly and she wondered for the umpteenth time if she should call Detective Terry and tell him what she'd remembered about seeing the Bolton woman at the same party as Peter. And for the umpteenth time, she talked herself out of it. Chances were that half the people at those events were from the same neighborhood, country club, church, et cetera. The wealthy moved in herds—eating together, socializing together, and if rumors were to be believed, sleeping together. The wealthy formed close-knit, inbred groups and they protected their own, as evidenced in the newspaper article by the comments of neighbors:

"We live in a gated subdivision with security systems, and still these people find a way to invade our neighborhood."

"You have to be careful who you hire these days. I do background checks and encourage my neighbors to do the same."

The locals, it seemed, were convinced the perp was an outsider, perhaps a gardener or a pool-maintenance worker. She doubted if any of them had considered the possibility that the murderer could be living among them, playing doubles at the club, raising money for his church, dropping his kids off at private school.

"Carlotta?"

She folded the paper with a crunch and looked up at a young woman carrying a clipboard. "Yes?"

"We're ready for you."

Carlotta rose, then made a rueful noise as she pointed to the paper. "Did you hear about the two women who were murdered?"

The young girl nodded, then leaned in to whisper, "I knew one of them."

Carlotta feigned shock and awe. "Really?"

"Yeah. Angela Ashford was a patient here."

"Did she by chance see the doctor I'm going to see?"

"Yeah," the aide said out of the side of her mouth. "Otherwise, you'd never have gotten in so quickly. Tuesday morning was her standing appointment."

Carlotta didn't have to feign surprise this time. A shudder threatened to overtake her at the realization that Angela should be there instead of her. Her conscience pinged with the eerie sensation that she was stepping into parts of Angela's life.

She walked into the tiny exam room, a little overwhelmed by all the mirrors and the oversize ads for prescription cleansers, oral medications, topicals and the countless before-and-after photos of cosmetic surgery procedures. In the corner sat a computer screen where the pathetic "before" pictures and miraculous "after" images merged to make it appear as if the transformation occurred within seconds, skipping over the surgery itself and the weeks or months of recovery.

Carlotta puffed out her cheeks in an exhale. If a woman had any confidence in her looks when she walked in, it was likely to be dashed within a very short period of time. She sat down and as the minutes clicked by, found herself staring into the magnification mirror sitting on the table. She scrutinized her pores, trying to remember how long it had been since her last facial. Then she was distracted by the fine lines around her eyes and mouth, conceding that some of the lines could no longer be defined as "fine." And the recent sleepless nights were taking their toll—soon the bags under her eyes were going to need luggage tags.

The door opened, snapping her attention to the man who strode into the room. Dr. Joseph Suarez was tall and barrel-chested—a definite possible fit for the men's jacket that Angela had purchased, Carlotta immediately thought. Pleasantly handsome, he looked to be in his mid to late forties.

Although, if he'd bought into his own procedures, the man could be seventy, she mused.

He removed the gum he was chewing and tossed it in a trash can, then smiled at her as he picked up her chart. "Miss Wren?"

"Yes," she said, suddenly nervous.

"What can I do for you?"

Before she could reply, he dropped into the seat opposite her and reached forward to cup her face in his hands.

"Um, I'm here for a consultation," she murmured, wondering what he was frowning at.

"Uh-hmm." He moved her head from side to side. "You have a lovely neck."

She swallowed hard at the bizarre remark. "Th-thanks." His fingers were butter soft, but strong and adept. She imagined them squeezing the life out of Angela and shivered.

"Are you cold?" he asked in a way that made her think he didn't really care.

"A little."

As expected, he ignored her response as he ran his thumbs over her nose and cheekbones. "I can fix that."

"The temperature?"

"No, the bump on your nose."

"I have a bump on my nose?"

He nodded and angled her head so that she could see her profile in the mirror. "That bump."

"That's not a bump," she argued. "That's a...hump." Her mother's hump, to be precise. "I don't want it *fixed*."

"Okay," he said easily, then proceeded to push and prod her skin as if she were a wad of Silly Putty. "Laser resurfacing will take care of the blotchiness, collagen injections will fill in your laugh lines and crow's-feet, and Botox will help those forehead wrinkles." Then he made a sorrowful noise. "I can't fix your teeth, but I can refer you to a good cosmetic dentistry group."

She tongued the familiar gap between her front teeth, then frowned. "I don't want to fix my teeth."

"Oh." He sat back and lifted his hands. "What then?"

The whole hard-sell routine had left her feeling a little blindsided, not to mention homely. With a mental shake, she reminded herself why she was there. "I'm interested in learning more about Botox. My friend Angela Ashford referred me to you."

The reaction was unmistakable. His eyes widened slightly and his mouth twitched downward before he reached for her file and pretended to peruse it—odd, since there was nothing to peruse other than her home address and phone number and the fact that the only medication she took was birth control pills.

Which was anecdotal, considering her lackluster sex life, but not particularly noteworthy.

"What…exactly did Ms. Ashford say about me?" he asked.

At his suspicious body language, her stomach fluttered with excitement. She paused for effect, then gave him a coy smile. "Angela said the two of you—how did she put it?—had a special relationship."

He fidgeted. "Were you aware that Ms. Ashford had… passed away?"

She nodded. "Everyone is torn up about it. Did you hear that the police had reclassified her death as a murder?"

More fidgeting. "I think I read something about it in the paper." He stood suddenly, then wiped his mouth with his hand. "I might have been too hasty, Ms. Wren."

"What do you mean?"

"I mean that you could postpone any work at all for at least another five years."

She perked up. "Really?" Then she realized he was trying to make a fast exit. "Hey, wait a minute, I paid three hundred dollars so you could tell me that I don't need any work?"

He walked over to a cabinet, opened the door and raked an

armful of bottles and jars into a plastic bag. "Here you go," he said, setting the bulging bag on the table in front of her. "That's at least a thousand dollars' worth of product. Have a nice day." Then he opened the door and walked out, not bothering to close it.

"You're not going to get a referral from me!" she shouted, but her pulse clicked like a timer. The good doctor was definitely guilty of something besides a bad bedside manner. But could it be murder?

She hefted her bulky bag of samples, not sure if she had enough information to pass to Detective Terry. Then she spotted the trash can and remembered the gum Dr. Suarez had been chewing—wouldn't the detective be impressed if she were able to provide a sample of the man's DNA? Probably not, she thought moodily as she set down her load and snagged a plastic Baggie from a dispenser. The man would probably just reprimand her again for "doing his job." She grimaced at the feel of the squishy gum through the Baggie, then stuffed it in her purse.

But as she walked to the door, a face on the computer screen caught her eye. The "before" picture wasn't familiar, but the "after" picture was: Lisa Bolton, post eye and chin lift.

Carlotta inhaled sharply. Coincidence?

"There is no such thing as a coincidence," Hannah declared over lunch.

"Yes, there is," Carlotta argued. "It's not a stretch to imagine that two wealthy women in Buckhead went to one of the most popular plastic surgery clinics in Buckhead. What's harder to imagine is why a successful plastic surgeon would murder two of his patients. But the man certainly acted strange when I mentioned Angela's name."

"If you ask me," Hannah said, "the entire population of Buckhead is one therapy session away from drinking the magic Kool-Aid. Most of these people are nuts, or have you forgotten so quickly the murder plot we stumbled into last fall?"

"As much as I'd like to forget being hauled to the police station and grilled like a piece of chicken, I haven't been able to yet." Then she clasped her hands together. "That reminds me—I got a letter from Jolie yesterday. She and Beck are doing great. She says she's never been happier."

"Do they have plans for returning to Atlanta?"

"Not anytime soon. And after everything she went through, I can't say I blame her."

"I know. And look how quickly that story disappeared from the headlines. Three people dead, and after the murderers were caught, the people in their social circle pulled in tight to keep it hush-hush. Unless someone was in the middle of it, like we were, they might not even know the whole thing had happened."

"The wealthy are masters at self-preservation," Carlotta said. "I'd be surprised if the police have any luck questioning the Martinique Estates residents about what might have happened. Even if anyone knows something, they're likely to remain silent just to keep property values high."

"A friend of mine told me yesterday that she once bartended a party in that neighborhood, and that by the end of the evening, everyone had traded partners and disappeared into bedrooms."

Carlotta winced. "Swinging?"

"Don't look so outraged. It happens all the time, especially in high circles where people feel entitled *and* bored."

"I know." Yet the thought of Peter and Angela indulging in something so sordid made her queasy. Maybe Peter hadn't loved Angela, but he had cared for her. And surely his own sense of integrity would have kept him from handing his wife off to another man. She rubbed her chin as another thought occurred to her. Was Peter so adamant that Angela hadn't had an affair because he didn't want his own shame to be revealed?

Her cell phone rang and she pulled it out, grateful for the distraction. The local number that came up on the screen was one she didn't recognize, but she pushed the call button. "Hello?"

"Is this Carlotta?" a woman's voice asked.

"Yes. Who is this?"

"June Moody, darlin', from the cigar shop. I thought you might want to know that one of the people who bought the cigar you asked about is sitting upstairs in my bar."

"Who?" Carlotta asked, worrying her lip.

"Dennis Lagerfeld. He's with a buddy."

Carlotta's mind raced. "I'd like to talk to him."

"Want me to stall him until you get here?"

Carlotta covered the mouthpiece and looked at Hannah. "Want to go on a field trip?"

"Hell yes."

She moved her hand. "June? I'll be right there."

29

"Try to look normal," Carlotta said on the sidewalk in front of Moody's, then took in Hannah's silver-studded black leather jumpsuit and sighed. "Scratch that."

"Don't worry," Hannah said with a flip of her striped hair. "I'll lie low."

Carlotta had her doubts but walked inside. She was surprised to find the shop crowded with men in suits and noted that it must be a popular lunchtime destination for businessmen in the area. Across the long, narrow room, June Moody caught her eye and made her way toward them.

"He's still upstairs," June said without preamble. "I gave him a nine-inch cigar on the house, so he'd have a reason to stick around."

"Thanks," Carlotta said. "I'll be discreet."

At her words, June stared at Hannah with a half smile.

"June, this is Hannah," Carlotta said. "Believe it or not, she can be discreet, too."

"It might help if you're smoking," June offered.

"I'll have the same thing I had the other night," Carlotta said. "An Amelia."

"And I'll have a Tamboril Torpedo," Hannah said.

June raised her eyebrows, apparently impressed. On the other hand, nothing Hannah did surprised Carlotta—her friend's travels and experiences would fill a book.

June left, then returned shortly with two cigars. "You can pay when you leave. You'd better get up there before he and his companion remember that there's an X-rated video store next door."

Carlotta gave her a grateful smile. "Come on," she said to Hannah.

"Okay, I love this place," Hannah said as they climbed the stairs and entered the bar area.

Most of the chairs and couches were occupied, but Carlotta's attention went immediately to the bar. Dennis Lagerfeld was impossible to miss, his big, athletic body taking up more than his share of space, his pale eyes latching on to her as soon as they walked in. She smiled a greeting, then slid onto a stool, leaving one empty between her and the businessman Dennis was talking to.

"He's still gorgeous," Hannah murmured.

Nathan was tending bar again today. "You're back," he said to Carlotta. "And I see you brought a friend. What can I get for you ladies?"

She ordered a cosmopolitan, and Hannah ordered scotch on the rocks.

"Put those on our tab," Dennis Lagerfeld said, then got up from his seat and took the empty one next to Carlotta. He was the only man in the place not wearing a suit, instead showing off his buff bod to perfection in flat-front trousers and a close-fitting knit shirt——Salvatore Ferragamo…nice. "I'm Dennis Lagerfeld," he said with a wolfish grin.

"I know who you are," she said, playing to his ego.

He grinned wider. "Then you have me at a disadvantage. What's your name?"

"Carly," she said easily. "And this is my friend Hannah."

"This is my agent, Patrick Forman," Dennis said, leaning back to allow the suited man to say hello. The guy looked a bit annoyed, as if he was accustomed to business meetings with Dennis being interrupted, but he nodded hello. The nod——and his wedding ring——were enough of an opening for Hannah, who made her way over to stand in front of him, all smiles.

"So, Patrick," she cooed, "tell me about yourself."

Carlotta almost felt sorry for the man, but focused on Dennis. "He's your agent?" She lifted her glass for a sip. "Are you still playing football?"

"Nah," Dennis said with a dismissive wave. "I retired from the rough stuff. Patrick handles all my endorsement deals and schedules my public appearances."

"Sounds exciting," Carlotta said, then picked up a cutter and snipped the end of her cigar.

"Can I light your fire?" he asked with a throaty laugh. He lifted a lighter and with a flick of his thumb, offered her a three-inch flame. Sometime between the time they'd sat down and now, he'd lost his wedding ring.

Smooth.

She smiled and moved in to light her cigar. The man's cologne was more overpowering than the smoke. She coughed lightly, then batted her eyelashes. "Thank you." She drew on the cigar, slightly dismayed at the way her body rejoiced when the first dose of nicotine hit her system.

"What do you do, Carly?"

"I work at Neiman Marcus at the Lenox Mall."

"Really? I shop there. I'm surprised I haven't seen you."

"I work in the women's department," she said. "And I see you aren't married, so I don't suppose you'd have a reason to be there."

His smile faltered a bit before he recovered. "Right."Then he whistled low under his breath. "There is nothing more sexy than a beautiful woman smoking a cigar."

She forced a little laugh. "Does that mean I could get your autograph?"

"Sure," he said, his eyes devouring her. "Is there anything special you want me to sign?"

Repressing an eye roll, she pulled her autograph book from her purse. "Here?"

He signed the book and handed it back to her. It read, To Carly—a woman who's hotter than the tip of her cigar. Dennis Lagerfeld.

She realized the man had moved closer—and that his breath smelled of brandy. "So, do you live around here?" she asked.

"In Buckhead."

"Buckhead's a big place. What neighborhood?"

"Why do you want to know?" he asked lazily. "Are you going to pay me a visit?"

Easing off lest she raise his suspicions, she took her time taking a puff and exhaling. "No, I'm just curious where celebrities live in Atlanta."

He grinned. "I live in Martinique Estates."

"That's a big neighborhood."

"Huge," he agreed.

"I know someone who lives there," she said with a little frown. "Or I should say, I *knew* someone. She died."

"Oh?"

"Angela Ashford, she was a customer of mine."

He drew back slightly and lifted his glass for a drink. "I heard about that. She drowned, didn't she?"

"That's what I was told...at first," she said, lowering her voice conspiratorially. "Then I read in the paper this morning that she might have been murdered."

His eyebrows raised, and then he smiled and shook his head. "Don't believe everything you read in the papers, sweetheart." His hand suddenly landed on her knee. "Why don't we change the subject to something more...personal?"

"Okay," she said silkily, lifting her cosmopolitan for another drink. "Do you come here often?"

"Not often enough, apparently," he said, squeezing her knee. "Maybe I would have run into you sooner."

She resisted the urge to slap his hand away and nodded at the long cigar he clamped between Erik Estrada teeth. "That's one huge cigar."

He grinned. "You ain't seen nothing yet."

Suddenly Carlotta remembered why she hated going to bars.

"I'm new to this cigar-smoking thing. Do you have a regular brand you like?"

He shrugged. "It depends. When it comes to cigars, you definitely get what you pay for."

"So you like expensive cigars?"

"Sure, because they're the best—Cohiba, Opus X, Cupido. I like to think that the pricey ones are made the legendary way—rolled between the thighs of virgins."

Carlotta squinted—was that even possible?—then laughed as if he were the most clever man in the universe. She made more small talk about cigars while their drinks were depleted. Then, not sure she was going to get anything new out of Dennis Lagerfeld, she tucked her hair behind her ear, the prearranged signal for Hannah to intervene.

"Carly," Hannah broke in, forcing Dennis to pull back, "I'm sorry, but I need to get back to work."

"If your friend wants to go on, I can give you a ride," Dennis offered.

"Dennis," his agent said, checking his watch, "if you don't mind, we really need to finish up."

Carlotta wanted to kiss Patrick Forman. "Thanks for the drinks," she said, pushing to her feet and peeling Dennis's hand from her leg at the same time. "And the autograph."

"You're so welcome," Dennis said, looking her up and down with appreciation. "Maybe I'll see you around sometime."

"Maybe," Carlotta agreed, then waved her cigar at him before turning to head back downstairs.

"Did you get anything?" Hannah asked. "I tried to listen, but couldn't hear anything other than the man purring."

"The guy's a player, but that doesn't mean he's a murderer. When I mentioned Angela Ashford, he changed the subject, but I couldn't tell if it meant anything, or if he was just trying to get into my pants."

"Maybe both."

"Did you get any info out of his agent?"

"Zippo. He's all business, seemed irritated that I existed. All I noticed was that he took care of the tab while Dennis was trying to stick his hand up your skirt." At the bottom of the stairs, Hannah looked up and stopped. "Did I mention how much I love this place?"

Carlotta glanced up and nearly stumbled to see Cooper Craft leaning on the lacquered black counter, talking to June. He wore worn, faded Levi's that hung low on his hips and a navy blue T-shirt that molded some impressive biceps. He noticed them midsentence, did a double take, then flashed a knee-weakening smile.

"Hey," he said as Carlotta wobbled closer, "fancy meeting you here."

June looked back and forth between them. "You two know each other?"

"My brother works for Coop," Carlotta said.

"Remember me?" Hannah asked Coop, her voice teenage-shrill.

"Sure—how's it going, Hannah?"

Hannah put her cigar in her mouth, sucked in deeply, then exhaled a figure-eight smoke ring. "Grrrreat," she growled.

"Uh…right," he said, then looked back to Carlotta. "I wouldn't have taken you for a cigar smoker."

She flushed sheepishly. "I don't suppose I could convince you not to mention this to my brother?"

He raised his eyebrows.

"I don't want him to know that I…smoke."

"He won't hear it from me."

She nodded her thanks, then squirmed, remembering their last conversation about crushes and her being smart. She pointed to the stack of cigar boxes on the counter. "You must have your own humidor to buy that much inventory."

"They're empty," he said, lifting a lid to show her. "June is nice enough to supply me with boxes for my hobby."

"What hobby is that?" Hannah piped up.

"Miniatures," he said with a shy smile. "I build miniature vignettes in my spare time."

"Vignettes?" Carlotta asked, suddenly feeling not so smart.

"Scenes," he explained. "I take a photograph and reproduce it in 3–D."

It sounded like an obscure, tedious hobby, but whatever floated his boat.

"I'd like to see one sometime," Hannah said, then clicked the tiny barbell in her tongue against her teeth.

Carlotta cast about for something to distract Hannah. Deciding against setting her on fire with the cigar she held, Carlotta asked Coop, "Do you live around here?"

"Not far from here—Castleberry Hill. You and Hannah should come by sometime. I'll show you my boxes."

Carlotta yanked on her friend's halter to circumvent whatever bawdy remark was about to roll out of her potty mouth.

"Ouch," Hannah yelped.

"We'll do that sometime," Carlotta promised, then looked at June. "I need to pay you for the cigars."

June rang up the sale on the cash register. "I hope you got what you needed," she said, her tone casual.

"It was useful, yes," Carlotta said. "Thank you very much."

"No problem," June said, handing over her change. "Come back and see me."

"I will," Carlotta said, surprised at the kinship she felt with this woman she'd just met. Then she turned to pry Hannah off Coop. "We need to go, Hannah," she said, concerned that Dennis Lagerfeld would come down and she'd be trapped again.

"I'll walk with you," Coop said, stacking up the boxes and thanking June. They left the shop with Hannah walking between them, chattering like a toddler.

"You know, Coop, if you ever need a hand moving bodies, just give me a call. In fact," Hannah said, whipping out an ink pen and turning over his hand, "here's my number." Then she proceeded to scrawl across his palm. "I'm as strong as a fucking ox."

"You don't say," Coop said, nodding.

Carlotta looked away to swallow a smile as they reached Hannah's van. "Bye, Hannah," she said brightly. "Call me tomorrow."

Hannah pouted, then said goodbye to Coop and climbed into her van.

"She definitely likes you," Carlotta said, her mouth twitching.

Coop laughed and looked at his graffiti'd hand. "She's hard-core."

"I'm parked over there," Carlotta said, pointing to her Monte Carlo. "But you don't have to walk with me."

He fell into step with her, though. "I actually wanted to let you know something about the Bolton woman's murder."

"Lisa Bolton?"

He nodded. "You're probably hoping the Bolton case will help to clear your—I mean, Peter Ashford in his wife's murder."

"It had crossed my mind," she admitted. "If a serial killer is on the loose, then the police will stop focusing on Peter."

Coop pressed his mouth into a flat line and studied her. "Do you know if Peter was acquainted with the Bolton woman?"

She weighed her words carefully. "They were neighbors. I assume he knew her."

"Okay, don't take this wrong, but I thought you should know...Lisa Bolton was pregnant."

The implication hit her like a punch in the stomach. Coop—and probably the police—suspected that Peter was the father... and the killer. Numb, she opened her car door and slowly lowered herself into the seat. What kind of fresh hell was this?

Coop closed her door and leaned down. "Just be careful, Carlotta. I'm not pointing fingers, but I'm not sure this Ashford guy is who you think he is." He wet his lips. "We don't know each other that well, but...I like you. I don't want to see you hurt—physically or otherwise."

She studied his sincere face, his intelligent eyes, and felt a little tug on her heart. Then as if he realized he might have confessed too much, he straightened and winked.

"Of course, maybe I'm just trying to get rid of the competition."

She laughed, happy for the break in tension, and started her car. "I'll be careful. See you around, Coop."

"I hope so," he said with a smile.

But as she watched him in her rearview mirror, she noticed that his smile faded to an expression of concern that mirrored the fearfulness building in her stomach.

Maybe Coop was right—maybe Peter wasn't the person she thought he was.

30

Wesley stood on the small wooden deck at the back of the town house, covering his cigarette and looking over his shoulder out of habit. Carlotta had already left for work, but if she knew he'd started smoking again, he'd never hear the end of it.

Although at the moment, lung cancer was the least of his concerns.

He'd arrived home late Monday night to find Carlotta sitting up for him. He'd felt helpless and ashamed when she'd told him about The Carver's thug jumping her and how that rich bastard Peter Ashford had saved the day. Then he'd gone to his room and reconsidered his plan to ask Tick for a few extra days on Father Thom's payment. When he was sure his sister was asleep, he'd snuck out, rode his motorcycle to Chance's and swallowed his pride. Chance, totally stoned and half-naked, pulled the grand Wesley needed out of his wallet and handed it over like it was nothing.

But it wasn't nothing. Chance had told him he'd be calling

today with details of a job Wesley could do in trade for the money he owed.

Wesley took a deep drag on his cigarette. He only hoped he didn't have to kill somebody. If he did, he'd have to work it in around the meeting with his probation officer today.

His cell phone rang and, as expected, Chance's number popped up. Wesley took a deep breath. Time to pay the piper. "Hello?"

"Hey, man, it's me. Ready to take on that job I told you about?"

"Yeah," Wesley said, hoping he sounded more certain than he felt. "What do I have to do?"

"It's easy, man. Just deliver a gym bag to a guy in College Park."

Alarm bells sounded in Wesley's head. College Park was one badass place. "That's all?"

"Right. I'll tell you where to meet the guy and what he looks like. He identifies himself, you give him the gym bag, and that's it. No money changes hands."

Wesley pursed his mouth—it didn't sound too bad...unless he thought about the likely contents of the gym bag. "Okay, but I have to meet with my probation officer first. I'll come by afterward. See you," Wesley said and disconnected the call before Chance could tell him something he didn't want to know.

The deck looked like hell, he thought, leaning on a loose handrail to take the last couple of puffs on his cigarette. The wood was weathered and gray, the only ornamentation was a rusted-out gas grill, minus the tank, and a few pots of long-dead flowers left over from a kick that Carlotta had gotten on last year after watching a celebrity gardening episode on HGTV. Conversely, Mrs. Winningham's deck had been converted into a gazebo, with ivy and flowers hanging freaking everywhere. The gay couple on the other side of them had enclosed their deck and turned it into a solarium sunroom.

He buried his cigarette butt in a pot of dried dirt. The Wrens were dragging down the neighborhood. Since losing the poker tournament, he'd been obsessed with the things he could've done with that twenty-five grand.

But easy come, easy go. There would be other games. He was sure a World Series of Poker bracelet was in his future.

He waited until he knew that Mrs. Winningham was parked in front of the TV watching *The Price Is Right* before walking his motorcycle out of the garage. The last thing he needed was for the old bat to mention something to Carlotta about the noise and busting him for driving. A half block down the street, he strapped on his helmet and climbed on, mentally mapping out a route to his probation officer's building that would keep him off main thoroughfares where cops might be trolling for jerks like him who were driving with a suspended license.

He made it to the building a little early and parked off the property so he could pretend he'd arrived on foot. While he sat in the waiting room for E. Jones to meet with him, the anticipation of seeing her again helped to dispel some of the dread accumulating in his stomach over the job waiting for him afterward.

"Wren," the lady at the counter called, "you're up."

E. Jones was sitting at her desk, engrossed in a file, when he opened her office door.

"Come in. Sit down," she said without looking up.

He sat, thinking how much better her red hair looked down, falling over her shoulders. She wore an aqua-colored shirt and she looked as if she'd gotten a light sunburn across her nose and cheeks since the previous week. From hiking? Biking? Sunbathing nude?

"Did you bring your paperwork?" she asked.

"Yeah." From his backpack he withdrew the employment status form that Coop had signed, plus the stub from his paycheck that he'd pissed away, and the payment schedule that he'd worked out with the court cashier.

E. Jones looked over the paperwork and nodded. "Good." Then she walked to the copy machine in the corner, giving him a glimpse of the contours of her rear end and thighs in a snug skirt—that fell just below her knees, dammit. Weren't short skirts back in style?

"How's your job going?" she asked.

He stabbed at his glasses. "Great."

She walked back to the desk and handed him his original paperwork. "Good, because I've spoken to the IT director who deals with the city computer systems, and it's going to be a few weeks before he can meet with you and assess your, um, strengths. Then you can start your community service."

He suspected they were still trying to figure out how much damage he'd done during his cyber break-in. "Okay."

"In the meantime, keep working, make your payments to the court and stay out of trouble."

"Okay."

She sat back in her chair. "How's your home life?"

He shrugged. "What do you mean?"

"I understand that you live with your sister."

"That's right."

"Is everything okay?"

"Sure, other than my sister busting my chops when I mess up."

She smiled faintly, then sat forward, giving him a glimpse of cleavage in the vee of her prim button-up shirt. "I talked to the D.A. about your case. He told me about your father."

He shifted in his seat. "What he probably didn't tell you is that my father is innocent."

Her fine eyebrows arched. "Are you in contact with your father?"

"No."

"You have no idea where your parents are?"

He gave a dry laugh. "Are you working for the D.A. now?"

"I work for the court system."

"What do all these questions have to do with me?"

"I just want to make sure you're okay. Did you know that you have access to counselors while you're on probation?"

He scoffed. "You want me to see a shrink?"

"I'm only letting you know it's available if you need to talk to someone." She gave him a tentative smile. "And I'm no doctor, but I'm a pretty decent listener."

His mind rewound through the countless school counselors, nurses and teachers over the years who had told him that he'd feel so much better if only he would talk about his parents leaving. But behind the concerned expressions he'd always detected a gossipy gleam in their eye that made him think they were more interested in the details of his father's criminal behavior than in helping him deal with the sudden loss of his parents. Besides, at the time, he'd been convinced that his parents would return any day, so why bother?

He studied the woman sitting in front of him, searching her green eyes for hints of ulterior motives. She looked sincere enough, and God, it was tempting to share with her some of the things he'd been through, if for no other reason than to be in the same room with her. But he had to remind himself that anything he said would likely be reported back to the D.A., and he simply couldn't risk a verbal slip that might make things worse for his dad.

"I'll keep that in mind," he said, then gripped the arms of his chair. "Are we finished?"

She nodded, but just before he left, she said, "Wesley...I really do want to see you do well. But for me to help you, you're going to have to trust me."

He hesitated, a little shaken by her intensity. She'd pity him if she knew how much he wanted to believe her. He conjured up a cocky grin and waved. "See you next week, E."

He drove to Chance's condo building by way of back roads, with his probation officer's words about staying out of trouble reverberating through his head. He had a couple of good things going that he didn't want to mess up: his job, and his impending access to the city's court records as soon as his community service got under way. And then there was the going-to-jail part of having his probation revoked—that would truly suck.

When he got to Chance's tenth-floor midtown condo and knocked on the door, his buddy answered, holding binoculars and flush with excitement. "You got to see this, man—a chick in the tower across from me is walking around her place buck-ass naked."

Wesley stepped into the poshly decorated three-bedroom condo. Nickelback blared from the top-of-the-line Bose stereo system. "I think I'll pass, man. I need to get going."

Chance frowned. "Dude, if I didn't know better, I'd think you were a fag."

Frustration billowed in his chest. He was about to put his freedom on the line, and all his friend could think about was T and A. "Come on, man, I just want to get this over with."

Chance sighed and set down his binoculars, then disappeared into his bedroom.

Wesley stepped to the door of one of the spare bedrooms, wincing at the sight of the disheveled, smelly bed and the debris of a partying binge. But he was gratified to see that all his good computer equipment was intact on the bookshelves. He stepped back out just as Chance emerged carrying a generic black gym bag. He handed it to Wesley, who tried not to notice that the bag weighed about ten pounds and appeared to be about half full.

"The guy's name is Hobbs," Chance said. "He'll meet you in front of the gas station at the corner of Smart and Livingston. Know where that is?"

"I'll find it. How will I know this Hobbs?"

"He's a short, stocky white dude. He'll be wearing a green ball cap."

"And all I do is hand him the gym bag?"

"That's all. Call me when you've made the drop."

The lingo didn't exactly ease his fears, but then again, if what Chance was doing was legit, he'd be making "the drop" himself. "What happens if he's not there?"

"Don't worry, he'll be there."

"Okay, I'll call you."

But Chance was already heading back to his balcony with the binoculars. Wesley shook his head and let himself out.

The gym bag felt bulky and conspicuous in his hand, and he worried that everyone he met on the elevator and in the parking garage knew that he was doing something he shouldn't be doing.

He wondered what was in the bag—drugs, for sure, but what kind? Pot? Coke? Crack? OxyContin? Ice? And although Chance drew the line at using heroin, that didn't mean he wouldn't broker it.

By the time Wesley reached his motorcycle, his palms and back were sweaty. His hands shook as he strapped the bag onto his bike. And he was so paranoid that at one point on the back-roads drive to College Park, he even thought someone was following him.

At the corner of Smart and Livingston, he slowed to cruising speed but didn't see his green-capped connection. He went down to the next block, turned around and stopped long enough to unstrap the bag so he could simply drive up, hand it off and drive away. Gone in fifteen seconds.

He pulled away from the curb for another pass. Up ahead he saw a guy with a green cap emerge from the gas station. With his heart thudding in his chest, he geared down and flipped on his signal to turn left across the trickle of traffic.

Preparing to turn as soon as a red Volkswagen Passat passed by, he frowned in confusion when the VW stopped next to him. The driver's-side window zipped down to reveal E. Jones's face, and he was so startled, he killed the bike's engine. Frantically, he tried to restart it.

"*Don't* drive away, Wesley," she shouted as his engine roared to life, "or I'll call the police."

He cursed inwardly and threw up the hand not holding the gym bag. "Okay, I'm cool."

She put her car in Park, then turned on her hazard lights. "Driving with a suspended license alone is enough for me to have your probation revoked, but what the hell is in the bag?"

He swallowed hard. "What bag?"

"The bag you're holding in your other hand," she said, pointing. "I followed you to the condo building in midtown, and saw you come out carrying it."

"You followed me?" he asked incredulously.

"I'm allowed to do that. I only expected to bust you for driving your motorcycle on a suspended license—by the way, the helmet hair you had when you came into my office gave you away." Then she leveled a stone-cold stare at him. "But when I saw the gym bag and followed you here, I realized that I underestimated just how stupid nineteen-year-olds can be."

"I don't know what's in it," he said in his defense.

"Oh, I suspect you know." She nodded to the green-capped guy on the corner, who now seemed to stand out like a siren. "And I suspect that he knows."

Wesley averted his gaze and wildly considered driving off

and ditching the bag. Even if his probation was revoked, going to jail for computer hacking was better than going to jail for drug possession.

"Don't do it, Wesley," she said as though sensing his thoughts. "Drive away and life as you know it is over. Or you can give the bag to me." She put her arm out the window and wiggled her fingers.

Sweat dripped down his back. Christ, he'd done it now. Go to jail and leave Carlotta alone to clean up his mess. Or trust his green-eyed probation officer, a woman he barely knew, who probably could advance her career by delivering the gym bag straight to the D.A. He goosed the engine.

"Wesley," she said, "make one good decision today."

He wanted to, dammit. He just wasn't sure which decision was the good one.

31

Carlotta sighed. Wednesdays were typically slow unless a sale or a holiday drove customers in. So much for making headway on her sales numbers.

There was another reason to dread slow foot traffic. When unoccupied, her mind snapped back to the Ashford and Bolton murders. She kept imagining both women as they were only days ago—living, breathing, going about their daily lives...shopping.

They'd both died in their designer clothes, Angela in those decadent black boots, and Lisa Bolton in exquisite lingerie.

Carlotta straightened and, on a hunch, walked to the lingerie department and began fingering through the racks and shelves. Ten minutes into her search she found the lightweight corset that she'd recognized on the dead woman. French, expensive and—yes, there was a God—exclusive to Neiman's.

She used a counter phone to call a friend of hers in inventory. "Jeanine, hi, it's Carlotta. I need a favor."

"You got a body you need to move?"

"What?" Carlotta choked out.

Jeanine laughed. "Good grief, it's a joke. What's with you?"

"Oh." Carlotta forced a laugh. "Good one."

"What do you need?"

Carlotta recovered—she was losing her mind. "A good customer wants to buy a piece of expensive lingerie that his wife admired, but wants to make sure she hasn't already bought it. He's not sure—you know how men are. Is it possible to look up an item number for our location, then track the purchase of each item back to a name on a credit card? I'd doubt if we carried more than a dozen of this particular item."

"It's possible," Jeanine said, "but it'll be a few hours before I can run a report. And if she paid with cash, you're out of luck."

"I understand." She gave Jeanine the item number and her cell-phone number. "Call me when you have the results?"

"Will do."

"I owe you one."

"You owe me about fourteen. When are you going to pay up?"

Carlotta bit into her lip. "How do you feel about skin care?"

"Huh?"

"I have cleansers, scrubs, peels, all of it pharmaceutical grade. Name your poison."

"Hmm—got any glycolic acid gel?"

"Twenty percent solution."

"You've got yourself a deal. I'll call you back."

Carlotta returned the receiver and walked back toward her section, wondering how angry Detective Terry would be if he knew she was still asking questions.

And that after tearing apart her bedroom and car she still hadn't found that damn cigar.

"Carlotta to the men's department," a woman's musical voice sang over the P.A. system.

Carlotta looked toward the ceiling, frowning at the hidden speakers. Pages were made only as a last resort—someone had obviously been by her station and couldn't find her. She hurried downstairs, perplexed. But when she walked into menswear and saw Dennis Lagerfeld lounging against a counter as if he owned it (and he probably could), she realized that she'd been "summoned."

"Carly," a menswear associate said, shooting arrows her way, "Mr. Lagerfeld asked that you assist him today."

"I'd be happy to," she said, trying to tamp down the nervousness that threatened to paralyze her. The fact that he'd come looking for her told her a lot about the man: He was predatory, accustomed to going after and getting what he wanted. She conjured up a smile. "Hello, Mr. Lagerfeld."

He splayed his large hands and she noticed that he wasn't wearing his wedding ring again. "Please, call me Dennis."

She nodded. "Dennis."

The other associate slipped away, leaving them alone.

Still leaning, he perused her skirt suit—yellow-and-gray-striped, with a lime-green T-shirt underneath, and gray T-strap high heels. It was, she relented, a great ensemble, but the man looked at her with those languid, pale eyes of his in a way that made her feel as if she needn't have bothered getting dressed.

"You're looking lovely today," he oozed.

"Thank you. You look nice, too."

He brushed a hand over the fine knit of his long-sleeve black shirt. In fact, he was dressed all in black, with every garment fitting his big, athletic body like a glove. She couldn't help but wonder if his leaning pose had been practiced in order to show off his long, muscular figure to best advantage.

"I have a guest appearance later today," he said. Gesturing vaguely to the racks of clothing around them, he said, "Meeting you yesterday reminded me that I needed some things."

"Suits? Sportswear? Shoes?"

"Yes," he said with a moneyed smiled.

Her return smile was genuine—a potential murderer's money was as good as anyone else's. Maybe she could repair her sales record while plying him for more information. "Then let's get started, shall we?"

She gave him a guided tour through every section of the men's department, making suggestions along the way, although she soon realized that Dennis Lagerfeld had developed an eye for what types of clothing complemented his large physique. She could see how a woman could get caught up in his aura, she decided. Just watching the man move was a treat—his physicality suggested he'd probably be a great lover. Plus, he was undeniably handsome...and rich.

And married, she reminded herself. And on the prowl.

And quite possibly, a dangerous man.

He shopped for shoes first, flirting with her while he walked around picking up exquisitely made styles. "I wear a size fifteen," he announced, "but I like a tight fit."

She squirmed, unable to stop from visualizing the exact image that he'd intended. "I'm sure we can accommodate you," she murmured, wondering what it would be like to be the mistress of someone like Dennis Lagerfeld. He seemed like someone who enjoyed the chase but would probably tire of the conquest.

A chill settled over her when she returned with a selection of size fifteens and knelt before him. Was he pursuing her because he'd recently rid himself of a mistress and was in search of a new one?

His cell phone rang and he answered while working his foot into a black ostrich-skin lace-up dress shoe. "Yeah, Patrick, what's up?"

Carlotta tied the shoe slowly, shifting when she realized that Lagerfeld was trying to look up her skirt. What a cad.

"I don't want to deal with this right now," Dennis said into the phone, his voice agitated. "Just make it go away, Patrick. That's why I pay you the big bucks." He snapped the phone closed.

"Trouble?" she asked lightly.

"Comes with the territory," he said. "There's always someone plotting to sabotage me or trying to get to my money—fans, competitors, strangers…even friends. It gets to the point that I don't know who I can trust."

"Sounds lonely," she observed.

"It is," he said, then leaned forward and gazed into her eyes with a pained expression so convincing she could see how a woman might fall under his spell. "More lonely than you could possibly imagine."

She smiled nervously, then stood and looked down at the two-thousand-dollar pair of shoes. "What do you think?"

He didn't even look down. "I think I'll wear them. You're a great salesperson."

She laughed, going along with his flattery. "Then let me sell you something else."

She led him into the suits section, accumulating armfuls of things he liked, eventually stopping next to a rack of cashmere jackets with a crest embroidered on the lapels—the same brand that Angela had purchased. She hung back, watching his reaction. He fingered the same jacket that Angela had purchased, even removed it from the rack, then frowned thoughtfully. Carlotta held her breath. Did he recognize the jacket?

"Nice jacket," she murmured. "Would you like to try it on?"

He glanced up, then grinned. "Only if you'll help me get undressed."

She blushed and delicately picked a hair off his sleeve. She was getting pretty good at DNA collection on the sly. "You're going to get me into trouble."

"Trouble excites me," he said with a low laugh. Then he donned one of those interested-in-an-offhand-way expressions. "Say...do you ever take back clothes that have been worn?"

Her mind flashed back to the days when she'd returned worn clothes herself. She made a rueful noise. "Not unless there's a defect...although funny you should ask. A woman just returned that same jacket a few days ago, you know, the customer of mine who drowned." She frowned. "It was very strange. She caused a bit of a scene, so we took it back—not that it mattered in the end."

His eyebrows rose almost imperceptibly. "I'm curious. What happens to clothing that's been returned?"

The back of her neck prickled. Resisting the urge to run, she said, "In this case, I put it with our other returns. It was too... soiled...to be put back on the floor. Eventually it'll be sent back to the manufacturer, I suppose."

"Ah." He leaned down and wet his curvy lips in slow motion. "What time do you get off work?"

"S-six."

"Let's go somewhere," he said. It wasn't a question but a foregone conclusion in his mind.

"I can't," she said. "I...already have a date." He didn't have to know it was with her brother and a plate of lamb chops.

Dennis pouted. "I promise I'll show you a better time than he can."

"Maybe some other time," she said and conjured up a hopeful smile.

He continued to flirt while he tried on the clothes and then she rang up his sale. When she told him the total, he shook his head and handed over his credit card. "This is the most money I've ever spent just trying to get someone to go out with me."

"Really? I pictured you as a generous guy—lingerie, perfume, the whole bit."

He grinned. "Well, I admit, I do have a weakness for a beautiful woman wearing beautiful lingerie. I've purchased quite a lot of lingerie here, in fact."

Her pulse picked up, but she played the demure flirt as she handed back his card. "Well, I'm not so sure I want to be part of a harem. You probably have ladies falling all over you. I bet you don't even have to look farther than your own neighborhood to find a willing woman."

In the span of two seconds, his expression morphed from playful to panicked. He jammed his credit card back into his wallet. "It's not like that."

"Come on," she said, baiting him. "A celebrity like you—you're probably fueling the fantasy of every housewife in your zip code." She gave him a sexy wink. "Women talk, you know."

His swarthy coloring faded to a sickly green-gray. "You don't say." He glanced at his watch. "I didn't realize it was getting so late. I need to go or I'm going to miss my speaking engagement."

She handed his bags over the counter. "Thank you for shopping with us. See you around?"

"Yeah," he muttered, then picked up his shopping bags and strode away.

Carlotta crossed her arms and watched him walk away, wondering if Detective Terry had questioned Dennis Lagerfeld, if he'd given any credence to her information that a man who smoked the same cigar that she'd found in the pocket of the returned jacket just happened to live in the same neighborhood where both women had been murdered. And who seemed inordinately interested in what had happened to a jacket that had been returned.

She held up the Baggie with the hair she'd plucked from Lagerfeld's sleeve. The detective would probably be furious with her if he knew she was still poking around, but she'd resigned herself to the fact that the man was in a perpetual bad mood where she was concerned.

As she walked back to her department, her cell phone rang—
it was Jeanine.

"Got those names for you," she said.

"Go ahead," Carlotta said, certain now that Dennis Lagerfeld's
name was on the list and that she had cracked the case.

"Six garments sold, two of them cash sales. The credit card
sales were in the names of Rebecca Bright…Regina Lon-
don…Robert Kenny…and Peter Ashford."

Carlotta froze, her vital signs going haywire. *Peter?*

"Are you there?" Jeanine asked. "Does this answer your
question?"

"Yes," Carlotta managed on an exhale. "Thanks, Jeanine."

"When will I get my gel?"

"It's in the mail," Carlotta murmured, then disconnected the
call, feeling as if she were moving in slow motion. Peter had
bought the lingerie that Lisa Bolton had been wearing when she
died? She recalled something that Angela had said on her last
shopping spree when she had bought some lacy underthings.
Peter likes me in black.

Perhaps he liked *all* of his women in black.

She covered her mouth, afraid she might be sick. Had Peter
been having an affair with Lisa Bolton? Had he gotten her pregnant? Had Angela found out? And had both women died at his
hands? Had he always possessed the capacity for violence and
she hadn't seen it, or had he changed after they'd parted? Feeling light-headed, she considered crawling behind the counter
and curling up in a ball. But no, she could—and would—collapse later. Right now she had to make a phone call.

She picked up the counter phone, dialed the police station and asked to speak to Detective Terry. After a few minutes, his voice came on the line.

"Terry here."

"Detective…it's Carlotta Wren."

"Yeah. What's up?" She could hear him shuffling papers in the background.

"I need to talk to you."

"So talk."

"Not now—I'm at work. But I get off in an hour. Can I meet you somewhere?"

"I'm leaving soon, too, and I need to make a few stops. How about I meet you at your place?"

"My brother will be there."

"Even better. I'd like to talk to him as well."

Why did she have the feeling that he had more questions about her parents? She sighed and massaged her temples. "Okay, I'll see you there."

Somehow she made it through the next hour without flying apart. But by the time she got to her car, her feet and her heart were dragging. She was terrified that Peter might be waiting for her again, but thankfully he was nowhere in sight. Still, when she climbed into the car, she locked the doors.

Gripping the steering wheel kept her hands from shaking, but the day's events were beginning to take their toll on her. She backed out of the space jerkily and made a wrong turn before exiting the garage into traffic. She settled in for a stressful commute home, her brain running a constant loop of images of

Peter, past and present. No matter how hard she tried, she simply couldn't reconcile the man she'd fallen in love with all those years ago to the man whose ties to the dead women could no longer be ignored.

About a mile from the town house, she was jarred from her fog by a set of headlights behind her that seemed to be approaching at high speed. She tapped her brake a few times, hoping her flashing lights would signal the driver to slow down, but the car kept coming. She gasped and gripped the steering wheel hard as the car whipped around her just before impact, then veered right to sideswipe her car. Sparks flew as metal ground against metal. Carlotta screamed, pumping the brake and struggling for control as the dark car tried to force her onto the shoulder.

An air horn blasted. She jerked her head up to see a large delivery truck barreling toward them.

Impending crash—minus ten points.

32

Carlotta screamed at the sight of the oncoming truck. She slammed on her brakes just as the other car pulled away and slid in front of her, narrowly missing the blaring truck. Her seat belt pulled her up short of bouncing against the steering wheel. Other car horns sounded behind her and cars screeched to a halt to prevent a pileup.

She gasped for breath, her mind numb as she tried to assimilate what had just happened. When she realized that she wasn't bleeding and how close she was to the town house, she straightened the car and pulled away slowly, her arms trembling with the force of clinging to the steering wheel.

Someone had nearly run her off the road. Accident, or premeditated?

Her vital signs had yet to return to normal when she pulled into the driveway leading to the garage. As the garage door went up, she saw Detective Terry emerge from his car across the street.

God help her, but she was glad to see him.

She climbed out of her car on unsteady legs to survey the damage to the car under the overhead garage light. Long, horizontal scratches marred the dark blue paint job, and the rear fender was badly dented. She tried to recall the amount of her deductible on her car insurance. Five hundred? A thousand? Christ, would she ever be out of debt?

"Gee, what does the other car look like?" the detective asked wryly as he walked up.

She frowned at him. "I wish I knew—the driver almost killed me."

He sobered. "What happened?"

"Someone tried to run me off the road about a mile from here."

"Are you sure?"

She crossed her arms. "Does it look like I imagined it?"

He pulled out his notebook. "Describe the other car."

She sighed and touched her forehead. "I don't know. It all happened so fast. Dark, maybe."

"Dark? I'm going to need more than that to go on." He bent and ran his hand over the scratches. "Looks like green paint. Was it a car, an SUV, a truck?"

"A car."

"Two-door or four-door?"

"I don't know."

"Did you see the license plate?"

"No."

"Not even the color of the plate, maybe the state?"

She shook her head. "Sorry."

"Did you see the driver?"

She squinted, trying to remember. "There was only one person in the car, a man."

"Did you see his face?"

"No. He was wearing a hat...maybe."

His mouth flattened. "Tell me what happened."

Carlotta explained as best she could, but realized that little about her story seemed concrete, except the scratches. "But it felt...deliberate."

"Do you remember doing anything that might have triggered another driver's anger—cutting someone off, for example?"

"No. If I did, I wasn't aware of it."

He put away his notebook. "I'll file a report before I leave."

She put a hand to her temple. "Let's go inside. Wesley should be home."

But he wasn't. She'd expected to be met with the savory aroma of lamb chops, not the scent of maple syrup, because she'd left out the container this morning. In a flash, she recalled that the spot behind her Miata had been empty—Wesley's motorcycle was gone. *Christ, what now?*

"Is something wrong?" the detective asked.

She closed her eyes briefly. If she told him that Wesley was driving on a suspended license, the man would likely arrest him as soon as he arrived home. "Wesley must have been called out on a job." She turned on lights as they walked into the living room, then gestured to the couch. "Would you like to sit down?"

"Okay," he said, then settled where only a couple of nights ago she had been prepared to make love with Peter.

She averted her gaze and sat in the chair adjacent to the couch.

"What did you want to talk about?" the detective asked. "I assume this has something to do with the Angela Ashford case."

She nodded, then took a couple of deep breaths for strength. "I've...been asking some questions."

His eyebrows went up. "Surprise, surprise."

She glared at him. "Do you want to know what I found out or not? Because I'd just as soon skip this little conference and go to bed."

When the whisper of a smile lifted his mouth, she realized her gaffe. "I meant alone...of course."

"Of course," he said. "Yes, Ms. Wren, please, *please* tell me what information you found."

Ignoring his sarcasm, she told him about initiating a conversation with Dennis Lagerfeld at the cigar bar, and that the man had come by the store that afternoon. "He picked up the same jacket that Angela had purchased, then asked what happened to clothing that got returned."

"That's not exactly conclusive evidence," he said.

"But this might be," she said, holding up a little plastic sandwich bag.

He squinted. "What is it?"

She smiled triumphantly. "A hair from Dennis Lagerfeld's sleeve. I thought you could match it to any hairs you might have found on the jacket that Angela returned."

He looked incredulous. "Are you kidding me?"

"No, I thought you'd be grateful!"

He lifted his hand. "Okay, okay, I'll take it." He held up the bag, studied the single dark hair inside and wrote something on the plastic Baggie.

"Lagerfeld asked me what time I got off work. He could've had someone run me off the road."

The detective sighed impatiently. "Did he happen to ask you out?"

"Yes."

"No offense, but I suspect he was more interested in doing you than doing you in." He gave her a flat smile. "Anything else, Sherlock?"

She frowned and told him about the consultation appointment with Dr. Suarez and her conversation with him. "He said I had a *lovely* neck."

The detective stared. "That's all? You want me to target this guy because he's got a thing for your neck?"

"Don't you see? A man who strangles people would notice someone's neck!" She pulled another Baggie out of her purse. "Here."

He rolled his eyes heavenward. "Another hair?"

"Chewing gum. I saw the doctor take it out of his mouth myself."

He snatched the Baggie from her hand. "You are unbelievable."

"Why are you so hostile? I know that Angela was a patient of Dr. Suarez, and get this—I saw a picture of Lisa Bolton in the before-and-after pictures on his computer screen."

His eyebrows went up. "I didn't realize you knew the woman well enough to recognize her."

She swallowed hard. "I...remembered something."

"Oh?"

"I saw the Bolton woman before."

"Where would that be?"

"At the party...where I ran into Peter...a couple of weeks ago."

His expression hardened. "And you're just now remembering this?"

She held her breath and nodded.

"Thanks for the information," he said calmly. "And from now on, Ms. Wren, rather than putting yourself in potentially dangerous situations, why don't you let me do my job?"

She bristled. "So you've questioned Dennis Lagerfeld and Dr. Suarez?"

"I can't pin down Lagerfeld. I'm at a disadvantage because the man doesn't want to sleep with me," he said dryly. "But I interviewed Suarez over the phone yesterday. He couldn't seem to recall who Angela Ashford was. And honestly, the guy just doesn't fit the profile."

"What profile?"

"Most women are murdered by someone they know, usually a spouse or someone they're romantically involved with. Dr. Suarez swore that wasn't the case with Angela Ashford. He even offered to take a polygraph test. His strange behavior was probably a result of you asking questions after I did." He frowned harder. "Which is why you need to stick to selling overpriced clothes and leave the police work to me."

Anger spiked in her chest, and she briefly considered throwing him out then and there. Ungrateful brute. But Angela and

Lisa deserved justice, no matter what it cost her. "There's one more thing. It has to do with Peter."

Now he seemed interested.

In a halting voice, she told him about the piece of lingerie linking back to Peter's credit card.

He leaned forward. "Are you sure it was the same lingerie?"

She pulled out a piece of paper. "I'm almost positive, but here's the information on the garment we carry to compare to what Lisa Bolton was wearing."

"Thanks," he said awkwardly.

Carlotta moistened her lips. "I understand that the Bolton woman was pregnant?"

He looked surprised, then nodded. "DNA was taken from the fetus to help determine who the father is." He angled his head at her. "I don't suppose you have any DNA from your boyfriend you could share?"

She shook her head, thinking that Monday night she had come close to letting him deposit a sample.

"I questioned Ashford about the Bolton murder," he continued. "He said he barely knew the woman, but he seemed mighty reluctant to talk about his whereabouts Monday evening."

Carlotta stood abruptly. "I'd appreciate it if you'd take that accident report now."

He hesitated, then pushed to his feet. "Ms. Wren, I can't figure you out. I go back and forth between thinking that you believe Peter Ashford is innocent, to thinking that you could have committed this murder yourself and are sending me on a wild-goose chase with these so-called clues that you've conveniently uncovered." His eyes narrowed. "It even occurred to me that you might be so bitter over Peter Ashford ending your engagement all those years ago that you could be setting him up. Get rid of the wife and him, all in one blow."

She scoffed. "That's utterly ridiculous. And why would I kill Lisa Bolton?"

"Maybe because she was Ashford's girlfriend." He shrugged. "Or maybe the murders aren't even connected. Besides, who knows why people do what they do?"

She set her jaw. "My only goal is to help you get to the truth, Detective. Now—my accident report?"

He studied her for a moment, then said, "I'll need your license and registration."

She leaned over to pull her wallet from her purse and a card floated to their feet. When she realized it was the postcard from her parents that she'd been carrying around, she practically pounced on it. Unfortunately, his hand was there first.

She straightened slowly, her heart galloping in her chest as he held up the card, studying it.

"Well, well. A postcard from your long-lost folks. Interesting. Recent postmark, too."

Carlotta shrank under his scathing glare. "Wh-what happens now?"

"I haven't decided yet," he said, his voice dripping with sarcasm. "I'm still all choked up about your speech on how your only goal is to help me get to the truth."

Carlotta closed her eyes, wondering if handcuffs were in this season.

33

Wesley took a deep breath and banged on the door to Chance's condo, pulling at his sweat-soaked shirt. Man, what a day.

Chance flung open the door, his round face beet-red. "Where the fuck have you been? I've been going nuts wondering if you got your skinny ass killed or something. Hobbs said you didn't show."

"Sorry, dude, something came up, and my cell phone died." Cut off, actually, because he hadn't paid his bill.

"Where the hell is the stash?"

Wesley lifted the bag and thrust it into Chance's hands. "Untouched."

"What the fuck happened?"

Wesley dragged his hand across his forehead. "My probation officer happened. She followed me to the drop."

"Your probation officer is a chick? And she followed you? Ain't that illegal or something?"

Wesley stared at Chance, incredulous. "Dude, what *we* were doing was illegal."

"No money changed hands."

Wesley looked up and down the hallway to make sure no one was in earshot, then leaned in. "*Possession* is a crime, dude. I could've gone to prison!"

"Still, her following you don't seem right. What did she do?"

"She drove up in her car and told me she'd revoke my probation unless I gave her the bag."

Chance's eyes rounded. "So you just *gave* it to her?"

"Yeah." Wesley squirmed. "And then she…gave it back. Said she wouldn't look inside or report it if I brought it back to you."

"She knows where you got it?"

"She only knows the building. I didn't mention your name."

Chance frowned. "It's a good goddamn thing."

Wesley lifted his hands. "I'm sorry. I know you were counting on me, dude." He waited for a beat, holding his breath. Chance and his moods could be unpredictable.

Chance sighed, then slapped Wesley on the shoulder. "It's okay, not your fault."

Wesley let the air out of his lungs. "I feel bad owing you so much money."

His buddy chewed on his lip, then snapped his fingers. "Take my statistics exam in the morning, and I'll knock off five hundred."

Wesley weighed his options. "Okay. Tell me when and where."

Chance pulled a business card out of his shirt pocket and scribbled the info.

"Nobody will question that I'm you?"

"Are you kidding? I'm never in that class—it's at fucking eight o'clock in the morning. I need a B on the exam. I know you could ace it, but if I get an A, someone will start asking questions, got it?"

"Got it."

"You need a textbook or something?"

"No, I'm cool," Wesley said.

Chance shook his head. "Man, if you're so damn smart, why are you hanging around with me?"

Wesley frowned and jerked his thumb toward the stairwell. "Gotta go, man. She's waiting for me."

"Is she hot?"

Wesley hesitated, thinking of E.'s long, willowy shape and her take-no-prisoners attitude. "Yeah."

Chance chortled. "Enjoy."

E. Jones was waiting patiently in her car when Wesley got back to his motorcycle. "Any problems?" she asked.

He shook his head, afraid to say anything, still sure that this was some kind of setup, that a cop was waiting for him around the corner.

"Good," she said. "I'll follow you home."

Wesley climbed on his bike with acid churning in his stomach. Carlotta would be home by now and mad as hell that he was out on his motorcycle. If he arrived home escorted by his probation officer, she'd want an explanation, and E. Jones was likely to give it to her. He didn't want Carlotta to think he was messed up in drugs, and besides, she'd be happy to name Chance as the source of the transaction. He drove carefully on the way home, conscious of the woman in the red car behind him. At the town house, he eased into the driveway and waited for her to pull up beside him.

She zoomed down the passenger-side window. "Is this it?"

He nodded.

"Okay, I'll see you Wednesday."

Her nonchalance caught him by surprise. The window was halfway up when he said, "Hey, E., why didn't you look in the bag?"

She leaned down until she could see him. "Because if I'd seen the contents, I would've had to report it."

"So why did you ask me to give it to you?"

She gave him a little smile. "To see if you would trust me. See you later."

He nodded and watched her drive away, dazed and a little confused. She could've had his ass thrown in jail and been rid of him, not to mention scored points with the D.A.

He would never understand women in a thousand years.

Wesley pushed his motorcycle into the garage, frowning when he saw the damage to the Monte Carlo's bumper and side. Had Carlotta been in an accident? He jogged to the house in the waning daylight, breathing easier when he saw lights and heard movement in the kitchen. Carlotta stood at the stove wearing her fuzzy yellow bathrobe, stirring a pot. A box of macaroni and cheese stood open on the counter. She had to have heard him, but she didn't turn around.

"Hey," he ventured.

"Hey," she said, her voice low and tired.

"I saw your car. What happened?"

"Some jerk sideswiped me on the way home this evening."

His heart jumped in his chest. "Are you okay?"

"Yeah, I'm fine."

"What kind of car was it? Did you see the other person?"

She sighed. "I already gave my statement to the police. I don't know who it was." Then she turned. "Why? Do you know something that I don't know?"

He shook his head, but they were both probably thinking the same thing—it could have been one of his creditors leaving a message.

"Don't worry about it," she said. "It was probably a run-of-the-mill asshole Atlanta driver." She put a lid on the pot, then crossed her arms. "I was looking forward to those lamb chops."

"Sorry," he said. "I'll make them tomorrow."

"Where have you been and why are you driving? You know you're not supposed to."

"I know. But I had to meet with my probation officer today and run some other errands. I swear it won't happen again."

She leveled her gaze on him. "I'm going to have that engraved on your tombstone."

His throat convulsed, glad that she didn't know just how close he'd come to disaster today.

"Want some macaroni and cheese?" she asked.

He relaxed, relieved that she had let the matter go. "Sure. I'll make us a salad." He walked to the refrigerator and began removing ingredients. "And you know, you can dress up the boxed mac and cheese by adding real cheddar cheese, sour cream, brown mustard and a dash of Worcestershire sauce."

She sat at the table, happy to let him take over the meal, and he was happy to do it. "Is that why yours always tastes better?"

"Yup."

But as the small talk continued, Wesley had a feeling from the pinched look around Carlotta's dark eyes that she was getting ready to drop a bombshell.

He was right. After her first bite of salad, she announced, "I found the postcard from Mom and Dad that you were hiding."

The tennis-ball can in the garage—he'd tipped his hand to that particular hiding place when she'd visited him in jail. "I didn't think you'd want to know," he said carefully.

"Detective Terry has it now."

Anger sparked in his stomach. "You gave it to him? Why?"

"I didn't mean to. It fell out of my purse while he was here."

"What was he doing at the house?"

She sighed. "I had some information regarding the deaths of Angela Ashford and Lisa Bolton. Unfortunately, I may have also implicated myself."

He gaped. "How? Because you have history with that Ashford jerk?"

"Yes. And as you'll recall, that 'Ashford jerk' saved me from one of your thugs the other night, plus used his own money to get you off the hook."

Wesley looked down at his plate. "I know, but Jesus, sis, he's dragging you into a *murder* investigation."

"I'll be okay," she insisted. "They're only leaning on me to put pressure on Peter."

"Are you still in love with this guy, after all he did to you?"

She took her time answering. "Wesley, our breakup wasn't entirely Peter's fault. He was young, and he wasn't ready to deal with everything that Mom and Dad heaped onto me when they left."

"Meaning me," he said.

She wiped her mouth with her napkin. "That was part of it. But it was mostly the scandal that Dad created. Peter's family didn't want him to be associated with the headlines...and I don't blame them. Did you know that Peter is working for the firm where Dad used to be a partner?"

"No."

"That would never have happened if he'd married me. Breaking our engagement was the smart thing for him to do."

"If you ask me, it was the easy thing for him to do. He left you high and dry."

"No," she said through clenched teeth, "Mom and Dad left me high and dry. And you too."

He sighed—they could talk in circles all evening. "You still didn't answer my question—are you in love with him?"

"I don't know," she said, toying with her food. "The whole situation is so confusing."

"Do you think he killed his wife or that other woman?"

"No. The man I know couldn't have done it."

"But people change."

She nodded and went back to eating.

"Do you ever think about what your life would have been like if you'd married Peter?"

She shrugged. "Sometimes. I guess I got a glimpse the other night when we were at their house. A mansion, a pool." She gestured to the dated, cramped kitchen and laughed. "Compared to this, that life seems pretty glamorous."

"And dangerous," he added quietly.

Carlotta squirmed in her seat. "So—the postcard. Is it the only contact you've had with Mom and Dad?"

"Yeah. I'm sorry I kept it from you, but I was afraid you'd destroy it."

"Fair enough. But from now on, I want to know, okay?"

"Okay."

"Are you on call this evening?"

He lifted his eyebrows at the note of interest in her voice. "Yeah. And I have to be somewhere at eight o'clock in the morning, so I'll be leaving early."

She gave him a stern look. "As long as you don't drive your motorcycle."

"I won't."

He resumed eating, casting worried glances at Carlotta when she wasn't looking. In love with a murderer and possibly implicated in his crimes.

Between the two of them, man, they had trouble to spare.

34

Carlotta knew it was a dream, but she willed it to go on. He stroked her skin exposed by the pale blue see-through chemise, caressing her foot, ankle, knee. But his touch was unexpectedly cool, and she shrank from it, confused. Was it a sign, she wondered in her half-conscious state, that she had misjudged him, expecting him to be one thing, when he was something else altogether?

The coldness slid against her thigh and her eyes popped open in panic as she realized that something was very, very wrong. Someone was in bed with her.

No, not someone...some*thing*.

She froze, but the thing kept moving...sliding against her. Then the large black-and-white-spotted head of Wesley's snake emerged from the covers.

Pure terror seized her, paralyzing her for a few bloodcurdling seconds. Then she let loose a paint-peeling scream and levitated out of the bed, barely touching the floor as she flung herself across the room to climb on top of her dresser. There she scrambled to her feet and stood with her back to the corner, gasping for breath as all six feet of the massive snake slid from her bed to the floor.

And stayed there.

"Omigod, omigod, omigod," she murmured, running her hands up and down her arms. "Ew, ew, ew." How long had that thing been in bed with her? A full body shiver overtook her and she stared at the python, its exotically spotted body ridiculously out of place against her plain beige carpet. "Wesley!" she screamed. "Wesley, your damn snake is loose!"

No response.

"Wesley! Come and get your snake before I make a pair of shoes out of it!"

Nothing.

She glanced at the clock—seven thirty. He'd said he had to be somewhere at eight and was leaving early. Oh, God, she was here alone with a snake that could swallow her whole. And she'd taken Wesley to the emergency room more than once when he'd first gotten the thing to get stitches for bite marks to his hands and face.

He's just getting used to me, Wesley had said. *Besides, his bites aren't poisonous.*

But the bites bled, and they maimed. And were very likely meant to distract while the snake snapped itself around its prey and contracted like a giant spring.

"Shoo," she yelled at it. "Get out of here!" She threw a tissue box at it, but the mammoth reptile didn't budge, apparently liking where it had landed, between her and her bedroom door. Only his head moved back and forth, his tongue slithering in and out. Her skin crawled and she had decided that a crying jag was the best way to go, when she spotted her cell phone lying on the dresser near her feet.

"Oh, thank God," she whispered, and bent over to get it. She tried Wesley's cell-phone number, but he didn't answer and it didn't roll over to voice mail. She cursed and tried twice more before giving up. Thinking he was probably on a job with Coop, she called Coop's number and prayed while it rang.

"This is Coop," he answered on the third ring.

"Coop!" she yelped. "This is Carlotta."

"Hi, there. Are you okay? You don't sound so good."

"Is Wesley with you?" she asked. "I'm having a bit of an emergency at home."

"No, he's not with me," Coop said. "Is it anything I can help you with?"

The snake lifted its head and moved toward her a few inches. She inhaled sharply. "Um...how do you feel about snakes?"

"Snakes?"

"Wesley's python got loose and it's in my bedroom."

"I see," he said, sounding amused. "And where are you?"

"A-also in my bedroom...standing on the dresser."

He laughed. "I'd be glad to come over and return it to its container."

She went weak with relief. "Would you? No, wait—the front door is locked. How would you get in?"

"I'll get in," he said. "I'll be there in about ten minutes."

The snake inched closer to the dresser. "Hurry," she squeaked, then disconnected the call.

She looked down at her pale blue stretch lace chemise and matching thong and realized in mortification that Coop was going to get an eyeful of more skin than even her doctor normally did. What had possessed her to forgo her regular pj's last night in favor of this sexy little number? All that talk yesterday about lingerie?

But there was nothing to be done—her faithful housecoat was draped over a chair across the room. Besides, the man was a doctor and he dealt with corpses, for heaven's sake. To him, the human body was no big deal.

The snake slithered closer, its head up. She pressed her back to the corner and looked for a weapon among the clutter on her dresser to use if she had to. A ThighMaster, a white bra, an empty water bottle, a curling iron, a pair of Gucci sunglasses and two purses—one in snakeskin, which might give the creature pause.

One by one, she threw the items in its path, but the result was never more than a momentary hesitation. It was definitely seeking her out. She used the bra like a slingshot, which merely made the snake flinch. Too late she realized she should have put on the bra instead of flinging it—at least that much of her would have been fully covered when Coop got there.

Where was he?

When the snake stopped in front of the dresser and reared its head, she started to whimper—this wasn't a good way to go. She threw back her head and started screaming, "Help me! Anybody! Mrs. Winningham, can you hear me? Help!"

"Whoa," a voice said from the doorway.

She looked up and her knees nearly buckled in relief to see Coop. "Thank God you're here." She pointed at the snake. "Kill it."

He stared up at her for a moment, then turned his attention back to the snake and wiped his hand over his mouth. "I don't think that's necessary. He's not going to eat you."

"Then why did he crawl into bed with me?"

Coop grinned. "He's male, isn't he?"

Her face warmed and she was reminded of her state of near undress. And Coop definitely wasn't looking at her with the detached disinterest of a doctor.

"Are you going to leave me up here forever?" she asked.

He crossed his arms, unabashedly skimming her from head to toe. "Can't I at least enjoy the view for a minute or two?"

Under his appreciative gaze, her nipples budded and she felt an unexpected tug of desire in her stomach. She inhaled shakily to clear her head, then narrowed her eyes at him. "No."

He grinned, unfazed as he pulled a pair of heavy leather work gloves from his jeans pockets and yanked them on. Then he knelt and gently picked up the snake by its neck and thick body, his arm muscles contracting under the weight. "Where does it go?"

"Wesley's room across the hall," she said, pointing. "There's an aquarium."

He left the room, carrying the snake, and she sagged in relief. After climbing down from the dresser, she felt a little silly in the aftermath. She pulled on her robe and tied the belt, then walked out into the hall. Coop was closing the door to Wesley's room. "He's back in the aquarium, and I, um, fed him."

"Wesley said he's been fasting, whatever that means."

"Reptiles go through phases," Coop said. "He must have suddenly gotten hungry to have gotten out."

"I don't know how it happened," Carlotta said, shoving her hand into her messy hair. "Wesley always keeps his door closed—that's our deal."

Coop pushed on the door and it opened without even turning the knob. "The strike plate is off center." He frowned. "Looks like someone has taken a screwdriver to this lock. Have you had a break-in recently?"

"No," she said, then sighed. "The police must have done it when they confiscated his computer equipment." Something else she could thank Detective Terry for.

"Ah. Well, I put the pin back in the top of the enclosure, and he's full now, so I doubt you'll have this problem again anytime soon."

She smiled in gratitude. "Thanks for coming, Coop. I'm sorry for interrupting your morning."

His warm eyes crinkled behind his glasses. "Anytime you're in trouble, don't hesitate to call." He grinned. "Especially if you're wearing skimpy lingerie."

A flush climbed her face as she relived the moment of electricity between them. Understandable, she decided, in the heat of the moment. "I assumed Wesley was with you this morning."

He shook his head. "No. I'm picking him up later today."

She bit into her lip. "Not another body pickup at Martinique Estates, I hope?"

"No." He shifted from foot to foot, and she knew he was

thinking of her connection to Peter. "The memorial service for Lisa Bolton is this afternoon at my uncle's funeral home."

Wondering if anyone of interest might show, she murmured, "I'll try to make it."

"Okay, I'll see you then."

Carlotta shoved her hands in the pockets of her robe. "Um, Coop, you saw both bodies...do you have any theories about whether the same person might have committed both crimes?"

He adjusted his glasses. "I'm just a body hauler. I'm not supposed to be offering theories on the crimes."

Which was what he'd probably been reminded when he'd pushed for the autopsy on Angela Ashford on her behalf, she realized. "But did you see any connections?" She pressed her lips together, then murmured, "I need to know, Coop."

He hesitated, looking as if something was causing him physical pain. Then he exhaled noisily. "Okay, after viewing both bodies, it would be my very unofficial opinion that, yes, the bruises around the women's necks were made by the same person."

Carlotta's hand went to her own neck. A few days ago, that would have been good news because a serial killer would have exonerated Peter. But now...now she was starting to wonder just how far Peter would go to wipe his slate clean and start over.

With her.

35

Wesley went over the answers he'd written on Chance's exam four times because he didn't want to be the first one to hand it in and draw attention to himself. After a dozen people had turned theirs in and left, he walked up to the professor's desk and dropped the exam on the stack without making eye contact. He strolled out of the classroom and down the hall, soaking up the atmosphere of hurrying bodies and snatches of lectures leaking out of various rooms.

His pulse ratcheted higher and he experienced a pang of regret for not applying to college. At the time it seemed like a big time-waster, but now he was having second thoughts. Maybe he could apply for the fall, although he wasn't sure how that would work with his probation. And he'd have to apply for school loans, which he couldn't even consider until he paid off Father Thom and The Carver.

One of the best things about being on campus was that it was close to a blood center. He went in to donate plasma and came out an hour later with his belly full of juice and cookies and forty-five bucks in his pocket, enough to get his cell-phone service reinstated at a customer service center—also handily located on campus.

He took the Marta train to within a couple of blocks of Chance's condo, then rode the elevator up and rang the door-bell to report in. When Chance didn't answer, he rang it again. He'd started to turn away when the door opened and a busty blonde dressed—barely—in a miniskirt, halter top and five-inch heels came teetering out. She smirked and walked by him with the stink of sex, pot and booze still clinging to her. Wesley looked back to the door to find Chance standing there in a black robe, smoking a joint, his expression glazed. "Come on in, man." He turned and walked back into the condo.

Wesley followed and closed the door behind him.

"How'd the exam go?"

"You'll get a B."

"Cool. Hey, finals are just around the corner if you want to work off the rest of what you owe me."

"I'll think about it," Wesley said. "Man, isn't it kind of early to get high?"

Chance laughed. "Haven't been to bed yet. Cecilia kept me up all night, if you know what I mean."

"What are you doing, man? That girl looked like hell—you're going to catch something nasty one of these days."

"A pharmaceutical sales rep friend keeps me supplied with antibiotics. Besides, normally I go a little higher class, but my regular girl drowned, of all goddamn things."

Wesley raised his eyebrows. "Drowned?"

"Yeah. She told me her name was Kay, but I saw her picture in the paper and turns out she was a fucking debutante—can you believe it?"

Wesley's heart sped up. "What was her real name?"

Chance took a drag on the joint, held his breath until his face turned red and exhaled. "I don't remember."

"Dude, it's important."

Gesturing vaguely, Chance said, "Angel or Angie or something."

"Angela? Angela Ashford?"

Chance pointed. "That's it, man. God, she was hot. Gorgeous ass."

Wesley's heart was beating so fast, his hands started to shake. "Let me get this straight. You paid the woman whose picture was in the paper, Angela Ashford, to have sex with you?"

"Dude, which one of us is stoned here? Bitch charged five hundred a pop to do me in her pool house." He took another drag on the joint, held it, then exhaled slowly. "But she was worth it."

"Gotta go," Wesley said, then jogged toward the door. Outside the condo, he punched 411 into his cell phone for directory assistance and asked for the Atlanta Police Department.

"Connecting," the operator said.

"Atlanta PD."

"Detective Jack Terry, please."

"Who's calling?"

"It's Wesley Wren. Tell him it's urgent."

36

Carlotta hurried toward the entrance of Motherwell Funeral Home, checking her watch. The memorial service for Lisa Bolton was already under way, but she was planning to sneak in the back, if possible, and stay as long as she could on the remainder of her lunch hour. She fanned herself with her hand—as always, Atlanta had made the leap from spring to summer in the span of a couple of days. It was easily ninety degrees.

She opened the door and walked into the entryway. An older suited man greeted her and from the family resemblance, Carlotta identified him as Coop's uncle.

"Are you here for the Bolton family?" he asked.

"Yes."

"The service has started, but there are seats in the back if you'd like to slip in."

She nodded and allowed the man to open one of the heavy double doors just wide enough for her to slide through. An organist was playing a beautiful hymn, and the mood was melancholy. The pews were nearly full, but she stole into a padded folding chair in the back. From the other side of the room where he stood against the wall, Coop caught her eye and nodded briefly. Her face warmed when she recalled this morning's encounter. The man was attracted to her—and she was surprisingly intrigued by him. But she had way too much on her plate now to deal with a flirtation.

Not when the man she had loved for most of her life was suspected of murdering his wife and the woman lying in the mauve-colored casket in the front of the room.

White lilies covered the closed casket, and mounds of flowers flanked either side. Unexpected tears scalded Carlotta's eyes at the mundane routine of marking the end of a person's life: a pretty box, flowers, a set number of songs and a few nice words. She hadn't known Lisa Bolton, but she'd envied people like her and Angela. People living a seemingly luxurious existence, with the world at their feet. Had some deranged person targeted them for that very reason?

As discreetly as possible, she scanned the room for familiar faces, not entirely surprised to see some of the same people who had attended Angela's funeral service: Walt and Tracey Tully, along with Tracey's socialite buds. She didn't see Peter, and wasn't sure if that was good or bad, but her heart raced to see Dennis Lagerfeld a few rows ahead of her, with his arm draped loosely around the shoulders of a gorgeous blonde. Since he was wearing his wedding ring again, she assumed the woman was his wife. He glanced back and when he caught Carlotta's eye, panic darted across his face. Then he jerked his attention back to the front of the room where the minister was giving a eulogy. Carlotta smirked, thinking she'd probably seen her last commission from the big man on campus.

But was Dennis Lagerfeld there out of compassion for a slain neighbor, or out of a compulsion to revisit his crime?

Carlotta listened to Lisa Bolton's life story while continuing to scan the audience. Her gaze stopped on a familiar profile—Dr. Suarez.

How many doctors felt close enough to their Botox patients to take time out of a busy schedule to attend their memorial service?

A few rows away, another familiar face stopped her—D.A. Kelvin Lucas. Carlotta's eyes narrowed. Was he there for professional reasons, or personal?

The warmth and weight of a person settling in next to her distracted her. She turned her head to see Detective Terry wiping his forehead with a handkerchief—it made her think of the one that he'd loaned to her on the day of Wesley's arraignment and to wonder digressively how many men these days carried a handkerchief. He ignored her while he, too, methodically scanned the attendees, his rocky profile grim. After a couple of minutes, he shifted his weight closer.

"We need to talk."

"Can't it wait?" she whispered.

"No." He jerked his thumb toward the door and stood up. Her stomach churned at his urgency, but she followed him out into the entryway where it was quiet. Coop's uncle was gone, presumably outside to welcome other latecomers.

"What's so important that you had to drag me out of a funeral?" she asked.

"Some new information about the case has come to light—actually, from your brother."

Alarm seized her heart. "What does Wesley have to do with this?"

The detective looked over his shoulder as if to ensure they were alone. "He called me a few minutes ago, said that a friend of his identified Angela Ashford from a picture in the paper as a hooker he knew as Kay."

Horror and disbelief washed over her. "Hooker?"

He nodded curtly. "Which would explain why Peter Ashford would destroy his wife's things."

Incredulous, she touched her hand to her head. "You mean you think that Peter found out and that's why he might have... hurt Angela?"

The detective shrugged. "Or he might have known and gone along with it."

She shook her head. "Never."

His mouth became a thin line. "It's possible that Lisa Bolton was also prostituting herself."

"But that's ridiculous," Carlotta said. "Why would two wealthy women with everything going for them become prostitutes?"

"Like I said before, who knows why people do the things they do? I came here looking for Peter Ashford. His DNA has been subpoenaed to check against the fetus that Lisa Bolton was carrying. Do you know where he is?"

She was still trying to absorb the awful allegations that the detective had made, thinking Wesley's whoremonger friend was no doubt that loathsome Chance Hollander. "No. Why would I know where Peter is?"

"Because he seems to have disappeared. He hasn't been to work, and he's not at his home or in any hotel in the city."

Bile rose to the back of her throat. Why would Peter disappear if he had nothing to hide? "Well, I have no idea where he is."

The detective crossed his arms. "Just like you haven't heard from your parents lately?"

She gritted her teeth. "I don't know where Peter is, but both Dr. Suarez and Dennis Lagerfeld are sitting in there," she said, pointing toward the room where the memorial service was being held. "Don't you find that odd?"

"Yes, but thanks to you, we have their DNA, and they've already been ruled out as the father of the child." He smiled. "You keep leading us to Peter Ashford. If he calls you, promise me you'll let me know."

She pressed her lips together. "Peter didn't do this."

The detective's mouth tightened and he made a derisive noise in his throat. "I'd like to know how this man has such a hold over you that you can't see what's right in front of you, how he can invoke so much loyalty from a woman like you, who's ten times his worth." Then he shook his head and straightened. "Then again, maybe I *don't* want to know."

His cell phone rang and he yanked it out of its holder, then turned his back to answer it.

Shell-shocked by his words, Carlotta stood there feeling the way she'd felt when she'd realized that her parents had abandoned her and Wesley. Everything she'd known for a certainty had been obliterated, replaced by a gaping hole of chaos.

If Peter had killed those women, she'd never again trust her feelings for another human being.

The detective closed his phone, then turned, his expression one of bewilderment. "That was Ashford's lawyer. Peter just confessed to killing Angela."

Carlotta shouted the word *no* but no sound came out of her mouth. Her last thought was that Detective Terry's black shoes were very, very shiny as they rose to meet her.

37

Wesley walked into the town house, glad for a little peace and quiet for a few hours. Coop had a funeral this afternoon, so they wouldn't be on call until later. He put a frozen pizza in the oven and flopped down on his bed with a *Playboy* magazine—the Racy Redheads issue. It wasn't a stretch to realize why all of a sudden redheads had captured his imagination.

He'd just turned to the centerfold when the doorbell rang. He rolled his eyes. He pushed to his feet, tossed the magazine on his bed and made his way to the door, trying to pull his T-shirt over the erection straining his zipper. Some people had the worst timing.

He opened the door, then blinked in surprise to see E. Jones standing there, wearing jeans and a black jacket over a T-shirt that molded her breasts. "Hi, Wesley."

Her gaze went to the bulge in his jeans, which he covered by crossing both of his hands in front of him. "Hi. I...wasn't expecting you."

She smiled and stepped forward to push on the door. "That's the idea. I came by for an in-home visit."

He stepped aside as she walked in, then closed the door. "What does that mean?"

"That means that I'm making sure you're not breaking the terms of your probation—you know, using drugs, firearms, and, in your case, computer equipment."

He swallowed hard. "I don't use drugs."

She picked up his arm and pointed to the fresh needle mark in the crook of his arm, a pinpoint of dried blood. "Really?"

"It's not what you think."

"Then clear it up for me, Wesley."

"I gave plasma this morning," he said, embarrassed. "I needed the cash to get my cell-phone service turned back on."

She considered him thoughtfully. "You can prove it?"

"I have the slip they gave me at the blood center when I left."

"I'll need to see it," she said more gently, then released his arm.

Call him a masochist, but he hadn't minded being grabbed.

"Why don't you show me around the house," she suggested, already studying the living room. She walked over to the desk and opened and closed the drawers.

He frowned and crossed his arms. "This is the living room. The kitchen is right through there."

She walked to the couch and felt behind the cushions. "So it's just you and your sister living here?" she asked, walking into the kitchen.

He followed. "Yeah, just me and Carlotta."

"Pretty name," she said, then walked over to the fridge and

looked inside. She checked out the freezer, too, and all four canisters sitting on the counter, plus the cookie jar. She stole a chocolate-chip cookie from the batch he'd made a few days ago. "Mmm, this is good," she said, stooping to look beneath the table. "Does your sister have a boyfriend who hangs around or lives here?"

"No," he said. "Carlotta doesn't date much."

"What does she do?"

"Works at Neiman's at the Lenox Mall."

She smiled. "Really? Nice. Do you have a girlfriend?"

"No."

"Why not?"

He shrugged. "No reason." Then he panicked. "I'm not gay or anything."

She looked at him and laughed. "I didn't think you were. What's out there?" she asked, pointing to the back door.

"A deck." He unlocked the door and held it open while she walked out onto the weathered structure.

She gestured to the weedy backyard, leading to a patch of trees. "Nice," she said, munching her cookie.

"Not really," he said, shoving his hands into his pockets, nudging an abandoned flowerpot with his toe.

"It could be," she said, lifting the lid of the rusty grill for a quick look before walking back inside. Wesley waved at Mrs. Winningham who was in her gazebo, craning her neck for a good look. Then he followed E. back inside.

"Where's your bedroom?" she asked.

In any other situation, he would have given his spleen to hear her say those words, but he was sure they had two entirely different activities in mind once they reached their destination.

He led the way and when he opened the door, he realized with a wince that the Racy Redheads *Playboy* was lying on his bed. She lifted her eyebrows but didn't make any remarks. Wesley turned the magazine facedown and tried to will away his returning erection. The sight of E. near his bed, *touching* his bed, made him grind his teeth to rein in his fantasies.

She felt under his pillows, then under his mattress. She pulled out more porn mags, a triple X–rated DVD movie and a pair of pink panties that some girl at one of Chance's parties had given him. A hot flush climbed his neck. It seemed so juvenile now.

E. barely glanced at the items before putting them back, then she straightened and moved around the room, checking under his lamp, even squeezing the hems of his curtains, finding a hundred-dollar bill he didn't know he had.

She removed various books from his bookshelf, running her fingers along the spines. "Nice collection," she murmured, pausing at *The Catcher in the Rye* before taking it down and flipping through the pages. "One of my favorites."

"Mine, too," he said, annoyed that his voice came out sounding squeaky and adolescent.

Across the room, Einstein moved in his enclosure. He expected E. to freak, like most women, but instead she walked over, smiling. "An axanthic ball python?"

Wesley blinked. "Yeah."

"From the size, I guess it's a male."

"Right. His name is Einstein."

"Is he friendly?" she asked.

He nodded, but was unprepared for her to unlock the enclosure, then reach in and remove Einstein like a pro. "You're a big boy," she said, as if she were talking to a dog, then she handed him to Wesley and lifted the driftwood decoration. Wesley almost dropped Einstein. Shit. He'd forgotten about the gun.

She removed the base of the decoration, and a dozen lies leaped to his tongue to explain away the presence of the .38 special. Instead, Wesley gaped to see it empty.

What the hell had happened to his gun?

"Nice hiding place," she observed.

"I...yeah," he said, still reeling. He remembered the day he'd arrived home and thought someone had broken in. Had the intruder braved Einstein and taken his gun? But who would have guessed it was even there? He looked at Einstein, suddenly fearful—had his pet somehow swallowed the gun? He pivoted his head and realized that the live mouse was gone from its container. How had that happened? Carlotta would freak out if the mouse somehow made it into her bedroom.

He returned Einstein to the aquarium and replaced the locking pin as E. went into his bathroom and, from the sound of it, looked in his hamper and medicine cabinet. He grimaced, wondering if she'd noticed the full unopened box of Trojans on the shelf.

"Condoms have an expiration date," she said matter-of-factly when she emerged. "Can you show me the rest of the house?"

Wesley led her across the hall. "This is my sister's room."

E. peeked inside, but didn't go in. Instead, she pointed to the room at the end of the hall. "Where does that door lead?"

He hesitated. "It's my parents' room."

Her expression softened slightly. "May I see it?"

With mixed feelings, he led the way to the door, turned the knob and pushed it open. The room was frozen in the decor of the previous decade—he and Carlotta hadn't changed anything. His mother's perfume bottles still littered her vanity, his father's ties were still draped over his valet stand. E. walked into the room and to the closet. She opened the door, revealing their clothes, still hanging as they'd left them, crammed into the small space, the closet about a third of the size of the one in the house that they'd lost.

They had traveled light when they'd left.

E. closed the closet door and walked back to him. "I think we're through here," she said quietly.

He exhaled in relief, closed the bedroom door and followed her back to the living room where she picked up her purse. "I just need to take a look in the garage, and then I'll be on my way."

He grabbed the remote control and walked out to raise the door. Once in the garage, E. scanned the cluttered shelves, and cupped her hands to peek into the Miata. "Is this yours?"

"My sister's," he said. "But it doesn't run."

"Too bad," she said, then opened the door and pulled the lever to open the trunk.

The woman was thorough, he conceded.

She lifted a blond wig and a high-heeled boot from the trunk and looked at Wesley. He shrugged and she dropped them back inside, closed the lid and clapped the dust from her hands.

"Thanks for the cookie," she said with the faintest smile. "See you next Wednesday."

"Okay," he said, feeling oddly proud of himself as he watched her walk down the sidewalk to her car. But as she drove away, he remembered the gun, which wasn't even his.

Wesley removed his glasses and raked his hand down over his face. Where the hell could it be?

38

Carlotta was already awake when her alarm went off the next morning. Awake and miserable, having spent the night vacillating between hiccupping crying jags and nonsensical optimism that Peter's confession would somehow turn out to be a mistake, that the real killer would be apprehended, and that she and Peter would live happily ever after.

She would have gladly spent the day wallowing in bed if not for that pesky paycheck that she needed to earn.

Working for a living was so damn inconvenient sometimes.

She inched out of bed, her limbs heavy and her heart down around her ankles. Showering and getting dressed seemed to take forever, despite that since she'd cleaned out her closet she had less to choose from. To lift her spirits, she put on her most gorgeous and most uncomfortable shoes: a pair of Valentino leopard-print pumps that were a half size too small, but she'd had to have them. They were, she acknowledged, turning in front of a full-length mirror, devastating. She was still inconsolable, but she was inconsolable and exquisitely well shod.

Concealing the circles under her eyes required more makeup artistry than usual, although the bounty from Dr. Suarez's office came in handy.

While she made herself a cup of coffee and ate eleven chocolate-chip cookies, she thought about Peter and wondered if he'd turned himself in this morning, as his attorney had promised he would. She was wounded to the marrow that she had so grossly misjudged him, and worried that he might be desperate enough to do something to himself.

She pushed away the thought as soon as it entered her head— she couldn't imagine a world without Peter in it. Even if they weren't together all these years, it had been comforting on a base level to know that he was walking around, breathing in and out.

Like her parents.

When she walked out onto the stoop, she scanned the yard and the street, looking for green cars, mobster-mobiles and Detective Terry's black sedan. Nothing seemed amiss on this gorgeous morning, the sun already simmering around the edges as it climbed in a cloudless sky. The cheeriness of the day belied the gloom in her heart, its stark brightness only highlighting the eerie feeling of impending doom.

She frowned at the long scratches on the side of her car. Filing a claim with her insurer was just one more thing to do. When she realized how the episode might have ended, she shuddered. Worse was not knowing if it had been an accident or one of Wesley's thugs.

Gone was the theory of someone trying to shut her up—unless it had been Peter. She worried her lip. When he had come to her house the night that Lisa Bolton had been killed, hadn't he begged her to stop asking questions? Her thoughts flew to the dark loaner car in his garage. Had it, by chance, been dark green?

She swallowed hard and climbed inside the Monte Carlo, securing her seat belt tighter than normal. She kept an eye on her rearview mirror on the way to work, in between skimming the newspaper at red lights. The Buckhead serial killer story was on page three. The husband of one of the victims had confessed to her murder, the article said. Peter Ashford, age thirty-three, was expected to turn himself in today.

She was all cried out, but her face hurt from the pressure behind her eyes and nose and throat. By the time she reached the parking garage, she was shaking from the caffeine, the sugar and the stress. As she drove in, she waved halfheartedly at Akin Frasier, who patrolled the entrance like a mercenary. She drove up to the second level where she normally parked, and pulled into the space, thinking how ludicrous it was for her to go to work today when she was likely to get nothing done. Yet what else was there for her to do but maintain her routine?

It was, she had learned, how people coped with the unthinkable. They kept moving, pretending to be okay, until one day they *were* okay…or some version of it.

She'd just turned off the engine when suddenly the passenger side of her car opened. She cried out in alarm when Peter swung inside and closed the door. There was at least two days' worth of beard on his jaw and his clothes were disheveled. And he was very drunk.

"Peter," she said, gulping air. "What are you doing here?"

"I had to see you, Carly," he said in a monotone, his eyes glassy bright.

"I thought you were...turning yourself in today."

"I am," he said, his voice low and desperate. "I'm trying to make everything right."

"If you killed Angela," she whispered, "then turning yourself in is the right thing to do." Her throat constricted. "Why did you do it, Peter? Because you found out she was taking money for sex?"

His eyes rounded in horror. "You...you *know* about that?"

She winced. "A friend of Wesley's was the one who identified her from the picture in the paper. Wesley told the police yesterday."

He pressed his hand against his forehead as pure panic registered on his face. "You mean, everyone knows?"

"Not everyone," she whispered. "Although there's always the chance that it will get out to the papers."

"Oh my God," he said, bowing his head. "This can't be happening." He clasped his hands together so hard they shook. "I found Angela's appointment book in the pool house and figured out what she was doing. I couldn't believe it. When I confronted her, she said it was *my* fault, for not loving her, that I drove her to find companionship elsewhere. She said her johns made her feel...desirable." He began to sob. "And I knew who had talked her into it—Lisa Bolton."

Carlotta's heart shriveled. Oh, God, he'd killed Lisa, too?

He pivoted his head. "Why couldn't you just keep your mouth shut, Carly? If not for that stupid autopsy, they would have let Angela rest in peace. They wouldn't have started digging into our lives."

Tears rolled down her cheeks.

"If only you had left things alone, everything would have smoothed over, and you and I could have been together."

She reached for the door handle, but he leaned over and locked her door. Then he put his hands on her shoulders, turning her toward him. "I made a terrible mistake. But we can still be together."

"Peter." She tried to pull away and realized she still wore her seat belt. Fear invaded her organs. "You're scaring me."

"Why?" His combustible breath was hot against her cheek. "Are you afraid I'm going to strangle you, like you think I strangled Angela and Lisa?" His hands closed around her neck and he laughed as he applied pressure with his thumbs. "You have no idea how much you tormented me over the years, Carly, how I searched for some way to forget about you."

Terror descended, tearing a mewling noise from her throat. She struggled against his grasp and used her elbow to stab the car horn. The blast startled him, making him more agitated. "I just want things to be the way they used to," he cried, anguish in his eyes. "But that will never happen now, will it?"

She clawed blindly for the door handle. "Peter, don't do this. I...I love you," she gasped, not sure if she said it out of desperation or because she meant it.

He froze, the glazed look in his eyes clearing for a few seconds as a wondrous smile spread over his face. "You do?"

She wheezed under the pressure of his hands, then abruptly the pressure on her throat was gone, and Peter's mouth was on hers, kissing her as if his life depended on it.

Then all hell broke loose. A loud bang on the car momentarily distracted Peter, and then the passenger-side door opened and a pair of big hands reached in to drag Peter off her.

"Peter Ashford," a familiar voice said, "you're under arrest for the murder of Angela Ashford."

"This is a mistake," Peter said. "Call my lawyer. This is all a big mistake."

She saw him being handcuffed, heard the click of the metal and brought her fist to her mouth to stifle the cry of grief trapped in her throat. Then Detective Terry's face appeared as he leaned into the car. "Are you all right?" he asked her, his jaw hard.

She nodded, wiping her eyes. He disappeared from view and she watched him in the rear and side mirrors lead Peter to his car and put him into the back seat. Then the detective returned to her car. She fumbled with the door, but finally managed to unlock it. He opened the door and knelt to her level. "Are you really okay?"

She nodded, still feeling a little dazed. He reached around her to unbuckle her seat belt and she recognized on a visceral level that his touch was different than Peter's—aloof, yes, but...protective...safe. "Were you following me?" she murmured.

"Yeah," he said. "I figured Ashford might try to see you before he turned himself in."

"I guess you were right...about a lot of things."

A muscle worked in his jaw. "For the record, I'm not happy about it."

She averted her gaze, her chest and throat wracked with the pain of helplessness. Senseless murders, lives upended...and the nagging sense of denial that she still didn't believe what was unfolding in front of her own eyes.

Her love for Peter was blind...*and* deaf, dumb and paralyzed.

"Did he tell you anything?"

She looked up, expecting to see a smug look in the detective's eyes. Instead she saw...compassion? Maybe there was a heart hanging behind those hideous ties. She nodded.

"I'll need for you to come down to the station and make a statement. Are you okay to drive, or do you want to ride down with me?"

Her gaze darted to his car. Peter sat in the rear seat with his head leaning back, a man in total surrender. It was heartbreaking.

"I'll drive."

"Okay," he said, his expression solemn. "Carlotta, you did right by Angela Ashford, in spite of your feelings for her husband. I know it cost you." He gave her a little smile, then walked back to his own car and climbed inside.

Carlotta watched as the detective backed up, then pulled away. Peter turned his head and looked at her, his face beseeching.

Her heart twisted in her chest as the detective's words of praise rang in her head.

If she'd done the right thing, why did she feel so damn lousy?

39

"Breakfast," Wesley announced from the doorway of Carlotta's bedroom.

She groaned and threw back the covers. "It's too hot to eat."

He leaned on the door frame and gestured to her Betty Boop pajamas. "So why don't you wear something to sleep in that's less wall to wall?"

She frowned, remembering what had happened the last time she'd worn something other than full-coverage jammies to bed. She sat up and shook her finger at him. "If that snake of yours gets out again, both of you can get a new address."

He laughed. "What does Einstein getting out of his cage have to do with your pajamas?"

She swung her legs over the side of the bed. "None of your business."

"Hey," he said quietly, "how are you doing?"

Twenty-four hours since Peter had been taken into custody,

and she was still a little numb. "I'll be okay," she said, her voice more confident than she felt.

"Sis, I'm sorry that Peter isn't the man you thought he was. You can't blame yourself for not realizing how much someone could change. All you can do is put it behind you and move on."

A bittersweet pang stabbed her chest. "Well, listen to you, Dr. Phil." Then she angled her head. "Thanks."

He grinned sheepishly. "Breakfast on the deck in ten minutes."

"That nasty pile of wood? What will we sit on?"

"Don't worry. I got it covered."

Curious, she pushed to her feet and shuffled toward the bathroom. Her body felt leaden, burdened with guilt and shame and disappointment over the events of the past couple of weeks… over the last couple of decades…but like she'd told Wesley, she'd get through it.

History had taught her there was no other choice.

She washed her puffy face, holding a cold cloth against her eyes until her fiery skin felt soothed. Then she pulled her hair back into a ponytail and donned shorts and a T-shirt. She padded through the house barefoot, stopping at the front door long enough to pick up the newspaper, dreading the inevitable details inside.

She walked through the kitchen, opened the back door and exclaimed in surprise. The wood of the deck had been restored to its natural yellow color. A new gas grill sat in the corner, and the flowerpots were filled with blooms and grasses. A children's plastic wading pool filled with water sat between two orange beach chairs draped with brightly colored towels. Plates of fresh fruit and yogurt and tall glasses of orange juice sat on TV trays. Clad in shorts, Wesley reclined in one of the chairs, his face tipped up to the sun, his feet in the water up to his shins. "It's not exactly an in-ground pool but it feels pretty good."

She sank her teeth into her lip. He'd remembered her comment about the luxurious life she might have had if she'd married Peter. Her heart expanded with love for her little brother, who was not so little anymore. And that was okay because she felt privileged to be able to watch him turn into a man.

See what you missed, Mom and Dad.

She smiled wide. "Plus ten points."

He grinned.

Settling in the opposite chair, she stuck her feet into the cool water, snagged a chunk of fresh pineapple and opened the newspaper.

"I'll take the sports page," Wesley said.

She handed it to him, her thoughts wandering briefly to Dennis Lagerfeld and his connection to the dead women—had he been a john? It would explain why he'd acted so strangely. And what about Dr. Suarez? He also could have had a relationship with Angela or Lisa or both of them. And either man could have left that cigar in the jacket. Her money was on Lagerfeld, but it didn't matter. The women had exposed themselves to all sorts of dangerous men by opening themselves and their homes to strangers. Yet Angela's husband had proved to be the most dangerous man of all. And the question still remained if Peter was the father of Lisa Bolton's baby.

The story was on page two. The police had arrested Peter Ashford for the murder of his wife, Angela, and were questioning Ashford about the murder of a neighbor, Lisa Bolton. Meanwhile, an anonymous source reported that an accomplice might be linked to a cigar found in the possession of one of the victims.

Carlotta frowned. An anonymous source? The only people who knew about the cigar were her, Detective Terry, Hannah, June, Coop...

And Liz Fischer.

Carlotta fumed. Liz was probably also the person who had "leaked" the story of Wesley's arrest to the paper...maybe in an attempt to flush out their father? She was probably sleeping with a news reporter, too. Carlotta shook her head, vowing never to trust the woman again. How her father and Jack Terry both had been taken in by that manipulative ho, she didn't know.

Then Carlotta frowned. Who was she to talk? *She* had been taken in by a murderer, hadn't she? But in her head she could still hear Peter say, *This is all a big mistake,* and see his pleading face from the back of Detective Terry's car.

She looked up from the paper. "Wesley, about the information you gave to Detective Terry concerning Angela Ashford..."

He turned his head. "Yeah?"

"Well, I assumed that was from Chance Hollander."

He didn't respond.

"Did you ever..."

His eyes widened. "Me? No, I'm not into hookers."

"Oh. Good." She looked back to the newspaper, then back to him. "So, what *are* you into?"

He thought a minute then said, "Redheads."

"Oh."

From the kitchen she heard her cell phone ring. "Wonder who that could be."

"Probably Hannah. She's called you, like, six times this morning. I have to warn you, I think she's wearing Coop down on the body-moving thing."

"Oh, please don't tell me that," she said, stepping out of the water.

Wesley shrugged. "He needs another crew member—people are dying faster than we can pick them up. I told him we need a double-decker hearse."

She winced and went in to get her phone. A local number flashed across the screen, but it wasn't Hannah's. Curious, she punched the call button. "Hello?"

"Hi, is this Carlotta?"

"Yes."

"Carlotta, this is Amy Lin at Designer Consigner. I'm calling because I found something in one of the Coach purses that you brought in and wondered if you need it back."

Her pulse picked up—cash, she hoped. "What is it?"

"It's a cigar in a plastic bag. I didn't open it—it looks expensive."

Carlotta groaned inwardly. She'd emptied her purse on the bed, then taken it to the consignment shop, apparently with the cigar still inside. The cigar probably wouldn't have any bearing on the case now except perhaps to help identify one of Angela's johns, but she'd turn it over to Detective Terry. "Yes, Amy, I'd like to have it back. And thanks for not opening it. I'll be by to pick it up on my way to work, in about an hour."

"Fine, I'll be here. By the way," Amy said, her voice raising an octave, "did you ever find that big, strong man to protect you? The danger is still with you, I'm afraid."

Unbidden, an image came into her head of Detective Terry hauling Peter off her the day before. She'd probably never know if Peter would have hurt her, but he hadn't been in a clear state of mind, so who knew what he was capable of? But as far as Detective Terry being the man that Amy had envisioned—well, he'd really only been doing his job, hadn't he?

"I'm not sure," she said cheerfully. "But I'll keep an eye out."

"Good," Amy said. "I'll see you later."

Carlotta disconnected the call, then turned over her hand and studied it. She smirked. The only danger she saw was the slight stain of nicotine between her forefinger and middle finger.

She dismissed the woman's words and went to get ready for work, deciding to dress to the nines. It always made her feel better.

40

"Detective Terry, please," Carlotta said into her cell phone as she walked toward the parking garage, wondering if he was on duty, or if he had hooked up with Liz Fischer for a Saturday-night special.

The operator told her to hold and after a couple of rings, he answered with a curt, "Terry here."

"This is Carlotta," she said, then added, "Wren."

"Carlotta," he said with a sigh, "I know who you are—you're the woman who has single-handedly doubled my workload into the foreseeable future. What kind of trouble are you in now?"

"None," she said hotly. "I thought you'd like to know that I found the cigar that was in the jacket that Angela Ashford returned. I'm leaving work, so I could bring it by—unless you're too busy with your workload."

"Still trying to clear your boyfriend of murder?" he asked wryly.

She scowled. Insensitive brute. "I just don't want to be

accused of destroying evidence again. Do you want it or not?" She stabbed the button for the elevator.

"Of course I want it. Call me when you get here."

She disconnected, muttering under her breath. The elevator doors opened and she walked on, her Miu Miu pump–pinched feet dragging with fatigue. The muscles in her arms ached from carrying clothes to and from dressing rooms. Her prized Judith Leiber necklace, a gold-plated breastplate, had grown heavier and heavier as the hours had worn on. It had been a long day, but at least her sales had been good. She'd stayed late to make sure her paperwork was in order and now a glance at her watch told her the time was closing in on ten o'clock. A yawn overtook her as the elevator began to descend. She was thinking past dropping off the cigar to lying in bed watching *What Not To Wear* when the bell dinged and the doors opened again.

Akin Frasier stood smiling at her. "Hello, Ms. Wren." He puffed out his chest as he walked on, trying to fill the overlarge jacket he wore.

"Hi, Mr. Frasier," she said, too tired to be annoyed or amused by his marching-band pomposity.

"I guess you're feeling better now that Peter Ashford is in jail."

"Um, yes," she murmured.

"He's about the same caliber as that wife of his," the man said. "She was some stuck-up woman." He sniffed. "Some of those women who come in think they're too good to talk to the likes of me."

Unease pricked the back of her neck. It sounded like Frasier was harboring a lot of resentment toward people like the Ashfords.

"I'm sure it's unintentional," she said mildly.

"Maybe," he said, then cracked his knuckles.

She looked down and noticed he was clenching and unclenching his fists, and a tickle of panic stirred in her chest. He began to rock back and forth on his heels and that's when she smelled the faint scent of cigar smoke waft from his uniform.

When the implication hit her, terror wasn't far behind. She fumbled for her cell phone and dropped her purse, spilling its contents on the floor. The cigar went flying to a far corner.

"Let me help you," Frasier said, grasping her arm.

She screamed and yanked free just as the elevator doors slid open. She ran through the doors, smacking into a big body and bouncing off.

The person steadied her and she looked up, blinking in recognition at Patrick Forman, Dennis Lagerfeld's agent.

"Help me," she gasped. "I'm afraid for my life."

"You should be," Patrick said, then calmly removed a gun with a silencer from his jacket, leveled it at a shocked Akin Frasier and pulled the trigger.

Carlotta jumped at the pinging noise, and horror washed over her when Akin Frasier slumped to the floor of the elevator just before the doors closed.

She gaped at Patrick Forman. "It was you."

A cruel smile spread over his face. "It was me."

41

Carlotta stared into the barrel of the gun and lifted her hands high. "You were Angela Ashford's john, not Dennis."

He nodded, proud of himself. "That's right. For once, I got the beautiful woman, instead of whatever hag happened to be with the girl that Dennis wanted. And I wasn't just Angela's john—the stupid woman was in love with me."

Carlotta's mind raced. Perspiration trickled down her back.

"Until you got Lisa Bolton pregnant?" she prompted.

He nodded. "That shouldn't have happened. That bitch tricked me. She told Angela about the baby, and Angela was furious. We had a big fight, and she broke it off."

Her heart thrashed in her chest.

"And returned the expensive jacket she'd bought you." Dennis had recognized the jacket all right, as one his agent had been wearing. "With a cigar inside that Dennis had given you."

He smiled. "A cigar that has my fingerprints on it, which is why I need it back. Peter Ashford will take the fall and no one need ever know I was connected to Angela or Lisa."

She swallowed hard and decided to stall, hoping someone with a bigger gun would happen by. "Wh-what makes you think I have the cigar?"

"You show up at Moody's asking questions, talking about how you knew Angela. Then Dennis confronts me about the jacket and tells me that Angela returned it to you. It doesn't take a genius to figure out why you were snooping around. Dennis I don't have to worry about—I got so much shit on him, he'd never turn me in. But you...you need to learn to keep your nose out of other people's business."

"You tried to run me off the road," she said.

"Yes, but you can't seem to take a hint."

The fact that he didn't bother denying his crimes made her realize with cold clarity that he planned for her to take his confessions to her grave.

He shoved the gun so close to her face that she went cross-eyed. "Where's the damn cigar?"

She wet her trembling lips. "Why do you think I still have it?"

"If the police had it, they would've already traced it back to me." He shrugged and made a rueful noise in his throat. "My fingerprints are on file. I'm afraid I have a bit of a history with women that I'd rather keep under wraps."

Her blood curdled thinking about the women he might have killed in his lifetime, and how grateful she was that he hadn't latched on to Hannah that day at the cigar bar—although she'd bet that Hannah would have held her own with the psychopath.

She, on the other hand, was at a decided disadvantage. "Why did you have to kill them?" she whispered.

"They were no longer useful," he replied simply. "And they were trivial, insipid women—I honestly didn't think anyone would notice or care that they were gone. You, in particular, should've been glad, since Angela's husband was in love with you. And Angela told me she tried to run you down in this very parking garage."

Carlotta's throat constricted.

"The day she died, Angela was drunk and out of control— she kept saying that I had betrayed her with Lisa just as her husband had betrayed her with you. When she stumbled into the pool, I reached for her and actually considered saving her. Then I realized how much better it would be if she just…died. But I did have feelings for her. I held her under so she would suffer less."

Carlotta's eyes filled with tears. Poor Angela.

"Why you kept stirring things up, I don't know, but now you'll have to pay." He touched the cold tip of the barrel to her nose, and she wondered hysterically if he noticed the hump there. "For the last time, where is the cigar?"

"I-it's on the elevator," she said. "It fell out of my purse."

"Get it," he ordered.

She turned around and punched the elevator button, dreading to see Akin Frasier's bloodied body. But when the doors opened, a big hand reached out and yanked her inside and behind him. "Freeze," Detective Terry shouted, pointing his weapon at Patrick Forman. Forman shot into the elevator and

Carlotta screamed, covering her head, feeling a jolt to her chest before the *chink, chink* of ricocheting sounds stopped. She heard the detective fire twice and looked up in time to see Forman jerk back, then fall to the ground in a way that convinced her he wasn't getting up again.

Detective Terry put his arm around her and the elevator doors closed, cocooning them inside. "Are you okay?"

She patted herself down, feeling for spurting blood. "I think so." Then she looked down at her chest and gasped at the dent in her gold breastplate—the necklace had probably saved her life—oh, along with the detective. "How did you know what was happening?"

"Akin Frasier managed to call 911. I got here as soon as I could." He shook his head and puffed out his cheeks in an exhale. "Lady, you need your own security force."

She managed a grin. "Are you volunteering?"

He pursed his mouth. "I don't know. What are the fringe benefits?"

An unexpected surge of gratitude and desire warmed her. She looked up into his golden eyes and searched for something to tell her whether he was just doing his job or whether he had developed a soft spot for her. For a split second, she thought she saw the promise of something special, but then he looked away.

With the moment shattered, she lifted the end of his red-and-blue polka-dot tie. "Free fashion advice."

A sardonic smile tilted his mouth. "I'll think about it."

The elevator door slid open and she stepped off to see Akin

Frasier being wheeled to an ambulance. She ran over to him and picked up his hand. "Thank you, Mr. Frasier."

"I did it, didn't I?" he asked. "I saved the day."

"You certainly did," she assured him.

She thought of the abominable Patrick Forman and what he'd nearly gotten away with, and suddenly her heart took flight.

Peter was innocent.

42

Wesley lifted his hand from the van armrest. "So Peter Ashford didn't kill his wife after all."

Coop looked over from the driver's side. "Why did he confess?"

"He thought if he confessed to the murder, that no one would find out about his wife being a hooker. But I'd told the police about Angela just before he called them."

"And when he discovered that word about his wife's extra-curricular activities had already gotten out, it was too late to take back his confession."

"Yeah," Wesley said. "Can you imagine a guy being so hung up on his dead wife's name not being smeared that he'd go to prison to protect her reputation?"

Coop shrugged. "I think it's kind of noble."

"You sound like my sister. If you ask me, anyone that stupid *deserves* the needle."

"If not for your sister, he might have gotten it." Coop chewed on his lip. "I guess they're back together?"

"No. Carlotta said they both needed some space to let things settle down."

Coop perked up. "Really?"

"Yeah, but the window of opportunity is short here, dude, so my advice is to do something bold."

Coop laughed. "Maybe I will."

"Man, you got it bad for her—you're pathetic."

"It'll happen to you someday, too, friend. You'll meet a girl who'll make you do things you never thought you'd do."

Wesley looked out the window, not about to tell his boss that he thought he'd already met her, and she had his balls in a vise.

He was pathetic, too.

Coop pulled into the driveway of the town house, then put the van into Park. "Wesley, I have a confession, too."

Wesley lifted his eyebrows. "What?"

"I took that piece-of-crap gun from your aquarium so you wouldn't hurt yourself or someone else."

He went limp with relief. "You did? Man, that belongs to a friend. I've been freaking out wondering what happened to it."

"It's in there," Coop said, pointing to the glove compartment. "Get it out of here and take it back where you got it. Maybe down the road—once you're off probation—you and I can go to the handgun range and you can learn how to shoot properly to defend yourself. Then you can decide which gun you'd like to save up for and buy."

Wesley stared at Coop and a warm feeling of appreciation flooded his chest. He was amazed that the man gave a damn about what he did. "I'd like that."

Coop smiled. "Good. Now get lost. And put in a good word for me with your sister!"

Wesley jumped down from the van and slammed the door. His cell phone rang as he was unlocking the front door. Chance's number flashed on the screen.

"Hey, man, what's up?"

"You still want to sell your bike?" Chance asked.

Wesley hesitated, then told himself that the decision he'd made last night was a good one—sell the bike and use the five grand to get caught up on his debt. It was just sitting there anyway, and Carlotta would be thrilled if he got rid of it. "Yeah."

"A guy will be there in ten minutes to look at it," Chance said. "He's got cash." Then he hung up.

Wesley shook his head. Chance was after every loose nickel in Atlanta. There was no deal he wouldn't broker and he wouldn't put it past his buddy to be more than just a john to some of his hookers.

Like Angela Ashford, for one.

A few minutes later, a guy showed up in a pickup truck and Wesley wheeled out his neon-green cycle for a dog-and-pony show. He threw in some extra equipment that he had never used but assured the guy was essential, and they struck a deal for slightly less than the five grand that Wesley had wanted for it.

He helped the guy load the bike in the back of his pickup, and after he'd pulled away, Wesley stood and stared at the wad of cash, feeling the familiar twitch in his fingers, the anticipation building in his chest.

If he could find a game, he could probably double his money.

43

"I didn't really think that you'd strangled the woman," Michael said. "That cop twisted my words. Forgive me?"

Carlotta glared at her friend, then gave a wry laugh. "Of course."

"All the drama, I just can't believe it. But how did Lisa Bolton's lingerie get on Peter Ashford's credit card?"

"Angela bought it with Peter's card. The police aren't sure if Angela got Lisa involved in the call-girl ring, or if Lisa got Angela involved, but Angela seemed to be footing the bill for Lisa Bolton's wardrobe."

Michael shook his head. "Why would two women who had everything get involved in something so sleazy?"

Carlotta shrugged. "Boredom…loneliness…money? Who knows why people do the things they do?" she asked, then frowned when she realized that she was quoting Jack Terry.

A scandalous light gleamed in Michael's eyes. "A friend of mine told me that this has been going on for a while, and that there were more Buckhead socialites involved in the call-girl ring and more celebrity johns to be revealed."

And to think that she'd once envied the Angela Ashfords of the world.

Her co-worker sighed dramatically. "Do you think that you and Peter Ashford will eventually get back together?"

"I don't know," she said honestly. "There's a lot of water under the bridge. I want to make sure that we have someplace to move forward to, versus just trying to get back to where we were. I told him that I need some time. Maybe a lot of time."

"And meanwhile?"

A sly smile curved her mouth. "And meanwhile...there are a couple of possibilities that I'd like to explore."

"Sounds intriguing," he said, wagging his eyebrows.

Her cell phone vibrated in her pocket and she pulled it out. "Talk to you later," she said to Michael, walking back toward the escalator. It was Hannah.

"Hello?"

"Oh. My. God. Guess where I am."

"Where?"

"At the magnetic-sign store."

Carlotta squinted. "Okay, why?"

"Coop hired me! I'm a body mover!"

She grimaced. "And what does that have to do with magnetic signs?"

"I'm getting two printed so that I can switch out the signs depending on what I'm hauling—bodies or food."

"Okay, you're sick, you know that?"

"I have to proofread these signs. I just had to share that with you. I'll call you right back."

Carlotta shook her head as she rode up the escalator. She had the feeling that Hannah was going to try to get her involved in her new enterprise, but she was ready for her life to settle down for a while.

The phone rang again and she punched the button. "That was fast."

"Carlotta?"

She frowned at the man's voice even as her brain sent vibrations of recognition through her subconscious. "Who is this?"

"Sweetheart, it's me…Daddy."

* * * * *

Don't miss a single move!
Look for the second book in the BODY MOVERS series
from Stephanie Bond and Mira Books in 2007!
www.MIRABooks.com
www.stephaniebond.com